The Lamentable Journey
of Omaha Bigelow
into the Impenetrable
Loisaida Jungle

The Lamentable Journey
of Omaha Bigelow
into the Impenetrable
Loisaida Jungle

EDGARDO VEGA YUNQUÉ

THE OVERLOOK PRESS
WOODSTOCK & NEW YORK

First published in the United States in 2004 by
The Overlook Press, Peter Mayer Publishers, Inc.
Woodstock & New York

WOODSTOCK:
One Overlook Drive
Woodstock, NY 12498
www.overlookpress.com
[for individual orders, bulk and special sales, contact our Woodstock office]

NEW YORK:
141 Wooster Street
New York, NY 10012

∞ The paper used in this book meets the requirements for paper
permanence as described in the ANSI Z39.48-1992 standard.

Cataloging-in-Publication Data is available from the Library of Congress

Book design and type formatting by Bernard Schleifer
Manufactured in the United States of America
FIRST EDITION
ISBN 1-58567-630-6
10 9 8 7 6 5 4 3 2 1

CONTENTS

Modern stupidity means not ignorance but the *nonthought of received ideas.* Flaubert's discovery is more important for the future of the world than the most startling ideas of Marx or Freud. For we could imagine the world without the class struggle or without psychoanalysis, but not without the irresistible flood of received ideas that—programmed into computers, propagated by mass media—threaten soon to become a force that will crush all original and individual thought and thus will smother the very essence of the European culture of the Modern Era.

MILAN KUNDERA, "Man Thinks, God Laughs"
Upon acceptance of the Jerusalem Prize
The New York Review of Books, June 13, 1985

There was so much else to include, and one must be firm in cutting out details. He had already chosen the title of the book, after much thought: *The Pacification of the Primitive Tribes of the Lower Niger.*

CHINUA ACHEBE
Things Fall Apart

"The Village is full of echoes. Perhaps they got trapped in the hollow of the walls, or under stones. When you walk in the street you can hear other footsteps, and rustling noises, and laughter. Old laughter, as if it were tired of laughing by now. And voices worn out with use. You can hear all this. I think someday these sounds will die away."

That is what Damiana Cisneros was telling me as we crossed the village.

JUAN RULFO
Pedro Páramo

THE NIGHT THAT OMAHA BIGELOW'S LIFE CHANGED FOREVER BEGAN quite badly. At around midnight on July 4, 2000, he was thrown brutally out of the Friendly Fire Club on Allen Street in the East Village. Technically, Allen Street is the Lower East Side, since it is the southern extension of First Avenue after it crosses Houston Street. The East Village esthetic, however, has seeped across Houston by two more blocks to Delancey Street. This is an odd area of New York City. The Chinese are marching northward from Chinatown, and the yuppies and artists are marching southward from the East Village. Bars and restaurants where young woman thespians average 8.7 percent trips to your table to determine whether everything is okay, and boutiques where you may purchase frilly slips to wear as a dress with combat boots, have sprouted along Ludlow and Orchard Streets, traditionally the site of shops where Yiddish has been spoken by merchants and shoppers for over a hundred and fifty years. A bit further north, in the middle of the East Village, is Loisaida, which is the name Puerto Ricans have given the area. The name Loisaida is a combination of a town in Puerto Rico by the name of Loiza and the Lower East Side. Linguistically exotic, Loisaida is a gallant and quixotic cultural attempt to dominate the geography even though renting is not the same as owning.

Omaha Bigelow was as high as a kite. Having consumed ten Rolling Rocks, taken no less than twelve tokes on several joints laced with a number of enhancements, and having innosed a line of Coca Cola at the Tenth Street apartment of his friend, Richard Rentacar, the leader of Carsick, the punk rock band in which he played bass, he was feeling no pain. Instead, Omaha Bigelow was feeling much too mellow to be permitted to remain in the club. The reason? He peevishly insisted on getting up on the stage and demanding from the bassist in Clowns Desirous, the featured girl's band, that she let him sit in. Between licks on the bass while they played their hit single, "Lick This," the insulted bassist, Rita Flash, backhanded Omaha repeatedly with her spiked right glove. She eventually managed to position him so that as the drummer slammed a cymbal she jumped up, and, as she was coming down, she kicked Omaha in the chest and knocked him off the stage. The dancers, delighted by this spontaneous entertainment, did not attempt to catch Omaha Bigelow as they usually did in punk rock venues. Rather than receive him in a welcoming gathering of upraised hands, they parted in tune with the music and watched him helicopter through the air and land thudly on his back. He crashed to the floor laughing, rolled around, grabbed at people's ankles, and attempted to get back up on the stage.

Mooko Pelujillo, the big dude who acts as peacekeeper inside Friendly Fire, intercepted Bigelow. The term "big" is too generic. Mooko makes Refrigerator Perry, the onetime 300-pound-plus pachydermian tackle of the Chicago Bears football team, look like a water cooler. With an appropriate bending of the left arm so that Bigelow's hand was up around the nape of his neck, Mooko escorted him to the door. Mooko explained to Omaha that he should stop fucking around and leave the bass guitarist of Clowns Desirous alone. When Omaha protested and said that he knew Rita Flash and that she had given him head plenty of times, Mooko increased pressure upward so that Omaha said fuck seven times in a row. Mooko then opened the door and spoke in Spanish to Tony Manganzón, the outside dude who was deciding who was coming into the club and who was not. Mooko outlined Omaha's behavior. Manganzón didn't respond in Spanish.

"Throw him the fuck out," he said.

"Word," Mooko said.

"Fuck," repeated Omaha.

When Omaha tried to resist, Mooko grabbed his spiky greenish hair with one hand, the back of his leather pants with the other, and lifted him up off the ground. Omaha Bigelow said he had as much right to get up there and play as that stupidass, Sting-looking Rita Flash. And who the fuck was he, big, stupid-looking, Puerto Rican doofus to be ordering him around, a fucking Nazi stormtrooper motherfucker? Mooko had no choice. Without even unhooking the velvet rope he heaved Omaha Bigelow in a rather majestic arc out into the summer night, catapulting him almost to the curb. Insult and injury, thought Omaha Bigelow. Fuck, he thought. Far out, he thought. What now? he asked himself.

He got up unsteadily and began walking. Turning the corner at Houston Street, he walked east across Orchard Street, past the Turkish falafel place, the pizza shop, and a new Japanese restaurant. At Katz's, the famous Jewish deli, he looked in the window and, grabbing his crotch, made a couple of pumping motions at the Puerto Rican guys serving up hot dogs and knishes behind the counter. They doubled up with laughter and threatened him with their knives, indicating that they were going to stick him in the butt. This made Bigelow laugh. He turned his back on them, lowered his pants and mooned them. They laughed some more and said he was a *pato,* a duck, which is what homosexuals are called in Puerto Rican slang.

Bigelow crossed Ludlow Street, thought about going to the Pink Pony or maybe stopping in at Nada to see if Aaron Beall could let him audition again for his theater group. He changed his mind and kept going. He tried to go into the Mercury Lounge, a bar, but was refused entry. The same was denied him at the Bank, a club, next door. Fuck, he thought. He stood on the corner of Houston and Essex and waited for the light to change. When it was safe to cross, he raced madly across the wide avenue and dove in front of two School of Visual Arts coeds about to go into Nice Guy Eddie's, the restaurant-bar on the corner.

"Let me lick your pussy," he said and wagged his pierced tongue at them.

"Get a life," said the chubby blonde.

"Little dick asshole," said the skinny shaved-head one, looking like she was fucking Sinead O'Connor, thought Omaha.

As the two girls went into the bar, Omaha Bigelow lay on the sidewalk laughing but wondering how the hell they knew about his dick and the Penile Asparaguitis from which he suffered. Did they know Carrie Marshack? The bitch had kicked him out two weeks before because what? He didn't have a job at Kinko's anymore? Like working at Kinko's with stoned poets and Puerto Rican JUCO students was supposed to be a career? Fine, Fly caught him sleeping in the back and he screwed up Sander Hicks's copies. Big deal. It wasn't like Allen Ginsberg died again or something. Or like he had dissed Iggy Pop when he came in that one time to copy his passport. Iggy was cool. People were nuts.

And then there was the Puerto Ricans laughing at him and the young girls pointing at his hair and saying: *gamara cura la mostaza cucaracha salsa tostones y pancaruco* or whatever. He should learn Spanish. What the fuck were the Puerto Ricans so happy about? They were totally fucked up, everybody thought they were stupid, and they were always laughing and having a good time. They probably knew about his small dick. Carrie Marshack didn't mind. Why should anybody else? She was an Off-Off-Broadway actress and had told him she'd read that Liam Neeson was really hung. So maybe she did mind and that's why she kicked him out. He'd seen Richard Rentacar when Rita Flash was giving him head, and he wasn't all that friggin big. Maybe Carrie had told everybody in the East Village that he had a small dick. Shit, fuck the bitch!

All at once Omaha Bigelow had three urges. He was hungry, he needed a drink, and his dick was suddenly screaming to either find a girl or spank the monkey. Omaha Bigelow got up from the sidewalk, walked up Avenue A, and started to go into Two Boots. Too crowded. He crossed the street and went to the Two Boots pizzeria, ordered two slices and a Pepsi. The Mexican behind the counter looked at him inscrutably.

"You want anything on the pizza?" he said.

"Mushrooms," Omaha answered.

"Regular mushrooms or the good shit?"

"The good shit," Omaha said.

"You got it, cowboy," the Mexican said. "*El Carlos Castaneda especial*," he shouted, turning around and speaking in his sing-song Spanish to the dude in the kitchen.

When the order came Omaha reached into his pocket but had only enough for one slice and the Pepsi. Looking at him like he was a dumb gringo prick the Mexican behind the counter took the second slice off the paper plate, scraped off the mushrooms into a sheet of tinfoil, folded it, and put it in his shirt pocket. He threw the extra slice into the garbage, which made Omaha think of his mother and the poor children of India.

"Sorry, man," he said to the Mexican.

"*No problemo, Americano*," the Mexican said, doing a deep Schwarzenegger.

"I coulda ate the other slice if you was gonna throw it out."

"*Sí*," said the Mexican.

Taking his food, Omaha slid clumsily into a booth and waved at some New York University students, three girls and a boy, sitting across the way. One of them, a blonde, looked remarkably like the actress Charlize Theron. Omaha told them he had gone to their school but hadn't graduated. When they smiled vapidly and said oh, yeah? he informed them that he had been kicked out of Tisch School of the Arts for making a twenty-two-minute black-and-white film of his repeated masturbations and one defecation which he then froze and supposedly ate. Two girls made a face and said ewww. The Charlize Theron look-alike said far out. Encouraged by the attention, Omaha Bigelow explained that he had shaped chocolate ice cream into turds and through "movie magic" he made it appear as if he was eating shit. Special effects, he said. He entitled the film "The Incredible Lightness of Being Omaha Bigelow." Spike Lee, at the time visiting the school, critiqued the film and said it was quite a personal statement. Lee added that Bigelow should've taken more care with the lighting, but his message regarding the plight of the white man in America was quite clear.

"What did you think of the eating scene?" Omaha asked Lee.

"I guess you had to have it," Lee said.

"Thanks," Omaha replied. "That makes me feel a whole lot better."

"They're gonna kick you out of school anyway," Lee said. "I'm sorry."

"No fucking artistic freedom in this country, man."

"You don't have to tell me, dude," Lee said. "I gotta go."

"Ciao, man," Omaha said. "Thanks for the critique."

Fuck, he thought. That was a long time ago. How old the fuck was he? Thirty-five? No fucking way. He was actually kicked out of NYU for distributing and posting leaflets asking a particularly sexy mathematics teacher at the school for head. He had her picture on the leaflet with a xeroxed copy of his enlarged, erect penis next to her mouth, which the big Oriental dude with the blue eyes at Village Copier on Twelfth Street helped him do. Timmy, who was the brother of the "Luka" folksinger chick, whatever her name was, he couldn't remember. He plastered the damn things all over the school's walls. No artistic freedom and no freedom of the press. Fuck.

He finished eating, slurped the last of the Pepsi and got up. He waved again at the NYU students, one of whom would probably give him the finger as soon as he turned around. Probably some literature major. The blonde smiled at him. Fuck, Omaha thought as soon as he stepped out into Avenue A and into a friggin late July blizzard. The snow was blinding and the wind was howling as he stepped through the snowdrifts watching tits bouncing inside girls' T-shirts, reading their tattoos and smacking penguins out of the way. Fuck. On Sixth Street a polar bear asked him for the time. It's obvious that polar bears and penguins don't exist on the same pole, but there were gaps in Omaha's education, and this was his mind. He looked at his watch and told the bear that it was one thirty in the morning.

"Thanks," the bear said.

"You're a polar bear," Omaha said.

"So?"

"How come you speak English?"

"Asshole," said the polar bear.

"What?" Omaha said.

"What am I supposed to speak? Spanish?"

"Sorry, dude."

"Dude?"

"You're not a dude?"

"Duh," said the polar bear, lifted up its T-shirt, and flashed two huge tits at Omaha.

"Sorry," said Omaha. "See you later."

"Retard," said the polar bear. "Get a life."

Omaha Bigelow continued walking until he got to Tompkins Square Park. At one time Tompkins Square Park was open at all hours of the night. The homeless slept there in Martha Stewart-decorated cardboard homes, people smoked grass leisurely and had all kinds of sex. Liberals and old socialists played nighttime chess under the lights, musicians played instruments, natives played drums, and it was lovely and hip and revolutionary and then the cops came and beat the shit out of everybody. Word has it that one night alone they killed 856 people and wounded over 2,500 others. They raped women, killed dogs, roasted them, and ate them with salsa and chips. They stole dope, shoved broomsticks up seventy-seven Haitian immigrants' butts, slapped gays, jeered lesbians, and even stole comics from kids. You think I'm exaggerating and using embellishment? Maybe a little. I don't know if all of it was true. I'm just saying what I heard. But Amadou Diallo happened, and Abner Louima happened, and Eleanor Bumpers happened, and that Rican guy in the Bronx who was choked to death happened. Don't tell me the shit at Tompkins Square Park didn't happen. It was a bitch, and Gordon videotaped the whole thing for posterity which they showed on cable before the Robin Byrd show. I'm sorry about the 9/11 cops, but history *is* a bitch.

Omaha Bigelow looked around. No cops. Good. He climbed over the fence and was running through the park to find a hiding place and sleep. If the cops caught him, they'd beat the shit out of him. He heard a siren and hid behind a tree. Fuck. The siren faded and he walked further into the park. He found some bushes, got down on his hands and knees, and crawled through. He hoped the rats wouldn't come.

He lay down and watched the snow fall all around him. He wanted to masturbate but was too sleepy. He thought about his mother back in Reliability, Kansas. She liked saying that they lived smack dab in the middle of the country. *We might as well be the umbilicus of the United States,* she'd say. Olivia Bigelow read James Joyce, had long slender hands, and painted her fingernails and toenails ruby red. He often sat on the floor of her bedroom watching her apply lacquer to her nails. The smell of the nail polish was intoxicating. Sometimes she sat cross-legged on the bed and painted her toenails wearing only panties and bra. She placed little cotton balls between her toes. Omaha was intrigued by the blondish fuzziness under the rayon of her panties. At times a sweet aroma wafted to him as he knelt penitently by the bed and watched as his mother hummed along with the classical music station. In Spanish the word for this perfume of estrus is called *almizque,* an Arabic word that means musk. Sometimes, impatiently, she would lean over, blow on her toenails, and her small breasts would threaten to fall out of her bra, the tiny pink nipples visible.

Omaha's mother taught the piano but for an extra two dollars gave older boys handjobs. Rather than a good American Legion baseball team, the town of Reliability had dozens of mediocre piano players. There was always a box of Kleenex by the piano. He liked watching his mother working on the boys. Bobby Hawthorne, Scotty Melville, or Terry Wadworth would come in and he'd say, *Mama, I'm gonna ride my bike down by the lake,* and off he'd go. *Be careful,* she'd say. The lake was about a mile away. One afternoon he got halfway to the lake when suddenly the day got dark. He heard the thunder, and lightning streaked the sky. He turned around and pedaled back furiously as the hailstones started to fall. He threw his bike under the porch, ran up the steps, slipped, and fell. As he was helping himself up by holding on to the bottom of a window, he saw his mother's hand. Her ruby-red fingernails were moving rapidly, but no sound was coming from the piano. He could only see the fingernails, so he crawled to the last window, and through the curtains he saw that she had a hold of Walter Fitzgerald and with her left hand was reaching for a Kleenex. Walter let out a moan, made an ugly face as his mother placed a tissue over the boy's sputtering organ. Fuck, he thought. It was the first time he had uttered this word as an expression of confusion. He was eight years old. He began spanking the monkey around that time. His mother stopped letting him watch her paint her toenails. Still, whenever one of the older students showed up, Omaha announced that he was going to the lake and hid to watch his mother give piano lessons. Sometimes for another dollar she let boys suck her conically pert titties.

As he began drifting off, he could hear the rats scurrying around in the dark. Maybe they were squirrels on a night peanut raid. Nah! he thought. They were rats. Maybe they would come and chew off his tiny dick. In a minute Omaha Bigelow was asleep.

F ROM HER PERCH IN THE TREE MARUQUITA SALSIPUEDES WATCHED THE weirdo below. She had been watching him for almost two months. He moved through the park like a dog, stopping in one place, looking around, sniffing the air, and going on. The siren sounded in the street and he hid behind a tree. She moved quickly on the branches, leaping quickly through the trees and following the weirdo's progress. Maruquita didn't know if he was the one. He could be the one. She liked his green hair and his little butt, and he had his tongue pierced. Maybe he would give her head on her *tontón papaya*. She had never had head. She had heard about head and imagined the green growth down there like blades of grass between her thighs and his tongue going at her, licking away like a pitbull drinking water. She would like to have head. She would also like to give head, but she wasn't going to pierce her tongue. That was wack.

The weirdo got down on all fours and crawled through the bushes. Maruquita leaped through the foliage of two more trees and watched. She waited until the weirdo fell asleep and then, in her monkey guise, she climbed down off the tree holding the stick. Her mother, Flaquita "La Bruja" Salsipuedes, had taught her many monkey tricks, and she could climb anywhere. She could even jump from her window on the fifteenth floor of the projects, grab the trees, and climb down. Even the squirrels were jealous of her and booed every time they saw her. Sometimes she became a squirrel and yelled at them in squirrel language. Fuck them, bushy-tailed punk mothafockas.

Maruquita sat cross-legged near the weirdo. She held the maglite she had boosted from the Jewish hardware store on Rivington Street in one hand and the *grayumo* magic stick from Puerto Rico that her grandfather, Rafael "El Gordo" Salsipuedes, had given her in the other, ready to bat the rats if they came too close to the weirdo. He could be the one. She knew they would bite him, and she didn't want that to happen. Maybe they would bite his *peepee bohango* and he wouldn't be able to give her a baby. He was a weirdo hippie punk rocko cocko but he could be the one. To stay awake she thought about what the baby would look like if she let the weirdo fuck her. She had doubts. Maybe the weirdo would give her an ugly baby. She wanted a nice looking Gringorican baby she could name something nice like Nathaniel or Christopher. Of course the baby wouldn't have green hair. She knew that. She liked his name, though. Omagaw Boogaloo was a very cool name. It didn't sound like a gringo name. She liked that. She found out his name one time when he was with other skinny-ass *blanquitos* in Odessa, eating red soup with big fat yellow bread.

"What is that shit?" Maruquita asked her aunt, Malta Duquesa.

Her aunt was only eighteen but she already had three children.

"What shit?" she said.

"That red shit the niggah's eating," Maruquita said, pointing a thumb behind her.

"Soup," Malta said, after taking a look.

"That shit look nasty. What kinda soup?"

"I don't know," her aunt said. "Axe the waitress. Gaw!"

When Flecka Modelewski came over, Maruquita asked her about the red soup.

"Borscht," said Flecka, her ancestral mind wandering crazily around the steppes of Eastern Europe after being raped by a Mongol with a huge kielbasa.

"Botch?" Maruquita asked.

"Yeah, Borscht," Flecka said.

"What it tastes like?"

"Try it," Flecka said, wondering if this stupid Puerto Rican girl with all the eye shadow, lacquered black hair, and big earrings had any brains. "I should bring?"

"Yeah," Maruquita said. "And bring a burger deluxe and a Coke. You want some botch, Titi Malta?"

"Forget it," Malta said. "I want blueberry blintzes with sour cream and a Diet Coke."

Flecka Modelewski wrote down the order and retreated, muttering Polish incantations that might turn the stupid girl into a dog. The other one wasn't too bright either. They reminded Flecka of Mongol barbarians.

"What food is that you order?" Maruquita asked her aunt. "Who makes it?"

"It's Jewish food. Blintzes. I like it."

"You gonna turn into a Jew eating them blinkers," Maruquita said to her aunt.

"Blintzes."

"Whatevah," Maruquita said.

When Flecka Modewleski brought their orders, Maruquita tasted the red soup, made a face, nearly gagged, and said *ewww*. She pushed the soup away and announced that it was cold and looked and tasted like sweet period.

"You tasted period?"

"Yeah. What's the big deal? It's my blood."

"Gaw, you're such a *puerca*. Such a pig."

"At least I don't have three babies from three different guys and you don't even know who the fathers are. Maybe you're the *puerca*."

"Shut up or I'ma tell your mother you eating period."

"I don't care. Taste it, Titi Malta," Maruquita said.

"It's *remolachas*," Malta said, after taking a spoonful. "Beets."

"Beet soup? That's fucked up," Maruquita said.

She put a big blob of ketchup in the middle of the French fries, popped a few fries into her mouth, and turned to see the guy in the green hair eating his red soup in the booth behind her. She got up on her knees and tapped the green-haired guy on his shoulder.

"Yo, you like that red soup? That botch?"

"It's pretty good," said the guy.

"I didn't like it."

"That's cool. What's your name?"

"That's for me to know and for you to find out," Maruquita said, looking at the guy's blue eyes and green hair. His tongue was pierced and so were his ears. He had a bird tattoo under his right eye. A weirdo for sure.

"So that's why I asked you," the guy said.

"What's yours?"

"I asked you first."

"And I axed you last."

"Omaha Bigelow," said the weirdo. "Now you."

"Maruquita Salsipuedes," she said, pointing at herself and leaning over to shake his hand so that her breasts spilled over the booth like live tapioca pudding all over Omaha's shoulder. "Who are the other bozos?" she inquired.

All of them cracked up and pointed at each other and said bozo.

"Oh, they're in our band Carsick."

"Carsick, like throwing up?"

"Yeah, yeah," they all said, scoping out the round and luscious Rican tits of Maruquita Salsipuedes.

"Oh, that's Richard Rentacar. He's the lead singer. The one with the pink glasses is David Bulemia, the drummer, and Pancho Vomit, the lead guitar. I play bass."

"*Bajo*," said Maruquita.

"Baho?"

"That's bass in Spanish."

"I should learn."

"Yeah. It's easy," said Maruquita.

"We're gonna play at ABC No Rio next Saturday. You should come."

"Where's that at?"

"On Rivington between Clinton and Suffolk. It's in the afternoon, when they're giving out food."

She felt Malta smack her behind and heard her hissing that she shut up and sit down. Maruquita said she liked Omaha Bigelow's green hair and turned back around. Malta Duquesa was not pleased with her niece's behavior. It was totally inappropriate for a Rican homegirl to be throwing herself at these gringos.

Maruquita and her aunt finished eating, went to the movies on Second Avenue and saw *American History X*, which they both thought was totally weird. They both covered their eyes during the prison rape scene, even though all the naked guys in the shower had nice butts. They ate pizza and eventually returned to the jungle on Avenue D. All she could think about was Omagaw Boogaloo. She loved his green hair, and thinking of his pierced tongue made her very wet, so that she felt like doing it to herself like Vicentica Valdez had taught her. Not actually touching her because they didn't want to be no *cachapera* lesbian girls, but Vicentica explaining while they were both under the covers when she stayed at her house when they were both twelve, telling her where she should put her finger. Vicentica was on one side of the big bed and she on the other. It felt good touching with her index finger, and then the bed was shaking and Vicentica was bouncing around saying *omagaw* and then it was too good and she said *omagaw* too and the bed shook some more.

Now she sat cross-legged sweeping the area with her maglite. If she saw a rat, she waved the stick and the rat scampered off. It could be that Omagaw Boogaloo was the one. She thought about it for a while. She was certain he was the one. He had to be the one because that was his name, Omagaw, and maybe he could make her bounce on the bed. She decided that she would ask her mother if she could bring him home and keep him as a pet. She was fifteen and ready to have a pet that could lick her and put his *coso* into her and give her babies and not run away like a *pendejo* and he could work and buy nice things like flowered shower curtains and microwaves and a nice stroller for the baby.

She had been following him, disguising herself as a pitbull one time and a Chinese delivery boy on a bike another time, and then a cop, and a wino, a girl scout, and a clown other times. Omagaw Bigelow was working at Kinko's, which was a nice job and it was air conditioned. She wasn't sure if she would let him stay working at Kinko's because many white bitches came in there shaking their skinny *culos,* talking all kinds of shit about going on additions, whatever the fuck that was but it sounded like they was movie stars and what-not and needed to add up their money. Movie stars came into the neighborhood. She saw Johnny Depp on Avenue A one time. He was cute. And she saw Angelina Jolie sitting at the Sidewalk Café on Sixth Street and she thought Angelina was some Rican girl with her big lips all painted purple or something.

She had seen Omagaw Boogaloo coming out of a building on Ninth Street with a skinny *blanquita* bitch with a *culo* that wasn't even as big as one of her own tits. She was arguing with him and making him feel bad and he was saying fuck over and over again so she felt like turning from a cop into a pitbull and biting the bitch's leg and running away into the park and turning into a squirrel and climbing a tree. Maybe Omagaw Boogaloo wouldn't like her fine J-Lo butt, which all the boys said was tremendous and spectacular. Maybe he liked them skinny-assed white bitches with their flat butts. She could change his mind big time. She could take him up into the mountains in the projects, and in the moonlight by the Rio Grande de Loiza she'd invite El Gran Combo to play, and she would dance naked for him, shaking her butt and her titties, and then he would get turned on and give her *mucha cabeza* in her *tontón creek.*

She remained on watch during the night, observing Omaha turn one way and then another and at some point grinding himself into the ground like he was wanting to wild-thing the earth.

OMAHA BIGELOW WAS VERY SURPRISED TO WAKE UP AND FIND A SMALL monkey staring at him. It was a girl monkey, and she was holding a little flashlight and a shiny black stick. He could see her *cuchi-cuchi*, tiny and pink, and that's how he knew it was a girl monkey. He blinked a couple of times and took a closer look, and it wasn't a monkey but a girl sitting cross-legged near him, but now he couldn't see her thing because she had on black panties. She was dressed all in black, with big lace boots and net stockings. The girl had a wonderful shape and was quite pretty in a spaced-out *mira mira señorita* kind of Spanish way. She looked vaguely familiar. He wasn't sure but he thought he knew her. Omaha also wasn't sure what he should say, but he had a great urge to put his tongue into the girl and make her moan. He wished Carrie Marshack hadn't been such a bitch. He gave her good head, and she kicked him out. Fuck.

"You go to ABC No Rio?" Omaha inquired.

"Yeah, I go. You're Omagaw Boogaloo, right?"

"Omaha Bigelow, yeah."

"That's what I said, you bozo. Omagaw Boogaloo."

"That's where I know you from," Omaha said, noting that the girl sounded like Rosie Pérez, although not quite as strident.

"From where?"

"ABC No Rio on Rivington Street."

"Maybe, but I seen you around. You work in Kinko's, copying booshit for skinny ass *blanquitas* going for additions."

"Yeah, I useta."

"No more?"

"I got fired for sleeping and fucking up copies."

"And you still playing *bajo* for Carsick?"

"Yeah, but the band's breaking up."

"For why?"

"David Bulemia got a gig with Godzilla, this Japanese punk band. He changed his name and dyed his hair black."

"The bozo changed his name?"

"Yeah, Hiro Buromika. He wears his hair all spiked up."

"That's fucked up."

"Tell me."

"But I like your green hair, and I seen you over there in the restaurant eating yucky red soup that look like period."

"Odessa, on Avenue A," Omaha said, pointing through the trees at the restaurant. "I was eating borscht with the band."

"That's right. Booshit botch soup. That shit is nasty."

"I remember you. You're Mariconcita," Omaha said, and felt a sharp sting where he had been slapped.

"What the fuck?" he said.

"I ain't no mothafuckin *cachapera* lesbian, *pendejo.* That's what the fuck. "

"What'cha do that for? Damn. That hurt."

"Then don't be calling me no names."

"I didn't call you no names."

"Why you call me *mariconcita?* For why? "

"I thought that was your name."

"Don't play yourself, Omagaw Boogaloo," the girl said, frowning at him, her teeth showing like she was going to bite him. "Don't play yourself. That shit mean girl faggot."

"What does?"

"*Mariconcita,* you bozo. Don't be calling me no lesbian. I don't be giving no head to no girl. That's nasty."

"I'm sorry. Maybe I forgot your name. What's your name?"

"My name is Maruquita. You knew that and you was trying to fuck with my mind."

"I'm not, really. I'm sorry. I had some heavy pizza. Was it snowing last night?"

"Snowing?"

"Yeah."

"No, it wasn't snowing, you bozo. You musta been smoking some bad shit. It's July. How it gonna be snowing in July?"

"It was the mushrooms. The real good shit the Mexican gave me. I talked to a polar bear."

"Omagaw Boogaloo, your head is fucked up. There ain't no polo bears down here. They got plenty of weirdos but no silly-ass polo bears. Don't be a asshole."

"I know, I know. I see shit sometimes."

"You do?"

"Yeah. It's weird."

"Splain how you see shit."

"I don't know. Sometimes it's like I'm not here. Like I'm flying around with butterflies and birds, stopping here and stopping there, and the music is going like violins and sometimes I'm walking around and people are turning into animals and that's why I saw the polar bear."

"For real?"

"Yeah, when I woke up, I thought you were a monkey," Omaha said, sitting up and looking at her. "But you're nothing like a monkey. You're a very beautiful girl."

"Don't get fresh, Omagaw Boogaloo," Maruquita said, wanting to put her tongue on the little silver ball on Omaha's tongue. "Don't be dissing me or I'm gonna smack you again."

"I'm not dissing you," Omaha said. "I'm saying that you're really pretty."

"Yeah?" Maruquita said, smiling.

"Yeah."

"Well, I gotta go and axe my motha for permission."

"Permission for what?"

"To let you give me head in my *tontón papaya* and keep you."

"Yeah?"

"Yeah, where you gonna be?"

"I'll be around here in the park. I gotta get me some change cauze I'm hungry. I'm going over to Second Avenue and handle a little."

"Handle?"

"Yeah, panhandle. Ask for change in the street. I'm hungry."

"You do that? You stand in the street and bug people for if they got change?"

"Yeah, I lost my Kinko's job."

"Yeah, you said that. They let you keep the cute shirt with Kinko's on it?"

"I still got it. It's over at Richard's house. I keep my shit over there."

"If I let you give me head, can I have it?"

"Sure," Omaha Bigelow said, brightening up.

"Okay, bye," Maruquita said, jumping up and racing east out of the park. Fuck, thought Omaha. Fucking A, he said out loud. He felt the meager erection in his pants and yelled, *Calm down motherfucker, your time is coming. Just shut the fuck up right now. We gotta make some change first.*

He got up off the ground, did two minutes of Kansas-style Tai Chi in which he moved awkwardly, like he was playing an imaginary bass, and crawled out of the bushes and into another East Village summer extravaganza. He asked a dude with a briefcase for the time. Fuck, he thought, it isn't even 8:00 A.M. Already in the morning there were bitches and dudes roller blading, people doing exercise, people selling dope, joggers going around Tompkins Square Park like they were training for the Olympics except that some were fat and would finish going around the park ten times and then go across the street to Odessa and order twenty-four potato pancakes and swallow them whole.

He came out of the park, crossed Avenue A, and walked on St. Mark's Place until he got to Second Avenue. A couple of raggedy-ass black bums were panhandling on his corner. He wanted to go and tell them off, but they'd call him a white motherfucker and kick his ass. He didn't feel like being a nonracist pacifist this morning. Fuck, he was really hungry. He searched his pockets and came up with fifty-four cents, stopped at a bodega, and got a bag of potato chips. He found a McDonald's box in a garbage can and continued walking until he got to Astor Place. Once under the black cube, he sat down, pulled out his little wire-rim sun glasses, put them on, and began acting like he was blind and singing Beatles songs. People rushed by on their way to work and, seeing themselves out of their dot.com jobs, empathized with this punk rocker and dropped coins into the McDonald's box with great there-for-the-grace-of-God-go-I ceremony. There was even one dude who sang "We All Live in a Yellow Submarine" with Omaha before crossing the street and going down into the Number 6 subway. By 10:30 A.M. when people stopped rushing back and forth, he had $13.77 to go with the four cents he had left after buying the chips.

Omaha Bigelow counted his change, put it in his pocket, and got up. He started feeling around, playing out his blindness, until a man came up and asked him where he wanted to go. He told the man he needed to go to Third Avenue. The man helped him cross the street. He thanked the man. When he was alone again, Omaha took off his glasses, placed them in his pocket, and crossed Third Avenue. He went to the pizza shop, bought a slice and a Pepsi, paid for it with coins, pissing one more New York City person off, not a difficult task. He wolfed down the pizza and left. He walked to Second Avenue, went into the Pakistani newspaper store, and changed some of the coins into a five-dollar bill. He then went down to Theresa's on First Avenue and ordered a full breakfast of eggs and kielbasa.

When he was done, he walked over to Suffolk Street, came to the old school, knocked on the door, and a big Puerto Rican guy with a mustache and glasses opened up and asked him what he wanted. He thought maybe the Puerto Rican was a ghost. Omaha pointed inside.

"What?" said the guy.

"I got a rehearsal," he said.

"What rehearsal?"

He pointed at the funeral-parlor-looking glass-covered board with a bunch of plays on it.

"The Magic Glasses," Omaha said quickly.

"They don't rehearse until this afternoon," the man said.

"I know. I just got off work and I wanna crash until they get here."

"You know John Macken and Richard Nash?"

"Yeah, I know them. Daedalus Theater Company."

"Okay, come in," the man said. "Don't crash in the lobby," he added pointing to the green hotel-lobby-looking seats.

"Sure," Omaha said, "I'll go in the theater."

"Watch the rats," the man said. "They'll eat your dick."

"I'll keep an eye out."

When the man was gone, Omaha Bigelow went into the bathroom, took a healthy dump, thought of spanking the monkey right there, but changed his mind. He thought about the naked body of Maruquita Salsipuedes and was instantly erect. He looked at his erection, puny and red with the darkish blond pubic hair around it, and eventually thought of his mother's brightly painted fingernails moving rapidly, and his erection disappeared. It was the one way he could calm himself down. If he thought of her ruby-red toenails, the erection would appear again. All he needed to do was think of her cherry-like toenails, and he would be hard. Even after having wanked himself ten or twelve times a day, all he needed to do was recall the red nail polish and little cotton balls between his mother's toes, and he was ready to go. Fuck, he thought. What the fuck was that about? Maybe his brain was really fried and he wanted to do his mother. It was radically Oedipal. Fuck. He washed his hands, came out of the bathroom, looked around the Como Coco Café, saw the Coronas inside the glass ice box, but the thing had a lock on it. He could use a nice brew but he didn't want to spend the little money he had.

He walked out of the big castle-looking building that everyone called CVS like it was the drug store and decided to stop by Kinko's. He walked down Suffolk past the yard with the big empty lot with the planted vegetables and the little house with chickens running around outside of it like it was Puerto Rico. That was what Fernández, the super in Carrie Marshack's building, had said. He felt like going to Carrie's building on Attorney Street and ringing her bell, but he heard that she was sleeping with some big Russian dude that was a bouncer in a West Side club. Igor Lumpenski or something like that. He didn't want any trouble. He kept going on Suffolk Street until he got to Meow Mix, which was a lesbian bar, waited for the light to change, crossed Houston Street, and went into Kinko's.

A thin Puerto Rican kid named Bobby with a fade recognized him.

"How you doing, Biggie," he said.

"Dude," Omaha said, bunching up his fist and knocking it against Bobby's closed one, but hating being called Biggie because big he wasn't. "How you been?"

"Oh, here and there," Bobby said. "Hitting the books and shit. Summer school at Boro of Manhattan. You know how it is. Getting an education."

"Yeah, I hear you. I'm working on that GED, bro."

"Get the fuck outta here," Bobby said. "I heard you was at Yale and NYU."

"Oh, yeah?"

"Yeah."

"Maybe I forgot. Fly's still working here?"

"Nah."

"Who's the day supervisor?"

"Molotov."

"Fuck!"

"I know. This is my last day."

"Do you think if I talk to him I can get my job back?"

"I don't know. This place is getting more fucked up each day."

"Bro, let me ask you something."

"What?"

"You know a girl called Maruquita?"

"Rican girl with a nice shape and big earrings?"

"Yeah."

"Fuck," said Bobby.

"What?"

"Stay away from her, bro. She lives over there in the projects."

"What's wrong?"

"Man, American people go in there and they never come out. They say that's like a jungle over there. Her people are all *brujos.* Father, mother, grand-mother. All *brujos,* bro."

"What's bruhos?"

"People that put shit on you and turn you crazy and you be barking like a dog or mooing like a cow. Don't fuck with those people, bro."

"You think Maruquita's a bruho?"

"*Bruja.* A girl *brujo.*"

"And they can do shit like that?"

"Yeah, they can do shit like that. One of my homeboys' father was mess-ing around with this lady, cheating on her and what not. This lady went to Maruquita's mother and got a *consulta,* and about a month later this guy's dick turned the size of a baby carrot like you see in the supermarket."

"Really?" said Omaha, intrigued.

"Yeah, no lie," Bobby said.

"Maybe they can do it the other way around."

"What you mean?"

"If a dude had a small dick, they could make it bigger."

"Maybe," Bobby said. "You know somebody like that?"

"No, I was just saying."

"Word," said Bobby. "Niggah could use a few more inches on his john-son."

"Gross," said a skinny redhead with a portfolio, who had come in and was standing next to Omaha Bigelow.

Bobby moved over to help the girl.

Omaha Bigelow waved to Bobby, went out of Kinko's, and walked around the corner to Avenue B, thinking of how his life was about to change maybe for the better. When he got back to Tompkins Square Park, he walked around looking for Maruquita. Maybe they could bruho his dick and he could have a big johnson like Barkuma Washington, who played on the Yale football team. That would be way cool. Just for spite he would go back to Carrie Marshack just to let her see it. Fuck, he thought.

MARUQUITA SALSIPUEDES LEFT TOMPKINS SQUARE PARK, TURNED INTO a chihuahua, barked at a few people, saw a pitbull coming, changed into a cat, and scurried down the stairs to a basement, saw a rat, had an urge to catch it, but concentrated and put it out of her mind. She changed into a fat white girl with lots of tattoos, a Mohawk haircut, a big tentlike dress and combat boots. She came out of the basement, walked down the street, stopped off at the Korean deli, bought a can of Colt 45 Malt Liquor, and drank it. She kept going on Sixth Street until she got to Avenue D and the city housing projects before changing into an old black woman and crossing the street. When she got to her building, she changed into a squirrel. Up a tree she went and changed into a monkey. Reaching the top, she hopped along the branches until she saw her window. It was closed. She said *baruka faruka maruka.* The window opened slowly, and she leaped into it. She landed on the bed, changed back into herself, removed her clothes, and was under the covers and asleep a few minutes later. Before she fell asleep she thought of Omagaw Boogaloo and how she was going to ask her mother if she could keep him for a pet because he was the one. Omagaw Boogaloo saw shit and people changing into animals and that was the sign. For sure he was the one. Unbelievable. A gringo *brujo,* although he probably didn't know much.

Maruquita slept until four in the afternoon. She got up, walked naked to the river, and dove into the clear mountain water before turning into a *burukena,* and then a small blue-and-silver fish. She walked back up to the family *bohío,* where her mother was sitting outside the thatch-roofed conical house making *kasave,* placing the large wet pancakes of taro flour on a stone that sat on a fire. She put out her hand, and her mother gave her one of the crackers.

"*Bendición,*" said Maruquita, asking her mother's blessing as she chewed on the taro cracker.

"The Lord Yukiyú bless you and keep you," her mother, Flaquita, said, turning from the stove where she was frying *bacalaitos.* "What you doing walking around naked? Go get dressed. You ain't no baby no more. You're a grown girl now with big titties and your *tontón* hairy. Don't be so fresh."

"There was no towels in the bathroom," Maruquita said.

"So? You shoulda thought of that before you went in. Go get dressed."

"Give me one, ma," she said.

"A what?"

"A *bacalaito*."

Her mother reached over with a paper towel, grabbed one of the crispy codfish fritters, and gave it to Maruquita, repeating her request that she go change before her father came home or her brother came upstairs.

"He's over there in Charas rehearsing his whatever."

"He's rehearsing his play."

"I know."

"He's a good boy. Every mother should have children like him."

"He makes money, Mami," Maruquita said. "That's all he does."

"Of course he makes money, *idiota*. That's good."

"He plays the spock market."

"Stock market."

"More booshit Star Trucks."

"Star Trek. Go change, I told you."

"Okay, okay. You don't gotta plex up."

With that Maruquita left the kitchen and went to change.

Flaquita Salsipuedes shook her head and wondered what the hell she had done to piss off Yukiyú so he gave her such a daughter. She had never seen such a stupid. The girl couldn't do anything right. Stupid in school, stupid for work, stupid around the house. She had bought the Great Books and the Encyclopedia Britannica for her son and daughter, but only her son had taken advantage of the books. She had as well, but not Maruquita. It drove her crazy that the girl was so lacking.

Flaquita took the last fritter from the boiling lard, let it drip for a moment, and placed it among the stack on the large plate. She stirred the beans, tasted the sauce, nodded approvingly, and placed chicken legs into the boiling lard where the fritters had cooked. With a potholder she lifted the lid from the large cast-iron pot and stirred the white rice. She smiled contentedly when she thought again of her daughter. She was stupid about a lot of things but not about their craft, the *brujería*. In that she was talented and fearless. She would go far. She could lead the battle to regain control of their ancestral islands. Flaquita had no doubt about that. She once again smiled. Yukiyú had his tricks. Don't give everyone the whole thing. Keep them humble. Her daughter, Maruquita, was a specialist, a professional.

Maruquita came back into the kitchen. She was dressed in shorts and a sleeveless blouse. Her hair was combed out and long, and she wore coral lipstick and small earrings. She had on thick socks and her hightop pink Reeboks. Without being asked, she began setting the table. When she was done, she made Kool-Aid just like her mother made it. Flaquita watched her and knew something strange was up. She didn't know what it could be. When she was done Maruquita turned on the TV and surfed around looking at bits of movies and made a face at MTV because Daisy Fuentes wasn't on. Daisy had a nice body, not like them skinny-ass white bitches that came on the screen and danced like they were retarded. Gaw she hated them. They looked like silly-ass Shorty Duval, Olive Oyl brooms. Her face softened as she thought again of Omagaw Boogaloo. She turned off the TV, went over to her mother, gave her a kiss, and said she was sorry for walking around *esnua*.

"I gotta axe you something important, Ma," she said.

"No."

"No?"

"No."

"I can't axe you something important?"

"No, not now. Jump out the window and fly over to Fourteenth Street and tell your grandma that dinner is gonna be served in a half hour. What time is it?"

"Five twenty-five," Maruquita said, looking at her watch.

"Go! If your grandmother don't come right away, your father's gonna eat everything and I'll have to cook again. She's his mother, but he don't give a fuck."

"Can I axe you something important later, Ma?"

"Yeah, yeah. Go, go. Shoo, shoo," said Flaquita waving her daughter away.

"Okay, okay. Gaw, you so crabby and bossy. Whatsa matter wif you?"

"Go, *idiota.*"

Maruquita went to her room, changed into a monkey, leaped out the window, grabbed a tree branch, and climbed to the top. When she was there, the brown fur became black and feathery, the flat face became pointy, and she turned into a crow. She lifted her wings and floated out from the tree before taking flight, soaring beyond the projects and over the tenements. Two minutes later she was circling a building on Avenue C and Fourteenth Street and landing on the roof. By the time her feet hit the asphalt, she had once again changed into herself. Her grandmother, Bizquita Salsipuedes, was sitting in a chair smoking a cigar and singing Protestant hymns in Spanish that had nasty words which made Maruquita laugh. *En la cruz, en la cruz donde primero me vení.* On the cross, on the cross where I first came.

"*Bendición, Güela,*" Maruquita said, smiling and kissing her grandmother's cheek.

"May the Lord Yukiyú bless you and keep you, Maruquita," said the old woman, dressed in jeans, cowboy boots, and a cowboy hat.

"Thank you, Grandma. Ma says you should come right away to eat, cauze Papi's gonna come and eat everything."

"Okay, let me get these *pendejos* and *pendejas* to come in," she said, blowing a big puff of blue smoke into the air and waving her hand at the sky where a flight of about five hundred to six hundred pigeons was circling overhead like a gray-and-white cloud.

She pointed to the cages. Maruquita began opening them. The old woman stood up, chomped down on her cigar, grabbed a long bamboo pole, whistled twice, and the pigeons circled and began descending onto the roof. Once they landed, nodding and cooing, they marched in a very orderly manner into the cages.

When the last pigeon was inside the ten large cages stacked against the wall of the stairwell, Bizquita twirled the cigar and it turned into a can of Budweiser which she offered to her granddaughter. Maruquita took it, drank from it, and gave it back to her grandmother, who drained it, gave the can another twirl, and the can turned brown, sprouted wings, and took off as a sparrow.

"You ready, Maruquita?"

"Yes, Grandma."

"You wanna go seagull until we get to the projects?"

"Sure."

"We can land on the roof and go down the stairs when we get there."

"Okay, Grandma."

In a blink of an eye the two women, one old, the other young, turned into seagulls, honked twice, and took off heading eastward.

"You think we got time for a little spin over the water?" said the old woman.

"Sure," said Maruquita.

They flew beyond the projects and out over the water. A cabin cruiser was making its way down the East River. On the deck a sticklike blonde was sunning herself, totally naked. You could tell she wasn't really a blonde. Maruquita thought of Omagaw Boogaloo and the skinny-ass, no *culo* bitches, and had a great urge.

"Can I bomb, Grandma?" she asked Bizquita.

"Can I join you?"

"Sure," said Maruquita.

The two seagulls swooped down until they were directly above the blonde lying on the beach chair on the top deck of the boat. They hovered there for a moment, counted one-two-three, and pooped simultaneously. Maruquita's salvo hit directly between the blonde's tiny breasts. Her grandmother's missile was more accurate and landed directly on the woman's face, mixing in a gray-green mess with her sunscreen. The two seagulls made a pass closer to the exasperated woman, who was now looking furiously up at them. They laughed, made a high arc, and climbed aloft before heading inland.

"Grandma, can I axe you something?" Maruquita said.

"Is it important?"

"Yeah. I wanna know."

"Sure."

"The pigeons? Are they all gringos and gringas?"

"They were. Mostly drug addicts, Wall Street types, but all college graduates."

"Can they turn back?"

"Nope, they're pigeons now. No more wild pot parties, no more herpes, no more ATM cards, no more bad dancing in discos, no more saying 'No problemo,' no more fucking with the people in this neighborhood. What they think we are, for them to be fucking with us and dissing us all the time?"

"They stay like that? Pigeons all their life?"

"Yep, cowgirl," said Bizquita Salsipuedes.

"You got punk rockers, Grandma?"

"Yeah, I gotta few."

"There's one boy."

"Yes?"

"He's got green hair and a bird on his cheek."

"Tattoo?"

"Yeah."

"I seen him. Is he messing with you?"

"No, *Güela*. He don't bother me."

"You want me to turn him into a pigeon? If he's messing with you, I can do that."

"No, Grandma. Oh, no, please don't," Maruquita said, her heart jumping so that she almost turned into herself, she was so frightened. "No, not him, please."

"Is he a *gringo*?"

"Yes, but I think he's the one."

"To keep?"

"Yeah, to keep. His name is Omagaw Boogaloo, and he sees shit and can see people turn into animals."

"For real?"

"Yeah, I think he's the one. I gotta axe Ma. But I'm pretty sure."

"A gringo white boy is the one?"

"I think so, Grandma. I gotta axe Ma, but she's always so nasty."

"You leave your mother to me," Bizquita said. "If he's the one, I'll handle it. I need to interview him. He needs to get tested."

"For AIDS and shit?"

"Yeah, that too. But I gotta test him to see if he's the one. Can you arrange that?"

"Sure, Grandma."

"Good. As soon as possible."

"Grandma?"

"What, honey?"

"You think I'll ever not be stupid?"

"You're not stupid."

"No?"

"Nope. You're the one."

"The one?"

"The one old people talked about."

"Really?"

"Yep. *La Bruja Mayor.*"

"Oh, my Gaw, Grandma. Me? For real?"

"It looks like it. Don't say nothing to your mother. Be a good girl until I can straighten this mess out. What's his name again?"

"Omagaw Boogaloo, Grandma," Maruquita said.

"Let me see what I can do," the old woman said.

The two seagulls were now near the north end of the projects. They circled the Con Edison steam towers and flew southward. After a few more minutes they landed on Maruquita's building. Two boys were playing with a pitbull puppy on the roof. Screaming and honking, the two seagulls swooped down until the boys, afraid of the seagulls, picked up the puppy and went down the stairs. Maruquita and her grandmother landed and turned back into themselves. Bizquita adjusted her cowboy hat, hoisted up her britches, and plumped up her breasts. She pointed for Maruquita to head downstairs. When they came into the apartment, Maruquita's father, and son to Bizquita, was about to sit down to eat.

"Hold it right there, partner," Bizquita said. "We need to give thanks for this here vittles."

"Yes, Mama," Roque Salsipuedes said, obediently.

A few minutes later Maruquita's older brother, Samuel Beckett Salsipuedes, walked in, carrying a script in one hand and a cardboard model of a set in the other. Even in summer he wore a purple cape and a wide-brimmed hat. He sported pink sunglasses and had a goatee. He was such a weirdo, thought Maruquita, now very hungry. But anyway she loved him, and he always gave her money to get clothes and go out. Anyway, he knew the spock market, which she supposed was very cool because he could make lots of money although she didn't know how typing on the computer could do that. Computers were weird.

OMAHA BIGELOW WAITED AND WAITED SOME MORE. WITH THE CONGA players going strong he finally fell asleep on a bench near the eastern side of Tompkins Square Park. Around four o'clock in the afternoon he woke up, went to Odessa, and had vegetable soup and a grilled cheese sandwich. He returned to the bench and at seven o'clock, with the day still bright, when he had almost given up hope of seeing Maruquita again, she showed up. Before he saw her he could sense her, since she had now entered his mind and sat there on her haunches like a little monkey, diminutive and furry, but her pretty señorita face smiling at him. It was strange that he could see her both as a monkey and as a girl in the same image. One face faded and the other took over, and once in a while they blended.

"Hi, Omagaw Boogaloo," said Maruquita, feeling shy and tickly inside.

"Hi, Maruquita," he said. "You look nice."

"Thanks," she said, wrinkling her nose and waving her hand in front of it. "You need a bath."

"I do?" Omaha said, feeling a tad embarrassed.

"Yeah, you smell like *chaleco de pordiosero.* Like *sillín de bicicleta.* Like *pantaletas de vieja cagá.*"

"Is that bad?"

"Yeah, it's bad. Very bad!"

"What does it mean?"

"*Falta de baño,*" Maruquita said. "You need a bath."

"Okay, I'm sorry. The other."

"What?"

"*Caleco, mocuco,* whatever you said."

"Don't make fun of me, Omagaw Boogaloo. Okay? Don't make fun."

"Okay, but what does it mean?"

"Oh, my Gaw. I was speaking Spanish. Why didn't you say something, you bozo."

"I thought you knew."

"I don't know. I'm crazy. I speak one and then the other and I go back and forth, and sometimes I forget you're a gringo white boy and everything. The first one means bum's vest, the next one, bicycle seat, and the last one old lady's shitty panties. It means you stink and I need to give you a bath right away."

"You do? Where?"

"We can go to my girlfriend Piloncita's house. Her mother went to work stripping, and she's home taking care of her little brother."

"Stripping?"

"Yeah, she takes off her clothes and guys pay to see her titties and her *tontón* that she shave."

"Her Tonto?"

"No, *tontón.* Her pussy. She just got a little bit of hair. She shave it."

"Oh, yeah?"

"Yeah, you wanna see my titties?"

"Sure."

"One only, okay?"

"Okay."

Maruquita looked around, saw that no one was paying attention, reached down, and extracted her left breast from inside the halter and blouse she was wearing. She let it sit in her hand and watched Omaha's eyes open wide. She quickly placed the breast back in her blouse.

"Oh, my God," Omaha said, instantly erect. "You're beyond belief."

"What means that?" Maruquita said.

"Tremendous. Formidable."

"Don't play yourself, Omagaw Boogaloo. Don't mess with my mind. Did you like it?"

"Yeah. It was the most beautiful breast I've ever seen."

"For real?"

"Yeah."

"Not like them skinny flat *fundillo,* itty bitty titty white *pendeja* bitches, right?"

"Right. You're the one," he said, pointing at her.

"I am?" Maruquita said, perplexed.

"Yeah."

"The one what?"

"It don't matter. You're the one."

"And you actually see niggahs turn into animals?" Maruquita said, liking what she was hearing.

"Yeah, I do. Sometimes."

"I can do that," she said.

"Do what? See people turn into animals?"

"No, turn into animals," Maruquita said proudly.

"No!"

"Yeah, for real. Pick something. Don't pick no tigers or lions, cauze they be chasing people and scaring the shit out of them, and niggahs got cell phones and call the cops. I don't do them cauze of that shit. I just do small animals and mostly birds. You know?"

"Okay, okay. A peacock."

"What's that?"

Omaha explained what a peacock looked like.

"Okay, I understand. *Un pavo real.* A real turkey."

"What?"

"That's what it's called in Spanish. *Pavo real.*"

"You said 'real turkey' before."

"Yeah, I translated. Real turkey."

"Maybe you mean royal turkey?"

"Yeah, whatevah. Anyway, I'ma do it quick, so pay attention. I don't want people freaking out. You ready?"

"Okay, yeah. Ready."

And then, in the blink of an eye Omaha was in the presence of a beautiful and majestic peacock. The bird emitted a small call and flared its tail to display the gold-and-green eyes of its plumage. Omaha shook his head in amazement, and a fraction of a second later there was Maruquita smiling at him.

"Did you like it?"

"Oh, it was beautiful," Omaha said so that Maruquita was reminded of a little boy.

"Let's go," she said.

"Go where?"

"To get you cleaned up so you don't be stinking up the joint, you bozo."

"Oh, okay."

Omaha and Maruquita walked out of the park, down Avenue B to Eleventh Street. They turned east and went up the steps of an apartment house. Junkies were hanging out in front. One of them said something to Maruquita. She turned to them, spoke quickly in Spanish, and they came down off the stoop, said they were sorry, and went down the street without another word.

"What happened? What did you say to them?" Omaha asked.

"One of them said I had a nice butt. I told them not to be fresh because I could turn them into *ratones.* That's mouses."

"You can do that?"

"They be cat sandwiches in a NY mini, honey. They be Cherries, and Tom be chewin' on their butts. What they think, they is dissing me that way."

They went up the stairs, she knocked on a door on the second floor, and a girl about her age let them in. The two girls hugged and kissed and gave each other high fives. Maruquita introduced her girlfriend, Piloncita, and told the girl this was her friend Omagaw Boogaloo. The girl said hi and said she liked his green hair. Omaha said thank you very much and wondered if the girl could turn into a monkey even though she wasn't as pretty as Maruquita.

"I'm sorry, Pilo. I gotta give him a bath," Maruquita said. "He smell so bad."

"Yeah," Piloncita said, holding her nose. "I didn't wanna say nothing."

"Can I use the washing machine?"

"Yeah. In the kitchen."

"Okay, you bozo. Go in the bathroom and take off all your clothes. Fill the baftub. Your sneakers and socks and everything. Take the money and everything out of the pockets."

"Now?"

"Yeah, now, before you stink up the joint."

"Where?"

"Over there," she said.

"Where over there?" Omaha said, feeling uncomfortable.

"Omagaw Boogaloo, don't embarrass me in front of my friend. You're supposed to be a smart gringo white boy that works at Kinko's and everything. Go down the hall and find the bathroom. *Vete.* Go."

When Omaha was gone down the hall, Maruquita shook her head and apologized to Piloncita again.

"He like playing me and acting like a *pendejo,*" Maruquita said. "But he's smart."

"Girl, whatcha doing with a gringo white boy?"

"I think he's the one?"

"For real?"

"Yeah."

"He gave you head in your *tontón papaya?*"

"No, not yet, but did you see his tongue?"

"Yeah, I saw his tongue. That's awesome. You get wet?"

"Yeah, I get wet. He's the one. I gotta axe my mother's permission, but my grandmother's gonna talk to her, and I think she's gonna let me keep him."

"A gringo white boy?"

"Yeah, what's wrong, girl?"

"I don't know."

"I told you I wanna Gringorican baby."

"Oh, right. And he's the one?"

"Yeah, I told you. Don't play yourself."

"Okay, girl. You don't gotta get ballistic and whatnot."

"I'm cool. I'm gonna give him a bath."

Maruquita went down the hall, walked into the bathroom where Omaha was about to get into the filled bathtub. Maruquita picked up the clothes, carried them to the kitchen, threw them in the washing machine, added detergent, and turned the machine on. She returned to the bathroom and watched Omaha Bigelow sleeping in the water, his green hair plastered to his head. She watched for a little while and then called his name. Omaha was immediately awake. He sat up startled and covered himself.

"Why are you in here?" he said.

"Omagaw Boogaloo, I came to give you a bath," Maruquita said, grabbing a big bar of Irish Spring.

"I can take a bath by myself," Omaha said.

"Omagaw Boogaloo, I don't think so," Maruquita said, beginning to scrub Omaha's neck. "If you could, you wouldn't stink like you been sleeping in garbage. Phew! Behave yourself and be quiet, or I'm going to pinch you like you was a kid."

"Okay, okay," he said.

She scrubbed his back and his chest and his arms and then told him to lift up his arms. Omaha wouldn't remove his hands from the front of him under the still clear bathwater.

"Lift up your arms, Omagaw Boogaloo. That's where the stink is hiding. That and in your *güevos*. Lift them up."

"I don't wanna," Omaha said in a little voice.

"Omagaw Boogaloo, don't make me get mad wif you. Okay? Don't be a bad boy. Lift up your arms."

"You're gonna laugh?"

"Laugh? Why for I'm gonna laugh? You got green hair under your arms? You got green *sobacos?* I ain't gonna laugh nothing."

"You're gonna laugh if you see me."

"What are you talking about? I ain't gonna laugh if you got green hair under your arms."

"Down there," Omaha said, pointing his head at his hands under the water.

"Ha, ha," said Maruquita. "You painted your *polla* green? Very cute. Let me see. Let me see."

"No, it ain't that?"

"What, you bozo? Tell me. Don't you want to give me head in my *tontón papaya*? Nobody ever even saw my pussy. I'm like Madonna."

"Like Madonna?"

"Yeah, like a burgen."

"Oh?"

"Let me see."

"Okay, but I don't want you to laugh."

"I won't laugh nothing."

"You sure?"

"Yeah, lift up your arms. You don't want me to look at your peepee? You're shy?"

"Yeah, I'm shy."

"Okay, I close my eyes but you gotta let me wash you so you don't stink, because that shit gross me out. You can't be a *gringo apestoso*, white boy. Gringos ain't supposed to stink like that unless they some useless white wino bum like they got sleeping over there on Avenue A across the street from that vegetaric Mexican place. That ain't gonna work."

Omaha watched her close her eyes and then lifted up his arms and Maruquita groped around until she found his underarms and scrubbed them furiously, sniffing and sniffing until all that was left was that manly Irish Spring smell of shamrocks and Guinness. She pushed his head down and rinsed him. The water was now clouded. Maruquita said that she had to wash below.

"I can do that," Omaha said.

"That's my job if you're gonna be my pet and give me head, Omagaw Boogaloo. Don't argue no more. Okay?"

"Okay," Omaha said meekly.

Maruquita dipped her hands into the tub until she found Omaha's pubic area and scrubbed with the bar of soap. She had a very strange look on her face. It was weird because although she had never seen a man's genitals, women said they were pretty big. This Omagaw Boogaloo felt so little. Maybe it got big, like women said it did. She finished washing his legs and feet and then put the soap away.

"Omagaw Boogaloo, I gotta axe you a favor," she said.

"Go ahead."

"I gotta make sure."

"What?"

"That you're the one. Can I kiss you and touch you?"

"Maybe."

"Close your eyes."

"Okay," Omaha said, closing his eyes.

Maruquita leaned over and kissed Omaha's lips, opening them with her tongue until she found the little stainless steel ball and let it roll around on her tongue. She then reached her hand down and found his erect organ. It was hard and thin like that of a monkey or a chihuahua. She opened her eyes and took it in her fingers under the water and caressed it until Omaha was moaning and then his back was arching up out of the water and the little peepee was shooting a stream of brightly colored fluid of magenta, silver, and pearl into the air, where it hung momentarily before crashing like delicate glass into the cloudy water. The ejaculation had looked like the feathers of a peacock to Maruquita. She was more than ever convinced that this was another sign.

"Omagaw Boogaloo," said Maruquita. "You're the one. Oh, my Gaw. That was beautiful. You make such beautiful come."

Omaha was wiped out and lay in the water wondering if he'd died and gone to heaven. She hadn't laughed, and he had gotten off. She had magical fingers, and for the first time in his life Omaha Bigelow was able to forget his mother's ruby-red toenails.

THE PUERTO RICAN NAVY AND
THE THEATER OF THE ABSURD

BIZQUITA SALSIPUEDES REMOVED HER COWBOY BOOTS AND SAT BACK ON her son's recliner. Roque had vacated his seat and had gone off to bed, which he did every evening around eight o'clock after watching the news. Bizquita made a *Bizquituka televisoruka*, and suddenly on the TV screen she was watching everything that had happened with Maruquita from the time she showed Bigelow her breast, did her peacock, took him to take a bath, until the magical realism ejaculation. There was no doubt that her granddaughter had chosen correctly. The only thing that worried her was the diminutive size of the young man's organ. She supposed that something could be done, but the price to be paid was an expensive one, and she wasn't thinking of money. What a talent Maruquita had! However, talking about money, her grandson was also quite talented in his own right.

Samuel Beckett Salsipuedes was in his room at the computer, trading stocks and other articles of importance. Thus far he had managed to acquire two destroyers, a cruiser, one submarine, four coast-guard cutters and was working on an aircraft carrier with twenty-four attack jet aircraft and four rescue helicopters. What a boy! Very quiet but very efficient. The Puerto Rican Navy project was in full swing. Although the work had not yet been completed, as Admiral of the Fleet, she had ordered the ships painted in nice bright colors. Gringos had no imagination in decorating a navy. Everything gray. Please! The destroyers were bright green, the cruiser was red, the submarine bright blue. The coast-guard cutters were yellow. She hadn't decided on the aircraft carrier, but maybe a nice magenta with silver trim might be nice. The attack jet planes would definitely be pink and the helicopters a nice lilac. She was very proud of her grandson. She wasn't so sure about SBS's playwriting and wished his mother wasn't such a theater enthusiast. SBS is what she called her grandson. He hated to be called Sammy and insisted on his full name, which had been given to him by his mother.

When Bizquita's daughter-in-law, Flaquita, was questioned about his name, she explained that she had once gone to the Tompkins Square Library to find a Lassie book because she liked reading about dogs. She was barely nine years old. Even though there was a library closer to her house, she liked walking to Tompkins Square Park to watch the hippies. It was a Saturday, about one in the afternoon. When she got ready to go home, it began to rain. There was thunder and lightning. It's nearly twelve blocks from the Tompkins Square library to the Lillian Wald projects on Avenue D, where the family lived. She didn't yet know how to fly, so going out was out of the question. The light of the day disappeared from the sky, the air grew dark, and rain fell in furious sheets, whipped by the wind. Some of the people ran out into the rain, but suddenly she knew that Yukiyú, Lord God of the Taino Indians, was upset and had sent Jurakán, god of the wind, to give her a message. She asked the librarian if she could stay until the storm was over. The librarian said it was no problem.

She went back to the window and stood looking out at the torrential rain. The drops were heavy and persistent. Suddenly the dark sky lit up and a tremendous burst of lightning exploded, followed closely by thunder. She later learned that a large tree in the Baruch projects further downtown had been struck and was nearly disintegrated by the lightning. It was as if the lightning itself had reached her. Shaken, she walked away from the window, went to the stacks and pulled out the first book she was drawn to. It was a copy of the play *Waiting for Godot*. She read it hungrily, the words hitting her with remarkable persistence. She went back for two weeks, each day reading the strange words and wondering what they meant. One night she stayed up reading the play. Toward morning she decided that she was waiting to get an answer, and the answer wasn't going to come. She decided that she liked the idea of trying to understand and waiting for the answer to reveal itself. In time it would come. Nothing came. Other ideas flashed into her head, but as interesting as they were, *the* answer never came.

One day she asked the librarian about the book. The librarian took her to a microfiche machine. She told her to sit down, went and got a reel, and placed it in the machine. She found the right article and told her to read it. It was a review of *Waiting for Godot* published on April 20, 1956, by the *New York Times* critic, Brooks Atkinson. In part it said:

> Although "Waiting for Godot" is a "puzzlement," as the King of Siam would express it, Mr. Beckett is no charlatan. He has strong feelings about the degradation of mankind, and he has given vent to them copiously. "Waiting for Godot" is all feeling. Perhaps that is why it is puzzling and convincing at the same time. Theatregoers can rail at it, but they cannot ignore it. For Mr. Beckett is a valid writer.

What did all this mean? She was as transfixed by what she read of the review as she had been by the play. She walked in a daze to the librarian and, tears in her eyes, she asked her to explain, feeling that she was Puerto Rican and therefore stupid, which is the impression she had always gotten from her teachers. *What it means charlatan, degradation, mankind, copiously?* she said. The librarian was at a loss to explain the review but said she should look up the words in the dictionary. She did. Nothing that she found explained the play. Flaquita walked around the East Village for months, totally perplexed thinking about the play. She went back to the library to inquire about Beckett's other works. In time she read about Eugene Ionesco and Jean Genet and eventually Shakespeare. She devoured everything. One day when she was twelve she wandered into a neighborhood theater during a rehearsal. The theater was down the street from the Fillmore East on Second Avenue. She stood listening to the words, dazzled by people actually speaking the lines to each other and moving around, at times showing disdain, disbelief, arrogance. The sight of this large-eyed, very thin girl standing in the theater made the actors stop their work. They were rehearsing Genet's *The Blacks.*

"What can I do for you, little girl?" said the stage manager.

"Nothing," she said. "I just wanted to watch."

"We're rehearsing."

"I know. You're rehearsing Jean Genet's *The Blacks.* That's why all of you all are black."

"Jawn," someone said. "Not Jean, but Jawn."

"Oh," Flaquita said. "It looks like Jean."

"Well, it's pronounced Jawn."

"Okay," Flaquita said, beginning to feel a bit strange. "Do you ever rehearse *Waiting for Godot?*"

"Godoe," the same person corrected.

"Samuel Beckett wrote it," Flaquita said, pronouncing it "Becqueé."

"Beckett, not Becqueé," came the voice again. "Beckett. No we don't rehearse *Waiting for Godot.*"

"Why not?"

"Because we're rehearsing *Les Negres.*"

"Los Negros," Flaquita said, joyfully. "That's in Spanish."

"Si," the director said, mockingly.

Someone was now shouting, "Places, people," and the actors began rehearsing again. Someone else came and asked her to leave. Flaquita went back out into the sunlight thinking about being inside the theater. Gringos were so snotty. It didn't matter if they were white or black. They were always snotty. She wondered if Puerto Ricans had any theaters? A few years later she saw a play in the Orpheum Theater called *El Piragüero de Loisaida* by Bimbo Rivas. All the actors were Puerto Rican. It was about an old man called Ernesto who had a *piraguas* cart. She remembered that the actor's name was Ed Vega and the girl who played his wife was named Brunilda. She had seen Bruni in the neighborhood and she was young, but they made her real old for the part. She understood the play and this bothered her even more. What good was a play if you could understand it, she thought.

But she continued to think about plays and theater and reading. Eventually she began to make people crazy with her questions. Three years later she saw a production of *Waiting for Godot* and came away as puzzled as always. Nothing much had changed since then. Life for her was exactly like the play. Nothing made much sense. For example, she thought: You knew you were going to die and still kept hoping about things like a nice plate of rice and beans with two pork chops and *tostones*, or maybe a nice pair of red shoes and a bag to match, or nice curtains, or a really dynamite orgasm. She wondered if she was a true existentialist. She knew she could be an actress. The profession required that you change yourself into someone else. She could already change herself into anything she wanted and could do it much better than anyone in the theater or in film. Maybe she could do other things. When she married Roque and got pregnant, she decided that if she had a son, she would name him after a playwright. She liked the name Jean Genet, but people would call her son Jeannie and make jokes about her son being a genie. She wasn't going to permit such a thing. She settled on Samuel Beckett, and this made her feel much better. When he was a baby she would sit by the crib and read from Beckett's work to her son. Gleefully she would watch her son's big eyes roll around in his head, and he'd make gurgling, laughing sounds. Maybe that's why he became a playwright. She was proud of this. But Maruquita worried her. Her daughter was as dopey as Samuel was bright.

Bizquita thought of how she would approach her daughter-in-law about Maruquita. Flaquita had just finished watching the Spanish soap opera in her room. She came into the living room, addressed her mother-in-law, and began her nightly review of the acting, directing, and weak plot points. Bizquita figured it was as good a time as ever to talk to Flaquita about Maruquita and her needs. She would have to eventually talk to the young man, but if Maruquita's mind was set on him, there was little they could do to prevent her from getting pregnant. The approval would be a formality, since Maruquita was talented in the arts of *brujería* in spite of her obvious empty-headedness about everything else.

Bizquita approached the subject of her granddaughter carefully, talking about several things such as the upcoming presidential election between George Bush and Al Gore and what impact each would have on the stability of the world economy. The two women were not exactly CNN material but fairly informed and accurate analysts.

"I don't think either of these two bozos is qualified to be president," Bizquita said. "I was watching the debate and both of them is plenty stupid. Gore is a big *pendejo* and Bush can't even speak English. You sure he ain't a alien? Not the ET kind, but not from the U.S."

"Yeah, I know what you mean," Flaquita replied, turning off the TV. "His brother married a Mexican, you know?" she added.

"Don't talk to me about her. Chalupa Bush is one of them rich-ass Mexican upper-class bitches. Did you see her son, Pancho Bush, talking in Spanish? Looks just like his old man."

"If Bush gets elected, that could help us with Vieques."

"They're all full of shit, Flaquita. They're trying to eat up our minds. The people in P.R. got Vieques covered. We're gonna win. We gotta concentrate on what we got here. When we get this under control, we'll take care of Vieques and the big island and everything else. Fuck the U.S. Navy. When we get our own navy going, we'll see *quién es más macho.* We'll kick their ass."

"Well, that's true, Mama," Flaquita said, deferring to her mother-in-law who was the Gran Kokoroka and overall in charge of all counterinvasion programs, not only in Loisaida but in all of New York and the other states.

"Do you know what SBS is working on?"

"I know, Mama," Flaquita said. "He's working on the cloaking device from Star Trek."

"That's right. We'll be able to sneak up on the gringos down in Vieques."

After they discussed the situation in the Balkans, the developing instability in South Africa, the World Monetary Fund, the Palestinian-Israeli situation, the Pope's health, Christiane Amanpour's recent marriage, Jennifer Lopez's derriere, and the possibility that Rudy Giuliani might change the city charter and remain mayor until his dick dropped off, Bizquita sat up in the recliner and said she had something really important to discuss.

"What is it, Mama?" Flaquita asked.

"Your daughter's ready," Bizquita asked.

"She's ready to flunk out of Seward Park High School, Mama. What's the matter with that girl? She is *so* stupid."

"She's not stupid."

"She's not?"

"No, she's only acting that way to keep them off guard when she needs to."

"With her own family?"

"Well, she's testing her powers."

"She's testing my patience."

"She's a talented *kokoroka*. Don't forget that. She's gonna help our people during the coming millennium."

"Fine," Flaquita said, not happy but having to admit that her daughter was quite talented in the art of change, which, everyone who had a grounding in logic knew, was the most important thing in the universe. She once again recalled the conservation-of-energy theory and decided her mother-in-law was right concerning her daughter. "What is she up to now?"

"She's ready to get down."

"Get down *get* down?"

"Yep."

"Did you choose him?"

"No, she chose him."

"Mama, she's only fifteen."

"She's precocious."

"I know, but she's so young."

"Have you seen her peacock?" Bizquita said.

"Of course. I taught her that when she was twelve."

"But she's perfected it. I don't mean to be hypercritical, Flaquita. You know that I hold you in the highest regard, but your peacock still lacks the *panache* that your daughter brings to the display of her feathers. When Maruquita flares that peacock tail, it's like watching the aurora borealis in the middle of the day."

"It is spectacular," Flaquita said, smiling proudly. "Birds are not my forte, Mama."

"I know, but in the history of our people there aren't two women who've been able to do a decent peacock in more than three hundred years. There was Burunguita in the 1740s. She's the one who comes closest. My peacock is at best mediocre. Maruquita's is spectacular. I certainly bow to her genius."

"Mama, I know you're right. She's very talented, but I have reservations about her getting down."

"Flaquita, your daughter is a nova in a firmament of minor stars. Forget Jennifer Lopez, Talissa Soto, or Rita Moreno when she was younger. Maruquita tops them going away."

"Jennifer's not a *kokoroka*, and neither are the others."

"No, J-Lo's talents lie elsewhere."

"She does have a magnificent *fundillo.*"

"Yes, she does."

"A tribal asset."

"I like that," Bizquita said. "Nice pun."

"I make it a pun to keep things on a lighter note," Flaquita said.

"Pun well taken, but let me pun something out to you."

"Ha-ha," Flaquita said. "Since you pun it that way, go ahead."

"The thing with your daughter has much more significant ramifications."

The room had grown quite tense, and the bric-a-brac appeared as if light had invaded them. The plastic seat covers on the couch became luminescent, the votive candles in the room suddenly were lighted and the *santos,* the plaster saints, began milling around. All at once doña Barbara was alive and dancing to the beat of Ray Barreto's congas. With that, the project walls parted and the brilliant sun of Borikén was on them. They were in a clearing in the Sierra de Luquillo with the sacred mountaintop of El Yunque staring down majestically at them. Both women knew a monumental truth was about to be revealed. They were suddenly naked, their breasts pert and their bodies a deep copper. Their heads were slanted to a point from having their foreheads bound as infants to achieve the conical beauty of their ancestral *cemíes.* They knelt and laid their foreheads on the red earth, their rears pointed upward as if giving themselves to the great god Yukiyú.

"We offer thanks, Yukiyú," Bizquita said. "You are the lord of lords and ruler of all within our sight and reach."

"We offer thanks, Yukiyú," Flaquita said. "And what Mama said."

"Rise," said Yukiyú addressing them. "Begin your dialogue. I will sit here, eat *platanutre,* and listen."

"O, great Yukiyú, we have been fucked with. We now wish to take our next step in the conquering of this land. We now wish to help our daughter prepare to become *kokoroka* of all *kokorokas.*"

The hills resounded with the crunching of plantain chips as Yukiyú chewed. When Bizquita finished speaking, Yukiyú smacked his lips, cleared his throat and simply said *"Palante como el elefante."* This was the Taino blessing to go forward. Go forth like the elephant. Now they had no choice. It is a known fact that there was a time when elephants ran free and trumpeted all over Puerto Rico. Why were there no more elephants in Puerto Rico today? Like everything else, the Spaniards were responsible for killing them. They killed the Indians and they killed the elephants.

When the two women were done invoking the Great God Yukiyú, they returned to the living room. Bizquita leaned back in her son's recliner and asked Flaquita about the projects. There is a very good reason why their dwellings were called the projects. All over New York City the people lived in the projects, and it wasn't simply about red buildings with faulty elevators and stone chessboards. When they were done they opened Budweisers, put on salsa, and danced. Dancing is how Ricans give thanks to the gods for their benevolence and guidance. Bizquita asked her daughter-in-law for an in-depth report.

FLAQUITA AND HER MOTHER-IN-LAW DECIDED THAT MARUQUITA COULD get down with her chosen. Maruquita would still be expected to ask her mother for permission, and there was a chance that Flaquita could say no. Bizquita sipped from her beer and asked for Flaquita's report. She was curious about the progress of what she had initiated three years ago.

"How's it going?" Bizquita said.

"Well, we got finished up to Thirteenth Street at the end of Riis Houses. It's all planted with trees up and down the hills. We got one more building to go. We're running the Loiza River through it, and we're almost finished. The coast looks beautiful, and we've planted over nine hundred young coconut palm trees, smuggled here from the island."

"You've done a great job, Flaquita. It looks beautiful down here in the Wald projects."

"That was totally fucked up for Moses to put us in these projects like he did."

"Totally fucked up."

What Flaquita Salsipuedes and her mother-in-law, Bizquita, were alluding to is what Robert Moses, the master builder city planner, who orchestrated the elimination of tenement buildings in major parts of the city, had done. He had destroyed neighborhoods in the Bronx, Manhattan, and Brooklyn. Moses sought to handle the increasing Puerto Rican migration and isolate Puerto Ricans within particular enclaves. Flaquita had recently read a review by Edgardo Vega Yunqué in a magazine called *City Limits* of the book *Selling the Lower East Side: Culture, Real Estate, and Resistance in New York City,* by Christopher Mele and published by the University of Minnesota Press, 2000, Minneapolis. The review of the book said:

> In explaining how the gentrification of the East Side came about, Mele also lays bare the causes for Puerto Rican social and political dysfunction in the area. The discrimination and lack of opportunities for Puerto Ricans in the last 40 years and the ghettoization of a people by master builder Robert Moses have been documented before, but not with such specificity and incisiveness.

By the time Flaquita had finished reading the review it was obvious that she had to read the book. She asked her son, Samuel Beckett Salsipuedes, to go to Barnes & Noble in Greenwich Village and get the book. As hard as she had tried to teach her son to fly and change into different animals and people, he was totally without the gift. She hoped he would be the first man with the gift, but it wasn't to be. He could do other things like his father, but complex *brujerías* were out of his reach. Her son had to take the bus or the subway like regular people.

SBS explained that he was in the middle of a plan to purchase part of Wyoming and did she mind waiting a few days for the book to be delivered. His mother said she was in a hurry. A few minutes later Samuel came out of his room and explained that he'd ordered the book from Amazon.com and asked them to deliver it next-day service. It was done. Two days later Flaquita, an extremely fast reader, had devoured the book during one afternoon spent lying on the grass of East River Park. On pages 129–130 she found the following. Needless to say she was appalled.

> With a dramatic increase of migrants between 1950–53 and, later, the declining economic opportunities in the manufacturing economy, political leaders in New York referred to the dire conditions as the "Puerto Rican problem." The ensuing construction (*sic*) of Puerto Rican migration as a threat to political stability and drain on economic resources echoed a previous call for migration curtailment in the early 1900s. Most of the public discourse, circulated in the city's press, in special reports, and in-depth exposés, chose not to focus on economic circumstances that contributed to poor labor conditions but on the size of the migrant flow and the decision to relocate to New York. In short, according to this discourse, the inflow of Puerto Ricans, not the excesses of the private low-income housing market or labor market instability, caused the reemergence and spread of the slum. Robert Moses and Phillip J. Cruise, chairman of the City Housing Authority, claimed that Puerto Ricans migration explained why slum conditions were worse in New York than in other cities. By 1953, as Puerto Rican migration peaked, city officials, planners, and slum committees were pressed to deal with the growing "Puerto Rican problem." Their solutions were sorely deficient. The Robert F. Wagner mayoral administration spent considerable time and other resources trying to convince Puerto Ricans on the island to relocate to cities other than New York. In 1959, criminal court judge Samuel Liebowitz claimed that Puerto Ricans were responsible for the rise in juvenile delinquency rates and posited that the city should make every effort to discourage continued migration.

Flaquita couldn't believe it. "The Puerto Rican Problem"? Is that what they were to these gringo people? She remembered her childhood and living in Spanish Harlem, and then overnight they had moved eight times in two years, staying with relatives in the Bronx, in Brooklyn, and then down here in the projects. On the one hand it felt good to be with other Puerto Ricans, but she knew that something was wrong. She knew that they had been herded into the projects. Flaquita was very proud that her mother-in-law, Bizquita Salsipuedes, had recognized her talents and, as *Gran Kokoroka*, had chosen her to marry her son. She read on, seething about what the book was revealing. In the next few pages her suspicions were confirmed.

If poor migrants from Puerto Ricans could not be discouraged from coming to the city, the government could wield land-use policy to determine those areas where they could and could not afford to live. Once sections of older neighborhoods were slated for demolition and renewal, already poor housing conditions tended to deteriorate further and at a faster pace. Absentee landlords withheld maintenance and vital services as a method to maximize profits before condemned buildings were scheduled to be pulled down. The displacement effects of urban renewal policy were pronounced. Urban renewal projects, nicknamed "Puerto Rican Removal Plans," forcibly relocated thousands of Puerto Rican families from one poor neighborhood into another. Displaced families doubled up and tripled up with friends and relatives in substandard apartments, moved into private low-income apartments in other neighborhoods, or waited for occupancy in the city's public housing units. Once renewal projects were completed in a given neighborhood, rents in new buildings were far too prohibitive for low-income families to return. Renewal, then, dispersed low-income minorities from certain areas and concentrated them in others. Increasing numbers of Puerto Rican residents encountered a tightening supply of low-income housing units confined to the poorest areas of New York, such as the satellite *barrio* on the Lower East Side.

Hijos de la gran puta, thought Flaquita. It didn't matter, she thought as she let the rage run though her body. What they had done in the ensuing years more than made up for it. One such development had been her home for more than forty years. This was the strip of projects that runs along the East River Drive of Manhattan between East River Park and Avenue D and north from Houston Street to Thirteenth Street. In one instance the city constructed the Lillian Wald Houses between Avenue D and the FDR Drive, from Houston Street to Sixth Street. The development, according to the book, had

1,861 apartments and some 7,168 people in sixteen buildings. The second development ran from Sixth Street to Thirteenth Street. It was called the Jacob Riis Houses, which were built with federal, state, and city funds. This second set of city housing projects had 1,768 apartments and has a supposed 6,865 people in nineteen buildings. The grounds were landscaped with fenced-in lawns and trees that today reached the height of the buildings.

Well, Ricans had turned all that around, Flaquita thought. She closed the book, got up from the grass, and began walking. She looked out over the river at Brooklyn and Queens. On the other side there were other Puerto Ricans in other projects. Up river was the Bronx with more projects. Her mother-in-law had people working in every city project building that had Puerto Ricans living in it. Looking northward, Flaquita thought of El Barrio, where little could be done, since the city had not permitted Puerto Ricans to move into those projects in large numbers. But down in Loisaida things were different. To the south were the Smith projects and the Baruch projects, and they had been developed by Ricans. Training facilities for the Navy, both for enlisted men and officers, were going forward. By day the kids looked like potential drug addicts, with floppy pants and fades, baseball caps askew, but when night fell, they were at their books learning navigation, armaments, electronics, radar, sonar. They specialized as SEALs, aviators, intelligence, counterintelligence, insurgency. Everything.

Turning away from the river, Flaquita placed the book in her bag, looked around to make sure no one was watching, and changed quickly into a seagull. She hopped up on the railing of the fence and pushed off. Now aloft, she flew out over the river to mingle with the regular seagulls, squawking with them. A couple of cormorants, black and discriminated against by most of the seagulls, were diving for fish. For a moment she felt like diving into the water to fish, but changed her mind and decided that she had a hungering for sushi. Promising herself that she'd go to Esashi on Avenue A and order the sushi deluxe that evening, she said goodbye to the other seagulls, peeled off, and flew west towards the projects.

She soared over the trees and the projects, dancing in the currents before gliding onto the roof, changing back into herself, and descending the stairs. Once down the stairs and on the fifteenth floor, she opened the door to her apartment and stepped into a glorious mountain landscape. She breathed in deeply the mixture of flowers and tropical fruits carried on the gentle winds. Beyond the canopy of trees that descended into the valley, she saw the blue of the ocean as the waves rolled to the shore. She walked along the mountain stream, stepped through a copse of trees and into a clearing. Up a gentle incline was her house, simple but welcoming. On the side of the hill were other houses in which Puerto Ricans like herself lived. It was an odd sensation knowing she could live in this dwelling winter and summer and leave the house to walk and take the subway to other parts of New York City. Giving thanks to the great spirit of Yukiyú, she entered the house.

She knocked on her son's door, and when he answered that she could come in, she saw that he was working at his computer. Rather than a room in the projects with their sterile beige walls, this room was like that of a business executive. There was a large desk with a computer and monitor, a phone with several lines, printer, fax machine, scanner, copier, and, on a large conference table, papers stacked neatly in piles. On a bureau there was the model of the theater piece that Samuel Beckett Salsipuedes was working on. Off to the side there was a small cot where her son slept three hours each night. He was such a strange boy.

"Samuel Beckett?" she said, deferentially, respecting his considerable skills. In a way she felt sorry for him because he couldn't change himself, or fly, but he was very talented. "Can I ask you something?"

"Yes, Mom," Samuel Beckett said without turning away from the computer.

"I need to find out about Lillian Wald and Jacob Riis."

"Mom, just sign on to AOL, get the Google.com search engine, and type in the names like I showed you."

"Thanks, Samuel Beckett," she said. "How's it going with purchasing the aircraft carrier?"

"Pretty good," her son said, taking his hand off the mouse, making a circle with thumb and index finger in the okay sign. "We're pretty close. Where are we going to find people to man these ships is another question."

"Don't worry about it, Samuel Beckett," said Flaquita. "Your grandma's working on that. We've started the Puerto Rican Naval Academy in the Baruch projects."

"Oh, I didn't know about that."

"We're doing our best," she said. "I made *sancocho* if you get hungry."

"Thank you, Mom."

"You're welcome, honey," she said, and paused before opening the door. "Oh, one more thing. How's the play coming?"

This time Samuel Beckett Salsipuedes turned around and jumped up out of his seat. He took off his pink glasses, went over, and showed her the model of the set. He explained enthusiastically how the stark nature of the set, the white walls and floor, represented the reality of eternity and how the clowns would play against that reality.

"Very postmodernist," Flaquita said.

"Mom, this is beyond postmodernism," Samuel said.

"What would you call it?"

"I don't know. Let the critics decide. It's a coulrophobic extravaganza."

"A clown play?"

"Yes," her son said.

"Fear of clowns?"

"Exactly," SBS said excitedly, walking over to the conference table and handing his mother a script. "I want to show the darker aspects of clowns. It's not a finished draft, but maybe you could look it over and give me your overall impression."

"Oh, thank you, honey. That's wonderful, SBS," said Flaquita admiringly. "You're such a genius."

"Let me get back to work, Mom."

"Okay, honey. 'Bye. Just let me know if you get hungry and I'll warm up the *sancocho*."

Flaquita once again watched her son admiringly and left the room.

He was definitely a genius, she thought.

She heard movement in Maruquita's room and knew she had returned. The girl never came in through the door except when she was flying, landed on the roof, and came down the stairs. Generally, she did the squirrel and then the monkey and she was in her room. Once in a while she did a little sparrow, but she didn't like the idea. Flaquita went to the living room and sat down with the script, sensing that Maruquita would come in to speak with her. A few moments later Maruquita came in and sat down across from her mother.

"Ma, I gotta talk to you," Maruquita said.

"You wanna drop out of school and work at McDonald's?"

"Yuck, Ma. That's so gross."

"Sorry. Burger King?"

"Yeah, Ma. I like their uniform better."

"Oh, great. Uniform preference. Anyway, what?"

"It's weird."

"What is it? You've become a Vista volunteer?"

"NO! Ma, listen. This is serious."

"Well, tell me and I'll decide how serious it is."

"Ma, I found somebody."

"Oh, really?" Flaquita said, faking surprise but eager to learn more about the chosen one.

"Yeah, he so cute. I think he wants to give me head in my *tontón papaya*."

"Wonderful! Aren't you a little too young?"

"No, Ma. I'm fifteen. I'm a woman. What I gotta do? I gots needs."

"What needs? What are you talking about, girl?"

"I need to get down, Ma. I need to get a baby."

"And you chose somebody."

"Yeah, Ma. And I want to keep him for a pet. I ain't never had a pet."

"What's his name?"

"Omagaw Boogaloo, Ma. Isn't that a beautiful name?"

Flaquita was up out of her chair.

"Are you crazy? You chose a *moreno*? *¿Estás loca?*"

"Ma, he ain't no *moreno*. You're so prejudice."

"I am not at all prejudiced," Flaquita said. "There are profound sociological and psychological reasons why I hold to the position. You have to understand the implications of choosing a *moreno*. Oh, never mind. Why am I wasting my time on a girl who is in her second year of high school and wants to drop out and get a job at Burger King. Who is he then?"

"He's a gringo whiteboy. He has green hair and little blue eyes like a cute monkey. He has a little tattoo of a bird under his right eye. He has earrings, and a little silver ball on his tongue. I want him, Ma. He's the one. I can take care of him, Ma. Please. I want a little Gringorican baby. Please, Ma."

"I'm so impressed. A gringo. As if we didn't have enough problems with them crawling all over our island and treating us like shit over here."

"Ma, please."

"You're too young, Maruquita," Flaquita said, turning her back on her excited daughter.

"Ma, why you being so mean?" Maruquita said standing in front of her mother. "He's the one."

Flaquita thought about the mandate to take the land a little at a time. This was as good a strategy as any. She knew her daughter's wisdom was operating in wanting to take in this gringo whiteboy and make him her pet. She steeled herself for what was coming.

"I'll have to think about it," she said.

Maruquita immediately threw her arms around her mother and kissed her effusively.

"Oh, Ma," she said, "you're the best mother in the whole wide world. Thank you."

"I didn't say yes."

"I know, I know. I gotta go."

"Where are you going?"

"I'm meeting Omagaw Boogaloo for dinner."

And with that she was out of the living room and back in her room. A few minutes later she came out in her bathrobe, showered, stopped off to see her brother, and "axed" him for one hundred dollars. Her brother peeled off a hundred and gave it to her. When he again reminded her that he could get her a credit card with a ten-thousand-dollar limit, she said as always that she didn't trust credit cards. SBS shook his head and, using his extensive knowledge of the Greek language, noted yet another human fear: *kartiaplastikophobia*. Maruquita returned to her room, got dressed, made up, changed into a monkey, and was out of her window and traveling along the branch of a tree.

FLAQUITA SAT ON THE SOFA AND OPENED HER SON'S SCRIPT. OUTSIDE, the night had been taken over by the *coquís,* their metallic call soothing. In the distance the surf crashed repeatedly against the shore. Flaquita read.

El Castillo de los Payasos
[Clown Castle]
a one act play with dire consequences
by
Samuel Beckett Salsipuedes

CHARACTERS

El Gato: An aging patriarch dressed in bright red footed pajamas with a Santa Claus hat that looks like a crown. He carries a bladder full of hot air with which he consistently bops other clowns over the head.

Matalina: El Gato's wife. She is dressed from head to toe in silver. Her hair, face, and hands are painted in silver. She is short and dumpy and speaks atrociously in disconnected phrases. She never gets people's names correctly and is imperious. She runs the show, although in the end she disappears mysteriously when she can't get her way.

Manny Morongo: A jester in a harlequin outfit with half his face black and the other white. He moves like a marionette.

Madreselva: An academic, she is dressed in a toga and mortar board, sits at a computer, sniffles and complains about her health. She speaks with a thick Spanish accent.

Ladroncito: A tall, mysterious Cervantine character. He is dressed like

Don Quixote and walks in and out of the scenes like a ghost. He carries what appears to be the script of a play and mutters lines as if he were memorizing them. At times he stops and whispers to other characters. They nod or make signs of assent.

Nalgas: The only gay in the play, except for a closeted one who shall remain unnamed, he wears a full evening gown throughout as he sneaks in and out of the scenes placing targets on people's butts and giggling malevolently. His movements are pronouncedly feminesque.

Betrayus: Thin, sinister. Dressed in a yellow banana suit so that he looks like some Fruit of the Loom apparition with thick glasses. He has a Spanish accent and smiles a lot, like a *pendejo*.

Tupiña: A bitch dog of undetermined pedigree, she belongs to Betrayus and barks at anyone who comes near her master. When someone makes the slightest move, she scurries away yelping. Brave this dog is not.

Smelly: An extremely rodential persona dressed in a mouse outfit. Her nose quivers a great deal and she speaks in a French accent throughout. She is married to Betrayus.

Parchaflaca: Daughter of Betrayus and Smelly. Very thin and rodential like her mother, she is naked, flat-chested and wears an apron with paint splattered over it as well as on her flat chest. She carries a palette and a brush. She is dyslexic. She is an artist.

MarcosDementos: Brother to Parchaflaca, also very rodential. He is so white that it is impossible to distinguish his costume from his face or hands. (A daring actor should be encouraged to play the part nude in white body makeup. He should appear spectral and behave ghostlike.) Throughout the play we see that there is an incestual brother-sister relationship between himself and Parchaflaca.

Jurakán: The spirit of the wind is dressed in strips of brown-and-green cloth that blow here and there when it moves. He spends most of the play twirling around in a useless dance for no apparent reason.

Margafrida Locust: A two-headed local politician of undetermined gender with breasts in front and back. A headdress should be constructed so that the entity has large penises as horns on its head. Throughout the play she gets down like a bull and attempts to screw people.

The Man with the Briefcase: An arts lawyer who attempts to take over surreptitiously.

The Ghost of Sam Smith: An honest man dead several years.

Chorus: Dressed like one-hundred-dollar bills, they come in and out of the play, sometimes mingling with the other characters, other times running around, most often standing in the background. Throughout the play they murmur unintelligibly. Towards the end of the performance the audience is aware that they're saying FUCK ART! FUCK ART! FUCK ART!

The Set
The set should be completely white. In the middle of the set is a model of an 1898 Neo-Gothic-style public school building with the letters VSC in front of it. There should be the thinnest of gauzelike material across the front of the stage. The audience should be able to see the actors clearly.

Lighting
Opaque, as if the entire action were being viewed in a liquid dream.

Music
Classical Fania All Stars circa 1970 and punk rock, played dissonantly against each other to create confusion in the audience. At no time should the music interfere with the dialogue, which will be confusing enough. One should have the sensation of being in an apartment in which on one side one hears salsa music and in the opposite one punk rock.

Admission
Free, like the best things in life. However, the clowns could beg on their knees for the government to assist them in their plight.

The Audience
The audience should be encouraged not to applaud the performance of the actors. Everyone knows that actors thrive on applause and therefore for the sake of the next performance, the players should be as depressed as possible, since everyone knows that clowns are constantly in pain and they act the clown in order to assuage their perennial sorrow. Anytime you meet a clown and he is a positive force in the environment, you should know that this is a counterfeit clown and should be stripped of all clownishness and excoriated, reprimanded, and ridiculed extensively so that he or she understands that clowning is a serious business, and people should be very afraid of clowns, Jesus Christ.

Caveat

This is not a morality play. It is a clown rehearsal that must be played out by people who mean well and are deluded by the society into believing that they're important. They are in fact grains of sand scattered on some beach contaminated by deceit. As such they wash up on shore anonymously and are trod upon by history. *Juega!*

Scene One

As the lights go up, we see EL GATO *pacing up and down the stage, smacking the hot-air bladder against his leg. After a few times he stops, bops himself on the head, and rebukes himself.*

EL GATO

What the hell are you doing? You're supposed to bop other people on the head with that thing. (*Answering himself*) Oh, leave me the hell alone, you old fuck. Don't talk to me that way. I'm the king. (*Grabbing his crotch*) King this, dummy.

NALGAS

(*Approaching skulkingly on tiptoes, he is carrying a target which he shows the audience. He moves behind* EL GATO'*s back and attempts to place the target on his butt.*)

EL GATO

(*Turning around suddenly*) Greetings, Nalgas. What news have you?

NALGAS

(*Hiding the target behind his back*) Oh, nothing, your majesty. Just trying to figure things out. The Artists Dalliance are acting up again. I just saw Betrayus and Smelly whispering outside the palace. They were talking to the man with the briefcase.

EL GATO

The same one you went to talk to?

NALGAS

Yes, that same one. Maybe I shouldn't have gone. It's a messy business.

EL GATO

(*Bops* NALGAS *on the head with the bladder*) You are a bad clown, Nalgas. Yes, you are.

NALGAS

(*Cloyingly*) Yes, I am. I'm so sorry, your majesty. I'm a very bad clown.

EL GATO

Go and be gay, you bozo.

NALGAS

(*Bowing ceremoniously*) Yes, your majesty. (*Makes a grand exit, his high heels clicking.*)

The chorus enters stage left. They mill around, mumble, consult with each other, and pass in front of EL GATO. *He doesn't see them and continues his musings.*

The stage goes dark.

Scene Two

BETRAYUS, SMELLY, PARCHAFLACA, *and* MARCOSDEMENTOS *are sitting on the floor. They are playing jacks. Off to the side the dog,* TUPIÑA, *sleeps.* MARCOS-DEMENTOS *is trying to touch* PARCHAFLACA*'s meager breasts. She ignores him. You can tell that they're artists because they look worried and are trying to figure out if they're seriously committed to something.*

As she was reading the first scene of her son's play, Flaquita's pager rang. It was her sister calling, very likely to say that she was ready to go out to dinner. As in *Waiting for Godot,* Flaquita had no clue where her son was going with this play, but she loved it. She marked her place with a hibiscus flower from her garden and hid the script in the kitchen cupboard. She telephoned her sister and they agreed to meet at the restaurant. She showered, dressed, combed her hair, and fifteen minutes later she was a bat flying in the summer night. Landing on the Two Boots building, she monkeyed down to the street, peopled again into herself, crossed Avenue A, and entered the Japanese restaurant.

Bejuquita and her girlfriend Carterita were already there. They kissed and hugged, all of them looking stunning and making the mostly Caucasian men drool sexually but deep inside feel an uncommon fear that they would be left without substance were they to enter into the most minimal physical contact with these Puerto Rican witches. Flaquita's girlfriend, Banderita, walked in while they were being seated in the back. More kissing and hugging. Once they had ordered they caught each other up on family, love, and shopping. After miso soup and salad had been disposed of, Banderita tapped Flaquita's arm and pointed at the window.

Outside, looking spiffy, Maruquita was talking with two gringo white-boys. The three women looked at Flaquita with a what's-up-with-that look. Flaquita shrugged her shoulders and gave them a combination you-know-these-kids look.

OMAHA BIGELOW COULDN'T BELIEVE HIS LUCK. WHAT A GIRL! MARUQUITA! He was freshly bathed, his clothes were clean, and she was taking him to eat sushi. Fuck! He hadn't eaten sushi in six months. He climbed the stairs of Richard Rentacar's building, knocked on the door, and waited. A minute later Richard opened the door, totally naked. He had an erection and was stoned. On the dirty mattress was Rita Flash, passed out with her mouth open. She was totally naked and her pubis was shaved except for a wisp which made her genitals look like a kewpie doll. Omaha pointed stupidly at her.

"Fuck, man. You're not wearing a rubber," he said.

"I was fucking her in the mouth, man," Richard said. "What do you want? The band is fucked. I think I'm leaving for the coast."

"Fuck. In the mouth?"

"Yeah, you wanna try?"

"No, man."

"What the fuck's wrong with you, dude? You're all cleaned up and shaved and your hair is combed. You trying to get your job back at Kinko's?"

Richard Rentacar had returned to sliding his erect penis into Rita Flash's mouth.

"No, man, but I gotta find something, man," Omaha said. "Yo, Richard, you gonna come in her mouth?"

"Yeah, man."

"Man, she's passed out. You could drown her."

"You know something, man?"

"What?"

"You're one superstitious motherfucker."

"That's not a superstition, man. That's a medical fact. You never heard of someone drowning in their own puke?"

At that moment Richard Rentacar shuddered and shot his load. He withdrew and a moment later Rita Flash was sitting up sputtering and spitting a combination of semen and bile.

"Fuck," Omaha said, pointing at Rita Flash. "See, see what happened?"

Richard had gone into the bathroom. Rita Flash recognized Omaha and pointed back at him.

"You fucking creep," she said. "You scumbag motherfucker."

"What?"

"You tried fucking up my gig at Friendly Fire, you bastard."

"I did nothing of the kind. I haven't been in that stupid club for weeks."

"You were trying to steal my bass, you fuck."

"You're crazy."

"I'm never gonna give you head ever again, you little dick punk," Rita Flash said. "I useta feel sorry for you because you had such a small dick and reminded me of my little brother when I used to play puppy with him."

"You gave your brother blowjobs?"

"Fuck you, you puritanical scumbag. He was only nine. But even then he was bigger than you."

Richard had come back into the room. He had taken a shower and was dressed. He announced that he was going out and if Rita wanted to crash there, it was cool. Rita Flash looked at Richard dumbly, spat at him and called him a bastard. Richard motioned Omaha and they left the apartment.

"You got any smoke?" Richard said.

"Fuck, Richard. I ain't got shit. I'm panhandling and sleeping in the park."

"It's the fucking economy, man."

"Tell me about it."

"Can't you get your job back at Kinko's?"

"Fuck no. They banned me for life. I heard they got my picture on the Internet. I could go to fucking Kinko's in Anchorage, Alaska, and they wouldn't hire me."

"What about the Village Copier over in the West Village?"

"You gotta have an MFA to work there now. It's all Adobe Photoshop, Aldous Page Maker, and other bullshit. I don't know that shit. Ask me to make eighty-five thousand copies of one document and I'm a fucking whiz."

"I know, man," Richard said. "You're a specialist."

"Yeah, a specialist. I should've stuck with film, man."

"Fuck," Richard said. "What about Carrie? I know you're not going out with her anymore, but aren't you still friends?"

"She's got some big fucking Russian living with her. Some underworld dude. Probably a hit man, ex-KGB commando fucker who's an avant-garde poet."

"We gotta get some smoke, man," Richard said. "You got any money?"

Omaha pulled out a couple of bills and extended them to Richard, who took them and, together with a few more bills of his own, folded them and put them in his pocket. Down the street they found a *tabaco suelto* salesman on the corner and bought a couple of joints. They walked over to an empty lot, lit up, and fifteen minutes later they were stoned and laughing as they walked west on Houston Street.

"Yo, Richard, I gotta ask you something."

"Shoot."

"Did you ever do a Rican girl?"

"Me?"

"Yeah."

"Forget it," Richard said before turning north on Avenue A. "I ain't gonna mess with no Rican girl, man. I want my balls intact."

"What do you mean?"

"You mess with them and they get it in their head you're cheating and they'll fuck the shit out of you, and when you go to sleep, they'll cut your nuts off. That happened to Mike Fuller."

"The Brushman?"

"Yep, some girl named Basurita," Richard said. "She got him stoned, fucked him, and when he woke up his nuts were sitting right there next to his head on the pillow like two bloodshot eyes staring at him."

"Fuck," Omaha said. "That's fucked up."

"Tell me about it," Richard said. "Why are you asking me about Rican girls? Don't tell me you found one."

"Yeah, I did. She's really young."

"Really young? What, she's still in grammar school?"

"No, high school, but she's only fifteen. She's gonna be sixteen in a couple of weeks."

"That's jailbait, man."

"I know. I don't know what to do."

"You don't know what to do, you dumb fuck? What you do is march your ass down to the squatters buildings and get counseling about how to get on a freight train and get the fuck away from New York."

"Fuck! She's beautiful, man. I'm supposed to meet her."

"When?"

"Right now at the Japanese restaurant on Avenue A."

"I wanna check her out."

"No, man. I don't want you bird-dogging this girl on me."

"I ain't gonna bird-dog nothing. I just wanna check her out. Dude, you are so paranoid."

"She's really nice, Richard. And she can do all kinds of magical-realism shit."

"Get the fuck outta here. A Puerto Rican girl that does magical-realism shit. No way. I don't want to diss nobody, but the fucking people can barely make change, man."

"I'm not joking."

"Wait, man. Magical realism? Like in García Márquez, with fucking butterflies in the whole town and seafood walking outta the sea and going into people's houses and shit?"

"Yeah, like that. Fuck. She did a peacock that was out of this world, man."

"Dude, a peacock? How?"

"Man, right there in Tompkins Square Park. One minute she was standing with me, and the next minute this beautiful peacock was in front of me and it flared its tail and I thought I was gonna die. I thought my heart was going to come out of my chest, I was so happy."

"Far fucking out."

"It was incredible."

"And other people saw this."

"Dude, no way. She's amazing. The whole thing lasted only about ten seconds, but the peacock was there and then it was gone."

"So what does she want?"

"She says I'm the one."

"The one?"

"The chosen, she said. She wants me to give her head?"

"You better get a dental dam."

"She's never been with anybody, but I've never kissed anybody like she kisses. She gave me a bath at her girlfriend's house. I didn't want her to see me, but she said don't worry, and she gave me a handjob and I shot my load, and the shit was like a firework display."

"You really got off."

"Yeah."

"Underwater?"

"Yeah, but it was really multicolored, and when it hit the water, it broke up like colored glass. Green and silver, man. It was spectacular."

"What kind of soap?"

"Irish Spring."

"Far fucking out," Richard Rentacar said. "Dude, I gotta check out this *chiquita.*"

"Richard?"

"What?"

"Don't fuck this up for me, okay?"

"Don't worry. I just want to check her out. You introduce me, and then I'll take off."

Omaha Bigelow agreed and a few minutes later, after they had walked past the Korean deli, Omaha came back and with his last couple of dollars he bought a red rose for Maruquita.

"You're really fucked up about this girl, Om," Richard said. "You got a look on your face like some little kid at Christmas time. Jesus Christ, man. You're thirty-five years old. Get a fucking grip."

They were now in front of Esashi, the Japanese restaurant. Maruquita was standing there looking more beautiful than he could remember. She had on a short skirt with striped stockings and combat boots. She wore a loose, low-cut Ukranian blouse she had picked up in a thrift shop. Her hair was combed out. It was long, black, and lustrous. Her eyes were like two huge black olives and set back behind high cheekbones accentuated by delicate makeup. Her full lips were glossed in copper. She carried a small patent-leather chartreuse bag about the size of a small book. She may have been fifteen, but she looked like the hipppest twenty-four-year-old on the scene. She was oblivious to anything but her brand of elegance. Other women who came by stared admiringly at her and hit their boyfriends for looking too long. As soon as she saw Omaha Bigelow, Maruquita's expression changed from that of a tough East Village homegirl to one of utter admiration and love.

"Omagaw Boogaloo, you late, honey," she said.

"I'm sorry, Maruquita," Omaha said. "I had to meet Richard to talk about the band."

"Hey, I know you," Maruquita said. "You're the bozo that was with Omagaw Boogaloo in the restaurant. You was eating red soup too. You're Richard Rentacar. I seen you play at ABC No Rio with Omagaw Boogaloo. That's some loud shit y'all play."

"Hey, I remember you too," Richard said admiringly, staring fixedly at Maruquita's ample and pert bosom.

She ignored the insolent look, and turning to Omaha, asked him if he was hungry. Omaha nodded and she turned to Richard and said that he should please excuse them. Taking Omaha's arm, she turned quickly away from

Richard and left him standing on the sidewalk. Omaha opened the door and, recalling his mother's instructions, pointed for Maruquita to enter ahead of him. Omaha turned to look, but Richard was gone. The Japanese waitress told them they had a couple of minutes' wait while they cleaned a table and got it ready and did they mind waiting. Omaha shook his head, and they sat down on the bench across from the sushi bar.

"Omagaw Boogaloo, I gotta tell you something," Maruquita said.

"About Richard?"

"Yeah, that bozo be dissing you."

"I didn't like what he did," Omaha said.

"Yeah, he looked like he wanted to suck on my titties."

"Shhhhhhh," Omaha said.

"It's true," Maruquita said. "The niggah better be cool or I'ma axe my grandmother to turn him into a fuckin' pigeon. That's some stupid shit. Like I'm your girl and everything and he's pulling that booshit."

"You're my girl?" Omaha whispered.

"Of course, you bozo," Maruquita said, snuggling up to him. "Did you like what happened in the baftub?"

"Oh my God. Don't talk about that."

"Why? You getting excited?"

"Of course."

"Me too," Maruquita whispered this time. "I want you to give me really nice head, Omagaw Boogaloo. My *tontón papaya* wants only you."

"I will, but don't talk about it right now, please."

"Okay, okay. I know, I know. Time to eat sushi, not pussy. But I gotta tell you something."

"What?"

"Sometimes sushi smell like pussy."

"Shhhhhh! Don't talk like that in public."

"Omagaw Bigelow, nobody can hear me."

The waitress motioned, and they followed her to a table in the back. As they walked by another table, Maruquita recognized her aunt Bejuquita and her girlfriend Carterita. She couldn't see the other two women at the table. Maruquita went over to her aunt, kissed her, and then kissed her friend. She was about to introduce Omaha Bigelow when she realized that here was her mother, Flaquita, and her girlfriend, Banderita.

"Ma," she said. "Look at you. You look so beautiful."

"Oh, so do you. You look like a doll."

"Ma, this is my friend Omagaw Boogaloo," Maruquita said, pulling Omaha forward and making the introductions, including her mother.

"Hi, ladies," Omaha said. "*Muchas gracias.*"

The women all laughed, looked at each other and pointed their chopsticks at him.

"Nice green hair," Carterita said. "You did it yourself?"

"No, a friend of mine."

"Well, we're hungry," Maruquita said. "'Bye."

They sat at the table, and Maruquita couldn't stop shaking her head. After they had ordered, Omaha asked her what was the matter.

"I already axed my mother about you, and she said she was going to think about it," Maruquita said. "And now I show up with you, and it's gonna look like I'm dissing her."

"You want me to leave?"

"No, you bozo. Just be quiet and let me think."

The waitress set their miso soup and salad together with a shumai appetizer on the table.

"Omagaw Boogaloo, can I axe you a favor?"

"Sure, anything."

"Don't axe for a fork. I've seen gringo white boys axing for forks. That is so fucked up. Just be cool and eat with the chopsticks. Don't fuck up, please. You already made me feel ashamed in front of my mother."

"What?"

"*Muchas gracias* means thank you, you bozo."

"Oh, right. I should learn Spanish.

"I'll teach you, but be quiet and eat. Let me think."

They ate in silence. The sushi was wonderful, and Omaha stuffed himself. Maruquita asked him if he wanted more, but Omaha shook his head. As they were beginning to eat their green-tea ice cream, Maruquita's mother came over and told Maruquita not to come home too late. She smiled at Omaha. Omaha smiled back.

"Do you know who Jean Genet is?" she asked.

"Yes, he was a French playwright," Omaha said. "He wrote such works as *The Maids*, *The Balcony*, and *The Blacks*. He's considered part of the post-modernist, avant-garde European movement that includes Samuel Beckett and others."

"Where did you learn that?" Flaquita said.

"They let me hang out at Yale and then at Tisch."

"The School for the Arts at NYU?"

"Yeah."

"Spike Lee went there."

"He gave me a critique once when he came back to visit the school."

"Far out," Flaquita said, approvingly. "You go, guy."

Flaquita smiled contentedly and leaned down to kiss Maruquita. When her mother and the other women were gone, Maruquita took Omaha's hand and squeezed it.

"Omagaw Boogaloo," she said. "I think my mother liked your answer."

"She did."

"Yeah, she's a theater nut. You know that shit?"

"Yeah, I was a theater major. I wanted to be a filmmaker."

"To make movies?"

"Yeah."

"That's so cool. And you mentioned my brother. That was good. She probably thinks y'all are friends and whatnot."

"I did? When?"

"When you was talking to my mother, you bozo."

"Your brother's name is Genet?"

"No, dopey. His name is Samuel Beckett Salsipuedes. He makes plays."

"Your brother?"

"Yeah, finish your ice cream. It's melting."

They finished their meal. Maruquita gave Omaha the hundred dollars to pay the bill. When he attempted to give her the change, she refused it and told him to keep it because she didn't want him panhandling anymore. They walked in the summer night, went to the park where they kissed, and in the grass Omaha Bigelow buried his face in the fragrance of Maruquita Salsipuedes's loins for the first time. She moaned and held him and said that she loved him.

Fuck, he thought.

A LITTLE BEFORE MIDNIGHT MARUQUITA LOOKED AT HER WATCH AND said they couldn't stay in the park. Omaha asked where he was going to sleep if not in the park. Maruquita said he shouldn't worry. She wanted to go dancing. She asked if he wanted to go to Friendly Fire. Omaha suddenly recalled the previous night and said he didn't want to go there. She wanted to know why, and he explained that he was banned from the place. She told him that her cousin worked at Friendly Fire.

"What's his name?"

"Mooko," Maruquita said.

"Fuck," Omaha said.

"Don't curse, Omagaw Boogaloo," she said. "That's not nice."

"Bad habit."

"Chill, okay? It doesn't look nice for a gringo whiteboy niggah to be talking like that."

"Okay, but maybe we could go someplace else."

"Fine, we'll go someplace else."

"Maybe The Bank."

"Okay, The Bank. But don't be saying fuck no more. You sound like some white rash, trailing park lowlife niggah."

"Trash. Trailer."

"What?"

"Nothing. Let's go."

They left the park and walked down Avenue A, crossed Houston, and went dancing at The Bank on the corner of Houston and Essex Streets. The guy at the door, recognizing him and noting that he was sober, let them in and enjoyed a good look at Maruquita. Even though he didn't look any different from anyone else there, Maruquita was appalled by Omaha Bigelow's dancing. My God, she thought: this was a very disorganized boy. Even for a gringo whiteboy he moved like a broom with cerebral palsy. She was going to have a very difficult time with him. She tried to put a *bukura mukura* on him, but it made him start doing *merengue* steps, and she took it off. He looked awful. His arms were going every which way, and his head looked like it was going to fly off his head. There were other gringo whiteboy weirdoes dancing who looked like they watched MTV, but Omaha wasn't even close. She looked around, and he was by far the worst dancer on the floor. She made believe she was dancing by herself. Omaha was oblivious to her discomfort and was starting to let loose. He looked at Maruquita and her breasts were bouncing beautifully inside her Ukrainian peasant blouse. Just looking at her made him erect. Fuck! he thought. He had never tasted anyone like Maruquita. It was like diving into the sea. A muff diver he was.

Omaha was sober for the first time in two days, and this concerned him because he was starting to feel frightened. He imagined being a full-time bum, living homeless in the street and pushing a shopping cart with his belongings in it. The idea of going to furniture and appliance stores and obtaining a large refrigerator box to live in during the cold months didn't appeal to him. Having to wear seventy-five layers of clothing in order to stay warm didn't appeal to him either. Suppose, as good as this Maruquita was, she got bored with him. Fine, he could give her head, but when it came to the wild thing, she would find him lacking. Having a small dick was not pleasant. He remembered being at Yale with Sally Crenshaw from Gooseberry, Oklahoma, or some fucking place. She tried putting a condom on him, but when he went to put it in her, it slipped off. She fell out of bed laughing, her big tits bouncing around. He asked her what the hell was so funny and she said that she had finally met him.

"Met who?" Omaha Bigelow said, outraged.

"The character my uncle, Randall Washburn, used to talk about."

"What?"

"You're him," she said pointing at his now flaccid penis.

"You're Needledick, the bug fucker," Sally Crenshaw said and laughed some more.

Omaha had an urge to urinate on her. Instead, he went into the bathroom, thought of his mother's toenails, and got himself off. When he came out, Sally was dressed and reading Darwin's *On the Origin of Species*. He got dressed and left. He heard Sally Crenshaw had an affair with Pat Robertson and was teaching Creationism at a small fundamentalist college in the Midwest. Fuck! Omaha thought. This was a touch-and-go type situation. Fuck, he thought again. He wanted to scream fuck seventy-seven times, but thinking about Maruquita, he chilled. But it wasn't all bad news. He was feeling good. He felt free, and his body was alive with hope for the future. He became very creative in his dancing, and pretty soon people were watching him. Most of them were convinced that he was on ecstasy and had flipped out. Even the band stopped playing and watched him, not quite convulsed with laughter but amused in a sort of philosophical I-may-not-have-it-totally-together-but-I'm-not-that-far-gone kind of concern.

Maruquita could no longer stand the embarrassment. She called his name several times and finally he looked at her. Word had gotten around that he was the bassist for Carsick, and now everyone was saying Omaha Bigelow like the fans in right field at Yankee Stadium called out the players names—OMAha BigeLOW—and clapping in unison to the four-beat chant. More embarrassingly, they were imitating his erratic way of dancing. The band started playing again, and everyone was still saying his name and waving their arms around like neurotic whooping cranes being attacked by giant shrimp. Maruquita walked up to Omaha and smacked him on the head.

"Stop it, you bozo," she said, grabbing his arm. "Let's go."

Once outside she was huffing and puffing as she crossed Essex and continued walking east, past the playground on Houston Street.

"What's the matter, Maruquita?" Omaha said.

"Nothing," Maruquita said.

"No, something's the matter."

"I told you, Omagaw Boogaloo. Nothing. Don't bug me. Okay?"

"You're pissed, aren't you?"

She stopped in the middle of the sidewalk and put her hands on her hips.

"You could tell?" she said, her eyes furious.

"Yeah, I could tell. You look beautiful when you're pissed."

"Omagaw Boogaloo, I am disappointed in you," she said, crossing the street in the middle of the block, with the traffic coming at her from both directions. "Let's go."

Omaha followed Maruquita. The traffic stopped to let her cross. Across the street, rising thirteen stories above Houston Street was Red Square, one of the ugliest buildings in the entire history of modern architecture. Reminiscent of the stark, state-sponsored apartment buildings found in the former USSR, it loomed like a totalitarian behemoth among the squat tenements surrounding it. Satirically, perhaps, the building sported on one corner of its roof the only remaining standing statue of Vladimir Ilich Lenin, or V.I., as he was known when he played the position of striker on his soccer team: The Union for the Liberation of the Working Class (ULWC Humpbreakers) back in the late

1890s, when he was exiled for three years to Shushenkoye, Siberia, for Communist agitation. The prisoners would clear the snow, and using a makeshift soccer ball made from a pig head wrapped in a blanket, they held great matches under, to say the least, adverse conditions. Subsequently Lenin was joined at this labor camp by his fiancee, Nadezhda Krupskaya, whom he married in Siberia. After the marriage Lenin lost interest in soccer. Nothing more is known of what could have become a world-class soccer career that may have equaled that of the great Pelé. People make choices.

When they were on the other side, Maruquita continued walking past the entrance to Red Square, past Blockbuster, until they were in front of Kinko's.

"What?" Omaha said.

"You're getting your job back."

"I am?"

"Yes," Maruquita said, ringing the night buzzer.

When the manager, a chubby girl, buzzed them in, Maruquita walked up to her. A Puerto Rican girl and a Chinese boy working at their machines stopped and looked up. Omaha knew Paganini Ling, the half-Italian, half-Chinese guy. Ling recognized him. Omaha, standing behind Maruquita, put an index finger to his lips. Ling agreed that his lips were sealed.

"What can I do for you?" the night manager said.

"He wants his job back?"

"I'm sorry. I don't do the hiring," the fat girl said.

"Let me talk to the hirer," Maruquita said.

"Excuse me?"

"Excuse me?" Maruquita repeated, mockingly. "Is that what you said to me?"

"Hello?" the fat girl said. "Is someone else talking?"

"Don't play yourself, Blimpona," said Maruquita. "Don't play yourself, or I'ma smack you upside the head."

"Are you talking to me?" the fat girl said.

"Again with this booshit? Who else I be talking to? You're the only one who could have Good Cheer or Fuchi written on her butt and be floating up in the air. Who you think I'm talking to, bitch?"

"What did you call me?"

"I call you Blimpona Maricona, you *perra puta* mothafocka," Maruquita said and right before everyone's eyes Maruquita turned into a bat, flew once around the place and tangled herself in Blimpona's hair. The fat girl screamed and fainted. Maruquita turned back into herself and stood watching the fat girl come to, totally freaked out.

"Take off your shirt and go home," Maruquita said.

"Okay, okay, take the money but don't hurt me."

"Just take off the shirt, Roseann."

The fat girl took off her shirt, handed it to Maruquita, and stood in her size 54F bra, with flaps of fat falling on one another. Maruquita again ordered the girl out of Kinko's and told her not to come back. When the whimpering girl left, she took the shirt and tossed it to Omaha.

"Go to work," she said.

"I can't do that, Maruquita," he said, timorously.

"You what?"

"I was fired. I could get in trouble."

"Omagaw Boogaloo, you're gonna be in worser trouble if you don't get behind the counter and go to work."

"But . . ."

"Niggah, put on the shirt. Don't be a bad gringo whiteboy. I'm not going to let you give me head anymore and you're not gonna get a big *bohango* if you don't behave yourself."

"I gotta ask you something, Maruquita," Omaha said, getting closer and whispering.

"What?"

"Are you really a bruha?"

"Yeah. . . . So?"

"The *bohango* is the thing?" he said, pointing at his crotch.

"That's the *bohango*. You have a *bohangito*. It's cute."

"Can you make it bigger."

"Yeah . . ."

"Could you please."

"Sure. My mother's an expert in that. I heard that she made one smaller than yours get bigger."

"Your mother?"

"Yeah, she can do that shit. Don't worry. Just put on the shirt. I'll see you tomorrow."

"And she can make them bigger?"

"Yeah, put on the shirt."

"Does it hurt?" Omaha asked, pulling on the shirt.

"Getting a bigger *bohango*?"

"Yeah, do they have to pull on it and stretch it?"

"No, it doesn't hurt, you bozo. Button your shirt."

Omaha buttoned the shirt. He looked at Paganini Ling. Paganini shrugged his shoulders and went back to work. At the door Maruquita blew Omaha a kiss and was gone. Fuck, he thought. What now? he thought. This is the *mucho grande* pickle, he thought. He asked Ling if there were any jobs pending. Ling pointed at the waiting-to-be-copied shelves. When he went by the Puerto Rican girl, she motioned him over.

"Pssst," she said.

"What?" Omaha said, noting that her name tag said Awilda.

"You know that girl?"

"Maruquita? Yeah, I know her."

"Oh, my gaw," said the girl.

"What?"

"She's a *bruja.*"

"I know she's a bruha."

"And you be hanging out with her?"

"Yeah, she's my girlfriend."

"For real?" Awilda said, crossing herself. "Your girlfriend?"

"Yeah, we hang out. We went dancing at The Bank."

"You dance?"

"Yeah, I dance."

"Far out. Can I tell you something?"

"What?"

"You should go real far away, like New Jersey. Tonight. Right now."

"Why?"

"You're gonna be in a lot of trouble if you stay with that girl. I'm telling you. I'm doing you a favor. You look like a nice gringo whiteboy. Not for nothing. Get away before it's too late. Didn't you see what she did to Pamela?"

"Pamela?"

"*La gordita,*" Awilda said puffing out her cheeks and splaying out her arms to indicate fatso. "She called her Blimpona and did a *murciélago* in her hair. That shit was awesome and scared me. It scared *el chino,* and it scared Pamela. She'll probably leave for Wisconsin tonight. She can get work references from Kinko's, but she'll be copying in Madison, Racine, Fond du Lac, or someplace like that. For real. Just take off the shirt and hit the road."

"I'm not going to leave. I'd be in worse trouble."

"Well, don't say I didn't tell you."

"Thanks. Okay?"

"Sure," said Awilda before turning away. A second later she had turned back. "One more thing."

"Yeah?"

"What's your name?"

"Omaha Bigelow."

"Nice name."

"Thanks."

"Another thing."

"What?"

"Nice green hair," Awilda said.

"Thanks," Omaha said, smiling and thinking that this Awilda had a nice butt with nice little titties and big lips, which could wrap around his future big *bohango*.

He found a job that looked like a Master's thesis. It was. On the cover it read, *Nervous Disorders in Working-Class Herzegovinian Immigrants and the Marginalization of the Eastern European Post-Modernist Ethos.* Fuck, thought Omaha. Far out, he thought. He noted the order and began loading paper into the big Matilda, seven thousand five hundred sheets-per-minute Magilla Gorilla copier.

WHEN FLAQUITA RETURNED TO THE PROJECTS AFTER A NIGHT OUT with the girls, she was smiling contentedly. She had declined a visit to a male strip club after dinner. Instead, she returned home to read her son's play. She was very pleased to have run into Maruquita and her chosen. He seemed a bit too weird, but he knew theater and that was exciting. Yale and Tisch School for the Arts were no joke. She didn't want to appear interested in such things but wondered whether Omaha Bigelow had known Jodie Foster when he was in school. Omaha retained a vague memory of the young Foster giving him a rather pitying look once, but perhaps she was concentrating on retaining a line from a play. He was never sure. Flaquita thought that perhaps he could help with Samuel Beckett's play. Maybe he could serve as his dramaturge. She knew SBS wanted to direct the play himself. That made sense, since he knew his characters. However, SBS could use a little help from someone who, contradictory as it sounded, understood absurdist theater.

There was no doubt in her mind that her son's play could be staged in any downtown theater. Her preference would be the Public Theater, and she wondered how she could go about getting the Public to produce the play. Maybe Maruquita's young man knew people there. It didn't matter. If it wasn't possible to find a theater that would produce his play, she would undertake the staging of *Clown Castle* herself, since she had enough money from her private investments to produce the play. How much could an Off-Off-Broadway production cost? Ten or twenty thousand dollars? That would be no problem at all. Rehearsal for a month and then a three-week, six-days-a-week run, with a Saturday matinee and evening performance and a Sunday matinee.

She went on reading *Clown Castle*, having at first no idea what the play was about, but that hardly mattered. She could visualize the characters on the stage moving and talking, and that was enough for her. A half-hour later she stopped reading, marked the page on the script with a telephone-bill envelope, placed it on the coffee table, and yawned. She reassured herself that she wasn't yawning at the pace of the play but because she was tired. The play was moving along quite well, she told herself. In fact, from the outset the play was tedious. Evidently, the plot had to do with a group attempting to wrest power away from the protagonist, El Gato. The group was composed of artists. Every time she heard the word "artist," her skin felt weird. One of the artists was Puerto Rican. His name is Betrayus. She wasn't sure if the names had any significance, but maybe they did. Maybe SBS was just being creative. Given his understanding of the Vieques situation in his consistent effort to purchase ships for the Puerto Rican Navy, the name Betrayus had some significance, since there was the word betray in the name. Then again it could be "betray U.S." So many things to think about in the symbolism of these kinds of plays. There was also an overtly gay character. The gay character intimated that the Puerto Rican may have been gay, but the Puerto Rican is married to the French girl. At one point the French girl tells the Puerto Rican artist that he should forget that he's Puerto Rican.

Smelly, the French girl says: "Betrayus, you have to be more serious. You are a great artist who has a mission in the world of art. Forget that you're Puerto Rican. That doesn't matter. You can overcome the stigma of coming from a colonial environment and emerge into the sunlight of creativity." She says *creativité*. Flaquita didn't know what SBS meant to say by including a French character. Was he alluding to the fact that Samuel Beckett was Irish but wrote in French?

Upon hearing the French girl, who is his wife, Betrayus responds by saying: "Smelly, you have nothing to worry about. I have forgotten all that colonial stuff. I am a postcolonial kind of guy."

Smelly wanted Betrayus to forget that he was Puerto Rican. Were they talking about that book *When I Was Puerto Rican*? She had read the book and was touched by some of the things in it. She was reminded of her own childhood growing up Puerto Rican and poor. But can you ever forget that you're Puerto Rican? Flaquita asked herself. Maybe there were people like that. How could she ever forget that she was Puerto Rican? Living in New York you could never forget such a thing. Especially, there in the East Village, these days. There were so many *blanquitos* moving in. They looked at Puerto Ricans with such contempt. Maybe that is why she felt so bad about Maruquita. She was the worst stereotype of a Puerto Rican homegirl. She was sure that the *blanquitos* made fun of her daughter. She hoped Omaha Bigelow didn't make fun of her. She hoped he really loved her. Everything told her the gringo whiteboy would do her wrong. She wished she could warn Maruquita about her premonition.

Flaquita stood up and thought once again about SBS's genius and nodded happily at having raised such a brilliant son. She stretched her arms and yawned once more. She then went into the kitchen, poured some milk into a pot, and retrieved a tin of Nestlé's chocolate from the cupboard for her nightly cup of hot cocoa. Flaquita then took out the butter dish from the refrigerator, opened a can of Sultana crackers, and placed four on a dish. She opened the butter dish and moved it a bit closer to the stove to soften it. Next she took out a *queso de bola*, cut herself a healthy wedge of the cheese, and set it on the dish with the crackers.

About 1:30 in the morning, as she began buttering the crackers, a monkey came running into the kitchen, jumped up on the counter, and moving her hand next to her mouth, pointed rapidly at it. The monkey then jumped on Flaquita's shoulder and kissed her cheek. Flaquita took the monkey by the scruff of the neck and set it back on the counter.

"Maruquita, change yourself and stop being silly," she said.

"Oh, Mami," said Maruquita changing back to her human form. "I'm so happy. Can I have some hot chocolate?"

"What are you so happy about?" Flaquita said, going into the refrigerator and pouring more milk into the pot. "You want crackers and cheese?"

"Yeah, sure. Did you like Omagaw Boogaloo?"

"Does he have a job?" said Flaquita, taking out the cheese and retrieving another mug and dish from the drainer. She cut another wedge of cheese and frowned at her daughter.

"Ma!" Maruquita said, turning away from her mother.

"Well, does he?"

"Yeah, he got a job."

"Where?" Flaquita inquired as she opened the can of Sultana crackers.

"I got him working at Kinko's again." Maruquita replied, turning to face her mother. "I had to do a *mukura bukura* on a fat girl."

"Kinko's? You have to be kidding."

"What, mama? They got them nice Christmas-candy-cane shirts and it's air-conditioned. The only thing I don't like is they got them skinny-ass *blanquitas* coming in there shaking their flat butts at him cauze he's also a *blanquito*, and they want his pierced tongue on their *tontón*. They better leave him alone, or I'm gonna have grandma turn their ass into pigeons."

"Maruquita, can I tell you something?"

"Is it about Omagaw Boogaloo?"

"Yes, it is."

"You liketed him?"

"This doesn't have to do with my liking him or not liking him. And it's liked, not liketed."

"What then?"

"Maruquita, don't you understand that Kinko's is the clerical equivalent of Burger King?" said Flaquita, shaking her head, obviously distressed by her daughter's ignorance. "Don't you see that?"

"What means that, Mama? Classical equipment? Why you gotta talk funny to me?"

"Forget it," Flaquita said, pouring the hot chocolate into the two cups. She then measured two teaspoons of powdered chocolate and five teaspoons of sugar into each cup and stirred the steaming chocolate. "Logical thought is wasted on you."

"What means that? You so mean, Mami. Why can't you talk like a normal mother? You talk like them gringa mothers on TV. I know you got white skin, but you ain't supposed to be talking like them white bitches and whatnot."

Flaquita shook her head and carried her cup and dish into the living room. Maruquita got hers and followed her mother. She sat on the sofa across from Flaquita, stripped the wedge of hard yellow cheese of its waxy red skin, and dropped it in the hot chocolate. She then broke off one of the buttered crackers and dipped it into the hot chocolate for a few seconds before bringing it to her mouth.

"Thank you, Mama," she said. "You make the best hot chocolate. Can I axe you something?"

"Axe? When are you going to rid yourself of that horrible accent? You sound like such a retard. The words is ask, not axe. Axe is something with which you chop wood. The English language is, admittedly, difficult but not insurmountable as a mode of communication."

"Okay, okay. So can I *ask* you something?"

"Go ahead, but it better be good."

"Grandma interviewed Omagaw Boogaloo and she says he's okay. Did you like him?"

"He has nice green hair. A little too skinny."

"He's been out of work. I'll fatten him up, Mama. Can I have him?"

"One condition."

"What?"

"You gotta finish high school. No GED."

"Okay, Mama. I'll finish high school," Maruquita said, jumping up and hugging her mother. "I'll even go to Borrowed Manhattan Communist College."

"No need to go that far, Maruquita. We don't want you hurting yourself."

"Oh, you're the best mother in the whole world. You won't be sorry when I give you a nice Gringorican baby. If it's a girl, I want to name her Gringocita and if it's a boy, Kevin."

"Oy vey," Flaquita said. "You're going too fast. Drink your chocolate before it gets cold. I'm going to sleep. It's late."

With that, Flaquita stepped out of the house and looked at the star-filled sky and a quarter-moon making its descent on the horizon. She took a deep breath of the clear mountain air. In the distance she heard an owl call and heard it flap its wings as it took flight. Maruquita saw her mother go up the hill to her *bohio* and let out a sigh of relief as she drank from the hot chocolate. She loved Omaha Bigelow so much and knew that she would be happy with him. The only thing that bothered her was that his little peepee *bohango* was so thin and small. She didn't want a shrimp for a son or daughter. She had to talk to her mother to see if she could make him bigger. Her mother could do those things but she wanted to wait and not freak her out too much. She didn't want to tell her that she'd given him a magical-realism handjob and that it had sparkled. It was her special peacock handjob. And she wasn't going to tell her about his tongue with the silver ball on her button either. That was so cool and it made her shudder and see butterflies and little green flying fish and her body felt wonderful. That was her own secret. Getting head was so wonderful.

OMAHA BIGELOW FINISHED COPYING THE LAST JOB, OBVIOUSLY AN attempt at poetry. One hundred copies of *Marketable Breasts*, an eighty-page self-described attack on the commercialism of female mammary nudity by someone named Clytemnestra Griswold. After reading several poems, he decided he'd heard better punk lyrics than what was contained in this self-published chapbook. He finished the job, placed the copies in boxes, and stretched. Practically out on his feet, he had been in a zone, the rhythm of the copying machines driving him hypnotically forward each hour. As Omaha finished packing the last box, Valery Molotov, the day manager, came in. He was not happy to see Omaha. Molotov looked like a very pale, blondish Ichabod Crane. He spoke with a nondescript Baltic Republic accent.

"Dude, what you're doing here?"

"Working."

"Where Pamela Fox, night manager is found?"

"The fat girl?"

"Yes, young overeating woman. Where she can be founded?"

"She quit," Omaha said, looking over to Paganini Ling and Awilda Cortez.

"Yeah, she quit," Ling said, looking at Awilda.

"Just walked out after midnight," Awilda said. "Like a bat was chasing her. 'I quit,' she said. She ripped off her shirt and split, man."

"Just like that you are telling?" Molotov asked.

"Yeah, just like Awilda said," Omaha replied, shrugging his shoulders.

"And who said you come back to work at Kinko's store near Red Square building of which does not want you in this collective?" inquired Molotov. "Who proclaimed such startling directive with statue of V.I. Lenin observing impudence of such majority?"

"I felt a strong obligation to serve the people," Omaha said, inspired by the fear of Maruquita's disapproval.

"You are committed to great ideal of noncapitalist labor for which this Kinko's collective pay small sums?"

"Yes, I am," Omaha said. "I feel great pride to wear the Kinko's shirt and serve the people."

Molotov nodded approvingly several times. "I like that. Good socially progressive disputation of labor problem. I make strong commitment to putting good word for you, dude," he said. "I make new name tag."

"Thank you, Mo," Omaha said, aware that Molotov liked his American nickname.

"No problemo, Om," Molotov said, noting how neatly their nicknames sounded. "I am noting how our short names coordinate in socially significant manner. You are Om and I am Mo. You are a good socially conscious brotherman. Give me high fingers."

"Yo, Mo, my brother," Omaha said, placing his hand up for Molotov to palm.

"You want to work the gravy yard shift, my brother?"

"No problemo," Omaha said. "I'll come back at midnight tonight."

"Paganini?"

"Yes, Mo," Ling said.

"You want night manager position of responsibility in this Kinko People's Collective Unit?"

"Sure."

"I recommend strongly. This okay?"

"Totally, dude."

"Good," Molotov said. "Everything progressing in forward socially responsible manner."

A few minutes later Ludmilla Alexandrovna Zubova, Victor Kovalev, and Olga Martinolovna Karpotseva came in, greeted Molotov in Russian, changed into their shirts, stood at attention to be inspected by him, and began the day shift. Omaha went over to Molotov and inquired about the possibility of a small loan until payday. Molotov went into his pocket and extended two twenty-dollar bills to him.

"This sufficient advancement?"

"Yes, thank you very much. I'll see you tomorrow, Mo. I'm going to Odessa to get breakfast. If anybody comes looking for me, tell them I'm in the park. Okay, *tovarich?*"

"You going too far, brotherman," Molotov said, seriously.

"Far? Odessa is on Avenue A between Seventh Street and St. Mark's," Omaha said.

"That, Russian immigrant joke," Molotov said. "You like Om?" he added, clapping Omaha on the back. "Odessa is in Ukraine. Too far to travel for ingesting morning comestibles."

"Oh, right," Omaha said. "Odessa. Maybe I'll go to Kiev instead."

"Very good! You make joke in synchronization of comrades," Molotov said, straightening his body in military fashion, and pumping his fist in the air. "Today is a glorious day of labor. I begin my mission. Have adequate relaxation period, but stay in progressive groove, dude."

Fuck, Omaha thought as he left Kinko's. Maybe his luck was changing. He headed west on Houston Street until he got to Avenue A. Rushing like he was on speed, he made it to Odessa's in ninety seconds, sat down, ordered challa bread French toast, a glass of milk, a Western omelet, and an order of kielbasa. He immediately put his head down on the table and fell asleep. Before he fell asleep he realized that he did didn't have to borrow the forty dollars, since he still had money even after paying to get in at The Bank. During his sleep he dreamed that he was a Cossack riding through the steppes of Russia with his father, who was none other than Valery Molotov. The absence of a father in his life had always loomed specterlike in his awareness. He wasn't asleep five minutes before Frieda Modelewski awakened him with his order.

"You for sleeping or for eating?" said Frieda.

"Fuck," Omaha said, rubbing his eyes and taking a deep breath.

"That cost extra," Frieda whispered, her bosom heaving like two bellows as she laughed.

"Sorry."

"Just joking. I am married woman, with husband hung like Przewalski stallion, mother to healthy Polish girls working hard like their mama."

"Sure, thanks for sharing," Omaha said and began eating.

"My daughter, Flecka, working here too."

"Cool," Omaha said, cutting a piece of kielbasa.

"People always making jokes about Polish people," Frieda said.

"That's true. Polish jokes."

"Yes, Polish jokes. I know best Polish joke. You want to hear?"

"Sure," Omaha said, looking up.

At this point Frieda Modelewski took two quarters out of her apron pocket and placed them on her forehead. Everyone knows that it's quite easy to get coins to stick to one's forehead because of the naturally adhesive skin oils and the flatness of most foreheads. Frieda pointed to the quarters.

"What you call?"

"I don't know," Omaha said, taking a drink from his milk.

"Polish Headquarters," Frieda said, mirthfully.

Omaha guffawed mightily and two streams of milk came shooting out of his nose. He couldn't stop laughing. People in the restaurant turned to look. Suddenly, Maruquita was there looking at him disapprovingly. He looked around to make sure he wasn't imagining things. He then pinched himself to make sure he hadn't fallen asleep and was hallucinating. Finally he realized that Maruquita was there in his mind. She was wearing a police uniform except that it was transparent, and she was magnificent in her nudity. Fuck, he thought. He had to get serious and work on getting a big *bohango*. He also had to activate his America Online account. Once he got his big *bohango*, he would make up a new screen name and e-mail. No more OmahaBigelow@aol.com. He would now be ElBohango@aol.com. And then he wouldn't have to sit in the Authors Divan, the Authors Lounge, the Book Shelf, the Writers Café or the Script Writers chatrooms and have to feel his face redden when they started talking about penis size. And then the e-mail and the constant announcements about penis enlargement. That drove him crazy. But like Sam Smith said, it wasn't like it was a long drive and he had to pack a suitcase. But fuck, he didn't have a computer anymore. He didn't even have a place to live. Maybe Maruquita's mother would double his size, and then he could be five or six inches. He wasn't greedy. Maybe the thickness of the kielbasa. That would be really good. He imagined holding the tumescence in his hand, the weight of it exciting.

He couldn't believe that he had let Didi Lujak put his dick in a bowl of ice to make it shrink even more. He was stupid to let her put her Indianhead ring on it and then give him head. The ring fit and then she wanted him to put it in. Didi Lujak had three major interests: Egyptology, her motorbike, and screwing as many guys as she could. They went at it, and he guessed it hurt her because she said for him to stop for a little bit. They were high and fell asleep. When he woke up he went to the bathroom, urinated, and realized that the ring had slipped off. He woke Didi up and pointed at her pubic area. *What?* she said. *The ring,* he said. *Oh, my God,* she said. *Get it out. Get it out,* Didi screamed and spread her legs. *Just put your hand in there and slip one of your fingers into it. Pull it out gently. That thing hurt like hell. You need a bigger dick so I don't have to become creative. You know?* He put the middle and index finger of his right hand in Didi Lujak's vagina. For the next ten minutes he dug around until he was finally able to get his index finger into the ring and bring it out. During the interim Didi had managed to have three minor climaxes and as Omaha withdrew his finger, the feathers of the ring's headdress touched her G-spot and she exploded in a writhing mass of motorbike babe that nearly woke up half of New Haven.

He finished eating and motioned for the check.

"How your kielbasa?" Frieda Modlewski asked, winking at him.

"Pretty soon," Omaha said, smiling. "I mean, pretty good."

"Hot enough?"

"Yeah, sure," Bigelow said. He got up from the booth and paid his check.

He went to the bathroom, took a dump, nearly fell asleep on the pot, and banged his head on the wall. When he came out of the restaurant, he went into Tompkins Square Park, found a bench, and fell asleep. Five hours later he woke up and immediately saw Maruquita's face in his mind. He did some exercise and saw that John the Revelator was looking at him from a bench across the way. John was wearing striped pants, a red union suit, and a tuxedo jacket. On his feet he had size-fourteen high-top Nikes and on his head a lady's wide Easter bonnet construction with wax grapes.

"How you doing, John," Omaha said, waving at the old man.

"You ain't gonna win the lottery, you punk," the old man said, waving his hand at him in derision. "You ain't gonna win nothing with that green fucking hair, you loser."

"I have a girlfriend, John," Omaha replied.

"I seen you with that Porto Rican hunny bunny," John said, taking out his penis, which resembled a long length of uncooked Italian sausage. "She's pretty sexy. I like to stick my bazooka into her." With that he began masturbating furiously until he made a big grunting sound and up came his seminal fluid, the stuff reaching powerfully almost to where Omaha was sitting. A couple of roller-blading women in shorts and tight T-shirts stopped off to watch the hourly spectacle. When John was done, they skated through the baby-making miasma on the concrete and went off in lesbian disdain, still stone-faced, uncaring, and obviously unimpressed. Omaha had always turned away from watching the Revelator, but this time he watched him intently and wondered if maybe he could go for a few more inches when he asked Maruquita's mother. Maybe seven or eight inches. It would be nothing like John's, but it might help. Like his mother often said: *It doesn't hurt to ask.* He would be bold and ask Maruquita if her mother didn't mind giving him a truly magnificent *bohango* that they both could be proud of.

He didn't have long to wait because a squirrel came down from a tree and turned into the biggest pitbull he'd ever seen. The dog leaped at John the

Revelator, bared its teeth, and growled at the old man. John the Revelator gave the pit the finger but walked off quickly, out of the park and down Avenue B. Omaha looked to see if the pitbull was going to go after him. The pitbull suddenly dissolved. Maruquita was standing in front of him dressed in tight jeans, a sweatshirt, high-top black sneakers, yellow socks and her hair in braids that were tied neatly on top of her head with yellow ribbons.

"Hi, Omagaw Boogaloo," she said sweetly. "You worked all night at Kinko's, right?"

"Yeah, that was cool," he replied. "I got my job back, I think."

"I knew it. You're a good person, Omagaw Boogaloo. I went over there, and the Commie pinko guy told me you was in the park."

"Thank you. You look beautiful, Maruquita."

"Oh, thanks. I ain't no MTV girl, but I know how to dress. I came to get you."

"To get me?"

"To go see my mother about you know what."

"The *bohango*?" Omaha whispered.

"Yeah, she's down with it. We're gonna monkey, though."

"Monkey?"

"Yeah, I'ma turn you into a monkey and we're gonna go to my house. We going like regular people until Avenue C and then I gotta turn you into a chihuahua like I'm walking you and whatnot. Then a squirrel to go up the tree and then we both go up as squirrels and then we be monkeys and go in my house. You down?"

"I'm down," he said, even though he was quite frightened at the prospect. "Let's book."

"Cool, let's book."

"I book, you book, he or she book, they book, y'all book, we book," Omaha said giddily and did a little dance.

"Omagaw Boogaloo?"

"What?"

"What are you doing?"

"Conjugating?"

"Don't start nothing weird, okay?" Maruquita said. "Just stop all the weirdness. My mother don't like no weirdness, especially from gringo whiteboys. My grandmother is gonna be there and she don't like weirdness even worse. She turn you into a pigeon and you be eating seven-day-old rice from the sidewalk in front of the Chinaman restaurant on Avenue B. Concentrate and stop the weirdness. Okay?"

"Okay, I'm sorry."

"I love you, Omagaw Boogaloo," she said. "We gonna have so much fun."

"I love you too, Maruquita," Omaha said, his heart expanding as he imagined a tremendous *bohango* standing up in all its splendor.

They walked out of the park with their arms around each other. When they reached Avenue C, Omaha was all of a sudden on all fours with a small collar around his neck. He looked around nervously at this huge world and had an enormous desire to bark at total strangers. The smells around him were fantastic and incredibly confusing. He saw a rottweiler approaching him, with a skinny girl on the end of a thick leather leash. He felt his testicles shrink and expand and he wanted to rip the bigger dog's throat out. His Aztec ancestry was churning around inside him and he knew he could kill his enemy. He set up a furious baring of his teeth and barking as he strained at his leash. He heard Maruquita admonish him. *Stop it, Marlon Brando. Stop it right this minute. That dog ain't done nothing to you. Why you acting all bad? Stop it!* The rottweiler went by, totally unimpressed by the strident barking. *I'm sorry, honey,* Omaha heard Maruquita say to the girl. *He need to get laid and he nervous. You know? Kewl,* said the girl, already stoned at three in the afternoon.

Maruquita and her chihuahua crossed Avenue D and went into the projects. Kids were running all over the place, old people were sitting on the benches, and some teens were hanging around deciding what they should do next. A couple of them greeted Maruquita. She returned their greeting and kept going into the landscaped grounds. When they were in a secluded area behind some storage bins, Maruquita did a *buruka maruka* and she turned the chihuahua into a squirrel first and then she joined him and went scampering up a tree. Omaha followed her, not feeling any trepidation at all. Within seconds they were at the top of the tree, traveling swiftly from one treetop to another until they were near Maruquita's building. At that point she did another *buruka maruka* and he was a cute rhesus monkey and then she turned herself into one. She did a *sesameruka maruka,* and the window to her room opened. In one leap she made it inside the open window, turned into herself, and urged Omaha to jump. The monkey shook his head, fearful that he couldn't make the ten-foot leap. At that point Maruquita had no choice. She locked the door to her room, took off all her clothes, and lay down on the bed with her legs open. The monkey became quite excited and jumped into the window, landing on the bed. Maruquita immediately turned him back into Omaha Bigelow and he stood there admiring her.

"Head," she said pointing down at herself. Dutifully Omaha went to work.

Within minutes she was shivering. After she was finished, Omaha asked if she could do him. Maruquita shook her head and said she couldn't until they saw her mother and she decided how much work she had to do. Maruquita saw the look of distress on Omaha's face. She reassured him that there was nothing to worry about.

"But . . ."

"But what?"

"I have to ask you something."

"Axe."

"Do you think that your mother can give me a really big *bohango?*"

"How big a *bohango* you want?" Maruquita asked, a bit startled.

Omaha extended his left hand and with his right one measured up to just above the wrist.

"Ten or twelve inches," he said.

"Omagaw Boogaloo, you trying to kill me? I'm so little."

"Okay, so maybe not that big. Maybe nine or ten."

"I'll axe my mother, but I gotta tell you something."

"What?"

"You put your *bohango* in another girl and I'ma have my mother take it away."

"No, no," Omaha said. "I'll never do that. My *bohango* is only for you."

"Okay, I'll talk to my mother. Eight or nine inches?"

"Yeah, but thick, though."

"Like a *morcilla?*"

"What is that?"

"The black sausage in the *cucifrito* place," Maruquita said.

"Or like a plantano," Omaha said.

"*Plátano,* you bozo," she laughed jumping up from the bed. "You better learn Spanish."

"I will, I will."

"It'll help you with *cuchicuchi* if you speak Spanish."

"I'll learn then. How long will it take before I have the big *bohango?*"

"I don't know. Axe my mother. She knows that stuff."

"When am I gonna see her?"

"Right now. Take off all your clothes."

"No way, Maruquita. I'm not gonna meet your mother naked."

"Forget a big peepee *bohango,* then."

"No, wait."

"Just take off your clothes. I'm gonna be naked too. Here, put this on," she said, and tossed him a skimpy brown thing with strings like an apron.

"What is it?" Omaha said, catching it and holding it up.

"It's a *taparabos.*"

"A what?"

"I don't know what it's called in English," Maruquita said and began putting on her *taparabos.* "It means 'cover your tail.' Just take off your clothes and put it on. It'll cover your butt and your peepee. Go ahead."

When Maruquita had put on her loincloth, she brushed her hair and put on lipstick. Omaha took off his Nikes and the rest of his clothes and put on his loin cloth, tying it on the side.

"What's it made out of?" Omaha said. "It feels so smooth."

"Iguana," Maruquita said.

"Iguana? Oh my God," Omaha said, shaking his hands like he had touched something hot. His face got white. "No way."

"Yes, way, you bozo," Maruquita laughed. "It's dead. It ain't gonna do nothing to you."

"It feels funny on my skin."

"Omagaw Boogaloo, you're gonna have to be a little more brave. You starting to get on my nerve! Stop being a big baby and let's go. Out the door."

"Dressed like this to meet your mother?"

"That's right. Stop being a *pendejo.*"

They went out the door to meet Flaquita and get a consultation on Omaha's new *bohango.*

Oh, a little note before going on. Okay, so you're wondering why is this guy making fun of Polish people. I have to tell you something, sotto voce and all that, because we don't want Puerto Ricans to hear this, but in my opinion Puerto Ricans are the Poles of Latin America. Everyone makes fun of us. I started using Edgardo Vega Yunqué again because too many Ed Vega's were turning up: a poet, an astronomer, a Hollywood designer, a choreographer who died and scared the hell out of my friends because they thought it was me. So I went back to my long Spanish name. So what happens? Do you believe in cosmic jokes? One night I'm tooling around the Internet trying to figure how many sites I'll find with my name. So I put in Edgardo Vega Yunqué and since I've been using my long name for about four years, I found maybe ten. Then I put in Ed Vega, which I used as a pen name for a while longer. I found about fifty sites. One that I ran across was quite interesting. I am not making this up. It's real and I'm a little freaked out about it. I have no idea what it says because it's in Polish, but here it is:

Ed Vega

. . . OnetPilot Czat Poczta Onet.pl. onet.pl › Film ›

Osoby › **Ed Vega**, . . .

Szukaj: **Ed Vega**

Biografia Galeria Wywiady Artyku?y Wiadomo?ci

Plotki Czat Strona oficjalna, . . .

From what I can gather, evidently, in some parallel Polish universe, there's a filmmaker named Ed Vega. For all I know, Polish people tell Puerto Rican jokes and I'm one of them. I wouldn't be surprised.

OMAHA COULDN'T BELIEVE WHAT HE SAW WHEN HE CAME OUT OF Maruquita's room. He took two steps and he was walking on a sandy beach with water that was blue and emerald rolling in on white foamy waves. The sky was clear and cloudless and the sun brilliant. The air smelled of flowers, fruit, and the sea. A row of palm trees that had grown on a slant from the winds extended along the beach and curved out to a point. In the distance there was a ridge of mountains with one prominent peak. He took a deep breath and watched Maruquita walking a bit ahead of him, her prominent buttocks swaying as she walked and her pert breasts enticing and full. He could feel himself growing excited and couldn't wait until he had his ten-inch *bohango*.

"Maruquita, where are we?"

"Luquillo," she said.

"Where is that?"

"P.R."

"For real? We're in Puerto Rico? I've never been. It's beautiful."

"Yeah, we're in Puerto Rico."

"How did we get here?"

"We've always been here."

"In the projects?"

"Yeah, in the projects. That's where I live."

"And there's a beach?"

"Yep, right here. Why you think we so tan even in the winter?"

"Where are we going?"

"We are going to see Yukiyú where he lives in the mountain."

"Is it far?"

"Yes."

"Is your mother there?"

"Yes, she went ahead to speak with Yukiyú so he can give permission for you to get a bigger peepee *bohango*."

"Suppose we get hungry?"

"The people will feed us. There will be a feast. Don't worry. Anyway, you can't eat nothing before the peepee *bohango* ceremony."

"I hope it doesn't take long, because I have to be at work tonight at midnight, you know?"

"You'll make it," she said, and stopped suddenly. "Listen."

In the distance Omaha heard a hollow sound. It sounded like a trumpet.

"What is it?" he said.

"It's the *fotuto*," said Maruquita.

"What is that?"

"It's the conch shell telling the people that you're coming," Maruquita said, placing her cupped palm to her ear. "Shhhh. Let me see what it's saying."

After a while, when the conch had ceased blowing, Maruquita smiled and nodded her approval.

"What did it say?"

"It said that Princess Maruka is coming with the man with the parrot feathers and everyone is invited to the *bohango* ceremony."

"Parrot feathers?"

"Yeah, your green hair. That's your name. Kotorrokoko."

"Oh, cool. I like that. But wait."

"What?"

"You're Maruka?"

"Yeah, with a 'k' in Taino and a 'c' in Spanish."

"I get it. Maruquita is little Maruca."

"That's right."

"You're a princess?"

"Yeah, no big deal. Let's go. We don't wanna be late."

They continued walking, first beyond the beach, past the palms, and then into the thick jungle. Above them birds chirped and chattered. In the undergrowth small animals scurried about. They heard a waterfall in the distance. They began their ascent into the mountain, walking on a small trail until, an hour later, they arrived at a large clearing made of tamped red clay. No one was there. Around the clearing, an obvious ceremonial place, there were long stones embedded in the ground and placed at intervals. Maruquita guided Omaha to the center of the round plaza and asked him to close his eyes. Omaha did as he was told and then, his eyes closed, he could feel them approaching. Fuck, he thought. And then he heard the drumming and the singing. It sounded like *"Oye como va,"* or something like that, but he couldn't understand it. This was freaking awesome and so anthropologically cool. It was better than a Santana concert or eating pussy or blueberry blintzes for that matter.

"Open your eyes," Maruquita said, nudging him.

"Oh, my God," Omaha said when he opened his eyes. What he saw was as if the pages of a *National Geographic* had been animated. On the edge of the plaza, standing in front of the stones, were men and women who looked like Maruquita, all of them the color of light coffee. Their eyes were very serious. They all had loincloths, but the women's breasts were uncovered. All of the men had clubs. The drums got louder and the people began dancing. Maruquita pushed him and told him he had to dance, but not that wild punk stuff, she said. Omaha began moving to the rhythm of the music, letting himself go and synchronizing his movements with the bouncing breasts of the women. Maruquita was pleased. The dance went on for about an hour, until Omaha was nearly exhausted. All of a sudden the drumming stopped. The conch made three long sounds. Maruquita pulled Omaha back into the circle, and the people went back to their places in front of the stones. A man then stepped forward and spoke.

"Who is that?" Omaha asked, a bit too loudly.

"Quiet," Maruquita said. "That's Kacike Agüeybaná, the Grand Kokoroko of the Taino Indians. He's the chief. Stop being such a bozo and listen."

"Oh, Yukiyú, father of all our people, we come to you on this day seeking your help for the chosen of our beloved Princess Maruka Gran Kokoroka of the Kokos. We ask that you help us with this *bohango* ceremony to make him a man. The white god has given him a small peepee *bohango*, and our beloved Princess Maruka Gran Kokoroka of the Kokos has asked her mother, Flaka Gran Kokoroka of the Kokoriko, to help her with the Ceremony of Enlargement. Give us your wisdom, oh Great Yukiyú."

"Loa loa loa," the gathering murmured.

"What are they saying?" Omaha whispered.

"Shh!" Maruquita said. "They're praying for you. This is the *Bohango* Council."

"Remove the covering," said Agüeybaná.

"Take it off," Maruquita said, elbowing Omaha in the ribs. "Take off the *taparabos.*"

"Here? They're gonna see me."

"Now, Omagaw Boogaloo. Don't be ashamed. The people understand that you're a gringo whiteboy."

With great hesitancy Omaha pulled on the strings of his loincloth, and the iguana skin dropped to the ground. Immediately there was murmuring and sadness in the crowd. They had never seen such a thin and meager peepee *bohango*. Some shook their heads with pity. Tears came into Omaha's eyes.

"What is your wish, Omagaw Boogaloo?" said the chieftain.

"Answer them, Omagaw Boogaloo," Maruquita said.

"What am I gonna say?"

"Tell them that you want a bigger peepee *bohango*."

"They're not gonna understand me. I don't speak Spanish."

"They're not speaking Spanish."

"They're not? What are they speaking?"

"They're speaking Taino, you bozo."

"I don't speak that either."

"Omagaw Boogaloo, you're pissing me off."

"What?"

At that point Maruquita held up her hands and made a T.

"Time out," she said. "Let me talk to this bozo."

The conch shell sounded. With that, Maruquita dragged Omaha out of the center of the plaza, made her way through the gathering, and stepped into the jungle. From beneath her loincloth she took out a cellular phone and, seething, dialed a number. She waited a while and then exploded.

"Vega?"

"Yes?"

"It's Jennifer Gómez."

"J-Go!"

"Never mind all that J-Go hype nonsense. Don't try to get me out of character."

"Okay, Maruquita. How's it going? How's your brother's play?"

"Going? You're asking me how it's going? What kind of question is that? Why did you put me in this thing with this gringo idiot? I'm gonna call my agent and tell him that I want out. And never mind my brother. Call him if you wanna know about his play."

"I'm sorry, honey."

"Don't honey me, Vega."

"Sorry. What's the problem?"

"This idiot, Omagaw Boogaloo, is pissing me off big time."

"Omaha Bigelow."

"Whatever," Maruquita shot back. "This doofus doesn't want to explain about his sorry-ass dick, and the people are getting pissed. He says they're not gonna understand him. Where the fuck do you get these people? Vega, will you tell him that this is a friggin book?"

"Sure, it's a book. I'm writing it, and don't think it's easy."

"Oh, great, Vega! Pull that retrograde 'I am an author' Nuyorican Poets Café, East Village literary bullshit on me."

"Don't get insulting and start with your Hunter College Drama Department method esthetic, okay? I suppose you'd rather have me write some degrading, icky, when I was, spidery, mean-street, ghetto novel, right?"

"I didn't say that, either. But this is some weird shit, Papa. It's like some kind of derivative Gabriel García Márquez magical-realism crap."

"Let's say I'm paying homage to a tradition."

"It's still pretty friggin weird."

"I can understand your concern. Let me talk to him."

Maruquita handed Omaha the cell phone. He took it hesitantly.

"Mr. Vega?"

"That's me. What's the problem?"

"I don't know if they're gonna understand me."

"Of course they will."

"Are you sure? You knew I didn't speak Spanish. I mean I'm picking it up, but my situation is a complex one. There are a number of psychological ramifications, and I'm not at all certain that, given this particular Amerindian environment, I'll be able to help them understand my lifelong sexual predicament."

"Omaha, relax. Do some breathing exercises, some preperformance warmups. It's a book, a postmodernist rendering of metareality and all that crap."

"Yeah?"

"Of course, but you know this. I'm just reminding you. Remember the course 'Hermeneutics and Linguistics in the Modern World' when you were a junior at Yale and you were going out with that cute, bony, ash-blonde from Chevy Chase with the serious feminist esthetic?"

"Kinda."

"Well, it's like that."

"Oh, right. So it's a book and you're writing it and it doesn't matter what I'll be saying because everybody understands everybody else no matter what they're speaking, right?"

"That's right. The important thing is the message that's being conveyed."

"And what is that?"

"Aha! That's for me to know and for you to find out, dude."

"Mr. Vega?"

"Yes."

"Why did you give me such a small dick?"

"It's a metaphor."

"For what?"

"You didn't take the follow-up course, did you?"

"Which?"

"'The Meaning of Metaphor within the Vagaries of Western Civilization.'"

"No, I didn't. It was an elective."

"Anyway, it's a metaphor, but I assure you that you'll be quite happy when the ceremony is completed."

"I will?"

"Yes, you will. Maruquita really likes you, you know?"

"I know. Thank you, Mr. Vega. She's a wonderful girl. I guess it's okay about our age difference."

"Of course."

"Okay, thanks, Mr. Vega," Omaha said, smiling and handing the cellular back to Maruquita.

"I'm glad you feel better, Omagaw Boogaloo," Maruquita said to Omaha. Snatching the phone back, she spoke once again into it.

"Did you straighten him out, Vega?"

"He's smiling, isn't he?"

"Yeah, but you're putting me through a lot of changes."

"I'm supposed to do that. Otherwise we're gonna end up with some silly ass Puerto Rican ghetto story, right?"

"Yeah, you're right, boss. That's all we're known for. Sorry I got plexed up. Is my man gonna get a real dick or not?"

"I think so. You know I wouldn't leave you in the lurch. Trust me."

"Very funny."

"What?"

"I thought you were going to say 'leave you hanging.' Get it? Hung? Which I hope this gringo whiteboy is gonna be after the ceremony."

"Interesting the way your mind is working these days."

"Well, I'm getting a little desperate. Thirteen chapters, and I haven't really gotten down yet."

"There's time."

"You got it, boss. Catch you later. You think they're gonna publish this thing?"

"I don't know, but I gotta write it. Talk to you later. The Blonde Exotique is calling me."

"You and them gringa whitegirls with their small butts. See you, Papi."

"Not this one. Bye, baby."

Maruquita closed her cellular and put it back under her loincloth.

"Let's go, you bozo," she said. "Back to the ceremony."

They returned to the center of the plaza, the conch sounded, and the chieftain once again asked the question.

"What is your wish, Parrot Feathers?" he said.

"Honored chieftain of the mighty Taino nation," Omaha said, speaking in a pronounced and theatrical accent. "I come to you humbly to beseech you in my quest for happiness and sexual fulfillment. Ever since I was a child, I have suffered from Penile Asparaguitis, a condition that has caused me insufferable psychic pain and social embarrassment."

"Omagaw Boogaloo?" whispered Maruquita.

"What?"

"What the fuck are you talking about?"

"You said fuck."

"Yeah, and I'm losing my fucking patience with your lame-ass shit. Yadda yadda yadda. What are you trying to do? Blow this thing? Is that what you're trying to do?"

"I'm explaining."

"Tell them that you want a bigger *bohango*. That's all."

"Oh, okay."

"Do it!"

"I want a bigger *bohango*," Omaha said, a little too loudly, making the people titter.

"How big?" came back the voice of the chief.

"Ten inches and as thick as a sausage."

The gathering gasped collectively and the women covered their faces.

"Vienna, cocktail, wiener, frankfurter, Italian, Polish, or *morcilla* thickness?" said the chieftain.

"Polish kielbasa, ten inches," Omaha said.

The conch shell sounded ten long blasts and the chief spoke.

"We will now break for lunch and retire into executive council for one hour to deliberate on the request and method of enlargement."

"I'm starving," Maruquita said.

"Me too," said Omaha.

"You can't eat until it's over, but you can watch," Maruquita said.

"That's not fair."

"Fair? You want to go the rest of your life with a little monkey peepee *bohango*?"

"No, but I'm hungry."

"Well, get over it. You'll eat after."

Beyond the plaza there was another clearing, and here there were several pits with roasted pigs. Cauldrons of boiling vegetables and tubers were cooking over another fire. In the coals there was manioc root, yams, ears of corn, breadfruit, lobsters, and crabs, all of them being roasted. People were carrying gourd bowls and plantain leaves and loading up on pieces of meat and the other food. There was no flan. Flan came with the Spaniards, and they had not yet arrived with desserts, influenza, and Maja soap. All Omaha could do was watch, salivate, and lick his lips. He wished he were little again and his mother was saying grace at the table and then there was meatloaf with mashed potatoes, gravy, peas and carrots, and raspberry Jell-O with tangerine slices for dessert. People were stuffing themselves and burping and farting at will, laughing and singing songs, and here he was starving and sitting around with his small dick hanging out and people touching his green hair and smiling understandingly at him. Fuck, he thought. Maybe they wouldn't approve his request. But then again, they might. That would be awesome, to have a ten-inch kielbasa *bohango*. The hour was over pretty fast. The conch shell sounded once more, and the chief returned. He pointed to a hut beyond the clearing, and Maruquita took Omaha's hand and led him down a path and into a conical dwelling.

IT WAS DARK AND COOL IN THE LARGE HUT, WHICH HAD BEEN BUILT OVER a stream. Sweet reedy music and soothing drumming drifted in from somewhere. In the middle of the hut was a pool of water with aromatic leaves that gave off a wonderful fragrance. Maruquita motioned for Omaha to get in. She removed her loincloth, and after Omaha stepped into the pool, Maruquita followed him. The water was warm and the fragrances soothingly pleasant. Maruquita kissed Omaha gently on the lips. A minute later Maruquita's mother walked into the hut. She was naked and was carrying a ceremonial stool and a double-faced rectangular statue that sloped on either side. Both were made of smooth black stone. Flaquita placed the statue at the side of the pool. Omaha asked Maruquita what it was and she said it was a *cemí,* the household god of the Taino Indians, which would oversee this part of the ceremony to ensure that everything went all right. At that point Flaquita placed the squat ceremonial stool, which Maruquita explained was a *duho,* next to the *cemí* and sat down with her legs spread, so that Omaha could see the pink yawning hairy maw of her *tontón papaya.*

"Oh, my God," he said and was instantly erect.

"Is he standing?" Flaquita asked.

Maruquita reached down and touched Omaha's erect penis.

"Yes, Mama," Maruquita said.

"Empty him," said her mother.

Maruquita began stroking him until Omaha laid his head back on the edge of the pool and emitted a loud groan. The water became multicolored, and a beautiful tune emerged from its surface.

"Again," said Flaquita.

Maruquita once again began stroking him until Omaha was once again spent. She repeated this part of the ceremony twenty-two times, until Omaha lay exhausted in the tepid water.

"Is he empty?" Flaquita asked.

"Mama, my arm's about to fall off." Maruquita said. "If he ain't, I'm gonna need a relief wanker. This man is too much. He's gotta be the one. He could wear out three womens."

"It appears so," Flaquita said. She clapped her hands twice, and two big brawny Tainos came into the hut with a straw mat. They laid the mat on the tamped red earth away from the pool. Quickly they went and took Omaha's limp body from the pool and laid him on the straw mat. They got down on their knees, bowed to the *cemí,* kissed Flaquita's *tontón papaya,* and left.

Flaquita now went to work in earnest. She said several *flakura mukuras* and began singing, not an enlargement song, but a shrinking song. Maruquita couldn't believe what she was seeing. She wanted to protest but knew better than to interrupt her mother when she was working. Right before her eyes her Omagaw Boogaloo was shrinking. This went on for the better part of an hour until Omaha was the size of a small banana, still perfectly formed with his green hair but totally tiny. His little peepee *bohango* was miniscule. He looked just like a Ken Barbie doll except that he had a little dick.

"Bring him to me," Flaquita said.

Maruquita went to the straw mat, and gingerly picked up the narcotized Omaha. Carrying him in the palms of her hands, she brought him to her mother. Her mother took him, kissed him, placed him in her mouth, head first and then feet first. When he was well lubricated, she spread her legs wider and introduced him, head first into her *tontón papaya* until his tiny feet disappeared into the pink-and-black gullet. She now stood up and began breathing deeply and then dancing and chanting *mukuras* and singing. For the next nine hours she stood singing and dancing, until she was nearly exhausted and her belly was enormous. Then she slowly slid into the pool and began groaning and pushing until a while later she coughed several times and the water started bubbling, and up to the surface floated the tiny figure of Omaha Bigelow. Flaquita motioned Maruquita to take him out of the pool. Maruquita rushed to the water. She removed Omaha and placed him on the straw mat. She smiled contentedly because even as tiny as Omaha was, she could tell that his *bohango* had grown. After her mother had rested and got out of the water, she put on a loin cloth and said a complex *mukura* of enlargement, and slowly Omaha Bigelow was returned to his normal size. Maruquita couldn't believe it. He still had his green hair, but his *bohango* was large and supple although a little crooked. She wanted to touch it and see it erect but felt shy and was a little afraid to put her hand on it. She pointed at the *bohango,* inquiring why it was a bit off-kilter. Her mother explained that it was likely that it happened when she coughed.

That night the final stages of the ceremony were held. A huge bonfire had been built in the middle of the plaza. Omaha was given a headdress and a new iguana-skin loincloth. He was brought food and drink, and people were happy to see him. The men nodded and touched their fists to their chest. The women smiled approvingly and plumped up their breasts. The drums began again, and the people began a dance of celebration. When they were done dancing the conch *fotuto* blew again and Omaha was led to a straw mat and was asked to lie down. When he had lain down, Flaquita came over and lifted his loin cloth and said another *mukura* over him. He was instantly erect and a great rejoicing went up from the gathering. He took a look at himself, and he was magnificent. It troubled him that he didn't seem quite ten inches. After a while each of the women came and touched his erect *bohango* and nodded approvingly. The men waved their clubs in the air and shouted *ugomugo boogaloo.*

After a while Maruquita came to get him. He stood up, took her hand, and they walked away into the jungle. The people cheered and the drums grew louder. In the moonlight Omaha looked at Maruquita, and his heart swelled with love for her. They walked down the mountain path and back to the beach. The waves were phosphorescent, and there were a thousand stars in the sky.

"Now we can get down, Omagaw Boogaloo," Maruquita said, putting her arms around him. "You can put your peepee *bohango* into my *tontón papaya* and give me a beautiful Gringorican baby. Are you happy?"

"Yeah, I'm happy," Omaha said. "Did you see it?"

"I saw it. It is a beautiful peepee *bohango.*"

"It's a miracle."

"Yes, it is. Isn't my mother fabulous?"

"She sure is. Maruquita?"

"What?"

"I feel like giving you head."

"Right now?"

"Yeah, right now."

"Here on the beach?"

"Yeah, right here on the beach."

"Okay," Maruquita said, feeling shy and hugging herself to Omaha and immediately feeling the peepee *bohango* against her. "If you want to."

They sank to the sand and Omaha went at it until Maruquita emitted a long moan and shuddered. He was immediately inside of her, feeling as if he had his Little League baseball bat and he was putting it into her. Fuck, he thought. This is incredible. In no time at all he was screaming, his voice lingering in the starry night. They lay on the sand for a few minutes, and then he went at it again until he once again depleted himself.

"Wow," Maruquita said. "I think I'm pregnant."

"You are?"

"Maybe," she said. "That is a real *kakomakako bohango.*"

"What do you mean?"

"In Taino it means the real thing that is hanging but stands up to be counted," Maruquita said. "You are definitely the one, Omagaw Boogaloo."

"It was awesome, Maruquita," he said. "Thank you."

"But I'ma tell you something, Omagaw Boogaloo."

"What?"

"Don't cheat on me. Okay? Don't play me for a fool."

"No, I would never do that."

"Cauze if you do I will take the *bohango* back."

"You will?"

"Yes, I will. I will cut it off, *güevos* and all. They're not gonna sew it back on like they did with that Lorena Bobo fool of a husband."

"You don't have to worry. I'm not gonna cheat on you."

After a while they walked back through the beach, through the living room and into Maruquita's room, where he got dressed in his jeans and Kinko's shirt. He looked at his watch and realized it was twenty minutes to midnight. He kissed Maruquita goodnight and went down in the elevator and out of the projects. Outside, the homeboys whassuped him and knocked fists with him. He was like one of their own. The girls smiled and some of them winked at him. He walked quickly to Houston and up the three blocks to Kinko's. Paganini Ling was now the night manager, and Awilda was there along with a new girl with blond hair, a nice butt, and nice tits.

"Omaha, how you doing?" Ling said.

"Hi, Omaha," Awilda said.

"Never better," Omaha said.

"Omaha, this is Winnifred Buckley. She's in law school," Ling said. "She's just starting out. Can you help train her? Winnifred, this is Omaha Bigelow."

"Hi, Omaha," Winnifred said seductively, her lips pouty and her blue eyes suggesting all sorts of confusing things, like the importance of constitutional law and the ecstasy of delicate brace-free fellatio. She was a five-foot-ten shapely WASP amazon, perfectly and uncharacteristically sensual. Omaha's *bohango* was immediately on alert. "Did you go to Yale?"

"Yeah, I did," Omaha said, thinking that she seemed familiar.

"Me too," said Winnifred. "I graduated last year. Magna cum. Political Science. You can call me Winnie."

"Okay, Winnie," Omaha said, smiling but thinking all sorts of raging sexual thoughts. "Like Winnie the Pooh."

"Yeah, like that. That's what my Grandma calls me. It's cute."

"Anyway, did you hear about me at Yale?" Omaha asked, fearful that his reputation as a small-dicked doofus had followed him and this Winnifred was just curious to see a small dick. Boy what a surprise she'd get.

"No, nothing at all," Winnifred said. "But Paganini told me and he said you were real smart and played bass for a punk band. I play a little guitar. Nothing special, but maybe we could jam sometime."

"Sure," Omaha said.

"By the way. I really like your hair. It's so green."

"Oh, thanks," Omaha said. "Let me show you how the Big Matilda operates. That's the simplest thing, and maybe you could start copying some things. Not too many people come in at night, but we have a lot of overnight jobs to do."

He stepped over to the big copier and Winnifred followed him, looking admiringly at him. Every time she got a chance, she got closer and rubbed some part of her anatomy against him. She was also very touchy-feely, and she was constantly patting his arm and touching his chest and smiling at him. He got her started on a job, and she went to work on her own. He looked around to make sure no one was watching him. He then grabbed a ruler and stuck it quickly into his waistband and under his shirt. He moved around a little, found a big job and placed it into a machine and set it going. When the job was running, he stepped out from behind the counter and went into the bathroom. Once inside he took out his still erect dick and with the ruler he measured it. He was a full six inches long, supple and throbbing. He could imagine going into Winnifred's lovely little blond twinkie. But six inches? Maybe he made a mistake. By pushing the ruler a little further into his groin he was seven inches. Fuck. It was thick enough, but he had asked for ten inches. What the hell had happened? He had a strong urge to get himself off, but he held back. In retrospect he should have onanized himself, because Winnifred Buckley was determined to have her way with him.

When he came out of the bathroom, Awilda was smiling idiotically at him. He wouldn't mind having a go at her too. Fuck, he thought. What was going on? It was like they could tell that he was hung like a horse. But he wasn't. He had only seven inches—well, really six. He consoled himself with the fact that he was now bigger than Richard Rentacar. He wondered what Rita Flash would think when she went to give him head. Hey, what about Carrie Marshack? I bet she'd feel sorry that she took up with her Russian KGB Igor Dumbinsky, whatever his name was. He'd go see her just for old times' sake.

He was so excited he wanted to run out into Houston street, unzip his fly, and show his dick to everyone. Fuck! This was too much. It was an unorthodox idea, but he wanted to go back home and show his mother what had happened. He recalled his first year in high school, when he was with Millicent Argyle and they were necking in her attic while her parents were out of town and one thing led to another and they were exploring each other and she pulled down his pants and he was erect and she asked him how long it would take before it got bigger. Fuck! He shook his head and said that it looked pretty big to him. Oh no, she said. She had seen Russell Gifford's, and it was five times bigger. He wanted to cry and saw his meager erection disappear and curl down as if it wanted to hide. It was so sad. He had gone home that night and confided in his mother. She had held him and asked him if he didn't mind showing her.

"Mama, I don't know," he'd said.

"It's okay. I'm your mother."

"Okay," he said and removed his pants.

"Pull down your BVDs, honey."

When he had done so, his mother nodded sadly.

"Yes, it is very small," she said. "But it's not size that counts."

What a liar she was. There she was, stopping a lesson of some piece of music to grab Kevin Frost's dick and give him a handjob. He was the biggest of her piano students. Even when her hand wrapped around it, there was still about four more inches above her fingers. Maybe he always had a regular dick, and watching his mother giving other boys handjobs had traumatized him and stunted his growth. That was possible. But he would go home and show her. But that wouldn't be too cool, flashing your own mother. Maybe he'd take some Polaroid shots and send them to her. He didn't care if he was a little crooked. She would be relieved that he was normal. Yes, that would be the way to go. He felt happy and relaxed and ignored Awilda and Winnifred.

IMMIGRATION VS. COUNTERINVASION AND A HISTORY LESSON

FLAQUITA SALSIPUEDES WAS SO FATIGUED FROM HELPING OMAHA Bigelow to be reborn that she was confined to bed for three days. Having a gringo whiteboy inside of her *tontón papaya* and then having him grow inside of her produced enormous stress on her system. She had done the *bohango* enlargement operation fourteen times in her life. The previous thirteen had been Puerto Ricans, and everything had gone quite well. I've heard that one of these was an ex-governor of Puerto Rico. I already have had repercussions from standing up and leaving when an ex-governor was speaking after the presentation of his daughter's book at the Museo del Barrio. Well, the truth is that in spite of numerous inquiries on my part, Flaquita will not reveal the name. However, she's reassured me that it was an ex-governor and that is why he was able to marry a young woman at an advanced age. The council voted him a sizable *bohango* even though it's suspected that there was bribery involved to bring about a unanimous vote. It's very difficult for me to admit that there is bribery in my homeland. The Statehood Party has been in power during these offenses. That the Taino deities accepted bribes is shocking and very likely disinformation produced by these very same people.

In Omaha's case the executive council, the equivalent of the Supreme Court of the United States, had voted not to give him ten inches as he had requested. Such a body often makes mistakes. The vote was 5–2 against it, with the dissenting opinions written by Justice Guarionex and Justice Caguax. Chief Justice Agüeybaná created a certain amount of levity by calling the opinions of his two colleagues distenting opinions. Everyone on the executive council chuckled. A unanimous *bohango* adjudication was needed and the two votes doomed a ten-inch enlargement. Their reasons were reasonable ones. A ten-inch *bohango* would set off a panic in most men in the United States. Word was sure to get around that Omaha Bigelow had such a large *bohango* that in time people would start mythifying his organ, and pretty soon it would be a twelve-inch *bohango* and it could cause a downturn in the economy. A panic could set in and the United States could easily collapse, since it was such a phallic-driven society.

Some of the members of the executive council said that would be just fine, given that the U.S. had taken over Vieques and wouldn't leave, and what better way was there to exact vengeance on the United States than creating a penile panic? Chief Justice Agüeybaná prevailed and explained that the people would combat their enemies on an equal footing, without resorting to cheap tricks and facile subterfuges like a penis attack. He further explained that he was sure that, were such a panic to come about, the President would form an Anti-Penis Terrorism Task Force and declare a war on large terrorist penises. Wasn't it enough that the people, meaning Puerto Ricans, rather than considering their presence in the U.S. an immigration, viewed it instead as a counterinvasion and now had over 3.4 million people there, which was just about the same number of people on the island, bringing the total number of Puerto Ricans on the planet to 7.1 million. Now someone had leaked out that our people were not native to this planet and that our numbers are even greater. If the U.S. only knew our strength, they wouldn't be so cavalier about our situation. Once the Puerto Rican navy was ready, we would engage the U.S. fully in naval warfare and defeat them soundly. There was no need to create a penile panic. Omaha Bigelow was to be provided with a little better than average *bohango*. That's it.

Perhaps Flaquita's discomfort and fatigue, she thought, had to do with the fact that Omaha Bigelow was a gringo whiteboy. Perhaps there were DNA complications. Perhaps it had to with the fact that she had come so closely in contact with a gringo whiteboy. Would she now become more American? The prospect concerned her. She had no idea what was causing her malaise, but on the second night of her recuperation she dreamed about Martha Washington, the first First Lady of the United States. The dream was very clear, but she woke up confused and embarrassed. As she recalled, the scene took place on the Washingtons' wedding night. Martha had blown out the candle on the bureau and was already in bed. She had her sleeping bonnet on and was ready to lift her nightgown for George to enter her for the first time. According to the dream, George came into the bedroom with a candle holder in his hand. The holder had a lighted candle which illuminated the colonial-style chamber. He set the candle on the nightstand, removed his wig, and set it atop a bureau. He then lifted his own nightgown. Look at what awaits you, Dear Martha, he said. She looked at the rosebud of her husband's erect penis, and a fit of convulsive laughter attacked her.

At this juncture it's important to give a bit of background on Martha Washington. These facts were not known to Flaquita Salsipuedes until she was able to read about them in her Encyclopedia Britannica some days later. The truth of the matter is that Martha had been married before. She was born Martha Dandridge in 1731. At age eighteen she married Daniel Parke Custis, a man twenty years her senior. They had four children, two of whom died in infancy. When she was twenty-six, her husband died. The following year she met a young colonel in the Virginia Militia. The young man was George Washington, a six-foot-two athletic young man who was admired for his strength and horsemanship. They fell in love. Paintings of Martha Washington don't truly do her justice. They were done later in life by rather poor artists. There is speculation that Martha Dandridge very much resembled the African American movie star Dorothy Dandridge who, other than the café au lait color of her skin, looked like a European woman, and without question was one of the most beautiful film stars of her day. It must be assumed that the lovely Dorothy was obviously a descendant of these Dandridges who spawned Martha. There is also some speculation in narrower historical circles that, like the beautiful Ms. Dandridge, Martha was also a bit tinted with the continent of Africa. The U.S. does have problems with race, but I don't want to enter into conjectures regarding such matters.

Martha was used to her former husband's penis, which was without excess but substantial and pleasurable. But surely it would be impossible for her dear George to have her feel any pleasure with his meager appendage. She couldn't stop laughing, and in the penumbra caused by the insufficient candlelight the future first president of the United States became concerned with what he perceived to be his wife's fear. *Dear Martha*, he said. *Please don't cry. I will be gentle. I will not hurt you.* Eventually, George entered Martha and the marriage was consummated. Her reactions to that first night can be found in the secret letters of Martha Washington, documents that are in the custody of the Smithsonian Institution. I will not incriminate myself by admitting how I came upon these documents. Some will speculate that perhaps Puerto Ricans are possessed of some sort of breaking-and-entering genetic disposition, but let people think what they wish. I'm sure the Smithsonian is hesitant to release these documents into the prurient and sex-obsessed environment the United States has become. Be that as it may, there is a letter dated June 18, 1759, in which the newly wed Martha expresses concern to her friend Abigail Adams. Rather elliptical, the letter does not refer to George's insufficiency but instead talks about certain anomalies that occur in harvesting a field of corn. "Invariably, among normal six- to eight-inch ears of corn, there appear a few ears that do not exceed three inches. These we do not use for seed for the yield would be meager. I am distressed that I as a field will remain fallow." This is an obvious reference to George and his lack. Admittedly, this is an enormous non sequitur, but what else can be made of this?

It should be stated that George Washington, although he helped raise Martha's two children, produced none of his own. Or more precisely, none that could be claimed for the sake of white history. Of course the name Washington occurs with regularity in the U.S., particularly among African Americans. One has to assume some connection, whether directly or indirectly. George did have two half brothers. One has to imagine that they were a horny pair. I cannot be certain that all the Washingtons in the United States are of African descent, but in Brooklyn, where I live, the telephone directory lists well over four hundred Washingtons. There are some twelve George Washingtons, but no Marthas, although there are about ten Ms. I'm sure you're asking yourself where this overabundance of Washingtons has its origin. There are several theories. One is, of course, George's brothers. Another that George, in spite of his lack, was regularly in the barn at Mount Vernon, consorting with the shapely darkies. A more plausible answer could be that the present-day Washingtons are descended from Coo Washington, a magnificent Mandinke young man with what has been described as "physical sufficiency," a term that can only be construed as a sexual euphemism. He was 6'8" tall, a tireless worker, and even more tireless when it came to the pleasuring of women. It is my belief that the myth or reality of African American men being overly endowed genitally has a certain amount of validity. On the other hand I have been in communal shower rooms in high school, the Air Force, and college, and not all African Americans are overly endowed. This could give rise to the theory that George did have his way with certain female slaves and thus produced a strain of short-armed African Americans named Washington. If you're one of them, consider yourself a direct descendant of the father of the country and compensate for your lack that way.

Flaquita did not know of these details as she convalesced. I'm providing these facts in order to try to understand Flaquita's condition and her state of mind. Her dream was even more distressing when camels appeared in a caravan and there was, within the dream, an overpowering aroma of incense. What did this mean? She woke up startled and breathing heavily. Had she contracted a dread American illness? Would she now go around saying, "We're the greatest nation that ever developed on the planet"? Would she now boast that the

United States was the greatest military power ever assembled and could defeat anyone on Earth? It was frightening. When she recuperated fully, she was able to understand that in inserting Omaha Bigelow into herself and causing his rebirth, she had incorporated United States history and was now recalling it. When she was strong enough, she went to the Encyclopedia Britannica and found many of the facts cited above. Of no small importance, given the George and Martha wedding night dream, it should be indicated that George and Martha were married on January 6, 1759. This explains the camels in Flaquita's dreams.

I don't need to point out the significance of January 6 to Puerto Ricans, Latin Americans, or Spaniards, for this is Three Kings' Day, or the Day of the Epiphany. This is the day when the Magi came to Bethlehem bearing gold, frankincense, and myrrh for the child Jesus. Flaquita was relieved that in performing the enlargement ceremony, she had tapped into a repository of Americana that would serve her well in eventually wresting from the United States the Borinquen archipelago, her ancestral home.

So there it was. A good, healthy six-inch *bohango*, which was magnificent enough. Apparently, Maruquita was quite pleased. Just that morning she had come in and announced that she was pregnant.

"Mama, I woke up the next morning and knew I was *encinta*," she'd said. "Can I have my own apartment so Omagaw Boogaloo can live with me and the baby?"

"Sure, honey," Flaquita said. "Doña Pancha on the eleventh floor died last week. Let me see what I can do."

"Thank you, Mama," Maruquita said happily, going over and kissing her mother and almost knocking over the bottle stands that were feeding her intravenously, since she had no energy left to even lift a fork and feed herself. "I love you so much. You're the best mother in the whole world."

"Thank you, *mijita*," she said. "Please bring me your brother's play from the top of the TV."

"Okay, Mama."

She returned with the play and placed it on her mother's chest.

"Mama, I gotta axe you something."

"Go ahead."

"Do I gotta go back to Seward Park and finish high school?"

"Yes."

"*¿Preñá?*"

"Yeah, pregnant."

"Mama!" Maruquita said, stomping her foot and pouting. She crossed her arms and turned her back on her mother. "I don't wanna."

"Maruquita, don't let me get out of this bed feeling like this," Flaquita said. "You're gonna finish high school and that's all there's to it."

"Mama, why are you so mean to me?" Maruquita said, and stomped out of the room.

Flaquita couldn't believe her son's play. What was going on? She couldn't figure it out. This made her very happy. The less she understood about the play, the better she liked it. What was the use of going to a play that was dealing with everyday reality? For that, she could watch CNN and have Christiane Amanpour explain everything to her. Boy, she sure looked Puerto Rican. Maybe her mother was P.R. She liked that English accent. And she was tough. She was sure Christiane was Puerto Rican. Some Ricans say that Vanna White is P.R. but doesn't want to admit it. But Samuel Beckett Salsipuedes, her son, was writing a beautiful, postmodernist, absurdist play. When she was finished with it she was going to ask her new *bohango* son-in-law if he could read it and give her his opinion.

As she read, she wondered where SBS had gotten his ideas for the characters. They reminded her of something she'd heard about but couldn't figure out. The scene had shifted to what appeared to be a board of directors' meeting. It was obvious that Manny Morongo, Ladroncito, Matalina, Madreselva, and El Gato were all Puerto Rican. The only one who wasn't Puerto Rican was Nalgas, and he was gay. Maybe people would think he was also Puerto Rican. *Nalgas* means buttocks in Spanish. Was SBS saying that Ricans were homosexuals or homophobic? Both were true, but which one was the dominant aspect of the culture? The characters were very clearly defined. There was no confusion. El Gato was like a king of the castle. Matalina, his wife, was running things in the kingdom, but she's ready to quit at every turn and blames everyone for the failures of the group. All Ladroncito cares about, it seemed to her, was his acting career. An actor who is an actor within a play. Very interesting. Madreselva is a professor and is always sick with one ailment or another. Did this mean that SBS was saying that the academic community suffers from consistent illness? She couldn't figure out Manny Morongo. He was the strangest of the clowns. Maybe it would all be revealed later. But there was no question that the clowns in this group were the protagonists in defending the castle, and the others—Betrayus, Smelly, Parchaflaca, and Marcosdementos—were the antagonists. Wow! SBS was definitely one deep playwright. What a son she had spawned. Maruquita might be a brilliant Puerto Rican sorceress, but SBS was right up there in producing his own kind of magic. No mother could be prouder.

Flaquita drifted off to sleep and dreamed that she was back on the island when the Spaniards first came ashore. She was a little girl holding her mother's hand and feeling apprehensive about the strange bearded men. She wanted to run away and jump into the clear pool and remain there as a diminutive silver-and-green fish, swimming with the other fish and catching mosquitoes on the surface of the water.

Life was so friggin genetically complex, thought Flaquita. She swore that she'd never do another *bohango* enlargement ceremony for a gringo whiteboy. On the other hand, if she had been able to help George Washington and given him a larger *bohango,* maybe the country might have developed differently. Americans loved to point at the Puerto Ricans and talk about their machismo, but they couldn't look at their own male posturing. You could understand a colonized country with a geography that measured a hundred by thirty-five miles wanting to inflate its importance, but the United States was the third-largest country in the world behind Russia and Canada. The United States was fifty-one times larger than Puerto Rico and apparently a hundred times more insecure.

N O MORE THAN A WEEK HAD PASSED SINCE HIS *BOHANGO* ENLARGEMENT, and Omaha Bigelow was totally out of control. He had a constant erection, and his mind kept flitting from images of a naked Winnifred Buckley to an equally denuded Awilda Cortez or Carrie Marshack to an angry Maruquita with a machete in her hand. Here he had this big *bohango* and was not supposed to share it with the women around him. Fuck, he thought. It wasn't fair. What was he going to do? He could hardly keep his mind on his work, especially when each time he looked up, either Awilda or Winnifred were looking his way and smiling invitingly at him, seemingly urging him to swoop down on them and enter their twinkies. He felt powerful, and for the first time in his life the future had no limits. Although he didn't quite know in which direction he wanted to go, he could finally be all that he could be. Was it to be film, his long-cherished desire? Other Tisch School of the Arts alumni had gone on to film careers. Of course, he wasn't quite an alumnus, but what did that matter? He knew the techniques and he was certain he could write a good script. Perhaps that would be the way to go. But why couldn't he think of anything other than the enticing body of Winnifred Buckley? Around four o'clock in the morning he succumbed to his urges when Winnifred announced that she was hungry and was going to Two Boots pizza.

"Hey, I'll walk you," Omaha said. "Anybody want anything?"

"Nothing for me," Awilda said, turning her back on Omaha and saying, *Coño!* knowing this gringa whitegirl was going to glom Omaha Bigelow whom she already knew the *bruja* bitches had done a peepee *bohango* ceremony on. Everybody in the projects knew it. And it was likely that he now had a tremendous *kakomakako machukapapas bohango*.

"No, thanks, Om," said Ling. "I'm cool."

"Are you sure?" Omaha said, solicitously. "It's not a problem, you know."

"It's okay," Ling reassured him. "I brought a chicken parmigiana sandwich and some steamed wonton my mother made."

So with that, Ling let Omaha and Winnifred out, waved goodbye through the glass door, and off they went. Ling locked the door and shook his head.

"He's gonna fuck himself up," Awilda said.

"It looks that way," Ling said. "She's got that barracuda look in her eye like he's just meat."

"Word," Awilda said. "Dead meat."

Omaha and Winnifred weren't twenty steps from Kinko's when Omaha stopped.

"Did you forget something?" Winnifred said, standing under the awning of Red Square.

"No, but you want to see it, don't you?"

"Of course I want to see it."

"Okay, let's go in the playground across the street and I'll show it to you."

"Sure. Do you want to see mine?"

"Yeah, okay, but the offer doesn't include a *quid pro quo*, you know."

"I know, but *tempus fugit*," she said.

"Let's go, then. *Nunc aut nunquam.*"

"*Carpe diem,*" she shouted, gleefully.

With little traffic at that time of night, they ran across the wide thoroughfare and went into the playground on the south side of Houston Street between Norfolk and Essex Streets, across the street from the Orensanz Foundation Synagogue. They found a corner that was shielded by some shrubs but had light from the lamppost. Fully erect from being in Winnifred's presence, Omaha revealed himself. This quintessence of budding Wasp womanhood became unhinged.

"Oh, my God," Winnifred said. "What is it?"

"It's a *bohango.*"

"That is magnificent. A *bohango.* Of course. What else would one call something of such impressiveness. As soon as I saw you I knew we were going to have a thing. I am inundated with desire. I am liquid with lubricity. This is most unexpected. May I touch it?"

"No, I just wanted you to see it."

"Please. I just want to feel it and mentally retain the texture, the solidity, the utter manliness of what you represent in the barrenness of my Christian abstinence. Please, I beg of you. I shall die of grief if you won't let me touch you."

"I can't, Winnie," Omaha said, placing his erect *bohango* back in his pants. "Oh, my God. I'm dying," he said, mournfully.

"There's someone else, isn't there?" Winnifred pouted.

"Yes, I'm sorry," Omaha said. "There is."

"And you're engaged to be married."

"Yes, I am," Omaha said, carping the diem opportunity, even though the idea had not occurred to him.

"Well, I shall be brave and weather this most unfortunate storm," Winnifred said, taking a deep breath. "But I must warn you."

"Warn me?"

"Yes, I do not give up so easily," Winnifred said, smiling sweetly at Omaha. "I have untapped resources which I will call upon to overcome your reluctance. We are not Buckleys for nothing. I hope we can remain friends."

"Friends, yeah. Sure. That's cool."

They went out of the playground, crossed Houston, and continued to the Two Boots Pizzeria.

"What's her name?" Winnifred asked.

"Maruquita Salsipuedes," Omaha said.

"Oh, a local," said Winnifred haughtily. "How quaint."

"Well, yeah . . . kinda," Omaha said, growing uncomfortable.

"I'm reminded of the work of Joseph Conrad," Winnifred said, icily.

"Oh, which book?"

"Oh, I don't know. Let's say: *Heart of Darkness, Nigger and the Narcissus.*"

"Of the."

"What?"

"The *Nigger of the Narcissus,* that's the title. Anyway, she's not a Negro, or black, to be more accurate. She's Puerto Rican."

"A person of color, nonetheless. A colored person."

"I guess. I can't keep up with the designations. She's Rican."

"I see."

They were now in the restaurant, and the Mexican was asking for their order. Omaha looked at Winnifred. She ordered a plain slice and a Diet Coke. Omaha asked for one with mushrooms and a Pepsi.

"Regular mushrooms or the good shit?" the Mexican said.

"Oh, just regular," Omaha replied.

Fuck, he thought. That's all he needed. Tripping. Fuck. He'd stick his dick in every orifice that this Winnifred had. He'd Winnie her Pooh until she was raw. And if Maruquita found out he'd end up with his nuts and dick chopped off and stuffed into his mouth. Fuck!

"So when can I come and watch you play?" Winnifred said. "When's your next gig?"

"The band broke up," he said. "I had to hock my bass, and then one of the members joined a Japanese punk band, and Richard Rentacar is moving away, so no more band."

"You know Richard Rentacar?"

"Yeah, he's my friend. You know him?"

"Far out. Yeah, not me, but my sister, Muffy. They went to Dartmouth together." She put her right index finger to her lips to swear him to silence.

"I won't tell anybody," Omaha said.

"Muffy and Richard had a thing. She's married to a congressman and will deny it. But she told me that he was no big deal." She placed her right index finger at the top joint of her left index finger. "Nothing like yours," she said.

"Is that what your sister said?"

"Yeah. Size is not supposed to count but it does, I guess. You know? I haven't been with a lot of guys, but some of them are tiny. Well, I really haven't been with anybody. Just groping and touching. Not even fellatio. Not really. I'm still a virgin."

"Oh, yeah?" Omaha said, biting into the last of his pizza. "That's unusual."

"I'm an unusual girl," Winnifred said, smiling and rubbing his forearm. "I bet you've been with lots of girls."

"Not that many," Omaha said, feigning a modesty for which there was little need. He didn't consider nine women in fifteen years a lot, given somebody like Richard, who claimed to have bedded over five hundred women. "I'm pretty monogamous."

"Obviously," Winnifred said. "But you must know that it makes you even more attractive."

"I wasn't aware of that," he said.

"So, are you going to keep playing in bands or do you want to do something else?"

"Maybe do a film."

"Really?"

"Yeah, I studied film at NYU."

"No way. That's far out. You're a filmmaker. That is awesome, Omaha."

"We better get back," Omaha said, wishing he hadn't mentioned NYU like he had a degree. Suddenly he felt ashamed of his life. But he would like to make a real film. How he would do so, he didn't know.

They left the restaurant and walked back up Avenue A. There were still some people in the street, but the bars were closing and it was starting to drizzle. Winnifred ducked into a darkened doorway. Omaha followed her.

"Okay, here it is," she said leaning against him. "I live right there in Red Square."

"Right next to Blockbuster and Kinko's?"

"Yeah, I just got the apartment. You wanna come up after work?"

"I don't know. You know what'll happen."

"Yeah, I know. I've got condoms."

"We better not."

"Let me just touch it through your jeans, then," she said, huskily, her hand reaching for him as she leaned forward to kiss him.

"No, please," Omaha said. "I really like you, Winnie. I'm not kidding. It's making me crazy imagining what it would be like with you."

"So, let's do it. After work you can come to the apartment and see what happens. You can relieve me of the awful burden of my virginity."

"No, I don't want to hurt Maruquita."

"Oh, the white man's burden again," she said. "You know something?"

"What?"

"You are so noblesse oblige it makes my family seem barbaric," she said, and left him standing there and walked quickly up Avenue A. He ran up the street calling her name.

"You don't understand," he said, grabbing her arm as she turned into Houston again.

"No, I certainly don't," she replied, "and I'll thank you to release my arm. It is uncommon for a Buckley to throw herself at a member of the opposite sex as I've done, only to be rejected so brutally."

"I'm sorry," Omaha said, releasing her arm and following her. "Wait, let's talk."

"I am so ashamed of myself," Winnifred said, stopping a little past the Red Square building. She began weeping, her blond hair now plastered to her head in the increasing rain.

They were almost in front of Kinko's. Out of sympathy because Omaha was at heart a good person, he couldn't help himself and put his arms around her. Winnifred slipped easily into his embrace and sighed deeply, albeit rather theatrically. Omaha pecked her lips. Her tongue reached out for him but he broke off the embrace and continued until he was in front of Kinko's and tapping on the glass. Innocent as all of this was, the brief empathic episode had been observed by Awilda Cortez, who, feeling the smallish hell of a woman not yet conquered but nevertheless scorned, promised herself to avenge the slight.

The rest of the shift went without a hitch. Winnifred Buckley took to the task of copying as if born to it. And with her capacity for speed reading, she absorbed everything she copied. Of great interest was a paper which predicted a tight presidential race, except that rather than Florida the electoral debacle was to take place in Wyoming, a place in the United States with hardly a Cuban population. In spite of this novelistic non sequitur, Winnifred's highly developed brain immediately thought of her father and his friendship with the presidential candidate's father. Yes, she thought. "*Cogito ergo sum*," which for people who don't know Latin—myself included —means "I think, therefore I am." Not knowing a language has never prevented novelists from spicing up their work with little foreign phrases to create atmosphere and exoticism. I have seen some lulus when writers attempt to use Spanish. I have included Latin from having the benefit of the Internet. I went to a site and extracted several phrases which I am using to produce further character elaboration, hoped-for mirth, and light divertissement that is not too intrusive.

Malevolently, Winnifred Buckley thought: *Pares cum paribus facillime,* and agreed that "Birds of a feather do flock together." Winnifred did know Latin and ended her Machiavellian plan by reciting the motto of her alma mater: *Lux et Veritas.* Light and Truth. Yes, she thought, kneeling one knee on the floor in front of the Big Matilda, and with both fists together she pulled back on the right one as if she were pulling the lever on a cannon, the traditional and secondary sign when one has scored a goal in ice hockey, a sport with which she was familiar from having played it with her brothers, Pierce III, Drake, and Creighton, the three of them Division I players of moderate second- and third-line distinction. I have made a slight digression for the jocks who may be getting a bit confused and in need of a point of athletic reference. But Winnifred Buckley was delighted with her plan. Hahahhahaha, she thought in Pablian delight. Pablo is someone I know. She's an excellent playwright, and when she laughs it sounds as if a closet has been opened and has disgorged all manner of items.

But if Winnifred Buckley's upcoming scheme to ensnare Omaha was complex and far-reaching, it was meager when compared to what was taking place in Awilda Cortez's brain. She was convinced that Omaha liked her and that not only was he making a mistake in being with that *bruja* Maruquita Salsipuedes, but now he was cheating on her with this *blanquita* bitch, and that was totally messed up. There was no way she was going to go up to Maruquita and say that her man was cheating on her with some gringa whitegirl. Maruquita might think she was lying or jealous and she could get turned into a chihuahua or a chicken at the *vivero,* the live-chicken place over on Delancey between Attorney and Pitt. Or maybe end up in a pet shop as an iguana or a hamster. Shit, Awilda thought! That was messed up what them *brujas* could do.

She couldn't wait to get home to call up her homegirl, Bibi Cantaleta, and tell her that the gringo whiteboy with the green hair who was going out with Maruquita *le estaba pegando cuernos con una rubia,* meaning that Omaha had placed horns on Maruquita's head with some blonde. It was very likely that as soon as Awilda finished telling Bibi what she'd seen, Bibi would call up her cousin, Lillian Averiguada, who would call her lesbian girlfriend, Denise Bochinche, who would tell her mother, Mrs. Bochinche, who would phone her *comadre,* Mrs. Lengüetera, saying that she wasn't sure how true it was, but she had heard that Mrs. Salsipuedes's daughter, Maruquita, who was giving it away to a gringo whiteboy American weirdo with green hair, was being deceived by him cheating on her with a blonde girl who looked like Charlize Theron, who has a pretty nice butt for a white girl and was in that movie about golf when she walks away back to her table after sticking her tongue all into Matt Damon's throat, or when she's out there in the golf course and she walks away and her *nalgas* are swinging back and forth like she's the girl from Ipanema, which gave her old man, Ramón, a tremendous boner and he almost killed her that night thinking about this Charlize Theron, who has those nice thick lips and who the hell knows whether she's even a white girl. She could be one of those real white Rican girls from the mountains. Anyway, Maruquita's gringo whiteboy is definitely *pegándole cuernos,* and whatnot. *You don't know who Charlize Theron is? Girl! You know, in the film about golf with Will Smith, who is fine even if he's a moreno, girl. Bagger something. Yeah, they gave it at the movies on Second Avenue, homegirl. Anyway, he's cheating on Maruquita and I feel sorry for that gringo whiteboy and hope it's not true. And it don't matter that they did all that secret peepee bohango ceremony on him cauze they'll reverse the procedure, and do a trabajo on his butt. Yeah, a penisectomy, I think they call it in the medical field, which as you know I have done filing in Dr. Glickman's office on First Avenue for twenty years since I got out of Seward Park High School, and I know that kind of shit from hearing about it. You know, some weird shit that them brujas do.*

In any event it is quite likely that Mrs. Lengüetera would let it drop in passing to her overweight daughter, Conchita, who was burning the torch rather than the calories and madly in love with Samuel Beckett Salsipuedes, who had kindly said he wasn't interested in rescuing her from her gluttony as had Victor Collazo done for Marcelina Puente that the writer, Ernesto Mendoza, had told about in the story "Collazo's Diet," that he had studied at Hunter College with Professor Lópes Adorno. Conchita would tell her girl-friend Olga, and Olga would tell Milagros, and she would tell Margarita, and in turn Margarita would tell Beatriz, until the story would eventually reach Maruquita.

Awilda couldn't wait to get home.

M ARUQUITA HAD A PREMONITION, A SIGN, AN OMEN THAT SOMETHING wasn't quite right. Not even a week after she had gotten down with her Omagaw Boogaloo and was now pregnant with her Gringorican baby she had a horrible nightmare. In the dream she was in Central Park, pushing her perambulator with Kevin Boogaloo in it when all of a sudden Uncle Sam came out of the bushes where he had obviously been hiding and told her to stop. Uncle Sam was dressed in his usual red, white, and blue and looked like Robin Williams. He was with the Statue of Liberty, who looked like Phyllis Diller except that she was greenish like an iguana and was dressed in jeans and a T-shirt that said:

> I'll take the hungry,
> the poor, the
> wretched of the
> earth, but them
> Puerto Ricans,
> oy vey!

It is prudent, for a number of antipolemical reasons, that at this point the author issue a strong disclaimer. This doesn't constitute the author pulling his punches. The author has a lot of other issues to worry about. The fact that the Statue of Liberty says "oy vey" is not, in any way, an indication that Lady Liberty is Jewish or that there is some sort of hidden message about Jews. I know that Emma Lazarus, a Sephardic Jew, wrote the original words, not the ones paraphrased on the T-shirt. The Statue of Liberty is French, and you know about the French and their snooty ways. The "oy vey" indicates that the Statue of Liberty has adapted to New York after more than a century here and is familiar with this universal Yiddish phrase of chagrin, disappointment, and astonishment at the vagaries of life. Puerto Ricans have a similar phrase: *"Ay, bendito."* It is likely, however, that it will take another century before the phrase is in popular usage in New York City. When I asked Lady Liberty what she meant by the message on her T-shirt, she simply said: "Vega, sometimes you are such a schmuck." You can't deduce anything from that remark other than the fact that Lady Liberty thinks the author is an idiot. Fair enough! That's been proven many times over. Most literary authors are idiots, even though their caricatures appear on posters and bags at Barnes & Noble. To try to tell the truth through fiction is idiotic today. Some very fine people still make an effort to amplify an issue through fiction, but we're basically idiots, quixotic fools trying to save humanity from itself. What could be more idiotic!

Anyway, in Maruquita's dream the two of them, Lady Liberty and Uncle Sam, stood in front of the baby carriage, and Uncle Sam said they were going to take her baby. "We're taking him now," Uncle Sam said. "He's an American and loyal to the American Way of Life and we want to train him so he can help us combat worldwide terrorism."

When she protested, she saw the horrifying sight of huge planes hitting big buildings all over New York City. Any building over fifty stories was being knocked down, and people were screaming and crying and it was horrible. Of course, when it happened in September after the baby was born, Maruquita was shocked that she had had the dream, but by then it was too late.

"He's only a baby," Maruquita said in the dream. "He can't fight."

"Yes, but he's our baby," Uncle Sam said, pointing his finger at her. "He is an American baby and I want him!"

"That's right," Lady Liberty said, waving her torch at Maruquita and threatening to smack her with her book. "Aren't you patriotic, you creep?"

"No, I'm Puerto Rican, you lame green mothafocka," Maruquita said, growing angry. "Whyn'tcha leave us alone and while you're at it get the fuck out of Vieques, bitch!"

"Oh, that tired old bullshit," Lady Liberty said, acting all bad, like she was a homegirl instead of being related to Kermit the Frog. "You people are too much. Grow up and get over it. Ricans don't deserve to be a country. Shit, you don't even deserve to be a state."

And then there were helicopters above the park, and mothers and children ran out of the zoo and about one hundred Marines in full battle gear came down from the helicopters in ropes and one of them snatched the baby away, and a band was playing music that sounded like John Phillip Souza marches but with a punk beat, which sounded awful.

Maruquita woke up in a cold sweat like she had the flu or something. She knew exactly what the dream meant. Omagaw Boogaloo was messing around on her. She knew it. She could feel it. She didn't know why she had trusted him. He was like any Rican, sweet-talking her until he got into her pants, and then he was off chasing bitches. And he was the one, too. He was the chosen and she had picked him herself. She felt so deceived. What was she going to do? What time was it? By coincidence, and not as a novelistic convenience, it was roughly twenty minutes after four in the morning, when Omaha was just putting his *bohango* back in his pants after showing it to Winnifred Buckley. Really, not exactly at the same time, but almost at the same time. Maruquita was not aware of that image, but she knew something was wrong. She determined to go to Kinko's and wait for Omaha when he finished working.

She tried going back to sleep but the specters of Uncle Sam and Lady Liberty stealing her baby kept her awake. She tried reading a Spiderman comic, watching TV, drinking warm milk, but nothing worked. She finally turned into an owl and flew out the window to hunt rats. She was so angry that she would swoop down on the rats, grab them in her talons, and climb high above the walkway next to the East River. Once there, she would withdraw her talons and watch the rats smash against the asphalt. The next morning joggers had to step around the roughly one hundred and fifty rats with which Maruquita's owl had proved incontrovertibly, and in Galilean delight, that the law of gravity works on other than lead and feathers.

She returned to the apartment at seven fifteen, showered, had coffee and toast, got dressed, and was standing outside of Kinko's at 7:50 A.M. She could see Omaha working, and her heart gave a tug at how cute he looked in his striped pinkish Kinko's shirt and his green hair. He looked like a Neapolitan icey. She noted with interest that there was a blonde girl there who kept looking at her man and smiling like something was going on but he wouldn't look back at her. The Rican girl was also looking at him, but it was the gringa whitegirl that was the culprit. The sign was very clear. That dream pointed right at her. Five minutes later a big lanky man with blond hair and sad eyes came up to her.

"Good morning of the day," the man said. "We will be make doors to open soon for conducting business at this people's collective copying establishment."

"Hi," Maruquita said morosely.

"I offer you my presentation," the man said. "I am Valery Molotov. Manager of collective."

"How you doing?"

"You are very sad in most interesting Dostoevskian manner," Molotov said. "Is very appealing. What you are named?"

"Maruquita Salsipuedes."

"We have similar name in Russia. Marushka Salsinokova. Great tennis player but she change name to Anna Kournikova. The medias do not aware of this. Must be very discreet. I like better other name. But very nice to meeting you. I go inside now to begin daily mission of labor to helping the proletariat in their replication."

With that, Ling came to the door and let Molotov inside. A few minutes later three more people arrived, and now the door was open and Maruquita entered. She stood by the self-service machines and watched Omaha go into a door. Shortly thereafter the blonde with a surprisingly round *fundillo* butt followed him inside, but Omaha came out immediately. It was very likely, Maruquita thought, that they had exchanged information or kissed or copped a feel while they were inside the room.

Omaha came out, spoke to Molotov for a few seconds, started to leave, and saw Maruquita.

"Hi, baby," he said, sweetly, truly glad to see her.

"Hi," Maruquita said.

"What are you doing here?"

"I missed you," she said. "I had a terrible dream. Bad people came to try to steal our baby."

"Our baby?"

"Yeah, our Gringorican baby."

"No way."

"Yeah, way."

At this point Winnifred Buckley came out of the room, waved goodbye to everyone, and saw Omaha talking to a Puerto Rican girl. She immediately deduced that this was the local and the target that she would eventually obliterate. She walked deliberately up to the couple, and in a most coquettish way that would make any Latina feel enormous envy at the style which this gringa whitegirl was displaying, she patted Omaha on the arm.

"I'll see you tomorrow, handsome," she said, totally ignoring Maruquita. "Thanks for showing me things."

"Sure," Omaha said, avoiding looking at her.

"Oh, I'm sorry," Winnifred said as an afterthought. "I interrupted your conversation."

"That's okay," Omaha said.

"Oh, I'm Winnifred Buckley," she said boldly to Maruquita, extending her hand. "How do you do?"

"I do okay," Maruquita said, sheepishly, intimidated by the blonde's height. She was as tall as Omagaw Boogaloo.

"How charming," Winnifred said. "The local color is so *je ne sais quoi*," she added, turned away theatrically, and walked toward the door, her gluteal maxima accumulation within her jeans swaying in a very Charlizian and Theronic way.

Out of the corner of her eye Maruquita caught Omaha looking at the blonde's butt. She had the urge to turn the bitch into some lame-ass white poodle, but now that she was pregnant she knew she shouldn't use her *brujería*. Her mother had warned her that she could have bad results with her pregnancy. She would wait until she gave birth to use her *brujería*. Dayum, she thought. What was she gonna do? Maybe she ought to talk to her grand-mother and see if she could turn the bitch into a pigeon. That was it. That's what she'd do.

"Are you hungry?" Omaha said.

"Not really," Maruquita said, still hurt by what she knew was true.

"Will you come with me to Odessa so I can eat breakfast?"

"Sure."

They walked out, and Omaha immediately put his arm around her waist and told her how glad he was to see her and was everything all right.

"You seem sad," he said.

"It was the dream," she replied, and told him about it.

"Those are some very powerful images," Omaha said. "Very graphic and disturbing images that show how greatly affected the common people are by American symbols. It is an overwhelming reality."

"Omagaw Boogalaoo?"

"What?"

"Why you talking like that?"

"Like what?"

"Like you in a movie that was made by BBS?"

"PBS?"

"Yeah, Channel Thirteen."

"I didn't mean anything bad, Maruquita," Omaha said. "But it was just a dream."

"But they took the baby, Omagaw Boogaloo."

"Yeah, but it was just a dream. They can't really take the baby, because there is no baby."

"But there's gonna be a baby," she said, patting her belly.

"When you get pregnant."

"I already am."

"No way. Just like that?"

"Yeah, I think it happened the second time you did it to me."

"Are you really gonna have a baby?"

"Yeah."

"Wow, I'm gonna be a daddy," Omaha almost shouted. "That's great."

"Yeah, but I'm worried."

"About what?"

"I don't know."

"Well, tell me about it."

They went into Odessa, found a booth, and sat down. A couple of musicians from the band Gravitational Pull, who had just finished an all-night drug and sexual binge with six coeds from Ramapo College in New Jersey, recognized Omaha and said hello. He wanted to tell them that he was going to be a father but felt weird and just waved at them. He wondered if he felt ashamed that he was having a baby with Maruquita. He thought for a moment about Winnifred Buckley and shuddered. She was one scary babe. Fuck, he thought. He turned his attention once again to Maruquita.

"You know something?"

"What?"

"I love you."

"You do?"

"Yeah, lots and lots."

"You bozo," Maruquita said. "I love you too."

When Omaha had ordered and the food came, Maruquita became serious and said she had to ask Omaha a question.

"Sure," Omaha said.

"Are you cheating on me?"

"Cheating on you? No way."

"What's with that blonde?"

"Winnifred?"

"Yeah, whatever. What is she bisexy that she gots to have a girl's and a boy's name?"

"Funny. Winnie and Fred. It's just an American name."

"She's a asshole."

"Well, yes. I agree. A bit overbearing."

"What means that? What kind of bear is an overbear?"

"She's over the top?"

"The top?"

"Yeah, she's . . . I don't know how to explain . . ."

"She's *antipática* is what she is. A *sangrigorda, descará, pendeja, cara de yegua* gringa whitegirl bitch *blanquita maricona*. And you know what?"

"What?"

"If she start shit with me, I'ma smack her upside her silly-ass blond head. She was trying to dis me in front of you."

"Maruquita, she can't hurt you."

"That's right, and if she try, I'ma turn her ass into a pigeon. Not me but my grandma. She does that kind of shit. And don't try to play me, Omagaw Boogaloo. Okay?"

"I'm cool."

"I caught you looking at her butt."

"No way," Omaha said, automatically.

"You were looking at her butt. Don't lie, Omagaw Boogaloo. I caught you. Admit it."

"Well, just a glance."

"I knew it. Do you think she has a nice butt?"

"It's okay."

"Okay?"

"For a gringa whitegirl."

"But not like mine?"

"Not even close. You have a wonderful *culo.*"

"Shhhhh. Dont talk like that in front of people. You say *culito,* anyway."

"Oh, okay. I'm sorry."

"But it's true?" she said.

"About your you-know-what?" he asked to make sure they were talking about her derriere.

"Yeah. You like it?"

"*Magnífico.*"

"You gotta learn the accents, Papi. *Magnífico.*"

"Okay, okay. I'm learning," Omaha said and then leaned over and whispered *"Culito magnífico."*

"*Muchas gracias,* you bozo," Maruquita said and laughed for the first time since she'd had the dream. He was so wonderful, she thought. She watched him as he paid the bill. They went out into the street, crossed Avenue A, and entered the park.

"Can we go to your house?" Omaha said, getting out of the way of an awkward roller blader.

"Why, you wanna give me head?" Maruquita said, going behind him and grabbing his butt.

"Yeah, *mucha cabeza.*"

"Oh, okay," Maruquita said, seemingly excited about something else.

"What?"

"My mother got us a apartment," Maruquita said as they continued walking in Tompkins Square Park.

"Where?"

"Right there in the projects. Four floors under my parents."

"Far out. How much?"

"I think two hundred and fifty, but you gotta do something. I hope it's okay."

"What?"

"You have to grow a mustache and have black hair."

"Why?"

"The City inspectors come, and they see a gringo whiteboy living there, they gonna get suspicion."

"Suspicious."

"Yeah, that too. Anyway, that's what you gotta do."

"No more green hair."

"No way. We frizz up your hair so you can look down with the program."

"What about my mustache? It comes in blond."

"Comes out, you mean."

"Yeah, okay. But what about the blond mustache hair?"

"We paint it black. You gotta have your black mustache and act stupid. You can do that. I seen you act stupid plenty times. Just don't say nothing. You act like you just came from P.R. and you stupid. That's it. Don't open your mouth. But we can move in next week."

"We have to get furniture."

"No, this old woman died, and her daughter said she didn't want the stuff. There's a big bed and everything. We can see it if you want to."

"Sure," Omaha said, and kissed Maruquita when they were in front of the bandshell. "You are so incredibly beautiful," he said, not quite believing his luck.

"You bozo. How is your *kakomakako peepee bohango?* Let me see, "she said, reaching down and touching the front of his jeans. "My goodness," she giggled. "It's alive in there."

"Yeah! Like it wants to give you a thousand Gringorican babies."

"You are such a gringo whiteboy bozo," Maruquita said, laughing.

They went walking out of the park and down Seventh Street holding hands.

THE WEEKEND AFTER SHE BEGAN WORKING AT KINKO'S ON HOUSTON Street, Winnifred Buckley traveled to Sag Harbor, Long Island, to seek out her father's help at the family's summer estate. Omaha Bigelow had been rather distant, and the disdain irked her. He seemed totally focused on his work and avoided looking at her. Whenever she went near him, he would find a way to scoot away and keep her at arm's length. Each morning before they finished their shift, the big-butt poor-man's-Jennifer-Lopez-look-alike, with her big earrings and pseudo grunge Latino fashion statements, came and stood outside the store until Omaha came out. He'd kiss her and get moonstruck and they'd go off holding hands or with their arms around each other. At school she was distracted by her constant sexual desire to the point that in one of her classes she almost lost control and started to scream "Fuck torts" before she caught herself.

As if the rejection weren't sufficient to drive her up the wall, she had to put up with the bother of suffering from chronic premenstrual tension. During the weeklong bouts she had visions of previous incarnations, all of them fierce warriors in the employ of great chieftains. Her least favorite apparition was fighting on the side of Angus the Long of the Clan McDonald in 937 AD. In the Scottish heather she was Ian of Clagh, kilted, red-bearded, and robust. Ian died impaled on a lance wielded by a man who looked remarkably like Mel Gibson in *Braveheart*. Her favorite was her incarnation as Mangian, the feared Mongol warrior in the employ of Ghengis Khan, when he rode his stallion into battle. She loved the way her sword struck the neck of enemies and the headless body continued forward on the horse while the head flew through the air, the eyes startled, until it bounced on the dusty ground of the battlefield. She often wondered why none of her incarnations was a woman.

Emerging from her apartment in Red Square early that Saturday morning, Winnifred crossed Houston Street and retrieved her red BMW from the parking lot on Essex Street. She went east on Houston Street until she hit the

F.D.R. Drive, whereupon she sped uptown, entered the midtown tunnel, and for the next two hours raced east until she drove into the manicured grounds of the Buckley summer estate. There, among heirlooms and upper-class excess, she hoped to seek her father's advice and a small loan.

Pierce Buckley was a man of funereal mien and passable intellect. He was 6'4' tall, lean and angular, with long limbs and facial bones that each year grew more prominent. Not a particularly handsome man, he made up for it by a voracious sexual appetite. However, even on a bright sunny day Pierce Buckley looked as if he had been told an hour ago that he had a week to live or that his considerable wealth had been reduced to a trifle. People often remarked that it seemed as if all the joy had been siphoned out of his life.

And yet he was able to take nearly moribund companies, resurrect them, and inject them with new vibrancy. Nobody had yet figured out how Pierce Buckley accomplished this. Many people think it was Lee Iacocca and an infusion of federal dollars that turned Chrysler around. No! It was Pierce Buckley who managed this industrial miracle. He minded not one bit that Iacocca took all the credit. In the same fashion as he had worked quietly in espionage, he chose to remain in the corporate shadows. As for the success of Microsoft, he was too modest to take credit for that feat, other than to admit to himself that it was very likely that he was Gates's father. His reasons were genuine ones. To make matters worse in fueling the rumor, Pierce Buckley looked very much like an embalmed version of the founder of the software empire. Pierce Buckley was not an inspirational or charismatic figure. He was not an articulate speaker, nor was he a great financial wizard. He was, however, the ultimate upper-level bureaucrat, close-mouthed, cunning, and efficient.

When the president was choosing his cabinet, Buckley was short-listed for both secretary of the interior and transportation secretary. In both cases Buckley declined, citing health reasons. Nonsense. He was healthy and strong and simply didn't want to be bothered with the intrigue of life in the capital. He would have preferred an ambassadorship to West Africa; perhaps Guinea Bisau, Gambia, Senegal, or the Ivory Coast, since in the past two years he had developed a predilection for African womanhood. These countries had coastlines, and he wouldn't have to give up sailing. He couldn't imagine what it would be like to be surrounded by high-breasted, ebony-colored women with long legs. God help him if his mother found out. In any case, GW hadn't asked if he wished to serve as an ambassador, and he was not about to hint and impose on what he believed would be a difficult presidency. He did agree to oversee the CIA on an interim basis, to determine whether he could overcome the staid conformity which had seeped into the agency and which Pierce Buckley believed was placing the United States in a vulnerable position.

Winnifred Buckley parked her BMW near the guest house on her parents' estate, took out her knapsack, and set it inside the three-bedroom cottage where she would be staying. She then headed for the mansion proper, two hundred yards away. Once there, she was greeted by the housekeeper, Mrs. Cross, a frumpy and affable if at times absent-minded English woman. Winnifred returned the greeting, followed Mrs. Cross into the kitchen, and asked where she could find her mother.

"I believe she's in the library," Mrs. Cross said. "Then again, she could be in the greenhouse. Either that or she's gone waterskiing with your father."

"That's not very likely," Winnifred said. "Thank you, Mrs. Cross. Could you prepare some lunch for me?"

"I've made a lobster bisque," Mrs. Cross said. "No, wait. That was Friday. Yesterday. Today is Saturday, isn't it?"

"Yes, it is."

"I can make you a nice salad with a lovely chicken-breast sandwich."

"That's super, Mrs. Cross. "Thank you."

Being closer to the greenhouse, Winnifred went out the back door to find her mother. She dreaded seeing her again. Her mother, Amanda Mumford "Bootsie" Buckley, née Lancaster, was an athletic woman of acceptable looks, thin-lipped, and angular of body. If there was a striking feature about her it was her eyes, which held twin question marks, much as if everything she saw were a mystery. She had been so sexually promiscuous in her youth that she had to be kept in irons in her grandmother Sarah Lowell Lancaster's basement at her Vermont home for six weeks prior to her marriage. An excellent equestrian, it is rumored that she was once caught attempting to manually pleasure her jumper, Hummingbird, in the family stables in Mount Kisco, New York. At sixteen she had won third place in the Nationals and would have competed in the Olympics had she not broken her right ankle when Hummingbird missed one of the water jumps and she was thrown. Hummingbird also broke a leg and had to be destroyed. Bootsie Lancaster was never right after that. The loss of Hummingbird so injured her psyche that she turned to writing poetry. Well, perhaps it's not fair to categorize her writing as poetry. Most people have no clue what poetry is, and most of them are at best writing what can be described as "feelgood" or "nicethought" instead of poetry. Populism has many flaws and it produces many casualties. Poetry is one of its victims.

Winnifred had also heard that the reason that her mother married her father is that he reminded her mother of Hummingbird. Not only did her father have those large, sad, dreamy eyes, but she heard that he was positively equine, which Bootsie Lancaster had ascertained when she visited her brother, Grayson, at Yale and had happened in on Pierce Buckley being pleasured orally by one Angelina Bellacqua, an Italian language teaching assistant and an authority on Ezra Pound, another victim of populism. Bootsie ducked behind a dresser and watched the masculine magnificence that was Pierce Buckley. *My God*, she thought, *he's not even a quarter into her mouth and she's gagging.* The bullfighter in Spain with the huge organ was a child compared to Pierce. Shortly after, she watched Pierce withdraw from Angelina Bellacqua's mouth, bid her get on all fours, and like a stallion entered the teaching assistant whose buttocks were so marelike it caused Bootsie to nearly faint.

From that moment on, Bootsy worshiped Pierce, whose name alone connoted pleasure for her. Nearly out of her mind with lust, Bootsie ran out of the room, emerged into the late autumn chill, and began a year-long quest to ensnare Pierce Buckley. Just the memory of Pierce made Bootsy want to screw every male she met, knowing that she would find them lacking, thus impelling her to capture the prize that was Pierce Drake Buckley. The six weeks' confinement prior to the marriage had made Bootsie delirious, and she endured the wedding ceremony nearly babbling. It was not until they completed the tediousness of the reception, and were in the honeymoon suite at the Plaza Hotel in New York City before flying to Punta del Sol the next day for their honeymoon that Bootsie was able to release her pent-up emotion. As soon as Pierce entered her, she screamed so loudly that the hotel was nearly evacuated.

She once told her friend Amber Raleigh that she thought she was going to die from the sensation and all she could think of was poor Hummingbird, lying there half in the water and half out of the cross-country jump, his eyes frightened with the knowledge that he couldn't get up. Nevertheless, the pain brought her immense pleasure and kept her totally faithful for her entire marriage up until the previous year, when Pierce had made his confession about his new-found predilection for African women.

Not finding her mother in the greenhouse, Winnifred circled the house, opened the French doors from the garden and entered the library. There she found her mother poring over a large tome of the Koran.

"Hello, Mother," Winnifred said. "Studying?"

"*Salaam alekum*, Winnifred," her mother replied without looking up. "May the peace of Allah the compassionate be upon you."

"Please, mother," Winnifred said. "You are so utterly bizarre lately. Why are you reading the Koran?"

"I am *studying Al Quoran,* Winnifred. Praise be to Allah, and his prophet Mohammed, may peace be upon him."

"Mother, stop it!" Winnifred shouted.

"Oh, dear," her mother said, turning to look at her daughter, whom she saw as a young libertine with a touch of the opportunist. "You are miffed again."

"I am not miffed," Winnifred said, arching her right eyebrow and staring at her mother, knowing she was an upper-class twit of the worst kind and that it was likely that were she not careful, she could be easily transformed into her mother. That is why it was so important that she convince Omaha Bigelow, an obviously middle-class barbarian whose loins she ached for, to mate with her. "Do you know where Daddy's gone?"

"He said he was going waterskiing."

"Do you know when he'll be back?"

"No, I don't. Your father said it was likely that he'd be out all day. He plans to go sailing after lunch."

"Will he be coming back here?"

"No, I believe he'll take his lunch aboard the *Concordia.*"

"Drat," Winnifred said, stomping her right docker and wringing her khaki pants. "I have to find him. Goodbye, Mother."

"Will you be joining us for dinner, dear?"

"I don't know," Winnifred said as she went out of the library.

"Mrs. Cross is making roasted leg of lamb with mint sauce and couscous," said her mother.

Winnifred did not respond. In the kitchen Mrs. Cross had finished putting the final touches on Winnifred's lunch. She thanked the housekeeper, swept up the sandwich, and chewing with great zest, went out of the house, back into her BMW, and creating a wake of gravel in the driveway, headed for the marina to find her father. Once there, she looked for her father's favorite yacht, a forty-foot racing sloop. No sooner was she on board than she shuddered as she saw herself as the fierce Viking warrior Sven Lutefiskson as he raised his battle-ax and crushed the helmet of some Frisian, sending him brain-dead to the ground. This vision was caused by a series of occurrences that nearly made her scream.

Up the companionway of the *Concordia* came the blackest, fiercest, and most beautiful woman Winnifred had ever seen. She had to be well over six feet tall, with aquiline features and a closely-cropped head of frizzy black hair. Clothed in white shorts and a yellow tank top which showed off perfect abdominal muscles, she was majestic. Winnifred heard a slap, obviously to her buttocks, and then a giggle from the black woman. Directly behind her, making his way up the steps, was her father, Pierce Buckley. He was tying his swimming shorts and attempting to smooth his tousled hair. Obviously the two had been cavorting below, thought Winnifred. She couldn't be sure of the woman's age, but she was young, perhaps thirty or thirty-five. The woman was, in fact, forty-one years old.

"Hi, Daddy," she said.

"Winnifred, dear," said her father, totally unruffled. "What brings you out here?"

"I have to talk to you, Daddy," she said, avoiding having to look at the black woman. "Urgently."

"Well, I'm very happy to see you, darling," said Pierce, giving his daughter his cheek to kiss. "Winnifred, this is Dakulana Imbebwabe. She's visiting from the Ivory Coast. Dakulana, this is my daughter Winnifred."

"How do you do, Winnifred," said the black woman in perfectly accented Oxonian English.

"Ms. Imbebwabe," said Winnifred, extending her hand, but feeling like she was going to have another vision. This time Feng Li, the Chinese warlord in twelfth-century Shanghai, kept peeking out impishly from behind a curtain in the Imperial Palace. Whenever Winnifred thought he would come out and begin waving his sword, Feng would duck back behind the red-and-gold curtain. "How do you do?"

"I'm very well," said Dakulana. "Your father tells me that you're reading law."

"What? Oh, yeah. I'm in law school."

"Excellent," replied the black woman. "Your father tells me a great many wonderful things about you. He's very proud of you."

"My father is a very kind man. May I ask you something?"

"Of course," said Dakulana, smiling mirthfully and a bit too condescendingly.

"Are you fucking my father?"

"Winnifred!" said her father.

"As a matter of fact we have just finished moments ago and were lounging in postcoital delight," said Dakulana. "Since you've chosen to be a typical American liberated woman in spite of your petulance, I must tell you that your father is a remarkably virile man. This is the third time today that he has imposed his libido upon me with rather glorious results."

At that point Tsunesaburo Kashimoto, a fifteenth-century samurai, retainer of Makoto Irihara, the Mokuyoku of Kyoto, appeared, and Winnifred Buckley was there again, drawing her sword and emitting a blood-curdling scream. Rather than make a fool of herself in looking as if she were about to attack, she ran to the bow of the yacht and jumped into the water. Both her father and his lover went to the front and saw Winnifred coming to the surface and swimming back towards the boat.

"She's a little high-strung, isn't she?" Dakulana said.

"A little," Pierce Buckley agreed.

When she was back on board, Winnifred went below, removed her clothes and shoes, found shorts and a polo shirt, and got dressed. She brought her clothes and shoes topside and set them to dry atop the cabin. Her father and Dakulana were sitting on deck chairs. Winnifred pulled a chair over and sat down with them. She smiled at her father and Dakulana and explained that this always happened to her before she menstruated. Dakulana was very understanding.

"Do you feel like you want to commit murder?" she asked.

"How did you know? I have visions that I'm a warrior and I'm in battle."

"I have the same affliction," Dakulana said. "About a week before I menstruate I am in the veldt, spear in hand, and I am looking for lions to slay. It's a distressing ailment, shared by only a few thousand women in the world. I believe it's a genetic malfunction triggered by extra testosterone. It hasn't been confirmed, but Margaret Thatcher, the ex-Prime Minister of England, suffered from the ailment before she reached menopause. The Argentinians paid the price with their insistence on the Falkland Islands. You have a bit of a wait."

"I'm only twenty-three. That's another thirty or thirty-five years. What the hell am I going to do?"

"You have to find someone like your father," Dakulana said. "Someone who will not leave you alone, and makes you submit to his desire."

Winnifred looked at her father. Her father shrugged his shoulders. Even though he looked sad, his large brilliant blue eyes were filled with the most amazing light. It was as if all the happiness in the world were locked behind them and shining out. This was new for him.

"Really?" Winnifred said.

"It's true," Dakulana said.

"Can I ask you something?"

"Of course," Dakulana said.

"Are you Afrocentric?"

"Hardly," Dakulana said. "I read European literature at Oxford. And my PhD from Yale University is in comparative nineteenth- and twentieth-century literature, with a special emphasis on the novels of Thomas Hardy, Fyodor Dostoevsky, Émile Zola, William Faulkner, and the development of the urban environment within the complexities of living in an industrial and commercialized society."

"But you're so black, so African, so . . . I don't know . . . so . . . "

"Sexual?"

"Well, yeah . . . something like that," Winnifred said. "Maybe that's why I came out to see Daddy."

"Why is that, dear?"

"I think I'm sexually frustrated. I met someone, and I'm going crazy because he's being very reluctant. He's a filmmaker and he has this really great idea for a motion picture."

"Is he secure?" Pierce asked. "Financially, I mean."

"No, I don't think so. We work together at Kinko's, but he went to Yale and graduated. He also went to film school at NYU."

"At Kinko's? Whatever for?"

"I just had to be near him," Winnifred said sheepishly. "He's brilliant, Daddy. It's an incredible script about a punk rock musician in the East Village. And he's composed the film score. He's an *auteur* of remarkable sensitivity."

"That's wonderful, Winnifred," Pierce Buckley said. "We have stock in Kinko's, by the way. How can I be of help?"

"Daddy, I need twenty million dollars," Winnifred said.

"That's not a small amount of money," her father replied. "Why do you need this money?"

"I want to make a low-budget film of this boy's script," she said. "I think it'll be a commercial success if someone like Johnny Depp agrees to do it. He'd be perfect."

"How soon do you need the money, Winnifred?"

"Right away, Daddy."

"Very well. Leave me your bank account number and I'll have the money wired to it immediately. I would suggest, however, that you allow me to invest the money at a low interest rate, and you can draw on it as you need it. Call my lawyers and have them set up a company specifically for the purposes of handling the production and finances for the film. They can write everything off as a loss, and you'll be able to avoid personal taxes on everything."

"Excellent idea, Pierce," Dakulana said. "What do you think, Winnifred?"

"Sure," Winnifred replied. "That sounds super." She turned to Dakulana and smiled sweetly at her, except that her eyes had a look of utter contempt. "I have to be frank with you, Dakulana."

"Please do."

"You are really incredibly black," Winnifred said. "It's almost like you're blue you're so black. It's very disturbing. You truly give the term 'people of color' a totally new meaning."

"That's a very silly term," Dakulana said.

"It is?"

"Yes, it reduces people's humanity to a superficiality."

"Maybe you're right, but you're truly the blackest person I've ever seen."

"You need to go to Africa. Or even London."

"Maybe I do," Winnifred said absently. "Thank you, Daddy," she said, turning to her father and smiling.

Winnifred had enough of this. She was sick and tired of this black bitch lording it over her. She jumped up, thanked her father again, and kissed him proprietarily. When she was once again seated, she inquired whether her mother was privy to what was going on.

"I mean, does she know that you and Dakulana are doing the wild thing?"

Her father laughed heartily.

"What's funny, Daddy?"

Her father looked at Dakulana and then at Winnifred. "I guess you haven't met Ahmed, have you?"

"Ahmed?"

"Her Arab boyfriend," her father said. "He's from some royal family in the Middle East."

"Is that why she's studying the Koran?"

"Exactly," her father said.

He went on to explain that he and her mother had reached an understanding.

"She has her life and I have mine," he said.

Winnifred wanted to tell her father all about Omaha Bigelow but felt that it was important to first convince Omaha that they belonged together. Armed with twenty million dollars, it would be fairly easy to convince him that if he was going to accomplish anything in this world, he needed a good woman behind him and she was the one who could make him successful. An hour later her clothes were dry. She got dressed and asked her father if he was going to be at dinner that night. Pierce Buckley shook his head and said they were sailing across to Connecticut to a dinner for the Consul General of Cameroon.

"I've been retained by a French company to help revitalize several enterprises in West Africa," said Pierce Buckley. "I'm very excited."

"Well, it certainly shows," Winnifred said, dryly.

Winnifred stood up, shook Dakulana's hand icily, kissed her father again and drove back to the estate. Without going into the house proper, she got her knapsack from the guest house, got back into the BMW, and sped back to Manhattan. Once again at her apartment, she called up Gussie Armstrong and Lisolette LaFollette and they came over. They had sushi at a restaurant on Houston Street and then went dancing at Wetlands on the West Side. She danced until nearly four in the morning, whooping and hollering within the loud music. When she got home she was exhausted. She had the strongest urge to masturbate but fought off touching herself, as she always had. She found, however, that imagining Omaha Bigelow's erect organ in her mouth made her achieve a rather potent orgasm. Armed with the new knowledge of the aphrodisiac effects of Omaha's *bohango,* she fell asleep. Her last thought before falling asleep was that she was in the throes of a very powerful obsession.

She was right.

OMAHA BIGELOW COULDN'T BELIEVE HIS LUCK. TWO MONTHS HAD gone by since he met Maruquita and his life had changed drastically. He was in his own apartment, had gotten his job back, had a dynamite girlfriend, was getting laid regularly with his reasonably large *bohango kakomakako,* and was going to be a father. He also wasn't getting high and he hardly ever thought of getting drunk. And he didn't mind at all having black hair and a mustache. The apartment had two bedrooms, and Maruquita was already fixing the second one for the baby. He had access to a telephone, cable TV, a microwave, a blender, and a lot of really cool things including a washer and dryer and a dishwasher. Fuck! He had to call his mother and tell her he'd met a girl and wanted to get married. With part of his last paycheck he'd bought a Polaroid camera and two packets of film. He thought of telling Maruquita about the photos of his *bohango* he'd taken and was sending his mother, but she would think it was too weird. It was just that he had to show his mother that he wasn't still a puny little kid with Penile Asparaguitis anymore. Instead, he told Maruquita that he wanted to document the progress of her pregnancy. She posed for him and he even got her to do some nude poses, looking quite angelic and innocent, which aroused him when the photos developed. He even gave her head and, holding the camera in one hand, snapped a shot of her as she reached an orgasm. The photograph was very artsy, a bit blurred. Maruquita's face looked like a Mayan mask or maybe one of those weird Japanese faces from the Bunraku puppet theater. Maruquita looked at the pictures and shuddered. She thought it was all very strange, but this gringo whiteboy excited her with his weirdness. She couldn't believe he gave her so much head, and she was starting to like the other, when he put his *bohango* into her *papaya.* He was so cute with his mustache and black hair, although she missed his punkish green do. She was very happy anyway.

Omaha was also very happy. The only thing that worried him was that Winnifred Buckley was still pursuing him. Two days before, she had followed him on his lunch break and asked him what kind of film he'd like to make, even though he had already discussed it with her. They were standing in front of Blockbuster, which was now closed for the night. He reminded her that he had always thought a sort of fictional documentary might be interesting.

"I began the project at NYU a while back. It's got a strange title, so I might change it," he said. "My whole perspective about the purpose of film has changed. It was too . . . I don't know . . . scatological, angry. Too personalized."

"What's it called?"

"It's a stupid title."

"Tell me. I promise not to laugh."

"It's called *The Incredible Lightness of Being Omaha Bigelow.*"

"That's brilliant," Winnifred said. "A Milan Kundera reference. Very cool."

"I'm attracted to the Eastern European esthetic."

"It could be about a punk rock musician right here in the East Village," Winnifred said.

"Yeah, that's what I was thinking."

"Maybe you could get Johnny Depp to do the film."

"I was thinking more like Keanu Reeves."

"No way, Johnny Depp would be perfect. Maybe Winona Ryder as a sort of spaced-out druggie punk rock girl band member that's his girlfriend."

"Yeah, like Rita Flash."

"From Clowns Desirous."

"Yeah, I know. You seen the band?"

"Yeah, a few times."

"Cool," Omaha said, not wanting to establish too much of a connection between Rita Flash and himself. "So you like the idea of the film?"

"Well," Winnifred said. "This is a secret, but I think I can get you backing for it."

"No way."

"Yeah, way," she said, running her hand over his arm. "You want to come up to the apartment? I can tell you all about it."

He had closed his eyes in desperation because just the mention of being alone with Winnifred produced such spasms of desire in him that he thought he'd black out.

"I can't, Winnifred," he said. "You know that."

"I know nothing of the kind," Winnifred said, becoming immediately annoyed. Here she was ready to finance his whole film and he was still acting like one of her Puritan ancestors, say Increase or Cotton Mather. "What I know is that I need you. That's what I know. I'm willing to get backing for your film and you can't even provide me with a nice friendly defloration? What is that about?"

"I can't, Winnie," Omaha pleaded. "You don't know how difficult you're making my life."

"What about my life? What about my sexually starved life? Does it always have to be about you? My God. I have never encountered such selfishness in a man. Me, me, me."

"Well, no, but you know my situation."

"I know about your situation, yeah. But, what about me? Don't I deserve happiness? Don't I deserve to be torn apart like the sun devours the dawn? Am I not desirable? Am I not sufficiently adorable? Look at me," she said. She looked around and no one was in the street at that hour of the night. She raised her T-shirt to reveal perfectly round breasts and then pulled down her sweat pants to reveal her pantiless golden pudenda.

"God, Winnifred. You are beautiful. Spectacular, in fact. I can't imagine that any man who meets you wouldn't want to spend the rest of his life with you. I wish I had met you two months ago."

"You're a creative person, Omaha," Winnifred said, passionately. "Let's make believe that it's no longer September. Let's make believe that it's July and after work go to my apartment. Please. Let's just see what happens."

Her plea was so convincing that suddenly Omaha had doubts about the choices he had made. "Let me think about it," he said.

"Oh, Omaha," said Winnifred. "That makes me so happy. You wanna go for pizza?"

"Sure," Omaha said, "but pull up your pants."

"Oh, yeah," she said, reaching down to her ankles and pulling up the sweats. "By the way," she added as they began walking. "I really like you with black hair, and I love your mustache. You look so Continental."

They had gone to the Two Boots Pizzeria. It was no good. His stomach was upset, and the idea of cheating on Maruquita tore at his heart. He might as well give up on living, but something too great was raging inside of him. They ate, went back to work, and rather than Winnifred constantly looking at him, she concentrated on her work and pretty much ignored him. For Awilda Cortez this was a sure sign that they were doing it. What a son of a bitch, she thought. She wondered why it was taking so long for the message to get to Maruquita so she could deal with this *ingrato* bastard.

Omaha had reassured Maruquita that she didn't need to come and get him each morning and should instead rest and make a strong baby. He came home each morning right after leaving work, and after eating breakfast and making love, he slept until late in the afternoon. One early evening he called his mother and told her that he was mailing her some pictures of himself and Maruquita sitting in the park and at home in their apartment.

"More pictures?"

"Yes, Mama. Did you like the last ones?"

"Omaha, why are you sending me those kinds of pictures?"

"That's me, Mama. Didn't you read my note?"

"No, I was very upset by the photos."

"That's my peepee, Mama."

"I don't believe it," Olivia Bigelow said. "Are you in the throes of some latent Oedipal complex? I will have none of it, you know."

"No, Ma. It's nothing like that."

"I see e-mail on America Online all the time for penis enlargement. Don't tell me that you answered one of those ads."

"No, Mama. It just happened. Well, not exactly, but I met this girl. I'm sending you some pictures of me with my girlfriend, Mama," he said.

"That's great, Omaha," said his mother. "That's really wonderful. I'm very happy for you. What is the girl's name?"

"Maruquita, Mama," he said, happily. "She's Puerto Rican. Maruquita Salsipuedes. I'm thinking of getting married."

"Costa Rican?" Olivia Bigelow inquired.

"Puerto Rican, Mama," Omaha laughed.

"What is that?"

"It's people. From a little island in the Caribbean."

"Oh, like in that movie with Natalie Wood that she plays a Spanish girl and there are gangs."

"Yeah, like that. *West Side Story*, Mama."

"That was it. I remember. Are they dark?"

"Some are. But Maruquita is the color of light coffee."

"Like Lonnie and Rita Little Feather that had the hardware store here in Reliability?"

"Yeah, like them."

"They're Comanches."

"I know, Mama."

"They sold the store, got a trailer home, and moved to Arizona, I think."

"Really?"

"Yeah, and this girl looks like an Indian?"

"Yeah, a little bit. But they're Spanish people. I think you'll like her, Mama. Maybe we'll come and see you before the weather gets too cold. Maybe for Thanksgiving. You're gonna be a grandmother, you know."

"Oh, my God," Olivia Bigelow said. "She's gonna have a baby? Your baby?"

"Yes, Mama," Omaha said, excitedly. "Isn't that great?"

"You know something, Omaha?"

"What, Mama."

"My grandma used to say you could end up with striped children, honey."

"Mama, stop that. You don't believe that, do you?"

"No, I don't believe such things, but aren't there any white girls in New York?"

"Of course there are, but this is a very special girl, Mama. I really love her."

"Well, be careful. Maybe you're not the father."

"I'm the father, Mama. She was a virgin."

"Omaha, you are still such a nice boy," Olivia Bigelow said. "You trust everybody."

"Don't worry, Mama. I'll send you the pictures, and then we'll come and see you. Okay?"

"Okay, dear. Are you still wearing your rubbers when it rains?"

"Yes, Mama," Omaha said. "And eating an apple every day. I'll call you soon. Bye."

"Bye, sweetie."

Omaha hung up and asked Maruquita if she wanted to go to Kansas and see his mother.

"Where is that?" Maruquita said, looking up from the *novela* she was watching on TV. "Is that in New Jersey?"

"No, we have to take a plane."

"Oh, okay," Maruquita said, but she seemed abstracted, a bit out of it.

What Omaha didn't know was that word had finally gotten to Maruquita about his supposed dalliance with Winnifred Buckley. The previous day Maruquita was sitting on a bench talking with Bibi Escobar when Beatriz Fuentes came up to her and stood with her head turned away because she couldn't stand Bibi Escobar, who was going out with her father except that she didn't think she knew.

"How you doing, Beatriz," Maruquita said.

"Girl, I gotta talk to you," she said to Maruquita.

"Go ahead," Maruquita said.

"Private."

"Excuuuse me," Bibi said. She got up and waved her hand derisively at Beatriz. "I'll see you later, Maru," she said, bending down and kissing Maruquita's cheek.

"I'll catch you later, Mama," Maruquita said.

Beatriz sat down on the bench.

"S'up," Beatriz said. "How's your brother?"

"Same old same old," Maruquita said. "He's writing his play and whatnot. Whatcha gotta talk to me about?"

"I heard some nasty shit."

"About?"

"About your man."

Maruquita sat up straight. "You heard some shit about Omagaw Boogaloo?"

"Yeah."

"Who told you that shit?"

"Margarita Burgos that work in the beauty parlor on Avenue B. She said that Olga, that cross-eye girl that useta be in our class in junior high, told her. But it's bad."

"What?"

"Your man was making out with some blonde gringa whitegirl," Bibi said.

"What gringa whitegirl?"

"She say that it's some girl he work wif at Grinko's."

"Kinko's."

"Whatevah. Over there on Houston Street next to Blockbustah."

"No way, girl. My man don't cheat on me. You crazy."

"I'm just telling you what's in the street, girl. Don't get all ballistic on me."

"I ain't getting ballistic. I'm just telling you that my man don't cheat on me."

"I hear you, mama. I gotta book. My mother's babysitting and I gotta take the twins to the clinic."

And with that Beatriz left, and Maruquita sat on the park bench stunned. Now what? The sign came, and she knew something was wrong. Omagaw Boogaloo had told her not come to get him in the morning. So it was that blonde bitch he worked with. For some reason Maruquita didn't feel like blaming him. It was the blonde's fault for throwing herself at him. She wished she could turn the bitch into a poodle, but being pregnant, her powers were diminished and about all she could do was give the gringa whitegirl split ends, unruly hair, and a few zits. Anyway, dudes couldn't help it when their *bohangos* acted up. *Coño,* she thought. What now? What was she supposed to do? She didn't know how to talk to him. Maybe her mother knew what to do.

THE POLITICAL METAPHOR OF SPERMATOZOON NUMBER 54

T WAS BOUND TO HAPPEN. IT'S IMPOSSIBLE TO SCORN A WOMAN AND not feel the reprisals attendant on such folly. Nor is it possible for word not to get around that a man has settled down and to keep previous lovers from becoming interested in him again. Why with that hussy, that bitch, that woman, and not with me? they may say. In the first instance the scorned one was Awilda Cortez, who still wanted Omaha Bigelow. She knew he had to be powerful, since word was out that Omaha had already given Maruquita a baby. As she saw it, why should this *bruja* bitch be the only one in the neighborhood with a cute Gringorican baby? In the second instance it was a double whammy, since both Rita Flash and Carrie Marshack were suddenly very curious about Omaha. From a strategic point of view it's important to prioritize these threats to Omaha Bigelow. In order of danger Awilda was first, Carrie Marshack second, and lastly Rita Flash. Winnifred Buckley is not included on the list, since she was quite another problem, perhaps more serious than the three put together but belonging in a category with incalculable resources, which gave her what one might perceive as an unfair advantage.

What happened with Rita was that Richard Rentacar told her about Omaha's new-found enlargement to his heretofore meager penis. Two weeks before leaving for the West Coast, Omaha ran into Richard in Odessa, and they had coffee and chatted. Richard congratulated Omaha on going native.

"Nice soup strainer," Richard said, referring to Omaha's mustache. "That's what my old man used to call it. He's really a stupid fuck. I'm not looking forward to seeing him again."

"Yeah, most fathers are assholes."

"He thinks that because he's a millionaire, he can say any old thing. But you got the facial hair and got the black hair going, so it's cool."

"Yeah, I'm living in the projects, so I have to look the part."

"I heard. You got a good thing going. And you're working at Kinko's again."

"Yeah, but I'm thinking of working on my film. I'm looking for backers."

"So is you're little señorita happy?"

"Yeah, she's pretty happy."

"And no problem?" Richard said pointing at a downward angle into the middle of the table as if to direct a line to his groin. "She doesn't mind?"

"Doesn't mind about what?"

"The little johnsito," Richard said, holding up his right pinky.

"Oh, that's gone."

"The Penile Asparaguitis is gone?"

"Yeah, gone. Vanished."

"Get the fuck outta here."

"Really. I'm okay now."

"No way. You're lying."

"I'm not, Richard. I got a regular *bohango*."

"A what?"

"Never mind. I got a regular johnson."

"This I gotta see. Let's go over to Rita Flash so she can give you head."

"I ain't gonna do that, Richard."

"Then you're lying, man."

"I ain't lying."

"Then let me see. We'll pay our bill and go in the john in the back."

"I ain't going in the john with you."

"Oh, why not? You're scared to let me see it and have to admit that you're lying?"

"No, I don't want people seeing me going in there and thinking I'm some sort of fag."

"Are you saying I look like a fag?"

"I didn't say that. But that shit would look stupid. Two dudes going in the john together."

"Women do it all the time, and they ain't always lesbians."

"That's different. If there was urinals or something, then maybe it'd be different."

"They gotta urinal."

"One, and you gotta lock the door and the two of us would be in there. Forget it, man."

"Fine, then," Richard said, and then looked as if he had hit on an idea. "I'll make believe I dropped some change, you take out your johnson and I'll look under the table and see it."

"Are you crazy?"

"Nobody's gonna see you, man. Just turn toward the wall a little bit."

"Okay, but quick," Omaha said.

And so Richard fumbled with his keys, dropped them between his legs, said, oh, shit, and slid out of the booth's banquette and onto the floor. In the meantime Omaha had unzipped himself and took out his *bohango kako-makako,* which at the prospect of displaying himself publicly had become erect. Richard found his keys first and then looked up and saw Omaha's erection no more than a foot from his face.

"Jesus Christ," he said, rising up and banging his head. He slid quickly back up and pointed directly at Omaha's chest. "That's a rubber dick, dude. No way that's your johnson."

"Richard, it's my dick," Omaha said, quietly. "Get over it."

"Rubber duckie, dude," Richard said and began laughing.

Omaha couldn't handle the humiliation. He raised himself up in the booth and slapped the *bohango* on the table like he was John the Revelator about to beat his meat in Tompkins Square Park.

"You wanna cop a feel, Richard?" Omaha said. "Go ahead, dude."

Nobody saw Omaha do this but Richard had and that was enough. Waves of jealousy washed over him as he saw what he perceived to be a huge organ. He had seen it under the table, and it was now as if a leviathan had risen from the depths. Instinctively, as if he were Ahab and needed a harpoon, he reached into his pocket, drew out a ballpoint pen, and held it at the ready in order to combat the white whale. In the wink of an eye Omaha was seated again and had placed his *bohango* back in his jeans.

"Fuck," Richard said. "That was fucking awesome, dude. Did you have one of those AOL penis enlargement things done? I didn't know that shit really worked, man."

"It's natural, man," Omaha said.

"It's that Rican pussy, ain't it?"

"Watch it, man. Don't be dissin' my woman," Omaha said, in perfectly enunciated Afrorican.

"I'm cool, Omaha," Richard said. "You're totally into that shit, ain't you? Pretty soon you ain't gonna be white."

"Man, later for you," Omaha said. He threw two dollar bills on the table and walked out. As he walked out, a woman with a lot of piercings and tattoos sitting near the door pointed at his still opened fly. He quickly zipped himself up, crossed the street, and went into Tompkins Square Park.

Richard paid the bill, went to Rita Flash's apartment, and told her everything. At first Rita laughed and couldn't believe it. Richard insisted that it was true.

"That thing's gotta be at least ten inches long and as thick as my wrist," he said, trying to wrap his left hand around his right wrist and failing. "I'm not lying. The thing is huge."

"For real?" Rita Flash said, opening her mouth instinctively.

"Yeah, for real."

"You want a little head?" Rita said, growing excited.

"Nah," Richard said, certain that he wouldn't be able to get it up thinking about Omaha's johnson. "Can I crash here for a little while? I don't feel good."

Rita nodded and immediately called up Carrie Marshack doing word processing down at the World Trade Center. She told Rita all about Omaha's *bohango*. Carrie couldn't believe it.

"My Igor is about eight inches, and that's pretty big," Carrie said.

"Well, Richard said Omaha's thing was about ten inches. Huge."

"This I gotta see," Carrie said.

"Me too," said Rita.

And that was it. So now it was like the two of them were Thomas Cranky plotting a sordid submarine romance novel, perhaps called *The Hunt for Pink November in His Manly Pants*. Right! A cross-genre novel. This new-found determination on the part of Rita and Carrie, together with Awilda's enraged ovaries screaming to be impregnated by Omaha so she could have her own Gringorican baby, the odds for Omaha's continued fidelity were rapidly dwindling.

As for Winnifred Buckley, she was on the verge of a nervous breakdown or else giving in and masturbating. The latter was unthinkable, she thought and cursed her repressive morality. Did she need therapy? Was she headed for a prosaic existence like her mother? Fuck, she thought. Maybe she ought to go on Prozac. She would then become prozaic like her. If people only knew what a lunatic her mother had been in her youth. Oh, she was very much under control, but it was because she had been totally neutralized by the drug. She couldn't believe that her mother had married her father because he had a huge schlong. Is that what was attracting her to Omaha Bigelow?

It finally dawned on Winnifred that the reason she didn't dare masturbate was that she was certain she would think of her father and his enormity, which she had never seen but now that she thought about it, was obvious whenever he wore a bathing suit or tight pants. She didn't want anything so large. She wanted Omaha Bigelow. He was enough for her. She decided that it wasn't lust that she felt but actual love and it hurt like hell. She fell down crying on her bed, repeating fuck over and over again until she was exhausted and fell asleep.

Meanwhile, Awilda Cortez was planning her strategy. She knew that Maruquita shouldn't do anything while she was pregnant. She felt disloyal as hell, but she had gone to her cousin who was living with a Dominican livery driver from the base over on Clinton Street, and they had put her in touch with Tigerita Linares, a Dominican *bruja*. She went and got a *consulta* and the *bruja* reassured her that she could do a number on Maruquita and her people if they got out of hand. *They be dancing merengue for the rest of their life*, the Dominican *bruja* said. She promised that after she was done with them, they would only be able to walk sideways to the beat of merengue even when they were in the street. So Awilda felt confident when she began stalking Omaha Bigelow in the evenings before they came to work. Usually he was with the *bruja* Maruquita, who was now back at Seward Park High School and not yet showing that she was carrying her Gringorican baby. One evening in late September of 2000 she caught up to Omaha as he was coming out of Tompkins Square Park and walking near Charas. She walked up to him and pulled out a small automatic pistol.

"Don't say nothing, niggah," she said.

"Hi, Awilda," Omaha said, not yet noticing the gun.

"Just keep walking and keep your mouth shut," Awilda said, pushing the gun into Omaha's gut.

"Where we going?" Omaha said.

"We're going to my house," Awilda said. "My mother's in P.R. taking care of my grandmother."

"Awilda, please put the gun away?"

"Ha, so you can run away? No way, man."

"I'm not gonna run away. Why are we going to your house?"

"Cause I want a Gringorican baby."

"I can't, Awilda," Omaha said. "I'm gonna get married with Maruquita," he added, using the grammar of the Spanish language, in which you marry with someone.

"So?"

"So I don't wanna be cheating on her."

"Niggah, quit the shit!"

"What?"

"You a lying mothafocka. You already cheating on the bitch."

"No way."

"Niggah, I seen you with that gringa whitegirl, Winnifred *pendeja,*" Awilda said, sticking the gun under Omaha's chin.

"We're just friends," Omaha said, starting to get frightened.

"Just shut the fuck up and keep walking," Awilda said. "We're almost there."

On Avenue C they turned south, and two doors down they went into a walkup. They went up the stairs. It was a place where drugs were obviously dealt in large volume. The building was clean and well-lighted. On the first floor a young man came out and nodded at Awilda. She had put the gun away and nodded severely at the young man.

"My cousin, Pito," she said to the young man.

"S'up," Omaha said, touching his index finger to his mustache and pointing at the young man.

"S'up," said the young man and waved Awilda and Omaha by.

They went up two more flights and into Awilda's apartment. It was a traditional Puerto Rican tenement apartment, with linoleum on the floor, plastic covers on the furniture, at least seventy-five saints and one hundred votive candles of different colors burning in their glass containers, each placed seemingly with purpose.

"In the bedroom," said Awilda.

"Wait," said Omaha.

"Wait what?"

"How do I know you don't have AIDS or something?" he said.

"Niggah, what's wrong wif you. Why I be messing around with some gay dude?"

"Well, you never know."

"Shit," Awilda said, going into her purse and pulling out an envelope and handing it to him. "You gringos is so paranoid."

"What is it?"

"Read it, moron."

Omaha opened the letter with a logo on the left side of the page which had two nondescript green silhouettes embracing so that you had the feeling that it could be a male and a female, two males, or two females. Running around the logo were the letters NYCTAFYSH. Extending to the right of the page, also in green letters, were the words New York City Testing and Facilitating Your Sexual Health," a reputable and quick testing facility with an address in Greenwich Village. Omaha knew about the organization because he'd gone there with Maruquita to get tested. Everyone knew the letters NYCTAFYSH really meant *Now you can try and fuck your sweet honey.* Omaha read the letter confirming that Ms. Awilda Cortez had been tested and no trace of HIV had been found in her blood. He folded the letter, returned it to the envelope, and gave it back to Awilda.

"Okay," he said. "Now what?"

"In the bedroom and strip," Awilda said.

"Just like that?"

"Yeah, just like that. Inside."

"Suppose I can't get it up?"

"What?" Awilda said, not quite believing what she was hearing. "Haven't you noticed what kind of body I have?"

"Yeah, I've noticed."

"So?"

"So it happens sometimes that a guy can't get it up. What then?"

"What then?" Awilda said, losing her patience. "Is that what you're asking me, niggah? What then? I take you up on the roof, kill you, and throw you off the roof, you cheating mothafocka. That's what then. Get in the bedroom and get undressed."

"Okay, okay," Omaha said, going into the bedroom, where there were another twenty saints and thirty candles. "Get undressed now?" he asked.

"That's right. Get undressed now. And no coming to bed with socks on."

"Right,"Omaha said, and stripped.

When he was done he stood there in the candlelight and watched Awilda undressing, and immediately he was erect. She was truly incredible. It was as if she were bigger with her clothes off. When she was done, she ordered him to lie on the bed. She was breathing heavily, and after he lay down she was on him, straddling him and placing the *bohango* inside of her. She lay on him and began slowly grinding herself on him with such smooth motions that a few minutes later he had exploded inside of her. Awilda lay on top of him and began kissing him. He couldn't help himself but finally said he had to go.

"No," Awilda said, coyly now, no longer angry.

"Why?"

"Maybe I want twins."

"What?"

"Twins. Maybe I want twins, so we should do it again."

"It doesn't work that way."

"Maybe triplets? Did you like it?"

"Yeah, but that's not biologically correct," he said.

Awilda began moving again and this time he couldn't help himself and turned her over and nearly drove her through the box spring so wild did he become. Before long Awilda was going insane. When they were done, she was so sweet that he couldn't help kissing her and holding her to him. He asked her if he could shower. She nodded and he showered, got dressed, and went back out into the street. He walked around the neighborhood, called Maruquita, and made up some story about getting stopped by some old friends from the band. They'd gone and had a couple of beers and he was going in to work.

"You okay, Omagaw Boogaloo?" Maruquita said.

"Yeah, I'm okay," he said. "How about you?"

"I'm okay," she said. "You sound funny. You love me?"

"Yeah, I love you."

"I love you too, you bozo."

They hung up, and Omaha felt terrible. And yet it had been wonderful making it with Awilda, especially the second time. He couldn't believe that she thought by doing it twice she could have twins. He hoped with all his heart that she wouldn't get pregnant. Such was not to be his luck. The female mind has no known obstacles to its determination. Spermatozoon 54 of the second emission caught Awilda's ovum as it was sliding around and split it in two, causing the creation of two perfectly formed identical little Gringorican girls who would eventually become Estee and Libby nine months later.

You probably want to know if the 54 was chosen at random. I wish such questions wouldn't arise in literature. For people who just read novels for story, a writer can get away with certain things, but there are other readers who have to find meaning in everything. I'm not a mean-spirited person who will leave things unanswered and make readers search all over trying to find significance and symbolism in narrative. Okay, the number of the spermatozoon stands for something. But I don't want to be accused of using the novel as a political platform and of pamphleteering or of some sort of diluted form of socialist realism. Well, maybe. But here's the deal.

In the late 1940s and 1950s there was a strong nationalist movement in Puerto Rico which sought independence for the island. In an election the independence movement garnered nearly forty percent of the vote in the met-ropolitan area of San Juan. This frightened the insular government as well as the U.S. government. The United States, already in a post-WW II frazzle over the rise of worldwide Communism, passed the Smith Act to prosecute subversives. This gave rise to the House Un-American Activities Committee (HUAC), McCarthyism, Hollywood witch hunts, and other attacks on democracy. Fearful that Puerto Rico would become a satellite of the Communists, as would Cuba a decade later, the repressive laws of the Smith Act were transferred to Puerto Rico and practically verbatim they were read into law by the Puerto Rican Senate. This was known as Law 54 or *La Mordaza*, which translates as *gag*, thus becoming the Gag Law. The enactment led to enormous repression and eventually the systematic destruction of the independence movement in Puerto Rico, and the quelling of dissent through repression for the most minor offenses. Discussing independence, printing of material, placing flowers on the tombs of nationalists, among other offenses, were considered seditious. As such, people were arrested, indicted, tried, found guilty, and sentenced to jail terms.

Symbolically, although part of the plot, Awilda Cortez, insisting on having Omaha Bigelow impregnating her and screwing herself represents how Puerto Ricans contributed to their own colonial status. Let me totally disintegrate the fourth wall, step forward and address the audience directly. Why will the twins be named Estee and Libby? The names stand for Estado Libre, which is what Puerto Rico is considered politically. The twins also represent the confusing duality of the Puerto Rican identity and its incapacity for deciding its future. The full name of the "political" entity is Estado Libre Asociado, or Associated Free State. The place is neither a true state in the sense of a nation, nor truly free in terms of its own destiny.

Oh, now you're pissed because this is a political novel. Duh! You don't think I'd go to all this trouble simply to entertain you, do you? Anyway, deal with it. It's an interesting story thus far. It's going to get even more interesting. You can forget the politics and just read for story, like it was just another vapid novel with little importance other than to keep you from thinking about how much you hate being married or your job or the bills that keep piling up. You can think I'm an idiot for deciphering things because it takes the fun out of figuring things out. For the "intellectuals," go read Derrida and leave me alone with your pedantic arguments.

OMAHA BIGELOW CAME OUT OF THE HAIR SALON DOWN THE STREET from Kinko's after getting his hair dyed again for the second time. His blond roots were becoming a nuisance. With each day he felt as if he had been trapped into an identity that was more and more uncomfortable. His dark hair and mustache caused American people, whether black or white, to treat him with an extra measure of disdain. When they were not subtly rejecting him they treated him with enormous condescension. They either spoke to him dismissively, or slowly in simplistic English. They often approached him carefully, so that he wouldn't descend into a fit of Latin fury. It didn't help that Omaha was malleable in personality and had pronounced aural acuity. The reaction of Americans, a quasi benevolent people, was understandable. In order to fit more properly into his role, Omaha had begun affecting a Puerto Rican accent when speaking English. As time passed, his speech became more and more adapted to the local Spanish-inflected patois of the impenetrable Loisaida jungle. As a result his oral grammar became extremely bizarre. Phrases such as, *Why for you axe me that? Yo, yet and still, I don't gotta go if I don't wanna; I didn't did it; You don't gotta plex up; Don't play yourself, homeboy,* and *I stood in my house all weekend* had become part of his everyday speech patterns. It was as if with each step he took in code switching and absorbing of Spanglish, he became less socially acceptable to the predominant hip East Village bohemian milieu. On the other hand he had become quite adept at talking to Latinas, and they appreciated his attention: *You lookin fine, Mami; I be thinkin of you all day in the sheets; Whacha doin, puchunga? You ready to give up some of your bonboncito sweetness* became commonplace in his approach to neighborhood young women, every word delivered with head nodding arrogantly and lasciviously. His right hand clutching his now substantial genitals within his baggy jeans, the phrases were positive additions to his lexicon and manner as a Latin lover. In spite of the social ostracism that he experienced from his one-time peer group, he was quite proud of his new-found masculinity. He laughed often when spontaneous seminars arose concerning the term *machismo*. It was even more laughable when the gringos stopped discussing the term as he approached them.

In a democratic society everyone is entitled to opine freely. However, the attitude I dislike the most is that of people who say they want to help the downtrodden. They're in every neighborhood, ready to give counseling, do social work, commiserate, understand, empathize, and generally shake their head in sadness at the benighted condition of the fuzzy-wuzzies. Heaven forbid if the person whom they're attempting to help is brighter than they are and is making an effort to do things on his own. That is when what I've identified as benevolent racism intrudes, and these people become angry, disappointed, and even abusive at the attempts of little brown people to help themselves. For if these people can help themselves, what value do they have as helpers? What status do they have in the hierarchy?

It should be understood at this juncture that most of the English-speaking, European-descended American population of the East Village was conscious that one of their own had gone native. This description of "one of their own" should be parsed in order to avoid generalizations. There is a good-sized population of Euro-Americans living in the East Village of New York City. Some of these are descendants of Poles, Ukranians, Lithuanians, and others of those European regions. There are also some Italians who own restaurants and bakery-cafés such as Lanza's or De Robertis. In the last ten or so years Irish from Ireland have moved into the neighborhood. Some have opened public houses, such as Local 138 on Ludlow Street. Those are not the people in question. In the general area there are also Orthodox Jews who own businesses. Those people are not in question either. There are also older professionals and artists who moved into the neighborhood forty years ago when the East Village became fashionable. I am not referring to those. Instead, I am talking about a group of Euro-Americans between the ages of twenty and forty who are college students, actors, painters, filmmakers, or financial wizards, who enjoy living in a pseudobohemian atmosphere. Given the fact that there are Puerto Ricans in a solid band along Avenue D and the projects as well as throughout the neighborhood, and Spanish is spoken almost everywhere you go except yuppie restaurants and bars along Avenue A, for these young people it feels as if they are living in a foreign country.

It is not fair to discriminate against people because of their race, creed, color, religion, or any other characteristic which was foisted upon them by genetic destiny and familial pressure. They themselves call each other

Eurotrash, but I don't feel it's fair to label people with such a derogatory term, so I'll use the term that Ricans use to describe this group. I'll use the term *blanquitos,* or Little White Ones, to describe them in this demographic profile of the area. The term is not quite a racist one but more of a class distinction. It's really the difference between getting a boom box or a really cool Bose system. It should be noted that Ricans use the term *blanquito* to refer to non-progressive people of any persuasion, including Puerto Ricans themselves who think they're hot stuff and have forgotten their roots. People like Geraldo Rivera and Bryant Gumble are *blanquitos.* A statistical breakdown of the neighborhood would look something like this:

Ethnic Europeans	11%
Orthodox Jews	3%
Older professionals	2%
Puerto Ricans	27%
Dominicans	5%
Latin American illegal kitchen help	2%
Assorted Asians	5%
Indian Subcontinent taxi drivers	3%
Blanquitos	78%

I realize that this adds up to more than 100 percent, but this is not a sociological tract. It's a novel, and as such I can create whatever fiction I feel like creating. I've always felt more comfortable with Yogi Berra's logic when he said that playing baseball was eighty percent talent and the other half was luck. Anyway, it feels as if the *blanquito* population is 78 percent, especially in the evening, when most Puerto Ricans are indoors either watching *novelas,* sports, or porno flicks. In fairness, it should be stated that these figures shift drastically, during the three weeks prior to and the three weeks after the Puerto Rican Day Parade. During these times the figures change dramatically and the neighborhood looks as if it were twenty-seven percent *blanquitos* and 78 percent Puerto Rican.

In any case the *blanquito* population was in quite a frazzle. Word about Omaha Bigelow got around quicker than you can say Tito Puente. At a concert in the park one weekend they had seen Omaha Bigelow dancing real salsa, spinning and moving to the fast-paced music as if born to it. He was no longer one of those embarrassing spectacles of gringo whiteboy dancing who look disconnected and shake their shoulders instead of their booty. In the East Village word had also gotten around about Omaha Bigelow's studliness and genital substance. Not only were Rita Flash and Carrie Marshack lusting after him, but it seemed as if every other white chick was wired for Omaha. Tongue piercings went up dramatically, and pharmacies ordered extra condoms. This condition was causing boyfriends considerable psychic pain and making them go searching for rulers and measuring tapes. In one case a young man near Avenue C tried measuring himself with a metal tape. As you know, such tapes have an overhang at the end which can be placed, for example, on the edge of a table. The tape can then be pulled and the measurement taken of the table or other surface. Well, a young Methodist man from Ohio extended the tape along the top of his erect penis, hooked the metal part into the prepuce of his penis and by mistake hit the release on the tape, causing the metal to withdraw quickly and bring with it the hooding skin. Several Jewish clerics were consulted, and it appears that in nearly two hundred years of Jewish presence in the Lower East Side this was the only auto-bris ceremony ever conducted. *Are you sure of this?* I asked a rabbi on Rivington Street. *Moel or less,* he said, without cracking a smile. I know. I groaned as well. If you don't grasp the understated humor of the illustration, go consult someone who speaks Yiddish or Hebrew. They'll explain and probably mutter *schmuck* under their breath at your ignorance.

It was now the middle of October, and Maruquita was in the throes of morning sickness. She was starting to drive Omaha crazy with her complaints. More and more he made excuses to stay away from the apartment, claiming that he was working on his film. If her brother could work on his play, why couldn't she understand that he needed to work on his film? *You could work here, honey,* she would say. He'd reply that he didn't have a computer and they couldn't afford one.

In terms of the actual progress of the film, he'd had several preliminary meetings with Winnifred. Omaha had dropped a hint that it was difficult working on the film script without a computer. They went shopping at Circuit City on Union Square and Winnifred bought a computer with a large screen, printer, scanner, and a fax machine. The blond doofus Woody Harrelson look-alike from the commercials wasn't around to bother them about getting a Dell. Omaha also got a scriptwriting software program. They also went to Barnes & Noble and got a copy of Syd Field's book on scriptwriting, which Omaha had left at Carrie Marshack's pad when she kicked him out. Fuck! He couldn't believe it. Winnifred paid for the computer with one of her credit cards and said that she would have it picked up and brought to her apartment. She had already set up one of the bedrooms of the apartment to be the production office until they could find bigger quarters.

"I'll give you a set of keys, and you can go up there anytime you want," Winnifred said. "No pressure. I'm cool. I'm just happy that you're going to be working on your film."

"Okay," he said, certain now that he and Winnifred were just friends. "Thanks."

She looked down at him and lowered her face for him to kiss her. He reached up and did so. She smelled so sweet and clean that he had the strongest urge to go further. Armed with twenty million dollars, she was certain that she would now be able to capture Omaha. Sensing his desire, she didn't push herself on him but stepped back and became quite shy.

"You hungry?" she asked.

"Yeah, kinda."

"You like organic food?"

"Sure."

"There's a little place on Thirteenth Street, before you get to Village Copier," she said. "You wanna go there?"

"Yeah, sure."

"My treat."

"Okay."

So they went and sat upstairs and talked about the independent film industry and how important it was to get the film distributed and placed at film festivals and she was sure that Sundance would be a perfect venue for the film and did he want to shoot the film in black and white or in color.

"I think maybe a combination," he said.

"Cool," Winnifred said, touching his arm and looking admiringly at him. "That is brilliant."

"Yeah, like the tedium of the character's life as a musician in the East Village could be shot documentary style in black and white, but when he's performing music it could be in color, with all sorts of dazzling visuals like HBO concerts. What do you think?"

"It sounds terrific."

"Wait, let me ask you something that's been going through my mind the last few weeks. Let me know what you think."

"Sure, what?"

"Well, you know there's a lot of sex in the East Village scene," Omaha said.

"I wasn't aware of that," Winnifred said. "I certainly haven't been the beneficiary of such attention. I don't mean anything about us," she added quickly. "But no, I don't know."

"I know, but what I mean, it's risky, but maybe we could be breaking ground. I'm thinking that maybe we could do everything explicit with fellatio, cunilingus, intromission of both vaginal and anal orifices, but in cartoon form. What do you think? You know, we could get Crumb or someone like that."

Winnifred had never heard of Robert Crumb. Omaha explained but it didn't matter. She was on the verge of exploding with desire and she was premenstrual. Bratwurst Goering, the most feared Hun warrior, was smiting Romans to his left and to his right, screaming Proto-Germanic curses. She wanted to scream that she wanted to be fucked but retained her composure.

"I think it's vaginally brilliant," she said, quite spontaneously.

"Far out," Omaha said. "That's pretty good. Vaginally brilliant. So you don't think it would be too much?"

"No way. I think it would be very cool, especially if everything is edited well and the continuity is rapid fire, mixed media, collagelike."

Their food had come. Everything was flamboyant and verdant with exotic sauces and breads that attacked you with their wholesomeness. There were huge boiled carrots that reminded poor Winnifred of Omaha's penis. She grabbed one, placed it in her mouth and totally out of her mind began sucking at it, her breathing becoming more and more labored. Her eyes closed in near-ecstasy, she was now moaning softly.

"Winnifred," said Omaha softly.

"What?" she said still moaning and then opened her dazed eyes.

"Are you okay? You looked like you were falling asleep. You looked quite placid. Good carrot?"

"Perfect," Winnifred nearly shouted as she bit angrily into the carrot and chewed with great determination. She was so close to orgasm, and he had to interrupt her. It was like she was sitting in warm Jell-O she was so wet. She didn't want to start screaming and do something bizarre. Feng Li was peeking out from the red and gold curtain in the Imperial palace. He winked at her and ran his tongue libidinously over his lips. She muttered *fuck* and continued chewing. Why didn't Feng Li ever come out? Why did he torture her like this? Feng Li, you fuck, she nearly screamed. "Did you ever think of killing yourself?" she suddenly said, looking straight into Omaha's eyes.

"No, I never have," Omaha said, noting that something seemed to be changing in Winnifred. All at once he felt a great and overwhelming fear. "I've been depressed but never enough to want to end it all. Have you?"

"Yes, I have," Winnifred said. "Especially lately."

"Why?"

"I don't know, but it's getting pretty bad," Winnifred said, nearly on the verge of babbling. "Two days ago I went up on the roof of Red Square and stood next to the statue of Lenin and almost jumped. I have visions."

"You have visions?"

"Yes, terrible bloody visions."

God, why was she confessing these things to him? thought Winnifred. He would never want to have anything to do with her if he found out about her warriors. He was watching her now and knew that she was going to do something crazy. Omaha stared at her as she became even more fierce and frightening.

The look on Winnifred's face was one of total insanity. It was understandable. Moamar ibn Maharmoud, the most bloodthirsty warrior of the tenth- century North African coast and the scourge of the Almoravids, spoke to her quickly in Arabic. What worried her most is that she understood Moamar. *Tell him that you want to be mounted like the camel bitch that you are.* Without hesitation she spoke in English.

"I want to be mounted like the camel bitch that I am," she said.

"What?"

"I do," Winnifred said. She quickly collected herself and began explaining that it was dialogue for another film she was thinking they could do after they finished *The Incredible Lightness of Being Omaha Bigelow.*

"Really? Another film?"

"Yes."

"What's it about?" Omaha asked. "Does it have camel intercourse?"

"Well, yes. Lots of it, but not excessive," she said.

"Pitch it to me," Omaha said, using film-business vernacular.

"What?"

"Tell me about it," Omaha said, spooning some more wheatgrass miso soup into his mouth. "Like you were pitching it to me. You know? Like I told you about in Syd Field's book."

She began by saying that it is night EXT (which she spelled out). The moon is out, and a caravan is moving across the dunes. In the distance a dog barks, but the caravan moves inexorably forward up and down the dunes, the camels padding silently over the sand, their feet seemingly floating over it. In the next scene EXT oasis, palm trees and limpid water, the dog is lying still, the full moon high over the desert. She moved her hands in front of her and seemingly framed the shot, INT (which she also spelled out) and explained that we are in a tent and Zángana, a poor servant girl, is lying on a pallet of silks and cushions. She is totally naked, and her blond pubis is aflame with desire. At that point Omaha inquired: *She's blonde?* Winnifred replied that she was. *Maybe it's Charlize Theron,* she replied. Omaha said that perhaps they should go with somebody more like Minnie Driver, who definitely looked Middle Eastern. Winnifred explained that it was rumored that Minnie had a weight problem and he knew the rest with Ben Affleck and all that. Anyway, suddenly Moamar ibn Maharmoud comes into the tent, rips off his turban, shirt, and pantaloons, and there he is in all his Arab splendor. At that point Zángana cries: *Moamar, fuck me like the camel bitch that you know I am.*

"And like that," Winnifred said. "I haven't figured out the whole thing, but it's not a porno film."

"Far out," Omaha said. He couldn't believe he had become so aroused. "Could we finish eating and go back to your apartment?"

The words shocked Winnifred. "Right now?"

"Only if you want to."

"Sure," Winnifred said. "I'm not that hungry."

"Me either."

Winnifred threw three ten-dollar bills on the table. They rushed downstairs and out into the street. On University Place they grabbed a cab, and ten minutes later they were back in the East Village in front of Red Square. Once in her apartment, they took off their clothes and Omaha had her repeat the phrase. Obediently, thankfully, wetly, Winnifred said *Fuck me like the camel bitch you know I am,* and Omaha was driving his hungry *bohango kakomakako* into Winnifred and thus dooming himself to desolation.

MARUQUITA WAS BEGINNING TO PANIC. WHAT SHE HAD LEARNED concerning Omaha and the blonde was making her crazy. She wanted to go to Kinko's in the morning, change into a rottweiler, wait until Winnifred came out, and jump on her, knock her down, and rip out her throat. Maybe she would just wait until she was going into her building and maybe turn into a cockroach, jump on her jeans, and ride the elevator with her, go into her apartment, and turn back into the rottweiler, rip off her clothes, put the doggie *bohango* in her gringa whitegirl *papaya*, and then she'd get pregnant and have eight or ten ugly black-ass rottweiler puppies.

She had the urge to change into a monkey, go out the window, change into a squirrel, go down the tree, and hunt down the gringa whitegirl. But she couldn't because if she did, it could make the baby change too and then when she went to the hospital to take the baby out it could come out like an animal. Shit, she thought. This was so fucked up. She wished she hadn't gotten pregnant right away. What was she gonna do? She went out of her apartment, took the elevator, and went to see her mother. When she walked in, her mother was reading Samuel Beckett Salsipuedes's play. Maruquita stood in front of her mother and complained that she wasn't having any fun and she felt like changing into a monkey, a squirrel, a seagull, and whatever else she wanted. It wasn't fair that she couldn't change because she was pregnant.

"Why for it gotta be like that, huh?" she said, pouting.

"That's the way it is. Stop being so silly. What do you have? Another seven months?"

"Maybe I could get a abortion," she said.

"Say that again and I'm gonna slap you so hard you gonna hear little birdies."

"Mama!" Maruquita said, stomping her pink Reeboks. "No slapping. Okay?"

"Well then, why are you talking like a crazy?"

"Maybe something happen and you don't know about it?"

Flaquita sat up, put SBS's script down, and ordered her daughter to sit down. "What are you talking about?"

Maruquita sat down and explained that she'd heard that Omaha Bigelow was cheating on her with some gringa whitegirl *rubia* slut bitch and she was confused about what to do.

"What I'm supposed to do now?"

"Who told you he was cheating?"

"This girl. She said she heard it from another girl and now the whole neighborhood know."

"What proof do they have?"

"Proof?"

"Yeah, proof."

"What you mean?"

"How do they know it's true?"

"They saw him kissing this gringa whitegirl. She got blond hair and look like what's-her-name from that golf movie with Matt Dayum. What's-her-name? Charlie Therapy."

"Charlize Theron and Matt Damon. Maru, that's so silly."

"It's not silly, Mama. This is serious. We're not even married and he's cheating on me."

"Serious? You're kidding, right?" Flaquita said.

"No, I ain't kidding."

"Serious is winning a Lotto jackpot and finding out you got cancer and are going to die in six months, or maybe having a nice looking body and looking like Mike Tyson like Mrs. Pinto's daughter, Floralora, who has a better mustache than your father. That's serious."

"Yeah, but he's cheating on me."

"Maybe they're friends," Flaquita said to her daughter. "Maybe Omaha and the blonde are friends. You know how Americans are. They're all the time kissy-kissy. Maybe that's all it is."

"But what I'm suppose to do?"

"You're supposed to maintain your integrity as a woman and stop whining like a victim of your environment. Read Germaine Greer. Read Betty Friedan. Read Gloria Steinem. Read even Camille Paglia. I can't believe I gave birth to a girl with such intellectual limitations."

"What?" Maruquita said. "Why you trying to confuse me with them bitches?"

"Well, maybe them bitches could straighten out your head. I never see you reading."

"I'm reading."

"What? You're reading what?"

"The Harry Pottah book that Nina loan me. She likeded it."

"Maruquita, your cousin Nina is nine years old."

"I know that, Mama. So?"

"So this Harry Potter is for little kids and adults with addled minds."

"Mama, it's really nice. It's about a boy that is a which, a little *brujo*."

"A which? You're joking, right? Don't you mean witch?"

"What?"

"Witch, you airhead. Witch not which."

"That's what I said. Which."

"Witch."

"Whatevah, Mama. Anyway, I'm reading it and the boy fly on a broom and he do magic like we do even if he a little bit dopey. He live in Inkland. I think maybe it's make-believe, you know? It don't sound real. Inkland, like it's just writing. With ink."

"Oh, boy," Flaquita said, imploring the heavens.

"What, Mama?"

"Nothing. Just keep reading that crap, and maybe instead of Harry Potter you can become Carrie Puta. Don't you understand that those books are training children to read vapid formula novels when they grow up? I can't believe my own daughter is part of this conspiracy to devaluate literature. Don't you understand that so-called genre books are simply the same book over and over again? All this horror, romance, detective, technothriller, pseudoscience crap is making people stupid. I can't believe this. But you had a head start."

"Mama, why you being mean again? This hurt so bad. I'm supposed to read, and then when I tell you about a book I'm reading, you put me down. At least I'm reading."

"That isn't a book. That's friggin Fruit Loops. What ever happened to the classics?

"But they're fun."

"Right, entertainment. I mean, what does that say about this society? I'll tell you what it says. It says that a society that needs to be constantly entertained is an immature society. That's what it says. Where are today's William Faulkners, John Steinbecks, Fyodor Dostoevskys, Émile Zolas? Where are they? In Connecticut?"

"Mama, you are so nasty."

"I'm not nasty. I'm explaining a reality of modern life to you. You better finish high school and maybe go to junior college."

"I'm pregnant, Mama. I can't go back to high school."

"Well, what do you want me to do? Maybe I'll ask your grandmother to turn your boyfriend into a pigeon. What do you think of that?"

"No, Mama," Maruquita said. "I love him. He's my pet. You told me I could have him. You gave him a big peepee *bohango* and he gives me nice head. I see colored lights and birdies singing and it feels like I'm flying. Don't tell Grandma to turn him into a pigeon, please."

"Well then, stop being a ninny," Flaquita said.

"But what I'm suppose to do?"

"You're suppose to relax, watch a few *novelas,* go shopping, stop eating junk food, play some classical music so the baby can be born with some culture. That's what you have to do."

"You did that with me?"

"Yes, I did."

"Then why are you so nasty to me? I'm nice."

"Yes, you are. You're very nice, but you're so intellectually inadequate. Go take a nap."

"But he's cheating on me."

"You don't know that for sure. Anyway, that's what men do. They got that *bohango* and they're proud of it and want to share it with other women."

"Papi does that?"

"Your father tried it a few times, and we dealt with it."

"What happened?"

"That's between the two of us."

"Did you do *brujería* on him?"

"Yes, I did."

"And he don't cheat on you no more, right?"

"No, he doesn't. He is very well-behaved. As soon as he watches the evening news, he goes to bed. He gets up in the morning, eats breakfast, and goes to his *punto,* runs his numbers business, and comes right home, just like any other businessman."

"So maybe you could do something like that to Omagaw Boogaloo so he don't cheat on me."

"Maybe I could, but only as a last resort. He hasn't done anything that warrants that sort of reaction. When the time comes, that's what'll happen.

However, things have not progressed to that point. It's not yet time for the *baul.*"

"Mama, I don't understand what you said."

"Okay, okay," Flaquita said, annoyed. "He ain't done nothing so bad that he got to be sat down for good on the trunk. *El baul.* When he does, we'll chill him."

"Is Daddy chill?"

"Your father is chilled," Flaquita said. "Now let me get back to your brother's play."

"Okay, Mama," Maruquita said. "I feel a whole lot better. I'ma go downstairs and watch a *novela* and do like you said. No more Cheetos and Doritos."

Maruquita kissed her mother's cheek, returned downstairs to her apartment, and turned on the television set. Some girl was complaining to her mother that her boyfriend was cheating on her and she didn't know what to do. Her mother couldn't believe it. She went to a dresser, opened a drawer, moved the underwear aside, and pulled out a small silver automatic pistol. She reached down, shoved a clip into the pistol and looked sweetly at her daughter.

"He's mine," the mother said, aimed the pistol at the daughter, and shot her three times.

Commercials came on and Maruquita turned off the TV. Soap operas were so silly. Her mother would never do anything like that to her. She tried reading Harry Potter. Something wasn't right. The words seemed scrambled and funny, and she couldn't figure out what the hell her mother had been talking about. What did intellectually inadequate mean? She knew one thing. It didn't sound good. It was like an illness or something, and it felt very, very yuckie kaka. She opened a cupboard and found a bag of Doritos. She had a strong urge to open the bag but changed her mind. Maybe her mother was right and all the junk food made people stupid. Maybe they put shit in the junk food to make people dumb.

She thought again about the *novela.* The mother had shot the daughter and said that the girl's boyfriend was hers. Maruquita was shocked. Gringos were so weird. Maybe this was another sign. Maybe Omagaw Boogaloo was giving her mother head. All of a sudden the word "matricide" appeared in her head in bright neon letters. She didn't know what the word meant, but it bothered her.

Upstairs, her mother was reading SBS's play.

Nalgas and El Gato are pacing on the stage. They are nervous. A revelation is about to take place. Flaquita's heart is racing with the anticipation of what is to be revealed. Nalgas and El Gato are talking about the man with the briefcase. The man with the briefcase obviously represents American bureaucracy, thought Flaquita. El Gato is concerned with what the man has in his briefcase. The briefcase, thought Flaquita, represents the future. What is contained in the future? Does the briefcase contain weapons of mass destruction? A nuclear device? Does it contain chemical weapons which will cause illness worse than the plague? The future, it seemed to Flaquita, was a briefcase held by men in suits, and it didn't appear that they were up to any good. She suddenly saw not one but two men in business suits. One was dark, had a full mustache, spoke in Arabic, and looked like the father of the Frito bandido. The other was white, looked simian, spoke in English, had a smirk on his face, and was frowning severely. On each of the briefcases the initials WMD had been printed in large letters. She didn't understand the significance of the letters but knew the two men represented the duality of all things. Of good and evil. Of light and shadow. Of heaven and hell. Of Olympus and Hades. Of Eros and Thanatos. Amazing! What a brilliant play. I don't want to include the entire play, since it would interfere with the telling of the story of Omaha Bigelow, but it's important to include a page or two, since within the play there is a key to the novel.

Flaquita closed the script and breathed a long sigh. He was so brilliant. What a son this Samuel Beckett Salsipuedes was. No mother could be prouder. A financial genius and a playwright of considerable promise. It was wonderful the way he sustained the tension about the man with the briefcase. And she loved the repetitions. It was so Mametic. So real. She opened the script once more and read the discovery page again.

 EL GATO

How large were these condoms that the man with the briefcase had in his briefcase?

NALGAS

Very large.

EL GATO

Well, how large were they? (*Extending his hands with each phrase*) Were they large? Very large? Or very, very large.

NALGAS

I'm so ashamed.

EL GATO

Stop this, Nalgas. (*Without turning around, bops* NALGAS *on the head with the air bladder*) How big were the condoms?

NALGAS

Life size. They were life size. The man with the briefcase had life-size condoms in his briefcase.

EL GATO

And you saw that they were life-size?

NALGAS

Yes, we went into Tompkins Square Park. The man with the briefcase demonstrated the life-size condoms he had in his briefcase. He removed his jacket, Betrayus opened the package and put it over the man's head and Betrayus and Smelly pulled the condom until the ring was at the man's feet.

EL GATO

Very interesting. And then what?

NALGAS

What do you mean?

EL GATO

What happened next?

NALGAS

Nothing. The man with the briefcase looked like a penis, but a really large penis. I was shocked that someone could look so much like a penis. The man with the briefcase has a purpose. I think it has to do with the man with the briefcase trying to fuck the people.

The stage goes dark. The music goes up and then stops abruptly.

She loved the symbolism of the life-size condom and the man looking like a *bohango*. It was so obvious that the man with the briefcase meant to fuck El Gato, who was Puerto Rican, so that El Gato represented the people. What a truly amazing play! She couldn't wait to see it on stage, with the clowns bounding around. She was certain that she could direct the play. But it wouldn't be fair. She had no formal training. She had read considerably on different types of theater: Auguste Boal, the Noh Theater, Stanislavsky. She wondered what SBS would think if she broached the subject of directing his play.

O MAHA BIGELOW BEGAN CONSIDERING HIS OPTIONS. NOW THAT HE HAD entered Winnifred Buckley with such enthusiastic results, he couldn't stay away from her. Awilda Cortez was not a problem. All she wanted was a Gringorican baby, although that fact alone would add to the eventual troubles that Omaha would encounter. But how to manage Winnifred and Maruquita? More importantly, how was he supposed to write this film script, compose the score, work at Kinko's, satisfy Maruquita's increasing sexual appetite, and cope with the feeling of absolute satisfaction and artistic accomplishment that he felt when he was with Winnifred? Did he still love Maruquita? Yes, the affection was still there, and her Latin ardor sated something primitive in him. But Winnifred was something else. Winnifred was the quintessence of the United States dream of aspiration, of accomplishment, of economic largesse and multiple dwellings. He could see the society pages: *Omaha and Winnifred Bigelow of Sutton Place, Sag Harbor, Martha's Vineyard, Málaga, Greenwich, and Palm Beach announced a donation of $200 million to New York University's Tisch School of the Arts for the construction of the Omaha Bigelow Performing Arts Center in Washington Square Park. Mayor Giuliani, now 102 and in his 12th term as Mayor, has given his permission to build in the park. Mr. Bigelow is the successful and respected filmmaker whose films have garnered every national and international award for their insight into the psyche of the average American.* Did he love Winnifred? Passionately, unquestionably, with all his poor, middle-class heart. And they were both graduates of Yale. How sublime!

For the purposes of continuity, let us now dispense with plausibility, logic, or accuracy and instead add artifice to the purpose of novelistic intent. Our hero is an artist. This tells you a great deal about the condition of art in America these days. Don't be shocked. It's true. This condition is possible because fine art has not had a credible response to the proliferation of so-called pop art. While fine art should take a stand against convention, it has instead become accommodating to the tyranny of mediocrity and in many respects attempts to emulate pop art in all its hydran manifestations of music, graphics, TV, film, and writing. Nowhere is this more apparent than in the publishing of the novel. We've already taken a swipe at poor, defenseless Harry Potter, which J.K. Rowling likely couldn't care less about, since on America Online's Authors Lounge it has been proclaimed that she will likely be the first billionaire author. The ascendancy of this Brit probably pisses off American writers like Clancy and King majorly. However, even if they were to fall far behind Rowling's earnings, their achievement at the cash register is already legendary, even for a society that relishes excess. Along the same lines we've seen the burgeoning of the formula novel, as seen in the output of the cited authors and others who basically write the same novel over and over again, as if they were manufacturing Pablum for toothless adults. No *cerebellum dentata* there. Formula authors create vapid, mildly entertaining novels, which likely contribute to the ever-increasing dumbing down of this big puppy of a country while contributing to the deterioration of its already inefficient educational system. Of course there are still fine literary novels written by a few writers, and they're published, but they're not read widely. Not because these novels are linguistically difficult, but because while they may entertain, they also challenge the reader to look at his soul. So don't blame me, a Puerto Rican, for the ills of the art form, because I choose to write in this manner. You want to blame me, anyway? Okay, blame me.

But let me continue my useless onslaught on the condition of the American novel with even more vigor. I'll do so in the metaphor of Omaha Bigelow as a sort of sexual John Wayne. This should advance the plot considerably, which appears to be the purpose of the novel today. In other words, forget style, social concerns, philosophical importance, structure, and poetics and concentrate on telling a story that travels at breakneck speed toward a tired and conventional denouement so that it can be turned quickly into a major motion picture that grosses $75 million in the first weekend. In other words: fuck literary concerns.

If you're wondering why I have alluded to Maruquita's resemblance to Jennifer Lopez and Winnifred's to Charlize Theron, and you think I'm hinting at casting should someone be stupid enough to want to make a film out of this novel, you may also wonder why I do no such thing with Omaha Bigelow. The answer is quite simple. You meatheads reading this book are Omaha Bigelow. What? You're saying that maybe I'm also Omaha Bigelow? Me? An old, washed-up Puerto Rican guy wishing to be a young, white guy with a big johnson? I don't think so. You insist? Okay, fine, I'm also Omaha Bigelow. But let's put the symbolism aside and address the issues. Or as one of my most devoted detractors says: *Yunq has tissues.*

Whatever! Let's keep going and forget all this philosophical whining and social commentary. Let us accept that as an artist, the emission of passion contained in Omaha Bigelow's ancestral memory to copulate with the bitch goddess and the coincidence of Winnifred's convenient novelistic ovulation caused a monumental explosion in the uterus of this Charlize Theron look-alike, occasioning Winnifred to be immediately with child. As you can imagine, Winnifred's condition will complicate Omaha's life even more. He had now impregnated not only Maruquita Salsipuedes, a young woman of considerable magical powers, for the moment stymied but eventually to surface and be a major player in this *extravenganza*, but had also been forced to plant his lively seed in Awilda Cortez, a dangerous girl who not only had an axe to grind but was working herself toward an associate degree at a junior college. These two Puerto Rican señoritas could be handled with relative ease had he not also caused his spermatozoa to drive itself with considerable Euro-American vigor into the equally vigorous and eager ovum of Winnifred Buckley. This fact is important and will eventually cause Omaha Bigelow considerable anguish, psychic pain, loss of self-esteem and social position.

"What am I going to do, Winnie?" Omaha said during one of their lunch breaks at the Two Boots Pizzeria, the cold air of fall outside already fogging the glass. "I want to be with you, but if I leave Maruquita, I'm going to be in real trouble."

"Real trouble?"

"They'll kill me. They're witches."

"You mean witches metaphorically, don't you?" she said calmly. "Evil women who have ulterior motives and wish to have their harpish talons in you."

"No, nothing like that. They're real witches. They do weird stuff and turn into animals and put spells on people."

"Wait," she said, holding up a hand. "You're not reading Harry Potter, are you?"

"Well, Maruquita has it in the house. I glanced at it. But I'm not making this up. They're bruhas. That means witches in Spanish. They practice bruheria. It's spelled with a J but in English it would sound weird to use the J, you know? They're real witches, Winnie."

"Really?" Winnifred said. "How anthropologically interesting. I'll talk to my grandmother at Thanksgiving. One of her ancestors was Hester Prynne's girlfriend."

"Fuck! No way. From *The Scarlet Letter?*"

"No, silly," Winnifred said. "The real Hester Prynne back in Salem, Mass, circa sixteen ninety. Hawthorne simply extrapolated the real story of female persecution in a male-dominated society to write his novel."

"Your family goes back that far?"

"Yes, darling. Please don't worry. We Buckleys have our ways."

"You mean that you know witchcraft?" Omaha whispered, looking around the deserted pizzeria and leaning close to Winnifred. "Not all of those girls were burned at the stake, were they?"

"No, they were not," Winnifred smiled, smugly. "But we no longer call it witchcraft."

"What do you call it?"

"Social facilitation."

"That's really cool."

"It is very cool, but you have to promise me not to worry. I just haven't been trained. The tradition survives, and I will ask my grandmother to teach me what she knows."

"Okay, but I gotta figure this out. I wanna be with you and I wanna write my script so we can shoot it."

"I have an idea."

"What?"

"You quit Kinko's and . . ."

"I can't do that. That's the only income I have, and I have to pay rent and there's a baby coming and Maruquita's gonna freak out if I lose my job. There's no telling what she'll do."

"Wait, wait . . . hear me out," Winnifred said, amused by how in control she now was. "You quit Kinko's. I form the Lightness of Being Corporation for the express purpose of shooting the film, the corporation hires you to write the film at a salary of five thousand dollars per week, and you write full time. How does that sound?"

"Five thousand a week?"

"Is that sufficient? We can double it if you want. As a matter of fact, we should, since you're also going to compose the score for the soundtrack. Ten thousand it is."

"Yeah, but that's a lot of money. How much is that a year? That's like a half a million."

"It's not really a lot of money," Winnifred said, sweetly. "The backers think it's a worthwhile project to get this film produced. They've given me full and absolute authority to do as I see fit. I am the producer. That will be my credit and my honor."

"Incredible," Omaha said. "So I quit Kinko's, leave each night to go to work, but come to your apartment instead. In the morning I go home to Maruquita."

"Yes, exactly."

"But wait."

"What?"

"You won't be at the apartment. You'll be at Kinko's."

"I'll quit Kinko's and be at the apartment with you. I was simply doing a bit of research for a course on labor law that I'm taking. By the way, I've never worked a day in my life. It was truly informative to learn how the working class functions. In any case, you can write, and if you feel as if there is too much tension you can leave the computer and I will tongue you into oblivion. How does that sound?"

"Oh, my God," Omaha said, recalling the last time he and Winnifred were together. "Stop, just stop, Winnie. You're making me too excited."

"Hahaha," Winnifred said. "I excite you, don't I?"

"Severely," Omaha said.

They finished eating and returned to work. In the morning Omaha informed Paganini Ling that he was quitting work because he'd gotten a grant to finish writing his film. When Valery Molotov came in to work, Ling informed him of Omaha's resignation and emerging good fortune. Molotov went over to Omaha, grasped his shoulders, brought him closer, and kissed his cheeks, first one, then the other.

"This commissar is sad to see dedicated people's hero go but salutes effort to depict struggle of working class to combat capitalist system of oppressive organization through film mediums made sacred by great Russian film genius, Sergei Eisenstein, maker of *The Battleship Potempkin*, but also other memorable comrade directors like Alexei Balabanov, *The Castle*, Nikita Mikhalkov *Burnt by the Sun*, Karen Shaknazarov *American Daughter*, Pyotr Todorovsky *Moscow Country Nights*, and Marina Tsurtsumia *Only Death Comes For Sure*. You knowing these filmmakers, my brother?"

"No, but as soon as they come to the Angelika, I promise that I'll go see them," Omaha said.

"Well, go with blessings of motherland, my brother," Molotov said, grasping Omaha's shoulders once again.

And so it went. Omaha quit Kinko's and a week later so did Winnifred. Each evening about 11:30 at night Omaha kissed the somnolent Maruquita, left his apartment in the projects, walked to Houston Street, turned west until he passed Kinko's, and went to Winnifred's apartment in Red Square. One time Awilda stopped him and said she knew what he was doing. At first Omaha didn't know what to do, but quickly recovered his composure.

"Oh, hi, Awilda," he said.

"You quit and you're hanging out with that gringa whitegirl, ain'tcha?"

"I'm working on my film. How's school?"

"It's okay. I'm taking this course called 'Tangents of Existential Thought in Post-Modernist Linguistics,'" Awilda said proudly. "It's kicking my ass, but I'm hanging in there."

"Far out," Omaha said. "Are you going to go on to a four-year college?"

"I'm thinking about it, but with the baby coming and everything, you know."

"Oh, the baby should go to college too."

"The baby?"

"Yeah, the baby," Omaha said, and went into his pocket and took out five hundred-dollar bills."

"What's that for?"

"For the baby, so he can go to college. I'll give you five hundred dollars a week for the baby, and we keep our secret to ourselves."

"A week?"

"Yeah."

"That's two thousand a month. You sure?"

"I'm sure. Let me ask you something."

"Sure."

"Did you tell Maruquita what happened?"

"What happened with us?"

"Yeah."

"No way."

"And you don't know nothing about me quitting my job, right?"

"I don't know nothing about you quitting your job or that you hanging out with Ms. Gringa Whitegirl."

"Cool. I'll come to your house each Friday."

"Okay, see you," Awilda said happily as she headed for Kinko's. "Can we still make it? I likeded it."

"We'll see," Omaha said and winked at Awilda.

October came and went, and then November, and Omaha explained to Winnifred that he had to go and visit his mother and he didn't want to make Maruquita suspicious, since he had already asked her to go home with him. Winnifred pouted a bit but said that she would see him when he got back. She asked if he was still having relations with Maruquita. He lied, shook his head, and said no way. She nodded happily and resumed mounting him, her magnificent body monumental above him.

OMAHA BIGELOW AND MARUQUITA SALSIPUEDES FLEW TO KANSAS CITY on American Airlines Flight 107 the day before Thanksgiving. He had given her five hundred dollars to buy new clothes, and she was dressed not as if she were flying to the Heartland to meet her future mother-in-law, but to go dancing at a Latin club with a gaggle of her homegirls to show off their steps, and listen to the music of Johnny Pacheco or Tito Nieves or maybe La India. Her dress was a bit short, and both skirt and bodice had black, red, blue, and yellow *lentejuelas,* sequins that is, which shimmered and reminded Omaha of the plumage of a rather attractive turkey. She wore her hair in ever-increasing coils that ascended a full foot above her actual height, and she had earrings so large that finches or canaries could have easily perched on them. On her delicate feet she wore boots that reached all the way to mid-thigh. Redundantly, she wore red fishnet stockings. She was made up in dark rouge and mascara with black lipstick, accentuating her already Moorish looks. Several men, dark of visage, seemingly evil of intent, and obviously essaying a possible hijacking, eyed her with increasing desire. Fortunately, Maruquita had purchased a long black coat which covered the entire ensemble except when she made abrupt movements and the flaps of the coat flew open to reveal the bizarre outfit.

Maruquita had the window seat and was enthralled that the large airplane was flying above the clouds. She remarked that perhaps heaven was very near because the clouds were so large and fluffy. A swarthy-skinned, Semitic-looking man with dark eyes and a mustache sitting across the aisle said *Saalam Alekum* and spoke in whispers to Omaha in a language that Omaha later surmised was Arabic. Omaha threw up his hands in a gesture of surrender. He shook his head and said: *no comprendo.* The man muttered a curse that sounded like *malish, al kharah amerika,* put on his sunglasses and turned away. As an aside, I should tell you that I have very little understanding of Arabic, not uncommon for most people in the U.S. and perhaps a major failing given the U.S.

involvement in Arabic-speaking countries. However, my limited understanding of Arabic tells me that the man was saying *Shit, I hate America.* Don't quote me but I think that's what he said to Omaha. Maruquita drank the soda she ordered but saved the peanuts which the flight attendant had placed on her seat tray. She knelt on her seat and announced that if people were not going to eat the peanuts to pass them to her. She collected about twenty packages of peanuts which she stored in her large bag.

They landed in Kansas City around noon and took a twenty-five minute American Eagle flight to Reliability. From the airport they took a cab to Olivia Bigelow's house at 32 Nice Street. Maruquita was delighted and snuggled happily against Omaha, causing his *bohango kakomakako* to rise up solidly in his jeans. She asked him if he really lived on Nice Street. He nodded, and Maruquita thought the whole thing was like being on television. She wasn't far from the truth, except that there wasn't a sound track. Reliability was very much your typical American small town.

There had not been any violence in Reliability for well over one hundred years, since one of the James boys—no one was sure whether Frank or Jesse— got into an argument with the husband of a housewife with whom he was having an affair. He shot her husband in the foot when he attempted to make the man dance in front of Carruther's General Store when he said James was nothing but a cheap renegade. The Chamber of Commerce of Reliability, together with the Reliability Historical Society, had placed in front of what is now the Carruther's Mall a small plaque to commemorate the event. It sits there embedded in the concrete between the Burger King and the Dunkin Donuts, approximately where the James boy shot off the man's middle and index foot fingers. "Hey, Sooz!"—that's what Jesus sounds like in Spanish. It's just an expression of surprise. The people of Reliability are, for the most part, quiet and respectful of each other, law-abiding churchgoers and civic-minded folks who work hard, do not cheat on their income tax, and believe scrupulously in the Gospel and whatever the CNN anchors proffer to them as truth. This is not to say that everything was perfect in Reliability.

That there was a slight undercurrent of dissatisfaction was an accepted fact. The four therapists in the town were doing a booming business counseling people with sundry neurotic disorders, doing family therapy, drug management, and treating several cases of sexual and marital dysfunction. However dissatisfied the citizens of this good town may have been, most of them understood that dissatisfaction was a Christian burden, one that must be borne with resignation. For if one kept to the straight and narrow he would be rewarded in the afterlife. This dissatisfaction was no more obvious than in the youth of Reliability. They grumbled constantly about too much homework, the boredom of religion, parental restrictions, and there being little to do in the town other than go to a mall full of dweebs and nerds, a film theater that showed PG films, and an ice cream parlor that looked like something out of their grandparents' era with photos of the Beatles and other memorabilia of a time long gone.

In the middle of this rather calm but nonetheless seething hamlet there were no less than eight boys—all of them from two-parent, Christian homes, all law-abiding and strict in their offspring's fundamentalist upbringing—who felt the chagrin of living in Reliability more acutely than most. These eight had joined in a confederacy of discontent and had each managed to purchase, over the Internet, AK-47s, five hundred rounds of ammunition each, and a dozen hand grenades. They thought of buying several bazookas but knew they couldn't handle their weight, recoil, and cumbersomeness.

One such boy, Trent Ingersoll, the leader of the disaffected and puerile group, was fourteen years old and in the last stages of constructing an explosive device that he hoped to place in the home of one Lisa Gumpert, also fourteen. Lisa, was a plumpish, insecure girl with unruly red hair. At the time she was seeing a psychologist three times a week because she had visions of her Lord and Savior Jesus Christ on a motorcycle, riding around with Mary Magdalene in tow, and felt enormous guilt. Inside her, a voice she identified as the Devil's, was saying much too frequently: *Girlie, the reason JC was cruxed is that he was doing the wild thing with Mary M because Mary M was working at her uncle's pizzeria in downtown Jerusalem and the Romans didn't like an Italian girl like Mary M going out with a Jewish guy.* It drove her mad that she had these unbidden thoughts.

The reason that Lisa had been targeted by these bad boys was that she had rejected Trent's amorous attention and refused to go to the prom with him in the spring. Young Ingersoll was certain that Lisa really wanted to go with him but was lying to make him suffer. The eight had decided that this Gumpert *femme fatale* was a slut and a liar and had to be disposed of. According to the plan, Trent would leave for school with the explosive device in his knapsack. He would ride his bike to the Gumpert home, place the device in the basement shortly after Mr. Gumpert left for work, and set the timer for an hour later. This would take care of Mrs. Gumpert and the home-schooled nine-year-old dyslexic twin brothers of the perfidious Lisa. The father would die of grief. Lisa would be dealt with later on at the school.

Trent Ingersoll would then go into the woods behind the school to rendezvous with the other seven boy commandos, two of whom were twelve and one eleven. Once there, they would dig up their cache, dress in full camouflage fatigues and combat boots, blacken their faces so that they looked like raccoons, and armed with loaded AK-47s and grenades they would march on the school. They would enter the Neil Armstrong Middle School by opening a back door which Ingersoll had propped open the night before. Once inside they would go from one classroom to the other and wipe out the entire school population of 225 students and 56 teachers, administrators, and custodial personnel. "Just like those boys did in Colorado," they commented among themselves, reassuring each other that they would not fail as had those faithless amateurs. They called their operation "Ultimate Terminator." Were they well organized? You bet your Schwarzeneggering Clancy they were. Brilliant and precocious, the young Ingersoll had read of Japanese novelist Yukio Mishima's life, and after their deed he would assassinate his comrades in arms and then commit ritual suicide by placing an armed hand grenade in his mouth. The word lunatic is too mild for this young American, but ignore what's going on here and instead let's focus on the fundamentalism of other cultures and their religion. Here, in the Home of the Brave and the Land of the Free, everything is cool.

Maruquita was agog at the orderliness of the town. She loved the neat homes with their painted fences, outside mail boxes, and birdbaths, the snow shoveled symmetrically to create paths to the houses. There was no garbage in the street, no rats running along the gutter and disappearing into holes in the buildings, no loud rap music, and above all no homeboys running around grabbing their genitals. The black people she saw were subdued, their passivity comforting. They did not move with the swagger she was so used to seeing in New York City, and for this she was thankful. The girls she saw in Reliability smiled at her admiringly, and none of them looked like they wanted to kill her with their jealousy. She hugged herself to Omaha.

"This is so nice, Omagaw Boogaloo," she said as they rode in the cab. "For real. Anyway you live on Nice Street so why not, right?"

"You like it, huh?"

"Yeah, it's really cool."

The cab stopped and Maruquita got out. She looked at the neat two-story house painted in pale yellow, with its little porch and everything trimmed in white: windows, porch columns, and balusters. Right outside the gate there was a mail box painted white and trimmed in yellow like the house. On it there was the name *Bigelow* written in red script and below it the number 32. There was a large oak tree next to the house and a couple of small pine trees in the yard. Shrubbery ran behind the fence and on both sides of the steps leading to the porch. In the middle of the lawns on each side of the walkway that led to the house there were rose bushes now trimmed and bare, but healthy looking, giving an indication that in the spring they would bloom gloriously. The ground was covered with a light sprinkling of snow, but you could also tell that when the warm weather came again the lawn would be green and lush. In the windows of Olivia Bigelow's house there were decorations of Pilgrims, turkeys, and pumpkins. Up and down the street there were other neat houses, each of which had stately trees and a smoking chimney that foretold of a Santa who would clamber down its sootless passageway, which likely had a circular staircase within the brick structure that expanded conveniently to accommodate the fat man's girth. As Omaha opened the gate to let Maruquita in, she saw the yellow-and-white birdhouse next to the house and pointed at it. At that moment a bird flew out and headed for the oak tree. She let out a small shriek of delight.

"Look," she said. "It flew out. It was blue."

"It's the bluebird of happiness," he said.

"The bluebird of happiness?" Maruquita exclaimed. "Is he yours?"

"He belongs to everyone," Omaha said, not quite believing her naiveté. "Did you see the film *Blue Velvet*?"

"No, when did they give it?"

Fuck, he thought. What the hell had he gotten into? He led Maruquita up the steps and knocked. His mother opened the door and smiled with kindly understanding. Once inside Omaha introduced Maruquita to his mother. With typical American hospitality Olivia Bigelow greeted Maruquita warmly, letting herself be hugged and kissed by this strange girl. She had rented *West Side Story* and suddenly had visions of Maruquita bouncing around her living room looking like Rita Moreno dancing and singing "Everything Free in America." She asked Maruquita to take off her coat and make herself comfortable. Maruquita did so and Olivia Bigelow gasped. It was as if suddenly there had been an explosion in her brain and there was a crescendo of Leonard Bernstein's score. In spite of her shock at how striking and hot-blooded Maruquita looked, Olivia made the best of the situation. Needless to say this was a strange experience. Stranger yet was seeing Omaha with black hair and a black mustache. She hadn't noticed the change from green in the photos he'd sent her. She'd get used to it. Maybe he was in a play.

"Hi, Mrs. Boogaloo," Maruquita said, disengaging herself from Olivia. "You are so cute."

"Well, thank you, dear," Olivia giggled.

"I brought you a present," Maruquita said, and dumped twenty-one bags of American Airlines peanuts on the couch. "For you," she added proudly.

"Well, thank you again," Olivia said graciously.

"You're welcome," Maruquita replied. "You know something?"

"What, dear?"

"I thought you was gonna be a fat old lady and look like Roseann and whatnot," Maruquita said, stepping back and shaking her body, the sequins throwing off tiny beams of colored light every which way. "But you be looking fine, Mama. You be playing the movie star and whatnot. You looking *muy bonita* and whatnot. I bet you do your own hair and nails?"

"Well, yes . . ."

"You look beautiful, Mama," said Maruquita. "Your son be cute, but you some pretty-ass gringa whitegirl. Look out!"

"Thank you," Olivia said, warming to the attention, but still unable to imagine what striped children would look like. "You're very attractive yourself."

"Well, you know, we Rican girls got it. Know what I mean," she said, and shook her hips and prominent derriere.

Maruquita turned to Omaha.

"You got a good looking Mami, Omagaw Boogaloo. You should be proud. Give her a hug and a kiss."

Omaha moved forward and hugged and kissed his mother. Olivia Bigelow was in fact a well-preserved fifty year old, still slender and pretty in an inoffensive Martha Stewart kind of way. Olivia was in fact a devotee of the housewifely guru, and her house reflected her taste in its delicate Americana decor: doilies and figurines, curtains and picture frames all made by her own hands and office. Beyond the living room there was a dining room on one side and on the other, through French doors, was a room that held a grand piano, where she still received her students and those who had gone on to become captains of industry, barristers, elected officials, academicians, and pillars of the community, men who returned periodically to reminisce and play duets with Olivia, the ubiquitous Kleenex box within reach atop the closed piano.

"Let me show you kids your rooms," Olivia said, heading for the second floor.

"Oh, Mama, don't worry," Maruquita said. "We sleep together in one bed."

"Oh," Olivia said. "Hmmmmm."

"I gotta tell you something, Mama," Maruquita said, sidling up to Olivia and elbowing her gently in the ribs. "Not for nothing but your son give really good head."

"Oh, my," Olivia said. "I don't know what to say," she exclaimed looking at Omaha.

"She means that sometimes she gets headaches, and I massage her temples," Omaha said, grabbing their bags and ushering Maruquita upstairs.

Once upstairs Omaha explained that his mother was a very Christian lady and you couldn't talk about sex to her that way. Maruquita said she was sorry and said she would be cool and not say anything like that anymore. She was certain Olivia Bigelow was not getting any head and had not seen a *bohango* in years. How right she was about Olivia not getting head, but wrong about her not seeing a *bohango*. Olivia Bigelow had seen well over 10,000 *bohangos,* but only one had held her rapt, its memory spectral and mythical.

The visit went quite well, and Maruquita helped her future mother-in-law in preparing Thanksgiving dinner. That Thursday they gave thanks and then stuffed themselves on a truly wonderful turkey dinner, simple and nutritious and certainly befitting this great holiday of gratitude. Nothing of an untoward nature took place while Omaha and Maruquita were in Reliability. Truths were revealed between mother and son but American family values and the bluebird of happiness reigned supreme in the Bigelow household throughout the visit. Some people gossiped, but things dissipated when one of the girls who had seen Maruquita, when Omaha took her to the mall, conjectured that Mrs. Bigelow's son, who everyone knew was in show business, was engaged to Jennifer Lopez and they made the perfect couple.

F RIDAY EVENING, AFTER MARUQUITA WENT TO SLEEP, OLIVIA BIGELOW, concerned with Omaha's future, marital choice, and her sure-to-be-born grandchildren, or what she had chosen to call children of parallel color, inquired as to his plans. The entreaty gave Omaha an opportunity to speak in depth with his mother about certain things that had troubled him far too long. You're probably wondering, for example, why no mention has been made thus far of Omaha's father. As you have probably imagined, since you know about balance in the writing of a novel, the topic is a delicate one. Omaha's paternity involves questions of national security. Since I'm privy to such things but not at liberty to say why, it is incumbent upon me to be as careful as possible to protect those involved. As you can appreciate, having read considerably, fictional characters also have feelings, and they should be respected. It is simply unfair to say that Melville's Ahab was an obsessive or to dismiss the brothers in *East of Eden* as just two people suffering from sibling rivalry. Certainly, Popeye in Faulkner's *Sanctuary* had issues of sexual dysfunction and in his weakness resorted to using a corncob as a substitute for his impotence. No matter how bizarre his behavior, there should be compassion for this poor man's feelings. I hope you share these concerns and understand my hesitancy. My reluctance is based on the fact that the subject of Omaha's paternity was not one of Olivia Bigelow's favorite topics. For that reason I want to tell about this with as much delicacy and discretion as possible. You should also understand that there is no need on my part to create sensationalism in order to spice up this narrative. I will, therefore, go forth as elliptically as possible. What I have to reveal at this juncture is a reality, and whether or not you consider it far-fetched, I believe it the responsibility of reasonable people to examine the facts objectively and draw their own conclusions as to the truth.

As background to answering the question of Omaha's paternity, as you may have suspected, Olivia, like many women today, is a single parent. You should also know that Bigelow is Olivia's maiden name and in no way related to the Bigelow clock, carpet, or tea people. The Bigelows from whom Olivia was descended came to the state of Arkansas some two hundred years before and lived in the mountains. They eventually made their way from the mountains into the towns and villages of the state. Olivia Bigelow raised her son alone, moving to Reliability, Kansas, before Omaha was born, to get away from her status as an unwed pregnant teen. Cheap wedding band on her finger, she explained to people in Reliability late in 1964 that her husband had been killed as an advisor in Vietnam, a gross misrepresentation given the true military record of Omaha's father. Omaha was born in 1965.

"Omaha, could you answer something for me, please?" Olivia said, getting up from the sofa and going into the kitchen.

"What?" Omaha said, following her.

"This girl," Olivia said, taking a pie and whipped cream out of the refrigerator.

"Maruquita. Maruquita Salsipuedes."

"Yes, Marquita Saltandpeppa," Olivia said, cutting the pie and serving Omaha and herself a slice, and bringing a bottle of eggnog to the table. "Is she all right?"

"What do you mean?"

"She's a little young, isn't she?"

"She's in high school, Mom."

"Do you think it'll help?"

"Probably not, but I don't think it's important, Mom. There are different kinds of intelligence, you know. Talent, intellectual capacity, athletic ability, financial and political cunning."

"And this one has which of them?"

"Talent, Mom. She is amazing."

"What does she do? You're not talking about her peculiar way of speaking English, are you? Or does she have a special way of doing the mambo, or the tango?"

"No, listen, Mom. She's magical."

"Magical? She does magic tricks? She's a prestidigitator. Card tricks and such."

"Yes. She does amazing things. She can change into animals. Monkeys, squirrels, seagulls, hawks. Mom, she even turned into a peacock. It was awesome. I've never seen anything so beautiful. She's really something."

"She works with balloons, then," said Olivia, intrigued.

"No, Mom," Omaha said, laughing. "She actually changes herself."

"She's an illusionist," Olivia said. "That's excellent. She's in show business like you."

"Kinda," Omaha said. "Anyway, sometimes talent like that is inhibited by schooling. You've developed yourself without much formal training, haven't you?"

"That's true. And she's going to have your child?"

"Yes, she is. You're going to be a grandma."

"That's nice, dear. And you're really thinking of marrying this girl?"

"Well, I don't know now."

"That's just like your father. By the way, have you heard of statutory rape?"

"What do you mean?"

"Statutory rape. She's fifteen. That's under age, Omaha."

"Sixteen, Mom."

"Fine, sixteen. Still under age, and you could be criminally prosecuted."

"I know, Mom. But what about my father? You said it was just like my father."

"Oh, I was about her same age when I was pregnant with you," Olivia Bigelow said. "I wasn't fifteen yet. I was fifteen when I had you. Just like right now, except that your father was eighteen years old. He was a senior and I was a freshman. We were in high school back in Hope."

"In Arkansas?"

"Yes, we were in the music room jamming on Thelonious Monk's 'Straight no Chaser.' Just four of us. Jimmy Booth on drums. Tommy Armitage on bass. Your father on tenor, and I blowing piano. I was taking a solo when I looked up to let him know that we should trade, and he was looking at me all dreamy-eyed and smiling that beautiful smile of his, and we fell in love, just like that. I suppose my folks could've had him charged with statutory rape, but he said he would take care of us. Don't get me wrong, he has."

"I know. Veteran benefits," Omaha said. "Anyway, I'm not sure if I'm going to marry her, Mom," Omaha said. "I suppose I could get charged."

"You've changed your mind?"

"Something's come up."

"Something?"

"Well, someone," Omaha said, looking upstairs to make sure that Maruquita was not coming down the stairs. "She's wonderful, Mom. And she went to Yale like I did."

"While you were there? She'd be close to thirty-five? Certainly a step up in maturity."

"No, she just graduated, Mom. She's young. She's in law school. Really bright."

"Not as young as Rosie Perez upstairs. Mind you, I'm not a prejudiced person, and I have nothing against the girl."

"Mom, Maruquita's a nice girl. You have to understand the social conditions under which Puerto Ricans live. American society is rough on people like them. Look at the books they write in English."

"Well, we're not exactly privileged stock, you know. But we've certainly done well for ourselves. I can assure you that both sides of your family were dirt poor," she said cryptically. "But what about this other one? Is she as spaced out?"

"No, Mom, she's really bright and beautiful," Omaha said, his eyes lighting up. "Blond hair, blue eyes. She looks a little like Charlize Theron."

"The movie star that was in that golfing movie with Matt Damon and that young Negro actor? Will Smith."

"Yes, that's her. *The Legend of Bagger Vance*, but she was in *Devil's Advocate, The Astronaut's Wife, Reindeer Games, The Cider House Rules*, and a bunch more. She's a brilliant artist. And Ma?"

"What dear?"

"Black, not Negro. People don't say Negro."

"Well, I do. Some of the Negroes don't look black at all. But that's nice that your girlfriend was in all those movies."

"No, she wasn't. Charlize Theron, the movie star was. Winnie looks just like her. Not exactly, but a strong resemblance."

"See, that's more like it, Omaha. That's the kind of girl I've always envisioned for you. Someone who is worthy of your talent. Does she do Martha Stewart things?"

"I know, I know. No, no Martha Stewart stuff. I just have to figure this out. Winnie doesn't want people to know, but her father went to Yale with President Bush."

"The president?" her mother said, suddenly frowning. "Dubya?"

"No, his father. They were classmates. But he's met the son."

"He's an embarrassment," Olivia Bigelow said, shaking her head several times and snorting powerfully. "Your Marquita speaks English better than this electoral thief. Heaven help us. He's nothing like the previous president, I'll tell you."

"Anyway, Winnifred's helping me with my film," Omaha went on, oblivious to his mother's increasing discomfort. "That's her name, Mom. Winnifred Hancock Buckley. She's got backing for the project. We start shooting at the beginning of the year. We're in preproduction and I'm writing the script. Probably the score as well. The company's paying me well. That's how I was able to come and see you. I'm not working at Kinko's anymore. Her family's very prominent, Mom."

"And her father knew the president's father at Yale?"

"Yes, all of us went to Yale. The president, Winnie's father, Winnie, and me. Isn't that great? Anyway, I think it is."

"Other people have gone to Yale. We're not exactly trailer trash, you know," Olivia Bigelow said, increasingly miffed. "You don't have anything to be ashamed of. You're just as good as they are."

"What do you mean, Mom?" Omaha said, putting the last piece of his second slice of pie into his mouth and sipping from the eggnog in his glass. "I'm sorry I went on about Winnie's family. I mean, it's very impressive. Their family goes back to the Pilgrims and the Mayflower. And to people who signed the Declaration of Independence. In a small way I feel honored that I've met someone like Winnifred."

"You have nothing to be ashamed of, Omaha," Olivia said, passionately. "Being close to the president may have advantages, but you have something even more important."

"I know, Mom," Omaha said. "We come from honest, mid-American stock. Our people settled the West. We don't have to feel any shame at all. We can hold our head up."

"You bet," Olivia said, starting to freak out. "Damn, him, damn him," she repeated as she smashed her fist on her thigh. "I should've made him marry me. Or at least threatened him with rape. But it wasn't rape. It was wonderful. If I had known that he was going to go on and do what he did and wasn't just a terrific saxophone player, I wouldn't be sitting in some hick town in Kansas. I would've had my day in the sun. I don't know if I would've gone to Yale Law School or become a U.S. senator, but I would've done much better as his wife. I worshiped him. She doesn't give a damn about him. Sometimes he looks so sad."

"Mom, what are you talking about?"

"Damn him," Olivia said, not really paying attention to her son. "It was like he was trying to punish himself for leaving me, knowing I was going to have his child. No wonder he had to turn to those awful women and ended up getting impeached. I can't believe it. I should've been stronger."

"Mom, are you talking about a boyfriend of yours?"

Olivia went on as if in a trance. "I have recurring nightmares that I'm walking around the Rose Garden naked at night and suddenly it's daylight and there is a reception for a world leader, Maybe Menachem Begin or Anwar Sadat, maybe Margaret Thatcher, and the president says, ladies and gentlemen, may I present my wife, Olivia Bigelow Clinton. And there I am, naked as a jaybird and having to smile and curtsey and shake everyone's hand."

"The president, Mom? What are you talking about? In the Rose Garden?"

"Sometimes I dream that I'm moaning in the Lincoln bedroom and he's there on top of me, his heavy body on me, not so heavy but filled with passion for me. He loved fried bread in bacon fat with Karo syrup. I would fix it for him when he'd come over to our house and Ma was working at the mill and Pa was driving his truck to Little Rock, and we'd make love. He had such a healthy appetite. In all sorts of ways. That's how I got pregnant. But I was a foolish little girl and believed him when he said we'd come to New York and play in the jazz clubs with Charlie Mingus, Thelonious Monk, Miles Davis, and those folks."

"Mom?"

"And then I'm walking in the Rose Garden and you're holding my hand, and when he sees you, he calls your name, and you run to him and he lifts you up just like President Kennedy would do poor John John, who shouldn't have been flying that plane in such bad weather. Poor thing."

"Mom, stop it, please. Who are you talking about?"

"I'm talking about us, Omaha," Olivia said, her eyes glazed and tear-filled. "I'm talking about what our family could've been if I hadn't been such a young innocent girl."

"You're saying that my father could've been the president of the United States if he hadn't been killed in Vietnam?"

"No, I'm not saying that at all, Omaha," Olivia said, sobbing now. "I've lied to you. I'm sorry."

"What?"

"Your father is alive."

"Alive? No way. Where is he?"

"Chappaqua."

"In New York?"

"Yes, he goes back and forth from there to his offices in Harlem."

"Wait. That sounds like Bill Clinton."

"Yes, I'm so ashamed. I should've been stronger."

"Let me understand something, Mom," Omaha said, pouring himself some more eggnog and cutting his third slice of spicy pumpkin pie with whipped cream. "Are you saying that Chelsea Clinton is my half-sister?"

"Yes, that's exactly what I'm saying. I'm sorry."

"That's fucking amazing," Omaha said.

"Omaha! Your language!"

"I'm sorry, Mom. Tell me all about it. This is exciting."

"Well, dear, it's quite painful," Olivia Bigelow said, fiddling with her brooch, her red fingernails still perfectly lacquered. "Quite painful," she added.

"How did you meet him, Mom?"

"I'd rather not talk about it."

"I have a right to know, Mom."

"And I have a right to avoid talking about it."

"Mom, please," Omaha pleaded. "You've told me this much. You might as well tell me the rest."

Olivia finally relented and told Omaha how in 1964 she had entered high school and there he was, carrying his tenor saxophone case and smiling that wonderful smile, always happy to see everyone and shaking their hand, clapping them on the back to encourage them. They shared an interest in jazz and they had fallen in love, and then she got pregnant and he went off to college at Georgetown and then to England to Oxford University and then to Yale Law School and then he met that awful Rodham woman and they got married and the rest is history, but he always sent monthly checks to a charity in Kansas City and the money was sent to her as a scholarship and he made sure Omaha was well taken care of and eventually went to Yale. When she was finished, Omaha had an enormous stomach ache, having consumed his fourth and fifth piece of pumpkin pie and his fourth glass of eggnog during the telling. Omaha shook his head, not quite believing what he'd heard.

"Mom, are you sure?" he said.

"Of course I'm sure," Olivia Bigelow replied. "I've never had relations with another man. I still worship him. I wish you hadn't sent me those photos."

"The ones of myself with Maruquita?"

"No, the other ones."

"I'm sorry, Mom," Omaha said, sheepishly. "I just wanted you to know that I was okay."

"I know," Olivia said, blushing a little. "I'm not a prudish woman. God knows that I have my flaws and have not been the perfect Christian. But I have to tell you something."

"What?"

"You and your father share an anatomical peculiarity."

"We do?"

"Yes, your yinganyangos are a little crooked."

"Hereditary, huh?"

"Yep," she said, smiling shyly. "I saw the photos, and the pain of rejection rose up in me once more. I mean, I was happy for you that you were normal, and proud that you were so like your father, but it was painful."

"I'm sorry, Mom," Omaha said, getting up and going to his mother. He knelt on the floor and placed his head on her lap as he used to do when he was a little boy. After a while he looked up and his mother kissed his forehead.

"I kept looking to see if other boys were crooked like Billy," Olivia said. "Except for helping them I remained on the straight and narrow. I know I was wrong."

"Don't, Mom," Omaha said. "I know all about it."

"You do?"

"The Kleenex box on the piano."

"Oh," Olivia said a bit startled. "Okay. We won't talk about that, then."

"No, we won't."

"Okay."

"So theoretically my name should really be Omaha Bigelow Clinton."

"That's correct."

"Why Omaha?"

"Oh, we went up to Nebraska for a football game," Olivia said. "The Razorbacks were playing the Cornhuskers. We wandered off and went to a motel. That's when I told him that we were going to have a baby. He suggested that either way, boy or girl, we should name you Omaha."

"No kidding?" Omaha said.

"Really," Olivia replied, sadly. "He said that we would go on and have lots more children and name them Fargo, Detroit, Tuscaloosa, Valdosta, and like that because he loved America so much. And he does. Your father really loves the people of the United States. So you have nothing to feel ashamed about, Omaha Bigelow Clinton. You can hold your head up because you come from good American stock. Don't ever forget that. This doesn't mean that you should broad-cast this and cause your father further embarrassment. He has his plate full with his eight years under severe scrutiny and now throwing his lot in with the Negroes."

"I won't, Mom," Omaha said, his life suddenly cast in a different light.

"Can I ask you something, son?"

"Sure."

"Do you think I would've made a good First Lady?"

"Mama, I think you would've been a top-flight First Lady," Omaha said. "A truly wonderful First Lady. You would've given recitals at the White House and invited musicians to jam with you and the president. It would've been wonderful. It would've been a truly swinging White House."

"I know," Olivia said, wistfully. "Choices. A person makes choices."

"Mom?"

"Yes, son."

"Thank you."

"Don't mention it," she said. "Maybe I should've told you sooner."

"It's okay. I'm glad you didn't. I've had a chance to mature. Maybe I wouldn't have been able to handle it before. I've stopped drinking and doing drugs."

"That's good. There's a time for everything, I guess," said Olivia Bigelow, still a little weepy. "It takes a while for a person to come to her senses, and then you're old."

They said goodnight and Saturday Omaha and Maruquita flew back to New York. On the flight back Maruquita chattered away and Omaha listened absently, thinking about his pedigree and what this new information meant. He wondered if he should tell Winnifred when he got back. He better not. She was from Republican stock and no matter how liberal she was and how much resentment she might feel toward her parents, this information might cause problems. Fuck, he thought. This was really cool. No wonder he had musical talent.

I F THANKSGIVING AT OLIVIA BIGELOW'S WAS A MODEST ALTHOUGH OFFBEAT affair, the same could not be said of what took place at the Connecticut estate of Winnifred Buckley's family. The five Buckley children came from near and far, the married ones bringing their spouses and children. The Sag Harbor house had been closed for the winter, the caretaker and his wife remaining in their house on the property, ready to open the guest cottage and make it ready for use during the winter, which happened when someone wanted to get away to recall happier summer days, when innocence ruled. Should that someone choose to brave those winter Long Island Sound waters, a small twenty-foot sailboat lay lonely in the water near the private Buckley dock. The other Buckley yachts, the racing sloop *Concordia* and the stately ketch *Perseverance*, had been dry-docked. The larger hundred-and-ten-foot three-masted schooner, *The Puritan,* which at one time had plied, in trade, the waters from Jamaica to Boston, had been sent, with its year-round crew, to Palm Beach after the end of the hurricane season. There appears to be no truth to the malicious intimations of Afrocentrists that the good ship *Puritan* was a slaver and had brought thousands of unfortunates from the coast of West Africa to these American shores. I'm going to catch hell from the left. Let me explain. I'm not defending this family nor what it represents in its considerable power in contrast to the plight of African Americans. I simply don't have time to research the provenance of this allegation. Perhaps it is true. It sounds like more political rhetoric.

But concerning political rhetoric and entanglements, it is well-known that one of the sports of the left is to surmise that everything of a sinister nature that happens in the United States is caused by two entities. Either the Mafia is behind it or the malfeasance can be directly traced to the WASPs. I have to inform you that there is some truth in this. More serious yet is the fact that Winnifred Buckley, herself a White Anglo Saxon Protestant, may be the one person most responsible for what happened on September 11, when the twin towers of the World Trade Center were caused to collapse by insane people who crashed jetliners into them. There! I've gone and tackled the taboo subject. I'm not saying she was in league with the hijackers or knew about their plans, but sure as God created Starbucks, her machinations to ensnare Omaha Bigelow created waves that reached all the way into the White House and eventually caused the tragedy. This is serious. Far-fetched? Keep your eye on the ball and let me continue. You will be amazed at the complexity of this tale.

But first to a modern Thanksgiving in America. As it had been for years at the Buckley home, tradition reigned, and although none of the men were dressed in buckle shoes, long brown coats, and big hats, nor the women attired in black dresses with white collars, aprons, and caps, the atmosphere was one that reverently recalled that day in 1621 when the Pilgrims sat down to give thanks for the bounty of this great land. On that occasion the Wampanoag Indians were present, bringing with them to the celebration fish, fowl, and vegetables. At this gathering to commemorate the year 2000 Thanksgiving there were no Indians present at the Buckley home, although there was one sort of dusky young person, perhaps representing the memory of the Indians of that November day more than 350 years ago.

The food that was served at this feast was beyond culinary reproach. In 1621 the Wampanoag brought sea bass, lobster, and other seafood. They brought wild turkey and beans, corn, squashes, pumpkins, and other native vegetables. At this modern feast no fish or other seafood was served. Everyone knows that seafood is an aphrodisiac. Just the aroma of seafood alone is reminiscent of sex. We are, after all, from the sea, squirmy, pleasantly slimy, and wet. Have you looked closely at the structure and liquidity of clams and oysters? Come on. The Buckley clan was already sexually vital enough not to need further libidinous prodding. I'm Puerto Rican. I know about these things. Although these folks, descended from staid and repressed Pilgrims, seem extremely sedate, they are sexual maniacs just like Puerto Ricans. Don't get me started. The only difference between us is that they can afford to have as many children as they want. We can't. They breed like rabbits, and just the aroma of a tuna fish sandwich makes them horny. Our thing is *bacalao,* codfish.

So no seafood. Turkey, potatoes, giblet gravy, candied yams with marshmallows, squash, corn, cranberries, Indian pudding, pumpkin pie, mincemeat pie, ice creams, and delicate wines and ciders for the adults and juices, soft drinks, and milk for the children. No less than six turkeys had been prepared, half of them stuffed with *hayabunga,* the corn stuffing of the Indians. In the true American spirit of unity and Thanksgiving the entire family descended on the palatial home, its twenty bedrooms replete with this sexually overactive collection. In the interest of family harmony Amanda and Pierce Buckley, at least in name, became a couple again and presided over the gathering. Pierce's mother, Abigail, acted as emeritus head of the family.

Winnifred was moderately happy to see her big sister, Margaret, her husband Baxter, and their children, Baxter Griswold IV, whom he called Eye Vee, and Grace and Felicity. She was also mildly enthusiastic to see her handsome and successful big brothers, Pierce III, Drake, and Creighton, the three with their wives Heather, Samantha, and Ashley, and each with their five children in tow. Fifteen of them, together with Muffy's three, all but one indistinguishable in their blondness and wholesomeness. The only child who was different was an olive-skinned girl of ten with dark eyes and black hair. Officially she was explained as a genetic anomaly caused by the ancestry of a Spanish grandee in the Buckley genealogy. In fact she was the daughter, after an illicit coupling, of Samantha Wilton Buckley, wife to Drake. Sam, as she was called, had had a brief liaison with one Giovanni Escarole, a South Boston tough, while she and Drake were living in Cambridge and Drake was getting his MBA from Harvard Business School. A few meetings in a motel near Revere Beach and Samantha was *enceinte*. Drake, at the time deep in his studies and subsequently the CEO of a dot.com outfit which provides digital imaging to capture extraterrestrial visits, did not notice Angela's dark hair and Mediterranean aura until she was seven years old, when he came home one day and with a deep frown asked Sam if she had dyed the girl's hair. Sam shook her head and Drake said, *Oh, okay* and headed for his computer.

The eighteen children, ranging in age from three to twelve, scampered through the mansion, watching television, playing video games, hide and go seek, and other more intricate games of political espionage at which they were all quite adept. Of all the children, none was more formidable than eleven-year-old Browning Chase Buckley, son to Creighton, who had inherited his paternal grandfather's prodigious genital size and sexual appetite. Although he was slight of physique, socially shy, and bespectacled, it was common knowledge that during the past year he had devirginated no less than a dozen upper-form girls from three prestigious preparatory schools. Further rumor had it that he had also performed this same ritual on frosh coeds at Vassar, Bryn Mawr, Smith, and Barnard. There was no need for condoms since it's common knowledge that HIV does not attack WASPs. Furthermore, Browning was not yet seminal, so there was no fear of pregnancy. The eager young women flocked to him at parties as if he were the wizard Harry Potter, whom he resembled, and they wished to ride his magical broom.

While Winnifred was superficially happy to see everyone, in a deeper place in her life she felt empty and depressed. She missed Omaha Bigelow desperately and felt jealous that this Jennifer Lopez look-alike, Marsuckita Whatever, was off in the Heartland visiting the mother of her beloved. Oh, she could die from the feelings of vengeance that she wanted to rain on this harpy. She couldn't wait to get her grandmother alone and quiz her on what she should do to counteract the witchery of her rival. She did not want Omaha living with that linguistic disaster anymore. Omaha should be with *her*, not with someone else. Winnie and Omaha 4 Ever, she thought childishly and had a powerful urge to get cans of spray paint in different colors and spray a heart with their names inside it. She wanted him with her. All the time, damnit. He was hers, not that Puerto Rican's. Oh, she was so angry. She had put in a bid for John John Kennedy's apartment in Soho, and that is where she and Omaha should live, away from the Puerto Ricans, since they couldn't afford such astronomical prices.

Toward three in the afternoon Winnifred finally got to see Abigail Lindsay Buckley, née Barnstead, mother to her father. She was alone in the library, where she had taken refuge, knowing that her great-grandchildren detested books except for imported British nonsense of dubious wizardry. If she heard one more reference to this Harry Potter, she would have her will redone and leave them all out of it. And the arrogance of the British to even think that they knew anything about magic. Did they really think they were defeated through military strategy and some sort of colonial vox populi? Ha, little did they know that it was witchcraft that had ultimately done them in. Winnifred walked in, approached the large leather-stuffed chair, kissed her grandmother, and asked if she could talk with her.

"Of course, dear," Abigail said, removing her spectacles and closing a book on the mapping of the human genome. "Are you well, Pooh? You seem a little troubled."

"I'm okay, Nana," Winnifred said.

"You're not, are you?"

"Well, no," Winnifred said, and dissolved into tears as she sank into another large chair beside Abigail. "I'm miserable."

"Is it a man, Pooh?"

"Yes, Nana, it is. He lives with another woman, and I want him for the rest of my life. He's my soulmate. I'm so heartsick."

"How can I help you, Winnifred?"

"You're going to think that I'm crazy, but I want to learn everything you know and defeat this woman. I think Omaha Bigelow is a tremendous talent, and I want to help him achieve his potential."

"Is that his name? Bigelow?"

"Yes, Nana. Bigelow."

"Clocks, tea, or rugs?"

"None of them, Nana. He's very poor."

"Oh, dear. How tragic to be without financial resources."

"But he went to Yale."

"That's different," Abigail Bigelow said, sitting up straighter. "A Yale degree will always get you places. Look at our president."

"I know, but can you help me?"

"I think so. You're bright and a quick learner. Can you come up to the Cape for three months or so?"

"I can't, Nana," Winnifred said. "I'm in law school and we're in preproduction for Omaha's film."

"I see. Your father told me about the film. May I ask you something? Confidentially."

"Sure, Nana."

"Is your father seeing another woman?"

"Not that I know of," Winnifred said, without batting an eyelash. She felt a bit of pleasure knowing that she had information and did not have to reveal it. She didn't feel that she was protecting anyone but storing facts for use at a future time. This delighted her. "It's inconceivable, Nana."

"Harrumph," said Abigail Buckley. "I've heard rumors that he has developed an unnatural desire for Negroes."

"Grandma!" Winnifred said, feigning shock. "How could you think such a thing!"

"We *are* related to the Jeffersons. He was quite something. All his Negro children, you know."

"Yes, I know. But can you help me?"

"Well, I don't know how this will work, but give me your e-mail address."

"I'll write it down for you, Grandma. It's WinniePooh1@aol.com," Winnifred said happily.

"Oh, that's darling, Pooh," Abigail said. "I'm WitchyPooh07@aol.com."

"Wait, you're going to teach me witch stuff through e-mail?"

"Yep, and on IM if you'd like."

"Sure, Nana. Oh, that's fantastic."

"Well, you'll have to get a good firewall so that this information doesn't get out. You don't want our accounts hacked."

"Oh, okay. No problem."

And so it went. Winnifred Bigelow was overjoyed. She couldn't believe how truly fortunate she was. Throughout the dinner she was talkative and effusive, understanding of the children's silliness, her siblings' concerns, and her parents' obvious deceit in appearing to like each other. During the weekend she slept soundly and took long walks alone through the estate as she pondered how to extricate Omaha Bigelow from his predicament. She had no doubts that this witchery of Marsuckita, as she now called her rival, was real. She had a further consultation with her grandmother, and Abigail Buckley explained that although transformation into animals was something she was also able to do, it appeared that the people she described had mastered the technique and could prove to be formidable opponents. It didn't matter, Winnifred thought. She would learn all there was and defeat them in order to free Omaha from their clutches. How could Caribbean wizardry compare with that of the United States?

WHILE PIERCE BUCKLEY THOUGHT IT WOULD BE WONDERFUL IF
Dakulana Imbebwabe, Pierce Buckley's six-foot, cobalt-colored para-
mour, could have attended the Thanksgiving celebration, they both
agreed her presence at the Buckley home would have been highly inappropriate and unsettling to his mother, his wife, and his children. Additionally, she
explained that she had been called to Paris for a briefing concerning new developments in the Middle East. As an important cultural representative of her
homeland of the Ivory Coast, she was a deep operative for the French Sûreté.
She explained that the French intelligence service was onto something concerning the Middle East and wanted to brief her. Pierce asked her if it was likely that she would be given an assignment. Dakulana nodded gravely as she finished undressing and glanced admiringly at Pierce, who had shed his clothing
and was waiting for her on the bed of his pied-à-terre in the Trump Towers in
Manhattan. The week before Thanksgiving, Dakulana had flown to Paris.
From there she'd gone back to West Africa and her home in Côte d'Ivoire to
see her parents in the capital of Abidjan. She would remain there for a month
and spend Noel with them as they celebrated the commemoration of the birth
of the Child Jesus in French fashion. Additionally, she would meet with French
undercover agents to plan a mission that had been given top secret status by
the Sûreté.

As a service to Americans, who, it often seems, can learn geography only
by bombing places, here is a bit of information on the capital of the Ivory
Coast. It was extracted from the Encyclopedia Britannica. I bought the CD
and have had no other use for it, so here goes:

> Abidjan, chief port, capital, and largest city of Côte d'Ivoire (Ivory Coast).
> It lies along the Ébrié Lagoon, which is separated from the Gulf of Guinea
> and the Atlantic by the Vridi Plage sandbar. A village in 1898, it became a
> town in 1903. Abidjan was a rail terminus from 1904 but had to depend
> on the meagre facilities of Port-Bouët on the sandbar's ocean shore. It suc-

ceeded Bingerville as capital of the French colony in 1934 and retained that position after independence in 1960. Districts within the city include Plateau, Cocody (site of the National University of Côte d'Ivoire), Treichville, Adjame, Koumassi, and Marcory.

The Vridi Canal opened the lagoon to the sea in 1950, and the city soon became the financial centre of French-speaking West Africa. The first of two bridges linking the mainland to Petit-Bassam Island was built in 1958. Abidjan's modern deepwater port exports coffee, cocoa, timber, bananas, pineapples, and manganese. From the administrative and business sectors on the mainland, the city stretches southward to the industrial area on Petit-Bassam and the mineral and petroleum docks along the Vridi Canal. There are a number of wide, shady streets and gardened squares in the city; the university (1958) lies on the eastern mainland. Abidjan has a museum of traditional Ivorian art, a national library, and several agricultural and scientific research institutes. The city is a communications centre and the site of an international airport (at Port-Bouët, an autonomous municipality within Abidjan). North of the city is Banco National Park, a magnificent tropical rain forest. Pop. (1990 est.) 2,168,000.

I've provided this information so that people who read this account can learn about geography and don't get the urge to bomb other places. Please don't bomb these people. Although many of them are Francophones, they don't present a threat to the United States. Look, they are in Africa but they have a university, a museum, a national library, and many other neat things. Please don't bomb them. Okay, they speak French, but they're really cool people. And they have wonderful dances. They do not represent a threat to the United States. Other countries may, but not Côte d'Ivoire, okay? I mean, French is also spoken other places: Morocco, Algeria, Mali, Senegal, Martinique, and Haiti. Don't try to pin me down about which of these countries fall into the category of a threat to the stability of the United States. I don't know which countries specifically present a threat to the United States. I'm not pointing fingers or naming any countries. I don't know, okay! Why are you bugging me about these things? All right, already. You're making me feel guilty. Maybe some contiguous Latin American country creeping up on the U.S. Southern border and sneaking coyotelike into the United States to take lettuce-picking jobs away from good Americans could be considered a threat. Maybe those people. I'm not going to say their name. I'm just speculating. I don't know.

Maybe Puerto Rico represents a threat to the United States, but please stop bombing us. We're not that big a threat. Puerto Rico is a really small place. You can obtain a map of the country quite easily. The capital is San Juan. It's so small that my CD version of the Britannica is not able to provide me with an outline of Puerto Rico. Puerto Rico is also a colony of the United States, so it's a very cooperative country, and although quite small, because of the United States's influence, it behaves as if it were a major world power. It only has 3.7 million people, but it is the fifth-largest importer of American goods in the world. The larger body in this diminutive archipelago, the island of Puerto Rico, is only a hundred miles by thirty-five miles with nice beaches, piña coladas, *paso fino* horses, and girls with cute butts. In keeping with this genetic trait, the country has produced something like five Miss Universes in the last twenty years, as well as fantastic baseball players. A smaller island called Vieques is being bombed periodically by the U.S. Navy even though Puerto Ricans have done nothing to the United States except to provide it with its status as a colonial power.

I will offer a hint if the United States promises not to bomb the rest of Puerto Rico. I will now reveal certain things that will indicate why Puerto Rico should not be bombed. I'm not going to be explicit, but you can draw your own conclusions. For example: Puerto Rico has more universities than many bigger countries. In fact, Puerto Rico is so studious that it has the highest per capita number of college graduates in this hemisphere and possibly the world. I'm not kidding. It's true. Most people can't get jobs there, so they leave and come to the United States. In some cases they take jobs away from Americans, since they're better prepared and hungrier. The jobs are not lettuce-picking jobs. Puerto Rico may represent a threat in that regard. Many people, however, stay there, on the island, and sit around discussing modernism, abstract expressionism, the Human Genome Project, the conductivity of plastics, and other harmless subjects. Sometimes they go to Burger King or K-Mart. So don't bomb Puerto Rico, and stop bombing Vieques, please. Don't bomb anyone. You can't make people drink Coca Cola and listen to country music if they don't want to.

Anyway, Dakulana Imbebwabe went home to be with her parents during late November and December. Around the first of the year she would return to her flat in London and there await Pierce Buckley's visit on his way to meet with several Euromart officials, concerning the euro, the new monetary unit. Maybe they would see a few plays and visit with Dakulana's East Village lesbian playwright friend in London before going to La Costa del Sol for a few weeks. There is no need to infer that this lesbian friend and Dakulana are or were lovers. As far as I know, Dakulana is not bisexual, although she often shops for shoes with her friend, whose initials are PN and that is all I'll say. I have never met her friend, and my information comes directly from Dakulana because she trusts me. In spite of my insignificant status, I have developed some contacts.

So that I'm not accused of creating characters gratuitously, let me explain that it would have been an even greater affront to the unity of the Thanksgiving feast at the Buckleys if Amanda's lover had been invited. Amanda "Bootsie" Buckley's lover, Ahmed Gaziozhari, returned to his father's sultanate on the Arabian Sea after the playing of the World Series. He was madly in love with Bootsie, and upset that the Mets had lost to the Yankees. He was also puzzled as to why Mike Piazza didn't knock Roger Clemens down to the ground and stab him in the heart with the broken bat that Clemens threw at him. Fat vampire bastard. I tried to explain to Ahmed that stabbing people in the heart or any part of their anatomy was not part of baseball. He was disappointed. Fine, I have Arab friends. I also go to Atlantic Avenue in Brooklyn and eat Middle Eastern food. I should be watched as a dangerous person. Anyway, I root for both the Yankees and the Mets, and my loyalties are torn. It's the same as my love for the U.S. and for Puerto Rico.

Sadly, geopolitics is not the same as baseball. It could be, but it's not yet so. Let me explain. Ahmed was also angry at his failure to master an understanding of baseball. I know. In your need for sensationalism about terrorists, you would like me to say that Ahmed, because he is an Arab, went to the Middle East, reported to Osama bin Laden, and explained that he is learning to fly jetliners to crash into tall U.S. buildings. That was not the case.

Ahmed was too busy with understanding baseball and feeling Bootsie Buckley shivering in delight beneath him and saying Oh, God. Lately she was repeating Allah's name, and he didn't know whether this was within proper behavior for a woman while submitting to the act. That it sounded like Ooh Lah Lah annoyed Ahmed because, like Americans, he intensely disliked the French. The poor French! They'll never live down their predilection for Jerry Lewis and for Maurice Chevalier's singing the praises of little girls.

And yet more than Bootsie Buckley's multiple orgasms it was baseball that consumed Ahmed's every waking hour. Such a placid sport. All that grass in the outfield. Ahmed had unlimited wealth and influence in high places. He planned on using his wealth and influence to contact Bud Selig, the Commissioner of Major League Baseball, and suggest that perhaps each outfielder could have his own sheep to keep him company out there. It had to be lonely, standing and waiting to have a ball hit to them. Often the ball was hit either in front of them, to their right or left, or over their heads. The batters, it seemed, were doing this on purpose. They had no compassion for the outfielders. Sometimes the batters hit the ball completely over the fence and gave the outfielders no opportunity of catching it. Cruelly, and with no regard for the lonely outfielders, people in the stands cheered happily when this happened, especially at home. What kind of hosts were these people if they enjoyed torturing their guests this way? Maybe Mr. Selig would permit a small tent in each of the fields, for the outfielders to stay out of the sun in the day and the cool of the evening during night games. Baseball was a very American game, complex but relaxed. They had bases, in theory symbols of the military might of the U.S. And of course home plate was in the shape of The Pentagon, a delicate sublimation of force. During the game players sat in bunkers from which they launched their strategic attacks.

Ahmed was certain that if he could understand the game, he could bring it back to the Middle East and convince the Israelis and the Palestinians to play baseball instead of trying to wipe each other out. Of course they would need to make certain modifications to adapt baseball to the area. You couldn't expect men of dignity to wear those silly little caps instead of proper headgear. Maybe a nice checkered kaffiyeh, a head scarf held together by an *agal,* the tassel that held the scarf in place, always in the team's colors. He was sure he could get Derek Jeter, who was from Detroit, which has a larger Arab population than many cities in the Middle East, to model the new uniforms. Jeter looked very much like a Tunisian or Moroccan. It would also be foolish that players be expected to run in the desert heat. Camels would be provided for each runner to get from one base to the other. The distance from one base to the next would have to be lengthened, and instead of the white square at each base, there could be a small oasis with palm trees, water, and a tent with a few dancing girls inside for the players to rest and find an outlet for their pent-up emotions.

Needless to say, there would be no stealing, otherwise off came a hand, and how could you field, throw and hit with a missing hand? Well, there had been one player with only one hand, but it was a bit awkward. So no stealing. Ahmed wanted nothing but to truly understand the game. He was aware that it was complex and that average Americans had no clue about the intricacies of its rules. He had heard that not even all major-league players understood the game completely and were hard-pressed to explain the infield-fly rule. Ahmed sympathized with them, because it's very difficult to spot a fly more than a few feet away. Hitting one with a batted ball was nearly impossible. Of course with the addition of sheep in the outfield, there could be more flies on the field, and hitting one wouldn't be as difficult.

Also, it irked Ahmed that arguing about balls and strikes or other calls on the field flared up, and the umpires always had the final word. There was entirely too much arguing in baseball, with hardly ever a resolution. He didn't mind the haggling, which is commonplace in any souk or marketplace in the Middle East, but nothing ever came of the encounters. In order to resolve this issue, he would also suggest to Mr. Selig that players should be able to bargain with umpires on their calls. Out or safe. Strike or ball. Fair or foul. A ball caught or not caught. How could they be sure? The players earned so much more money than the umpires, so why shouldn't an umpire be offered a few dinari, rials, dollars, or maybe some stock options, to change his mind? There was no harm in that. He realized that a game, if played according to his rules, could last eight or ten hours. However, he would argue that a good deal of money could be made during that time in food and drink. This would be good for the small-market baseball teams. Why not introduce a little shish kebab, pilaf, falafel, and babaganoush to what you could buy at a stadium? There would already be sheep out there in the outfield. Why not have a roasting spit out in the bullpen? There were no cattle out there. And then again, why shouldn't there be? Why have a bullpen and no prime rib? He had been to the stadium in Baltimore and seen the smoke rising behind the right-field wall, and the smell of barbecue had wafted to him as he sat in a VIP box. He had many suggestions for Mr. Selig.

In Ahmed's defense it should be understood that he was also a bit of a visionary. Ahmed would return to the United States and continue to study and work on his "Baseball Training and Peace Proposal for Establishing a Lasting Serenity and Tranquillity in the Middle East." He envisioned the Middle East Major Baseball League. Teams in Baghdad, Aman, Cairo, Riyadh, Gaza, Damascus, and Tel Aviv to start. He hoped the Israelis wouldn't complain that they had only one team to the Arabs' five. This was the reality of the Middle East. Arabs outnumbered Jews. What was to be done? If the Israelis were adamant about the disparity, he would suggest that Israel could have baseball teams in Tel Aviv and Haifa. Also, for the sake of harmony and in consideration for Israel, the suicide squeeze would not be permitted in Middle East baseball. Home runs will not be called bombs. Later the League could consider expansion teams like Teheran, Casablanca, Algiers, Khartoum, and Tripoli. Of course there should be time for prayer and other religious observances during the game with mosques and synagogues adjacent to the stadiums. Sadly, there would be no Friday or Saturday baseball, to accommodate Semitic faiths. The schedule would be juggled to permit religious observances on both sides.

His plan was a challenge, but Ahmed promised himself to work tirelessly to make his dream a reality. The only thing that concerned Ahmed was the advantage that the Palestinians would have. He had seen boys eight or nine years old who could throw rocks with uncanny velocity and accuracy, two stringent requisites in playing baseball. He had even heard that executives for the Chicago Cubs, Baltimore Orioles, and Texas Rangers had sent scouts to talk with the parents of an eleven-year-old who had reputedly thrown a rock with such velocity that it had pierced the armor of an Israeli tank. They had clocked his throws. The speed gun had consistently registered in the 120 mph range. They got him to fire a baseball from about 65 feet, and he only was able to get up to about to 112 mph. They presented a very good deal to the family, but the boy didn't want to go to America and train to become a baseball player. He wanted to grow up and become a martyr. Someday, he said, he would wear dynamite and fight for the liberation of Palestine. What a waste. This had to stop, Ahmed thought. He had to complete his proposal.

Okay, by now you're probably wondering why I'm engaging in this kind of silly digression. Although it appears that the digression is a Latin American novelistic technique, I'm not doing it for that reason. The truth is that this Islamic thing is kind of scary. I don't want to be part of an agenda that says the United States is not at war with Islam when in effect it appears that this is exactly what's taking place. I'm already in hot water with a lot of people. I don't want to piss more people off. I'm obviously being a little bit cowardly and vacillating. I have no need to martyr myself and certainly don't want a *fatwa* issued against me as was done to Salman Rushdie by Iran. *You should be so lucky,* I can hear my detractors say. *Fatwa? Fat chance, buddy!* Frankly, I have no idea how the people who attempted to scare him even understood what Mr. Rushdie was writing about. He's a great stylist, and at least he's not writing about vampires, werewolves, dinosaurs, and submarines. I have to be honest, however. He does get a bit weird sometimes and goes off on these fantastic trips. I wish I had his facility with language, and even though I like his work, I have to confess that I also read him so I can impress mid-forties, sexually needy female literature professors. Notice the gender specific designation of my sexual orientation and subtextual disclaimer. Well?

At this point I feel like extending myself even more in this digression, because it's going to get heavy. I'm hesitant to continue revealing the details of what I've learned concerning certain recent world events. Given the frenzy over the latest developments in the United States: the rounding up of suspects, the curtailing of certain freedoms, the bombing of Afghanistan, the hunt for

Osama bin Laden, and other issues, introducing the details involved may further annoy certain people. However, what is more pertinent to this recounting is that as innocent and fun as all this is, with magical realism and the bending of reality, there are serious issues involved in this narrative.

For example, the fact that Puerto Ricans are in the process of creating their own navy right here in New York City and allegedly have figured out a cloaking device purloined from a Star Trek episode is a serious issue. I've already intimated that when fully operational, the Puerto Rican Navy could sneak up and attack the U.S. Navy at Vieques. This is no laughing matter. A war between the United States and Puerto Rico could make things a little messy, especially for someone like me, who lives here in the United States but was born there. My loyalties are already pretty divided. As I'm writing this, the Mets just traded for Roberto Alomar, who is Puerto Rican. By the way, Alomar is a Moorish name. All family names or the names of things that begin with *Al* in Spanish are Arabic. Some have drifted into English: algebra, almonds, etc. Did you notice that a couple of the 9/11 hijackers are named Alomari? But don't blame Robby for any stuff, okay? He's trying to convince the Mets to sign his buddy, Juan González, another Puerto Rican. González will likely play it safe and sign with the Texas Rangers. Too bad. Then again, his nickname is Igor. New York City is too cruel to pass that up as a joke. Also Jorge Posada and Bernie Williams are on the Yankees, and they're Puerto Rican.

Williams, I don't know about. I mean, he's Puerto Rican, but like we say: *el tipo tiene guille de americano.* He has a serious case of gringosity. I mean, what is it with that number 51 on his back, like he wants Puerto Rico to become a state? You have to know that his name is really Bernabé Figueroa Williams. Figueroa is not a middle name. It is a family name. This is the way it goes with Spanish names. You have your proper name, either one or two, and then your father's last name and your mother's last name. It's not like in the United States, where whatever last name you have is your last name. In Spanish we honor the father and the mother. That's why mailboxes in front of the houses in Puerto Rico have both last names, and people know that the first one is the father and the second the mother. It looks like Bernie is really Bernie Figueroa, unless his father's name is really Williams and he put his mother's name in the middle. I don't think so. I hate to get picky and bust chops, but U.S. hegemony and the need to homogenize everyone really annoys me. For example, Gabriel García Márquez and Federico García Lorca both had fathers with the last name García and mothers with Márquez and Lorca as maiden names. In the U.S. these two writers are known by most people as Márquez and Lorca. I don't care. That they have distinctive mother's names is great, and that they're known by their feminine side is a great honor for the mother, even though that was her father's name. So now we have to address male dominance, which is too long a digression. Anyway, I found something from the Internet which shows conclusively that Bernie should be Figueroa and not Williams.

It's sad to say, but Bernabe Figueroa's death may have saved his son's season. Williams just isn't a .221 hitter.

In another place on the internet I found this:

Bernabe Figueroa, father of Yankees outfielder Bernie Williams, died in Bayamon, a suburb of San Juan, Puerto Rico, following a heart attack. He was 73.

Why did Williams choose to be known as Williams instead of Figueroa? Maybe he wants to be accepted as more American, so Bernie Williams sounds cooler than Bernie Figueroa. Whatever, Bernie. Keep the politics out of baseball. Well, maybe I'm not cool in bringing it up. Maybe Ahmed Gaziozhari is not cool in attempting to use baseball to solve political problems in the Middle East. In any case, quit bombing P.R., okay?

FTER VISITING HIS MOTHER, OMAHA BIGELOW RETURNED TO THE
East Village inspired. Being the son of a man who has been president
of the United States filled him with a sense of accomplishment far
greater than he had ever imagined. He understood more clearly why he had
always felt a kind of regal sense about his person. It wasn't a feeling of being
part of an elite but more akin to having a special mission to accomplish. It was
a kind of overwhelming benevolence and a desire to help others, such as that
exhibited by his father. He now felt expansive and as if he were part of a group
of larger-than-life human beings on the planet who rated special attention.
Whenever people spoke to him, he smiled kindly and nodded. He was certain
that recognition would eventually come to him. The making of his film,
indeed his entire life, took on a different meaning. He thought that it was
important to find a metaphor for the central character of his film. Did his
character represent the United States? This character, who was autobiographical but at once a fictional creation, must have a greater mission as well.

And yet, what was that mission? he thought as he sat in Tompkins Square
Park and pondered the question. People stopped by, looked at him, wondering at his state as he sat in deep contemplation. Some Buddhist remarked that
he resembled Shakyamuni sitting under the Bodhi tree moments before he
achieved enlightenment. Astrologers said he had all his planets aligned and his
moon and sun had converged and he was in astral flight. A young woman
commented to her girlfriend that it looked like he was doing Reiki exercises and
sending the energy to Kosovo. Spiritualists said he was attempting to contact
Mother Teresa, Mahatma Gandhi, and Martin Luther King in order to get guidance about the world situation. Some people visiting from California remarked
that his aura was awesome. Squatters from the area were sure he was high.

It is imperative in a situation such as the one we have on our hands with
Omaha Bigelow to examine the issues on different levels. Besides the sociopolitical and psychological, philosophical and symbolic levels, there is another

with even greater significance if we are to understand the peculiarities of his character. I'm referring to the matter of hubris. The dictionary describes hubris as wanton arrogance, overbearing pride, or presumption. The word comes to us from the Greek, where, along with Latin, a good number of complex words in the English language have their roots. a word like *xenophobia*—dislike of strangers or foreigners, and *ethnocentrism*, the notion that one's own group, race, or culture is the best and gives one the right to measure other people by those standards—is another example of the Greek and Latin influences on the English language. The use of these two words as examples is not necessarily connected to other ideas, such as bombing places in order to learn geography, but they could be.

In truth, the application of hubris pertains to persons of consequence and not regular people like you and me. If we make mistakes we're usually punished by overdraft letters, eviction notices, or messages on our phone answering machines from really cool chicks telling us they just want to be friends. Kings, heads of state such as presidents, prime ministers, and politicians fall into this category of people of consequence. A second tier, composed of CEOs of large corporations, film and rock personalities, and superstar sports figures can suffer this malady as well. There is another tier for people like us, but we're usually explained away as schmucks. Some people who are done in by hubris handle it well, and others do not. Of course what happens on a grander scale affects little people as well. Seeing the downfall of the mighty, we guard against excessive bragging and displays of arrogance. Admonishments like "Don't you get too big for your britches, mister" or "Man, you're letting your ego get in the way" are leveled at people like us when we get a little too much. Sometimes a display of such arrogance is dealt with by dismissing the person with the word *asshole*, a stinging, albeit temporary, commentary on character. I don't want to use this word for those people who might complain that I should be concerned with advancing the plot, and forget attempting to create literary references and use the novel to advance knowledge. Oh, sure, the novel should be used solely to entertain and help people be even more empty-headed than they already are. Hey, just shut up! It's important to keep literature alive and not let readers be hoodwinked by a marketplace that is simply interested in taking their money and giving them Mickey Mouse crap.

There are components to hubris. For example, *hamartia*, or a person's tragic flaw, is one of them. In other words, hamartia is something in the person's character that prevents that person from seeing himself clearly enough to prevent his hubris from tripping him up. The Greeks loved instructing their citizens through theater, to help them guard against angering the gods. Theater, in many ways, was a means of religious instruction and observance. That it's used these days merely to entertain seems a pity. In one of the most famous Greek plays, *Oedipus Rex* by Sophocles, Laius, King of Thebes, is told by an oracle that his son will grow up and kill him. Fearful for his life, he and his wife Jocasta give the baby to a shepherd with instructions to abandon their son in the wild, hoping he will be killed by wolves or starve to death. The baby wasn't named Oedipus. I don't know his original name. Maybe Aristotle or maybe Thucydides. Maybe they called him Yanni, like the Greek guy with the long hair, the orchestra, and the elevator music. Instead, the shepherd gives the nameless child to another shepherd, who brings the baby to the King of Corinth. Oedipus is raised by that king and his wife.

He grows up, and during a gathering he is called a bastard by someone. He goes to Delphi, another nearby city, and consults the oracle there. He learns from the oracle that he will eventually kill his father and sleep with his mother. An oracle is like watching CNN. You get a lot of news but you really can't do much about it, since we're at the mercy of the gods and of producers, who are like gods.

Seeking to avoid the tragedy of killing his father and boinking his mother, Oedipus didn't even go back to Corinth but went on to Thebes, where there are many cool things going on and the city has loads of *koritizi* in short skirts who smile a lot and have nice butts. It hasn't helped the reputation of the Greeks that boys (*agouri*) also wore short skirts and had nice butts. Wouldn't you book if you knew patricide and incest awaited you at home? One day you come down for breakfast, your father says something weird, you bop him on the head with a two-by-four, and turn to your mother and say, "Let's go to a motel." Not a pretty HBO special. It sort of gives the word *motherfucker* a more classical, intellectual, and acceptable sound, but it's still pretty nasty. Eventually every son kills his father with disappointment and, in order to work things out with his mother, marries someone just like her. It rarely works out well.

On the way to Thebes, Oedipus gets into a fight with a man and kills him. Oedipus doesn't know that this man is the King of Thebes, in other words, his real father. He continues on to Thebes, arrives there, there's an opening for a king, he ingratiates himself with the court, and eventually marries his mother, Jocasta, and becomes king. Again, Oedipus doesn't know that Jocasta is his mother. I know, it would be pretty disgusting to marry your mother if she looked momserly like Shelley Winters. This is theater, so you have to imagine that the son is someone like Brad Pitt and the mother is Sharon Stone, forty-ish but still a fine-looking babe. Believe me, I would wash her panties in Woolite any time she wanted me to. I saw her with James Lipton on his Actors Studio Bravo interview series and not only did she look like a *tremenda mami*, but she was brilliant. Some people think she's a dummy, but that is one bright lady. You go, girl.

As the tragedy progresses, Oedipus has four children with Jocasta, his mother. Things are going pretty well and then a plague hits Thebes killing children, animals, and crops. Again we tune in to CNN and learn from Christiane Amanpour on assignment in Thebes that the plague has been caused by a terrible sin. "Well, Paula," says Christiane in her British accent, as she answers the ever-saccharine Ms. Zahn on the morning shift, "it is after dark here in Thebes, and although things appear calm there is a good deal of unrest in the city. The king, Oedipus, sent his brother-in-law, Creon, to Delphi to consult with the oracle. Creon has returned to Thebes and in executive session has informed Oedipus and his cabinet that the plague is being caused by a murder that has gone unpunished. In a radio and television address Oedipus has promised to save Thebes. He has named a head of Domestic Security, placed a curse on the evildoer, and has posted a twenty-five-million-dollar reward for his capture dead or alive. Everyone is excited, and even Geraldo Rivera has gone looking for him. From Thebes in the Greek mountains this is Christiane Amanpour reporting. Back to you, Paula."

By the way, Christiane is also a hell of a babe. Besides Charlize Theron and Jennifer Lopez, she and Sharon Stone are my favorite women in the whole wide world. I think Rym Brahimi of CNN is truly beautiful. If I were a girl, I'd want to be just like Christiane and Sharon. Or maybe Rebecca Lobo, who is like six foot five and cute, or maybe Robin Roberts from ESPN, who also played basketball and is superfine. Cammie Granato from the USA Women's Olympic Ice Hockey is also cute even wearing all those pads. And while I'm at it, so is that curly-haired amazon midfielder, Michelle Akers, from the USA Women's Soccer team. Also Gigi Fernandez, who plays tennis; Katarina Witt, the skater; and also Anneka Sorenstam, the golfer. I obviously like big healthy girls. Wait, I forgot Anna Kournikova and Hannah Storm, now at NBC. Anyway, when I think about it, the list gets longer and longer. Kristi Yamaguchi, the Nipponese-American ice-skating princess, has to be on the list. She is awesome. While I'm in the area of women who have an epicanthic fold, please put Tina Chen on there as well. This is much too much information about the author. Okay, more discipline. You think I'm using Omaha

Bigelow to work out my fantasies about multiple relationships. Hahaha! You think you're perceptive. How cute!

What happens in the play is that word comes that Oedipus's stepfather has died in Corinth, and Oedipus is now CEO of both Thebes *and* Corinth. He is relieved that he will not kill his father. He does worry that Laius, the ex-king of Thebes, has been killed at the place where three roads meet, where he did in some schmuck who told him to get out of the way. He seeks the counsel of an oxymoronic blind seer, Tiresias, who says the transgression is much greater than murder. Oedipus gets very unhinged and banishes the blind guy. Jocasta tries to reassure Oedipus by telling him that oracles are superstitions and that she and her husband had been told by an oracle that their son would kill his father. They had disposed of their baby and he had died in the wild, and her husband had been killed by thieves where the three roads meet. How accurate can oracles be? she chuckles. That's like listening to Lou Dobbs on CNN's *Money Line*. He's got nice lacquered hair, but who can understand the stock market? Oh, that reminds me. Put Willow Bay on the list. She is a lollipop. She's married to Michael Eisner, the head of Disney, so I have to be extra careful in case Hyperion Books might consider publishing this book. Hyperion is owned by Disney. Every important publishing house is owned by some large multinational. No wonder so much crap gets published. I know. I'm not doing myself any good, and my agent will probably want to kill me.

Eventually the shepherd who had originally taken the baby Oedipus to Corinth comes and reveals that the baby did not die but grew up as the son of the King of Corinth. Oedipus finally understands that he has killed his father and has seeded his mother with his own siblings. This did not happen in some obscure holler in Appalachia but in the cradle of western civilization. Scary, right?

Another aspect of Greek tragedy as it pertains to hubris is *anagnoresis*, or the recognition that, in the vernacular of the street, the dude fucked up. In Oedipus's case it is the revelation that he's wiped out his real dad and bedded his mom. The third aspect of hubris is called *peripitia*, or a reversal of fortune. From being king, Oedipus is now despised by the people. He loses everything. Having seen too much too late, he gouges out his eyes. To add to his suffering, he is exiled from Thebes. Lastly, the release of tension at the end of the play is called *katharsis*, a word with which people who've had therapy are familiar. In other words, *katharsis* is the release of emotion when you see Brad Pitt realize that he's killed Richard Dreyfus and has gone to bed with Sharon Stone. We almost had *katharsis* in the O. J. Simpson thing, when he was trying to make a getaway. But it didn't happen. Simpson stood trial. He learned that the

American judicial system has advantages if you can afford to pay for adequate legal help. If you're aristocracy, you get away with things and keep your money. If you're of the meritocracy, as Simpson prominently was, you can get away with the crime but they'll take your money. Simpson was acquitted of murder, but there was a civil suit and he had to pay. Instead of *katharsis* there is now mystery and distraction, which Americans embrace with more enthusiasm.

Brothers shouldn't get all bent out of shape at me using Simpson as an example. You're going to like what happens to Omaha Bigelow. Just be cool, okay, homes? Put away the blade, man. Damn, why don't you be like Denzel Washington or Wesley Snipes? See how cool they be under pressure? Just chill. Why are there no *negritas* on my list? Scroll up, dude. What does Robin Roberts got? Negro makeup? Oh, okay. I won't use that N word. You plexing up too much. Take that shit up with big-lip Stanley Crouch. He uses the word Negro consistently and with impunity. You don't know about impunity? Look the shit up. Check out your dictionary instead of your dick. Improve your ass and stop whining. Dayum! Let me get back to the shit.

I'm back. Folks is getting out of hand. You think I'm playing with you and this is heading in the direction of hubris catching up to the protagonist? Are we going to see Omaha Bigelow, a young man whom I've grown to like, and for whom you've probably developed a fondness, come crashing down? Maybe. Okay, I won't be cruel. The answer is: Yes! I won't reveal the ending yet because it wouldn't be fair, but you know that Omaha Bigelow can't live happily ever after, given what he's done. Well, I don't know. We'll see. He's already in enough trouble, so you know that something has to give. But the trouble he's in is minor when compared to what's coming. In any case, you can hope that like his father, Omaha will be able to survive his problems. By the way, I'm laying it on kind of heavy on Clinton, but I will deal with his successor in good time. Never you worry. You can't be Bill Clinton's son and not have heavy karma. By the way, most people have no clue what karma is. I'm not going to go into it, but people have no clue. What you do have to know is that Omaha Bigelow had heavy karma.

REFLECTIONS IN A
TARNISHED MIRROR

G IVEN OMAHA BIGELOW'S FULL-BLOWN NARCISSISM CONCERNING HIS *bohango,* it was not surprising that when Carrie Marshack finally caught up with him in Tompkins Square Park on a mild day at the beginning of December, his hubris was beginning to surface and he took another step that would eventually add to his undoing. I'm very sorry. You don't know what narcissism is? You need to study and probably could use counseling of some sort. The word comes once again from the Greek and has to do with a young man in Greek mythology. What? You don't know what mythology is? You do know. Good. Myths are very important, you say? Yes, they are. Whether people want to believe in them is of little importance. They're there to remind us of our folly.

In any case, here's what happened. The story begins with a nymph by the name of Echo. Zeus, who was the chief god of the Greeks, enjoyed seducing young women even though he was married to Hera, the head goddess. Hera suspected that her husband was being unfaithful with Echo. She was about to catch them in the act, but Zeus, being a God, sensed that his wife was approaching. He instructed Echo to tell Hera a story so he could slip away. When Hera confronted Echo with being involved with Zeus and aiding in her husband's unfaithfulness, Echo denied any wrongdoing and began telling Hera a very elaborate and convoluted story. While she told the story, Zeus was able to make his escape. Hera was very angry at Echo's involvement with her husband and her subsequent attempt to deceive her. Being all-powerful, she placed a curse on Echo. Henceforth the nymph could not speak her own words. Instead, the only thing she could do was repeat what other people said. So far so good. You know why we have the word echo? Correct. That is the origin.

Echo went around repeating what she heard. If she heard, "Roast the lamb well," that's what she said. If she heard, "Drink that hemlock, and the game's over," those were the words she spoke. Eventually she became distraught at people scolding her for seemingly mocking them and retired to the woods, hoping to get away from everyone. Enter into the tale a very beautiful young man by the name of Narcissus. One day, while Narcissus was walking in the woods, Echo saw Narcissus and fell madly in love with him. He was the most beautiful young man she had ever seen. Afraid that Narcissus would reject her because she was unable to speak except to repeat others' words, Echo observed him from a short distance. As he walked, Narcissus became thirsty. He leaned over a clear pool and saw his reflection in the crystal-like water. Overcome by his own beauty he said, *I love you.* Surprisingly, the image spoke to him in a clear and delicate woman's voice. *I love you* the voice said back to him. Exactly. It was Echo repeating his words. Narcissus again repeated the words, and again the reflection said, *I love you.* For the better part of the day Narcissus remained staring at his reflection, until he was convinced of the illusion. In time Narcissus fell in love with his own reflection. As many times as he said *I love you,* without fail Echo's sweet and love-filled response came back to him, reassuring Narcissus that indeed his image spoke the truth.

You would like to make a suggestion and cast Gywneth Paltrow and Leonardo DiCaprio as Echo and Narcissus? Also Russell Crowe as Zeus and Nicole Kidman as Hera? Fine, but my intent is not to create a movie. The words *narcissism* and *narcissistic* are applied to people in love with themselves. Artists, actors, politicians, sports stars often fall prey to narcissism. My aim is to perhaps cast some light on the myth as it pertains to the present world situation. In other words, I would like to help the United States examine itself and stop hearing the echo of its own voice proclaiming its greatness and instead begin listening to others, most of whom are friends. You say that this is a little too heavy, too didactic. Perhaps. A little preachy and obscure? Perhaps you're right. Fine, ignore my humanist pleas. It's your country. Okay, let's get back to the things that most Americans understand: sitcoms and canned laughter. Here we go.

Omaha was quite gracious, although a little abstracted at seeing his previous girlfriend. Carrie asked him how he was doing. He explained that he was fine and working again on his film. He had backers, and the writing and composing were going well. He inquired as to her health, and Carrie said she was fine and had broken up with the Russian, explaining that he had met a woman named Tatiana from St. Petersburg and they were going to get married. Igor was lying, of course, and, as Carrie put it, "The Russky bastard knew Tatiana back in Russia and was waiting until she could emigrate." Carrie Marshack didn't seem that upset. Instead she had the same hungry fuck-me look Omaha had learned to recognize in her. He was not only flattered but instantly aroused and eager to show off his *bohango* to Carrie, who had so cruelly kicked him out of her apartment six months ago, when he was at his lowest. She asked him if he had time for a cup of coffee. He smiled understandingly at her and explained that he did but perhaps they ought to go out of the neighborhood.

"I understand," she said, hopefully. "Where would you like to go?"

"Let's walk over to First Avenue and take the L to Brooklyn."

"Brooklyn?"

"Yeah, the L goes to Williamsburg," Omaha said. "One stop. It's like the East Village but more subdued. More laid back. It's like a suburb of the East Village. The same kind of people."

"Oh, okay."

So they walked over to First Avenue, took the L Train, and got off at the next stop, Bedford Avenue. By the way, Bedford Avenue is known alternately as SVA (School of Visual Arts) Avenue or Avenue E. When they came out into the street, it was just as Omaha had said. Little cute cafés, bars, and boutiques and a definite East Village esthetic. Same fashions and attitudes and pale, thin young women with delicate tattoos and piercings, who were experimenting with collage and bisexuality. They sat with equally thin, ascetic-looking young men who were poets, worked for dot.coms, and read comics. Everything was *très* cool. They sat in a café and ordered hot cider with cloves and ate organic carrot cake. By the way, for you old fogies, the phrase "going for coffee" is just a code for wanting to get it on. If you want to talk about midi software, or a new graphic platform for your computer, or serious stuff, or you want to hang out and just read quietly side by side, you usually say, "You wanna go to Starbucks?" In nearly ten years of Starbucks, there have been only seven affairs that began by men and women deciding to meet there. Only one marriage has come out of going to these places. In that instance the dude was from Virginia and was visiting his sister, who was going to NYU. The dude went there with his sister's roommate and they fell in love. They would have fallen in love by going to Taco Bell, so maybe Starbucks wasn't an influence. These are New York City figures; maybe it's different where you are. I think it's all that smell of coffee. I believe that the aroma reminds people of marriage, and they steer away from romance. The figures for affairs and marriage are much, much higher for sushi restaurants, where it smells like sex because of the fish.

Anyway, Christmas was approaching and there was an overwhelming smell of evergreen from fresh wreaths and a delicate tree decorated demurely with antique bulbs, colored ribbons, and an angel with the Star of David on its T-shirt. I'm sorry. You're still thinking about sushi. There were large pine cones at every table. Most people ignored Carrie and Omaha, but a couple of them glanced their way and turned quickly away, threatened by the presence of a Puerto Rican in their midst. Omaha was angered and wanted to shout at them that he was Bill Clinton's son and was just as good as they were, even if he looked Puerto Rican. He knew it wouldn't be cool. However, even stifling such an outburst it's obvious that his tragic flaw was beginning to surface.

"So, Carrie Marshack," he said, sipping from the hot cider.

"So, Omaha Bigelow," Carrie said, smiling her crooked smile and tucking her lank brown hair behind her ears. "How's it going?"

"It's going good, Carrie," Omaha said. "You look good. Are you still at the Ontological Theater at St. Mark's Church?"

"Yeah, still there. But I'm doing word processing down at the World Trade Center. I'm working for a big firm that does bond trading. You know. Data entry and stuff."

"Great," Omaha said.

"I like you with black hair and a mustache," Carrie said. "You look *muy Latino urbano*. I've heard so much about you."

"*Gracias,*" Omaha said.

"Hahaha. You speak Spanish."

"*Sí, un poquito,*" Omaha replied, modestly. "But you've heard about me? Really, what?"

"Oh, things," Carrie said, and giggled. "You know."

"No, tell me."

"You know."

"Oh, that."

"Yeah, that, you rat. What happened? Everyone's talking about it."

"I don't really know," Omaha said. "I was always a kind of nerdy kid, my head in the books and not really paying attention to life. I was always stressed out about one thing or another. One day I just said, 'Hey, life is passing me by and I'm not taking full advantage of my talent.' I think something clicked, and the next morning I woke up and there I was."

"No longer suffering from Penile Asparaguitis."

"Exactly."

"Omaha?"

"What?"

"I missed you," Carrie said, almost pleading with him.

"Well, we had something special."

"Oh, please don't say that," Carrie said, and began crying. "I should've been more patient. Even when you lost your job at Kinko's, I could've supported both of us waitressing at Baby Jupiter's until you got back on your feet. I was so impatient. Such a bitch. Really!"

"Don't blame yourself. Luckily, it was summer, and I slept in the park. I learned some things."

"Do you think we could try again?" she said, and immediately shook her head. "What am I talking about? You're living with someone. A Puerto Rican girl. She's very attractive. She looks a little like Jennifer Lopez. Some body! Wow! I can't compete with her. And then you and the blonde are pretty close, I guess. I can understand the attraction. She is gorgeous. She looks like Lisa Kudrow."

"Lisa Kudrow? From *Friends*?"

"No, not her. The girl in the golfing movie with Matt Damon."

"Charlize Theron."

"Is that her name?"

"Yes, Charlize Theron."

"Well, okay. That one. But I shouldn't be intruding."

"That's okay," Omaha said, permitting himself, although unwittingly and similarly unaware of the consequences, the same tragic flaw as his father, of coupling indiscriminately with females. Fortunately, Omaha had better taste in women and Carrie Marshack was quite attractive in a Holly Hunter kind of way. "Who knows what the future will bring?" he added seductively.

"Oh," Carrie said, not quite believing that there was a possibility she would get back with Omaha. "I'm watering the plants and feeding the cats for my friend, Nina McCauley, while she's doing an art film in Michigan," Carrie said. "You want to go with me?"

"Where?"

"The Village. She won't be back for another month."

"Sure."

So they went there and got naked and Carrie gasped at the size and magnificence of Omaha Bigelow's *bohango,* which Omaha's new knowledge of being a president's son had caused to grow even more. We don't have to have a measuring scene. Let's just use our imagination. They continued meeting after Carrie's work and before her rehearsals for one of Richard Foreman's plays about potatoes at The Ontological at St. Mark's Church. As fate would have it, Omaha caught Carrie on a day when she was ovulating and, kerpowie, she too became pregnant. This brought to four the women that our hero had now impregnated. Hey, with Bill Clinton's genes running around in his system, why not propagate? Who knew what the twenty-first century would bring? But he wasn't through. When Carrie Marshack learned that she was pregnant, she rejoiced and told Rita Flash. Rita was consumed with jealousy and vowed that she would also get Omaha to make her pregnant. I won't go into the details because I'd have to compare Rita to Shelly Duvall or maybe Olivia Newton John, and that's no fun, but that too came to pass, and now five women were carrying Omaha's future offspring.

This is sort of a Puerto Rican fantasy but it really happened, and it happened to this gringo whiteboy. Dayum! Don't underestimate these folks cauze they be snow bunnies instead of jungle bunnies. They be shaking and baking, too. *What? Niggah, sit down and put the motherfucking Uzi away. Just think of Bryant Gumble. You too could be wearing five-hundred-dollar suits and in spite of a double chin could be talking shit on TV. He, a oreo? So motherfucking what Bryant a oreo. He get paid good money and don't have to be hustling in the street like you. Fuck Bryant Gumble? Fine! Think Samuel L. Jackson or Morgan Freeman. They're real. Right! Morgan was the Count on The Electric Company when you was a kid. You learned to count with Morgan? Yeah, my kids too. Fact they went to school with Morgan Freeman's daughter at CCWS on Eighty-eighth Street and Ruth Messinger, who ran for Mayor later, was their teacher. You scored some shit on that block? I didn't know that. But just be cool! The shit's gonna work out. Just let me tell it my way. Don't go all cocolo PC Cornell West on me. You my brother and I love you, man. Yeah, I know this shit don't have brothers in it. I ain't gonna cut into Spike's shit. And truth is, there ain't that many brothers in the East Village. A couple of jazz musicians that like white pussy but that's about it. You don't be messing with them white bitches? I understand where you're coming from. And you don't eat pork cauze you a Muslim? I hear you. That's righteous shit. Yeah, I promise I'll do another book that has brothers in it. I'll write about the South Bronx projects and they'll be brothers and sisters talking shit all over the place. Yeah, I'll put you in it, my brother. I'm not bullshitting. Niggahs be doing rap, drinking wine coolers, and smoking erf. All very cinema verité nouvelle vague voulez vouz coucher avec moi ce soir and whatnot. Knowwhati'm saying? You mah niggah! Word up.*

It should be clearly understood that I do not use the N word in any context in real life. I find the word insulting and I'm merely creating a voice, much as if I were a character in this novel and were talking to an African-American street brother. In other words, a sort of interlocutor. I just looked up the word in my Funk and Wagnall's to make sure I'm using the word correctly. I wish I hadn't. Ironically, the second meaning of *interlocutor* is the center man in a minstrel show. Nice going, Vega. Hoisted once again on your own petard. I can't believe it. I'm not going to explain the phrase.

Go ask somebody. I know. Interlocutor this!

T HIS IS WHAT IS CALLED A TRANSITIONAL CHAPTER. HERE IS WHERE THE
reader gets caught up on what's happening with all the characters who
matter. We may need to return to Kinko's or some other locale and
have the minor characters appear, but only briefly. Awilda Cortez will remain
in the background for technical and plot-complication reasons. We need not
bother with Olivia Bigelow except for her appearance at the wedding of her
son at the Buckley estate and a frantic call that she makes to Bill Clinton's
Harlem office toward the end of the book, which I will not include, since
I'm telling you about it right now. The call is ignored by a Clinton aide who,
recognizing traces of an Arkansas accent, deals with the call as coming from
another disgruntled female from that state attempting to discredit the legacy
of a great American. Although alluded to, Bill Clinton does not appear in this
novel, so let me dissuade you from harboring such a hope. I could have him
come down to the East Village with his sax and sit in with some black jazz
musicians, since they share a predilection for mediocre looking Euro-
American chicks, but I won't cheapen this novel with such a scene.

President Bush does not appear in the novel either. His presence will be
felt through other characters, but he will not make an appearance. I have no
idea how I could possibly write dialogue for him and not be accused of treason,
sedition, or sour grapes for what happened in Florida during the presidential
election. I don't really care who won. I'm sure if Gore had become president,
this so-called war in Afghanistan would be more boring than the weather
channel. Not that war is that interesting. How many times can you show pictures of pilotless airplanes or interview androgynous woman jet-fighter pilots?
My chagrin is about the ignorance of the American electorate that the choice
would be between Gore and Bush. Let's take the men who lost the primaries.
Had McCain emerged as president, the war would have ended in three weeks.
He, instead of Geraldo Rivera, would have gone and extricated Osama bin
Laden from a cave, killed eighty-two Al Qaeda ruffians, wrestled bin Laden to

the ground, captured him, and put him on trial. McCain was a warrior and a prisoner of war and knows about these things. He would have probably chewed out Osama really bad and made him feel sorry he ever messed with McCain and the U.S. On the other hand, if Bill Bradley had become president he probably could have recruited bin Laden, and he could have proven that the six-foot-five bin Laden had nothing to do with 9/11 and that his name is really Cleon Merriwether, a graduate of an obscure black college. He would have had him shave his beard, cleaned him a up a little, told him to keep his mouth shut, and made him a point guard on the New York Knicks. Anyone with any sense knows Osama's presence in uniform would be an improvement over the present Knicks team. For whatever it is worth, George Walker Bush will not exit from this novel unscathed. He'll catch a bit of flak. As you noticed, I kind of zinged him a little already.

Most of Winnifred Buckley's relatives no longer have importance. For all intents and purposes we're finished with them. They have been presented as sort of light Thanksgiving divertissement. So we'll dispense with most of them, although they will return for Winnifred and Omaha's wedding. Of course they're going to get married. You don't think I'm going to pass up an opportunity to have the American Way of Life triumph over mostly brown-skinned immigrant rabble, do you? I may be Puerto Rican, but I'm not stupid. Of the Buckley family the only important characters, besides Winnifred—who is now central to the tale—are the grandmother, Abigail Buckley, who will attempt to teach witchery to her granddaughter through the Internet, and Winnifred Buckley's father, Pierce. We're finished with the mother and her Arab lover except as a leitmotif to keep alive the irrational fear that Arabs mean to harm the United States at a core level and institute a reign of terror in which people will have to wear cloth wrapped stylistically around their heads like a bunch of Ethel Mermans, celebrate Ramadan, and rather than turkeys American Thanksgiving tables will have poor, defenseless roasted lambs, head and all, as centerpieces. Sorry, Aly. Rather than cranberry jelly, mint jelly. Double yuck, right? Aly's my daughter and is against any kind of transgression against the genus ovine, especially little lambs. She would even cry when people sang "Mary had a little lamb, her fleece was white as snow. And everywhere that Mary went, the lamb was sure to go." *But maybe the lamb didn't want to go to the park and have kids make fun of the way she talked.* What about: "Baa baa, black sheep have you any wool? Yes, sir. Yes, sir, three bags full. One for my master, one for my dame, and one for the little girl who lives down the lane." In an elementary Marxist analysis of the situation it's obvious that the lamb of color is being exploited and the natural product of her effort is being shorn from her body and exchanged for some sort of slavish concession from the master. The one for the dame borders on further exploitation of womanhood by the master. Of course give the dame a bag of wool, since the master is probably bribing the dame to keep her quiet about the fact that, behind his wife's back, he's having a grand old time with the teenager down the lane, who gets the third bag for being compliant. But the one that really got Aly, being she's a Harvard alumna, is that awful Wiffenpoof song. "We're poor little lambs who have lost our way." How dare they use lambs for such a sick metaphor of their own misguided conservatism? Anyway, that's likely why Americans are so upset with the Arabs. The Arab Ahmed Gaziozhari stays, but with little involvement in the plot. Instead, he will appear gratuitously to further deconstruct baseball from the point of view of a Middle Eastern mind. Maybe. Well, let's skip the suspense. Ahmed goes to see the Commissioner and presents a plan. The Minnesota Twins and the Montreal Expos are not making money in their small markets. Why not move the teams to the Middle East? The Tel Aviv Twins and the PLO Expos. I don't want to spread rumors, but that is what Mr. Selig is attempting to do with this downsizing of Major League baseball.

Maruquita's family will also stay in the background, as they work on the Puerto Rican Navy project and prepare the ships for training exercises, a maiden cruise, and offshore maneuvers near Section 17 off Orchard Beach in the Bronx, a traditional summer gathering of Puerto Ricans. They will attempt to enlist new recruits for *La Marina Boricua*, the Puerto Rican Navy.

As for Dakulana Imbebwabe, she remains not only as an integral part of the plot, but as a latent reminder of African sexual and genetic power, something which is bound to piss off the saltines and their KKK mentality, who insist on racial purity instead of addressing the value of hybrid vigor. Anyway, Dakulana is sort of an ace in the hole, the importance of which I will not reveal at this time. Richard Rentacar has moved to the West Coast, and we don't need to know anything about him except that he's a PA (Production Assistant) for films and, as is the case with roughly twenty-two percent of the population of California, is writing a screenplay. As for Rita Flash, after gaining forty-seven pounds in the first trimester of her pregnancy, she returned to her parents' home in Bayonne, New Jersey, to eat potato chips and await the birth of an obviously pachydermic child. As for Carrie Marshack, she will carry her child to term, meet a thin poet and out-of-work dot.com programmer, marry him, and move to Williamsburg, where the poet shares a loft with his cousin, a chef at an organic restaurant in Chelsea. On the morning of September 11,

2001, Carrie, now Mrs. Eugene Doherty, will take her daughter Lisa, two months old, to Mrs. Gorenwicz, the Polish babysitter in Williamsburg. She will kiss her baby goodbye, take the L train to Eighth Avenue in Manhattan, transfer there to an E train, and a little after 8:00 A.M. report to her job on the eightieth floor of the World Trade Center South Tower. Carrie Marshack will not have a cell phone, so there will be no record of her last words before being vaporized and becoming fine ash.

All other secondary characters are of no importance. They've served their purpose and exited, stage left or right, their moment of glory done. If it's necessary to bring in a new character from now on, it will be in the form of man, woman, boy, girl, waiter, taxi driver, gaffer, best boy, presidential aide, reliable source, and such designations. If it's absolutely necessary to give the character a name, it will be done subtly and quickly before moving on. We're left now with a triangular plot in which Maruquita Salsipuedes and Winnifred Buckley will vie for the affection and control of Omaha Bigelow. There is no need to try to figure out what these three characters represent. I don't even think they're archetypes for anything, unless you want to drive yourself nuts trying to attach symbolism to them. From now on all attention will be concentrated on these three, with input from a few of the remaining characters mentioned above. The action of the novel will end roughly around mid-July of the year 2001. I will leave those sixty or so days in July, August, and the beginning of September for the reader to play time-juggling games with the fiction of this work and the reality which it purports to present vis-à-vis the historical facts of recent events. Quiet on the set. Sound. Rolling! Camera. Rolling! And . . . action.

About two weeks before Christmas, Maruquita noticed that she had become a little heavier and more content as she got through her morning sickness. The trip to visit Omaha's mother had done wonders for her. She loved her first contact with that United States so foreign to native New Yorkers, particularly those at the bottom rung of the ladder. Maruquita was one of these people, in spite of her great capacity for magic and transmogrification or, as we think of it in pop terms, morphing. She couldn't change during her pregnancy, in order to protect the baby, but she often thought about it. Although she didn't know it as a scientific fact, Puerto Ricans who are gifted in this area are able to do so on the basis of a very simple evolutionary fact. This fact is that ontogeny is the recapitulation of phylogeny—that is, a human organism in its gestative development goes through the process of evolution. People who are offended by evolution can skip ahead. The trick is to be able to morph at the right evolutionary level, compute rapidly the shape, inner workings, and outer covering of the animal, and say *cambio*. When you're done, you reverse the process. Maruquita was a natural and could rapid-morph better than anyone in the history of this peculiar Puerto Rican capacity.

Her grandmother had recognized the talent immediately and had begun training her. When she was younger, she made terrible mistakes and would end up half monkey and half squirrel or something like that. Awful looking things. She once did a beautiful peacock with a pitbull face. She would look in the mirror and laugh with great delight, and then her mother would come in and call her a crazy. It was a delicate business, and being pregnant, she had to be careful. By the way, if you see animals in New York City and they seem a little crazed and out of sorts, it's very likely they're Puerto Rican witches in disguise. Be careful around them. Oh, very funny. No, we don't do roaches and rats. Watch it! Maybe you do! Yeah? Your mother! *Tu madre, pendejo!*

Very little worried Maruquita these days. Omaha was away from the house more and more, and although she wanted to question him about his reasons for spending so much time out of the house, she held back, knowing that any protest from her would cause him to drift further away. Men were like that. They eventually returned home. If things got too bad, she would have to rein him in and sit him on the trunk. This is how Puerto Ricans think of a henpecked husband, someone sitting on a trunk at home, someone well-behaved. *Esa mujer tiene a ese hombre sentado en el baul.* Meaning: that woman has that man sitting on the trunk. Oh, it should be noted that most Puerto Rican men are sitting on the trunk and are permitted to act as if they're not. In public they order the women around, reprimand children, frown a lot, and talk quite seriously on issues as if they were really in charge. They're not. If they were, Puerto Rico would have been free a long time ago. This is not to say that women are not aiding in keeping Puerto Rico from being independent. It's always a cooperative endeavor to be the chattel of a world power. Anyway, it's a complex problem, and we should move on. Puerto Rican men, unlike Arabs, understand baseball and are remarkably good at it.

What? I'm now equivocating? Please! Oh, you think I'm avoiding the issue. I'm not! If I go on I'll be accused of pamphleteering, a terrible charge to level against any writer in a free and open society, which the United States is, despite major flaws, such as keeping fuzzy-wuzzies in tight little ethnic ghettoes of publication. You think I'm obsessed? I'm not obsessed, I'm pissed. I spent a good part of my life penning works of supposed lasting literary significance, and people still want me to write vapid ghetto stories with Puerto

Ricans shooting dope, running around in gangs, or losing their memory. I don't think so. You know what? Quit reading this book and sell it back to Amazon.com. Right! Have a nice day even though I know you've made other plans. Yeah, F*** U2. Sorry, Bono. I love Irish people and listen to Solas. They're cool. Afro-Celt is strange, but they're cool too. Okay, I haven't gone to see *Riverdance*, but I've seen the show in the comfort of my own home on VHS.

This is making me crazy, but as Sam Smith used to say: *It's not like it's a real long trip and you have to pack luggage and everything.* Poor Sam Smith. He was a good man. A leader of the squatter movement, a dynamite plumber, which was his trade, and a passable electrician. He died sleeping in East River Park after one too many beers. His mother had me order his body cremated. She came from Michigan for the burial. I ordered a Flowering Cherry to be planted in one of the huge flower boxes Sam had constructed in front of the Clemente Soto Vélez Cultural Center on Suffolk Street, down the street from Kinko's and Meow Mix and catty-corner from ABC No Rio.

The other squatters wanted to scatter Sam's ashes into the dumpsters outside of fine restaurants where they dug for unused food. People go hungry in America, but expensive restaurants dump perfectly good food in the garbage. The squatters in the East Village would go early each morning and meticulously rescue dozens of eggs, loaves of bread, fresh meat, fruits, and vegetables. They subsisted this way and were quite healthy. This communal culture has been wiped out from the East Village. The squatters were arrested, the buildings torn down as unsafe, and the last vestiges of the hippie culture made to disappear by the efforts of the Mayor of New York, Rudolph Giuliani, who post-9/11 transformed himself into a hero. Many of us will not forget the mayor's excesses, in spite of his generalship post-9/11.

When Sam's mother heard the suggestion to have Sam's ashes scattered, she refused. Instead, she asked me to dump the ashes into the hole we had dug for the tree. I was surprised but acceded to her request. I was honored that Sam would stay close by and that his ghost could wander the halls of the huge building. Sam's ashes went gently into the hole. There was no wind. We planted the cherry tree in the hole, the burlap covering the roots of the tree like a blanket over the cold ashes of Sam Smith. We then went into the Milagro Theater of the center for an off-beat memorial service. We heard music and drumming from the squatters and eulogies for Sam, another white man done in by a society that is color-blind because citizens, black or white, are inconsequential at a certain level. I had ordered twenty pizzas from the Greek pizzeria on Clinton

Street. The hundred squatters and members of Sam's family got free beer from the Como Coco Café, the contributions bar we ran in the center, so we could remain a self-sufficient arts institution. As I've said before: state-sponsored art sucks, whether in a totalitarian or a so-called democratic society. As there is a separation between church and state, so should there be the same separation between art and state. Why have I created this digression? I think it has two purposes. One is to get the business of the cultural center off my chest, but more importantly, to reassure you that this is not about race, but about something a lot more important: the cultural health of the United States.

But back to the lamentable journey of Omaha Bigelow.

Christmas came, and from Houston Street to Fourteenth Street along Avenue D there was a wonderful aroma of roasting *pernil,* boiling *pasteles,* and *sofrito* being confected with loads of garlic and onions for *arroz con gandules.* And this was the salty food. The sweet food had other spices. Whether *arroz con dulce* or *majarete,* cinnamon and cloves confused the senses with their delightful smells. I will not give the recipe for *coquito* here. Get to know Puerto Ricans and get it from them. I'll give you a hint. It's a type of eggnog with coconut milk and rum. It will knock you on your ass either from the 110-proof rum or the high sugar content.

As an aside, a lot of people think that the warming trend in New York City is caused by El Niño. I disagree and believe strongly that there is a cloud of garlic and grease that has risen above the city from Puerto Rican cooking. At last count Puerto Ricans constitute the largest ethnic group in New York City, supplanting the Italians and the Irish. Of course many ethnic groups marry Puerto Ricans, and for some odd reasons the children become Puerto Rican and shed their other ethnic identification. I think salsa dancing is a dominant genetic trait. In any case, this culinary miasma hangs over the city, preventing cold weather and snow from penetrating it. I suspect that eventually, perhaps around 2072, there will be a line of bowing palm trees along Orchard Beach and Coney Island, and people will be wearing *guayaberas* at Christmas and even going to the beach. I believe strongly, not from a sense of national pride in my homeland but from a clear politicogeographic analysis, that it was a mistake to allow Puerto Ricans to come into the U.S. in such large numbers. It's proving to be a counterinvasion of immense proportions and presents a real danger to the United States of myth, probably much greater than the Arabs. I'm being satirical, so don't pay attention to me. We're harmless, really. Okay, I understand you being a little paranoid now. Maybe that's good.

But to Christmas. All over the projects on Avenue D things were going full speed ahead. Nearly every window was decorated with Christmas lights, so that from a distance at night the complex of buildings looked like a galaxy. It may well be, given the activity there. A number of people left New York City and returned to Puerto Rico by plane. The people in the projects, many of whom could not afford the fare, simply stepped out of their apartments and were on the island. As other families did, beginning on about December fifteenth, Maruquita and others traveled through the mountains until they reached their relatives and sat with them and told stories of other *navidades*. They wished each other *felicidades* and a *próspero año nuevo*. They sang *aguinaldos*, *villancicos*, and *décimas* and ate and drank and brought *parrandas* to neighbors in the cool mountain nights, singing songs at the doors of the houses along the narrow paths, until the people opened the doors and let them in and fed them and gave them drink. It went like that for days until *nochebuena*, Christmas Eve, when the big dinner was served. The celebration continued until January sixth, *el día de los reyes*, Three Kings' Day, when children found presents under their beds. The celebration didn't end until eight days later, during the *octavitas*, when people who had been visited earlier returned the favor and brought *parrandas* to their friends.

Maruquita was exhausted from climbing the hills, but she did enjoy the family feeling and thought about when she would have her own family and could celebrate Christmas with them. A few times she wore her bathing suit and went to Luquillo beach with friends and waded in the warm water or relaxed on the sandy beaches, the sun making her feel languorous and sensual. At those times she missed Omaha. She had invited him to come with her, but he said that he was working on his film and couldn't go. Was he going to visit his mother? No, he just had a lot of work to get ready to begin shooting the film. Would he go away and see other friends? She didn't want to bring up any other girl he might be seeing. It pained her to believe it was possible that he was cheating on her. She hoped Omaha would settle down and be responsible to her and their baby. She worried that he wouldn't. When the holidays were over, she returned to her routine of cleaning her house, preparing the baby's room, going for checkups, and watching her diet. She had gained weight, and things were becoming a little more difficult.

WINNIFRED BUCKLEY SPENT A QUIET CHRISTMAS. SHE TRAVELED TO Vermont and had dinner with her grandmother. Early in the month she FedExed presents to all her relatives and each of her eighteen nieces and nephews. Additionally, she had a service mail with her stamped signature more than twenty-five hundred Christmas cards to friends and relatives. She returned to New York City on December twenty-sixth, and she and Omaha had a dinner prepared by her cook. She had given up on John-John Kennedy's vacant apartment and closed on a large loft apartment in the same Soho neighborhood. This was a twelve-room duplex with a private elevator, a sauna, a mini theater, and a superb kitchen. She staffed the apartment with a cook and a live-in maid and left the apartment on Red Square for Omaha to continue his work. In what was once her bedroom and the place where she had been gloriously devirginated she had a thirty-two track studio installed for Omaha to continue to compose his score for the film. Omaha was then very close to completing the script. She read it and was quite happy with the development.

As it then stood, the main character, Baby Blue, was a punk rock musician who had come from the midwestern United States seeking to make his mark in the New York downtown scene. While playing at an East Village venue, he meets a Puerto Rican girl who turns out to have magical powers. Her name is Tinanosaura Regina but we know her simply as Tina. At this point in the script Omaha has bracketed a note that the next sequence should be animated. Being a writer myself, I know that Omaha has run out of ideas and is clutching at straws. What happens is that using a rather silly joke Omaha has written the following: *They fall in love and the girl says she's a genie and their romance is fated to fail, but he has three wishes.*

We can obviously see that Omaha, in writing a failed romance, is slowly disengaging himself from Maruquita. Baby Blue tells Tina the genie that he wants a million dollars. She says that he will meet a princess with blond hair who looks like Charlize Theron. The princess, whose name is Glamora, will

234 Edgardo Vega Yunqué

launch his career as a musician, making it possible for him to earn a million dollars. Second wish: He wants to be important. Tina says he will soon find out that he is a descendant of Ludwig Van Beethoven from an illicit affair the composer had with a loquacious music copyist. This affair with the talkative young woman very likely caused Beethoven's deafness. Here we see Omaha's desire to reveal his pedigree. The incorporation of verisimilitude happens often with writers. They fictionalize aspects of their life. Don't try to figure out what it is that I'm disguising with this novel. I am a professional and know the intricacies of the creative process.

There is a note on the margin of Omaha's manuscript that suggests that the roles of Beethoven and Maria Bechtelwurfer-Ingleflunger, the copyist, have been specifically written for Robin Williams and Sigourney Weaver. As an afterthought, for reasons which I do not know, Williams's name is crossed out. The names *Mandy Patinkin or Steve Martin* have been written in.

The last wish: Baby Blue says he wants to make love to Tina. She says she cannot, because genies cannot have sex with just anyone. Baby Blue pleads and pleads, but Tina will not relent. Eventually Baby Blue says: *Well, maybe you can give me a little head.* Tina frowns and replies: *That I can do.* There's a puff of smoke, and Baby Blue has a tiny walnut-sized head. *Just kidding!* says Tina. *Wrong head.* Another puff of smoke, and we now see a shocked Baby Blue at a urinal where he realizes that his johnson has been shrunken to the size of a spider monkey's penis. Baby Blue is distraught. It's obvious that Omaha is beginning to feel the guilt of his unfaithfulness to Maruquita and is writing about his fears concerning losing his *bohango.*

Be aware that the introduction of certain elements at this juncture is called foreshadowing in the writing of the novel, be it literary or paraliterary. I dislike polemics, but sometimes they're unavoidable. While some people want to blur the distinction between the literary novel and novels written simply to entertain, the effort is simply a marketplace strategem. I cite from *The Oxford Dictionary of Literary Terms,* which states the following:

> **paraliterature,** the category of written works relegated to the margins of recognized literature and often dismissed as subliterary despite evident resemblances to the respectable literature of the official canon. Paraliterature thus includes many modern forms of popular fiction and drama: children's adventure stories, most detective and spy thrillers, most science fiction and fantasy writing, pornography and women's romances, along with much television and radio drama.

Today any defense of literature presents problems, since people are fearful of not only creating an atmosphere of censorship and a rejection of free expression, but of appearing to be part of an elite. It's odd that there is so much fear concerning this topic. In complex societies one can establish gradations of quality for wine, cars, jewelry, art, and many other areas of human endeavor. However, when it comes to writing, it's a free-for-all and today all novels apparently have the same value, not only in the marketplace, but in the minds of the people. Even the *New York Times* will include, with no distinction as to quality, in its Best Seller List for Fiction a romance novel and a literary one, without any specificity of content other than volume of sales, or at least orders by bookstores. Clancy or Ishiguro. Gordimer or Rice. King or Rushdie. It's all the same to some. That the construct of nondiscrimination falls apart under analysis means little to most people. One gauge that can be pointed to without any fear is that the authors of paraliterary novels basically write the same book over and over again. Such cannot be said of literary novelists, except that they're concerned with social or philosophical issues and have distinct styles in the manner in which the authors use the English language. In many cases of derivative examples of the novel, the style is generally poor. This fact can be established quite easily. The other aspect is that the preponderance of these paraliterary novels examine nothing about the human condition, the original purpose of the novel as expressed by Cervantes in *Don Quixote de la Mancha*. Fear sucks. Either one can defend a point of view logically or he cannot.

All right, enough of polemics. Back to the tale.

As Winnifred continues reading Omaha's film script, she recognizes that a genius, meaning Baby Blue, is being destroyed by self-doubt. While she realizes that the script is autobiographical, now that she is the woman behind Omaha Bigelow, he is sure to triumph, and any vestiges of self-doubt will disappear from him.

There is a note from Omaha that indicates that certain scenes will be shot in black and white. As such, there are suggested locales all over the East Village. There are costume changes but always black-and-white pans of the location, and closeups of Baby Blue in slow melting collages. Two Boots, Nice Guy Eddie's, the Turkish takeout place on Houston, and the falafel place on Avenue A, Esashi Japanese Restaurant down the street, Odessa up the street, St. Dymphna's, the Irish restaurant on St. Marks Place, St. Mark's Church during a performance of another derivative absurdist play, this time about cabbages. In each scene we see the further deterioration of Baby Blue. Johnny Depp and his natural angst would have been great, but instead they were able to cast a young man from NYU's Tisch School for the Arts. Notice that "a young man" was used. Maybe at some point you'll see the film and read the credits and figure out his name.

While he's able to perform in ever larger venues, Baby Blue becomes more and more despondent. The concerts are shot in brilliant and spectacular color. During these scenes Baby Blue is all right and doesn't display his growing despair. In the throes of an enormous existential dilemma Baby Blue turns more and more to drugs. A CD is released, and it climbs the charts. The hit single "Archetypical Behavior" is nominated for a Grammy. Although it doesn't win, Baby Blue becomes a household name. He goes on a world tour, playing in European, South American, Australian, and Asian capitals. The hit single is translated into Spanish and is given a revolutionary, magical realism twist. It becomes number one in many Latin American countries in which the people are oppressed by magical realism governments and people trade in butterflies rather than currency.

Needless to say for Omaha Bigelow, being a president's son, having a large johnson, a $10,000-a-week salary, a ready-to-shoot script with a twelve-million-dollar budget, with a cast working for scale, a score of brand new music and songs, a girlfriend who looks like Charlize Theron, another gorgeous girl in the projects, the two of them pregnant, plus three others expecting his children, had to make Omaha feel powerful and as if he could conquer the world or at least win a Palme d'Or or a Sundance Best Film. Fuck, he thought. He no longer went to have his hair and mustache dyed. In fact, he shaved his head, and about a week later blondish fuzz began to appear on his pate. He decided to let his mustache grow blond as well. Winnifred was totally turned on by this new development. Maruquita was too, since it reminded her of first becoming interested in him. She suggested he dye his hair green again, but he nixed the idea.

While it may appear as if Omaha Bigelow's life is on the ascent, what we're observing is simply a segment of this struggle, and what is being portrayed is the drive of the main character as he pushes the stone of his destiny up the hill. Much like Sisyphus, once he reaches the top and rests at the end of the day, the stone will roll down to the bottom again. In the morning, as in the myth, the struggle will begin anew. Can this myth be applied to individuals? Obviously, since the stone of mortality is present in each human. Can it be applied to nations? I believe so, although it is more difficult. Is the United States engaged in pushing its stone up the hill, or is it resting atop it, unaware that the stone has rolled down the hill and when the sun rises it will have to walk down the hill and again attempt to push the rock back up? Where is the U.S. in all this? You should figure it out and do something about it. Does the United States have hubris? That you should also figure out. As for Omaha Bigelow. he was definitely pushing the stone up the hill.

Through Maruquita, Omaha had hired two body guards from the neighborhood, Chucky and Rocky. Don't be misled by the cuteness of their names. These were people with whom you did not mess. Big, tough Ricans who were joint-hardened and unimpressed by rhetoric and useless threats. Silent and deadly dudes they were. Of course they were not only guarding Omaha but also reporting back to Maruquita on his comings and goings and how much time Omaha was spending with his blonde gringa whitegirl.

Trouble was fast approaching.

O MAHA BIGELOW'S FILM, *THE INCREDIBLE LIGHTNESS OF BEING AN ALIEN in Your Own Land,* began principal photography on January 15, 2001. The shooting schedule was six weeks. All black-and-white photography was shot first, with the actors improvising the scenes. Everything was filmed with hand-held digital cameras. The film would subsequently be transferred to 35mm without losing its quality. Most of the black and white scenes consisted of the four members of the band eating, hanging out, talking about sports, waiting to go on stage, smoking pot, taking pills, doing lines of cocaine, drinking beer, belching, farting, and being generally raunchy about different girls and their physical attributes. This was not exactly a Dick Clark American Bandstand scene. The United States had evolved. The Constitution had triumphed, and the youth of America was continuing to exercise its inalienable right to be free. The setting depicted a run-of-the-mill conventional punk esthetic. The girls were no less raunchy, enticing the band members to get it on. There was even a scene of four girls giving the four members head, but it was eventually cut from the film. The sequence was not left on the cutting room floor because it might affect the ratings of the film but because it was obvious that condoms were being used, and the contrast of safe sex against the background of the natural disorder of the punk life detracted from the overall feeling. Some of the actors didn't want to have piercings and tattoos, for fear they would eventually make it big in Hollywood and how the hell was one supposed to undo all that? Body doubles were used, and artists had to draw tattoos on the actors. East Village punk rockers came out in full, vying to be extras, now called "background actors" in movie making, blurring the distinction between the movie star status of Robert Downey, Jr., and Joseph Shmo, an extra. For those not familiar with the milieu, an appropriate response to this sort of rationalization is: *Yeah, whatever!*

During the time of the filming there was a city ordinance stipulating that film companies couldn't shoot north of Houston Street, meaning the East

Village proper. By the way, the East Village grows more staid and conservative as more and more rich people invade the neighborhood to live a pseudoexciting bohemian life. So Omaha, using Tisch School for the Arts students as crew, got around this obstacle by not using the big movie trucks and lights. No trailers or food rigs. Everything portable; lights and generators hand-carried, explaining that they were doing a student film. They set up a modest craft services table on the sidewalk with fruit, crackers, cheese, soft drinks, juices, and coffee; bagels and cream cheese in the morning. Meal money was provided for actors and crew at lunch and dinner time. Sometimes when they shot late they would order a hundred burrito dinners from Caliente Café or twenty-five pizzas from Two Boots. A production office was set up in an apartment on Ludlow Street around the corner from Katz Delicatessen. Graphic artists were hired to do story boards of the sex scenes so the animators could begin their work. These images were scanned and sent digitally over the Internet to the animators. Roughly one-third of the film was color animation, one-third black and white, and the other half, to paraphrase Yogi Berra, was beautiful and elaborate concert-quality production, at first in clubs like The Bank, ABC No Rio, Friendly Fire, Wetlands, the Ritz, and such venues. Later, bigger venues were used.

There was considerable cheating in background audience shots of concerts in places like Madison Square Garden in New York, Chicago Stadium, and other U.S. arenas. These were edited with the band on stage at a club during the day and then blended into the existing footage through blue-screen technology. For venues outside the country the same was done, and through special effects you saw the band in those venues. For the travel scenes you saw the band arriving at and going through airports in London, Dublin, Madrid, Paris, Oslo, Berlin, and other European capitals as well as Tokyo, Hong Kong, and Singapore and down into Australia and New Zealand and South America. The production did not leave Manhattan for any of its work. Movie magic.

Eventually Winnifred rented Madison Square Garden for a big concert. A public-relations firm was contracted for the supposed band, Undocumented Aliens. They plastered the city with huge posters. A concert was announced and promoted and tickets distributed for free. Photos of the band were given out at record stores and the neighborhood was covered with more posters with SOLD OUT slanted across them. T-shirts were printed, buttons appeared, sample CDs of the sound track showed up at record stores and were snapped up by eager fans. The CD cover was a drawing of the punk band members in ripped clothes, dyed spiky hair, piercings, and tattoos outside of an immigration office. Two very dour immigration service bureaucrats who resembled the often-parodied couple in *American Gothic* by Grant Wood were blocking their way. Omaha had given an artist a photograph of his mother and asked him to age her twenty-five years and stand an equally aged Bill Clinton next to her holding a saxophone. Everyone thought the reference to Clinton was hilarious. You and I know that Omaha was pushing it. Exactly. More hubris. The couple sternly admonished the band as its members tried to get past them to a door that in bright green letters said: GOOD OLE USA. In a bubble, one of the musicians is saying, "Me wanna grin car," which pissed me off a little bit because that's the way a Spanish-speaking person newly arrived in the U.S. might say "I want a green card."

Puerto Ricans don't need a Green Card. We are citizens of the United States. We not only have to put up with being colonials and being rejected by Americans for speaking Spanish, but we also have to hear it from other Latin Americans about how lucky we are. They always say this with subtle irony and smugness, because they have a seat in the United Nations and we don't. My grandfather Toño Yunqué always said being American made him feel cheap. *Barato.* Well, he was pretty cheap. He bought everything wholesale and kept it all in his room. Sacks of rice, beans, and cornmeal, codfish, canned goods, salt, spices. Each day my grandmother Suncha went to him with a shopping list. She knocked on the door, and when he appeared with his usual frown, she'd give him her daily request and like a penitent wait for him to fill it out. He would measure everything out on this old-time scale hanging from the ceiling and pour, where required, the goods into brown paper bags. When he was done, he closed the door. We had no idea what he was doing in his room, but we suspected that he was planning the revolution.

Okay, I'm being a little paranoid, and maybe Omaha didn't mean anything with the "grin car" business. But I have to tell you something: there is nothing wrong with being paranoid in certain situations. I'm not a big patriot regarding the United States for obvious reasons, but I'm willing to help out. Who is it that the CIA and FBI hire? They hire strait-laced goody-two-shoes people in cheap suits and outdated haircuts. Because they must look the part, they look serious and committed. They're nice people, who want to raise families and don't understand computer technology that well. What else can they do? They're nice Americans trying to do their best. They're just security guards with college degrees for the most part. Why doesn't the United States wise up and hire really paranoid people who suspect everyone of wrongdoing? I strongly believe that everyone serves a purpose, even paranoids. There's a Buddhist saying that the rice in the little bowl that you get when you order Chinese food has been handled by eighty-eight people before it gets to you. Okay, the English construction of the sentence is not the best, and it sounds a little unhealthy, but you understand what I mean. It means that it takes a good number of people, from the person who planted the rice seed to the waiter who brings it to your table, to complete the chain to your mouth. I know. More weird language. Humor me. I'm an immigrant. Bottom line: you should respect everyone.

Let me tell you something. The U.S. is in trouble. Two very important things which come naturally to human beings, and indeed, all animals, have been nearly eliminated from the American culture. In seeking to create a further blurring of reality, and giving everyone the semblance of equality and an I'm okay/you're okay kind of well-being, the U.S. has completely defanged itself. Number 1: you're not supposed to be judgmental. How curious! That means that people should have no judgment. Of course judging someone is not the same as sentencing them. In the judicious examination of people, their habits and utterances are open to criticism. It is the constitutional right of people to determine with whom they should congregate, whether to accept or reject their opinions and be suspicious of the motives for their actions. Poor Bill Maher and his cute celebrity-populist show. They took him to task for being logical about 9/11. Additionally, people are constantly warned against being paranoid. Justified paranoia was one of the slogans of the 1960s and 1970s. Amnesia has set in, and paranoia has no place in American society. Oh, yeah? Would that the CIA and FBI and the entire intelligence community had been paranoid and judgmental. Maybe 9/11 would have been prevented. So I say in all sincerity, give the CIA, the FBI, and all other intelligence outfits nice, harmless desk jobs and hire paranoids to protect the country.

Back to the tale. These asides are exhausting me. But don't get paranoid. Don't be judgmental. Hahahaha! Or ROFLMAO, as they say online. You don't know what that means? Get an AOL account and get with the program. No, Time-Warner doesn't pay me to say these things. I just think it's funny that AOL keeps growing, and people are spending more time online and less time in the bedroom screwing. And it's mostly Euro-Americans. So if that population dwindles, don't blame anyone but AOL. Having a mouse in your hand is not the same as holding a breast or a penis. So in a way I'm saying "AOL 4Q." Go ahead and invoke the Terms of Service and try tossing me this time. One time on AOL these two harpies, TPoopC and TornadoC, gave me three violations in one hour and caused me to lose my account because I wouldn't stop arguing constitutional rights. They said I was monopolizing the chat room. In all I lost nine AOL accounts for arguing freedom of expression. AOL had so many complaints and lawsuits that they eventually chose to loosen their tight-ass, conservative, hoosier grip on free expression. No disrespect to Indiana, but I'm glad Bobby Knight is gone. Once, visiting the island, he smacked a Puerto Rican cop. He was lucky he didn't smack a Rican cop in New York. Julio, Carlos, and Miguel don't mess around, homeslice. Okay no more whining for a while.

Baby Blue's band made appearances at record shops, and there were photo ops around the city with Indian subcontinent taxi drivers with magnificent turbans, Africans from Senegal and Mali, Chinese, Mexicans, and other Latin Americans. Omaha played bass on the sound track. An actor played someone by the name of Tommy Bigfella, a spaced-out dude with green hair, obviously a sexual reference. I know. More hubris. The big Madison Square Garden concert takes place toward the end of the film when the protagonist, both at the height of his professional success and his existential despair has had an epiphany as he walks in the rain up Avenue A, past the falafel place and other restaurants and shops. It is at that point that he decides to enter a monastery and dedicate himself to a life of silence, self-abnegation, and sexual abstinence, in which the only music he will allow himself to hear are madrigals and liturgical compositions. It's quite touching. The rain scene would have eventually proven to be a stroke of genius in Europe, where such things in black and white are received well, particularly in the Nordic countries. In Italy, however, it would have caused giggling and people in the audiences to yell at the screen: *"Cretino, la pioggia, la pioggia. Va dentro."* "Hey, dummy it's raining. Get inside."

In private screenings, before the release of the film, critics almost unanimously agreed that in this low-budget independent film, at times a bit amateurish and self-conscious in its production values, Omaha Bigelow, in his writing and directorial debut, had plumbed the depths of American artistic life and had made a statement about the incredible emotional void and dearth of meaning in the youth of America. The editing was masterful, and through further special effects the black-and-white sequences blended into the color. The color animation flowed masterfully, with the actors creating spectacular morphs into cartoon characters. Crumb, who had done *Fritz the Cat* so brilliantly, and whom Winnifred contacted at Omaha's suggestion, wanted artistic input, a reasonable request. Winnifred, protecting Omaha's vision, wouldn't give in. Omaha agreed. Instead, they found a couple of disgruntled Disney animators who vowed to outdo Disney and go beyond, in their words, "the studio's retrograde and mindless drivel and childsish drawing." Sorry, Mr. Eisner. I know you're the head of the company and everything, but that is what they said. You can't really blame them. You have to admit that the Disney film of *The Hunchback of Notre Dame* was pretty pathetic. I saw *Fantasia* when I was a boy in Puerto Rico and was awed. The disgruntled animators were right. The drawing for the *Hunchback* film and the *Pocahontas* one was pretty weak. I know the studio was going for the washed-out, hip, pastel children's-book illustration look but IMHO (in my humble opinion) the result sucked. I know I'm a poor schmuck and you're a powerful executive, Mr. Eisner. I'm just saying.

Anyway, the animation scenes of actual sex were amazing. It was brilliant pornography, with screaming musical orgasms, glisteningly moist vaginas, thickly veined penises spurting seminal fluid that traveled dozens of feet and exploded like fireworks and lit up girls' heads when in the act of fellatio. The actual fucking scenes were awesome, with female genitals turning into flowers, which had delicate tendrils that grasped the engorged penises and danced. There was one sequence when Baby Blue and his girlfriend Giselita were getting it on. The young woman, by the way, is a Herzegovinian, black-haired gypsy, an immigrant actor playing a Puerto Rican girl with a perfect NYC Rican accent. I could protest the casting of a Herzegovinian instead of a Puerto Rican, but the young woman is a gifted actor. By the way, you can't say *actress* anymore, because feminists bunch up their fists, get very indignant and say nasty things like "porcine motherfucker." In one sequence the cartoon girl (read, *young woman*) removes her clothes, and her vagina slides down her leg so she's left looking like a Barbie doll. The vagina saunters over to Baby Blue with his spiky blue hair. He is erect, and the vagina starts singing really raunchy and punkish like maybe Courtney Love: *I'm gonna take you in and chew you up, chew you up, chew you up and vomit you! Vomit you, yahhhhhh! Vomit you. Chew, chew, chew, chew you, chew you up! Chew you up and vomit you. Vomit you! Throw you up! Throwwwww you up! I'm gonna throw you up!* The penis detaches from Baby Blue, and the vagina and the penis do a brilliant slam dance that culminates in a mutual orgasm.

When the screams of delight stop, the animation blends back into black and white, and we see the two actors in postcoital exhaustion on a futon in Baby Blue's disgustingly filthy East Village apartment, with empty bottles of Rolling Rock and oily pizza boxes from Two Boots on the floor. Two Boots gets credit on the thank-you list of the film. The owners of Two Boots are lovely people. They close their pizzeria at 1:00 A.M., but because Omaha Bigelow is using the place as a location for his film and I for my novel, they've kept it open for us until four in the morning. Two Boots is a fun place. I love their jambalaya with Cajun sausage and their cornbread. The owners have opened the Pioneer Film Theater next to Two Boots Pizza after they had to scrap their film shows at Charas once Mayor Giuliani and the City sold the building on Ninth Street. Bummer! Winnifred thought that it might be cool to have a private screening there. Anyway, Omaha saw the slam-dance animation sequence and was overjoyed.

So the film was finished only a week over schedule, and now the post-production process began. It was likely that the film would be X-rated, but they were hoping for at least R, which meant that 17 and under required a parent or guardian to be along. Punk kid demographics indicated that the average age is about fourteen. It wouldn't help much, since punk kids didn't even want to be seen with their parents in the same room at home let alone in public. They would accept NC-17. The tag for the film, which would appear on the posters, would say in bold red letters: "Punk Rock, A Cultural Revolution or the End of the American Family: A Documentary." This would draw millions of people with a need to experience life vicariously. It was all good.

B Y THE TIME OMAHA BIGELOW'S FILM WRAPPED, WE WERE INTO MARCH. The weather was warming, and the East Village was once again thriving with outdoor activity. We have to stop now and reckon date of delivery for the women Omaha had impregnated. While you may find that Omaha's sexual vigor strains credibility, you need to study the animal kingdom and then compare cultures in which men are permitted several wives. No, it's not only Muslims or Arabs, but Mormons. I guess they figure that if you have the genes, you may as well share them. They have a number of wives and dozens of children. In June 2001, right before the Olympics, the State of Utah tried Tom Green, a practicing Mormon, for polygamy. Green had five wives and to date had fathered twenty-five children. So Omaha Bigelow was a Boy Scout compared to Mr. Green.

But back to determining when these young women are due. Here we go. Okay, first Maruquita. She became pregnant in August, so roughly 280 days later, she was due in May. Don't start with the astrological signs, okay? I don't care who the woman is, if she begins a conversation with, "Hi, what's your sign?" I take a breath and very likely say nothing or make believe someone is waving to me across the room. If the woman insists, I swear, I don't care how much of a babe she is, I tell her she doesn't want to know. If she still insists I say: "My sign is NO PARKING KEEP MOVING" and watch her get unhinged. Anyway, Maruquita in May. Awilda got pregnant in September, so she's due in June. Winnifred got pregnant in October, but, through witchery, she has a short-term pregnancy of seven months, and she also gives birth in May—just in time to get married in June and avoid the embarrassment of waddling down the aisle. Carrie Marshack supposedly got pregnant in December and has her baby in March, giving rise to speculation that the father is not Omaha but perhaps Igor the Russian, or perhaps Eugene Doherty, whom she'd known for a number of years and with whom she'd been intimate during the last few months of living with the Russian. Not at all true. A DNA test would have proven conclusively that Omaha was the father and that Carrie got pregnant before she kicked him out of her apartment in June. Rita Flash got pregnant around December and had her child at the end of September. She gave birth to a huge, healthy forty-two pound baby girl whom she named Carrie after her girlfriend who had perished in the World Trade Center attack.

I'm not being cruel in bringing up 9/11 so casually. It happened. I'm still outraged, but it's a personal thing. Of course I feel compassion for the families of those who lost their lives. But the thing that bothers me each day is how these people have taken a piece of the graphic memory of my city and left this fuzzy picture postcard of the magnificence of the twin towers. I had been there many times. I had gone all the way up and watched the view in amazement. I'd stood in the plaza between the towers and marveled at their majesty, assuredly not great architecture but incredible ingenuity and courage. I don't hate anyone, so it's difficult to get with the program and become part of the collective piranha that the government and media are hell-bent on creating. I don't believe in war. It's as simple as that. All violence begets violence. I have been violent, and for that I am deeply ashamed. Organized violence is barbaric. I'm a stupid person, but that is what I believe. I'm not a turn-the-other-cheek kind of person, but neither am I an eye-for-an-eye person. I'm just someone trying to get through this difficult journey of existence with a little integrity about the things I was taught by other writers in the personal dialogue that is the novel. I know. I'm getting a little maudlin and defensive. I'll stop. What a mess. It's so sad.

How can I go back to the task of making you laugh after that. I can. I'm a professional. At least I like to think I am. As such I'm going to switch gears. WBGO is playing John Coltrane blowing solo on soprano, and he is beyond belief. He's doing "Afro Blue," and I am out of my mind with delight. What inspiration. Jazz is so incredible, and so few people support it. I have a theory. The masses don't support jazz because it is improvisational, unexpected, a glorious decanting of the human spirit that is spontaneous and heroic. The masses need monotony, so that they don't rebel. Certain music is repetitious, and the repetitiveness habituates people, narcotizes them. It's the same principle as the formula novel. Provide people with mind candy, so that they're groggy from the sugar high and don't have to recognize how they're being robbed of their dignity and socialized to accept conformity and not educated to seek truth.

Anyway, by March Winnifred was getting lessons from her grandmother with moderate success. Here are two sample e-mail communications that I was able to obtain. No I didn't hack their accounts. I have friends. First the AOL e-mail from Winnifred to her grandmother.

Subj: Good News
Date: 2/21/01 1:40 PM Eastern Standard Time
From: WinniePooh1
To: WhichEPooh07

Grandma,

I am ecstatic. The knowledge you've imparted to me is simply amazing. By saying *turn* I've been able to stand across a room, concentrate on the person whom I wish to contact, and invariably the person will walk over and say: "What is it, Winnie?" When I've felt in a jocular mood I've replied: "What do you mean?" The person has said: "Didn't you call me?" I've smiled and said. "Of course not. Did you hear me call you?" The person is then nonplused and will exclaim: "I was sure you had called me." This power is extraordinary. Is it telepathic? When will you be online so we can chat in private through IM? I'm full of questions regarding this new-found power.

Love, Winnifred (your loving and grateful granddaughter) :)

Later on that evening, while doing research on wedding dresses, Winnifred received the now familiar YOU'VE GOT MAIL. It never ceased to thrill Winnifred. She clapped her hands gleefully, retrieved a container of Haagen-Dazs Cookies and Cream ice cream, and some dill pickles, and returned to the computer in her luxury apartment. Omaha was lying down in the bedroom after he had brought her to incredible orgasm, which continued for nearly eighteen minutes. She was so in love and was certain that she would be able to tear Omaha away from the witch Marsuckita. She moused over to the mailbox and hit READ MAIL. Her grandmother's reply appeared on the screen.

Subj: Re: Good News
Date: 2/21/01 6:07 PM Eastern Standard Time
From: WhichEPooh07
To: WinniePooh1

In a message dated 2/21/00 1:40:02 AM Eastern Standard Time, WinniePooh1writes:
<<I'm full of questions regarding this new-found power.>>

My dearest Winnifred,

Congratulations on your new-found powers. Without an iota of scolding in these words, I must warn you that these powers should not be used in jest. What you did is a natural tendency in apprentices and will do no harm. However, if used indiscriminately and with evil intent, the results may cause one's powers to wane and possibly lead to insanity. I strongly believe this is what took place in Salem so many years ago. Girls became enamored of these wonderful gifts and began to use them recklessly for mirth and sport. As you well know, they became quite mad, turned against the teachings of the Church, were entered into by the Devil and became community spectacles to be despised and scorned and eventually burned as witches.

The world has changed considerably since those days but if you're not judicious about your gifts you could go mad and end up appearing in one of those awful, undignified shows such as Larry Springer, Maury Povich and that woman, Sally Jessie Raphael, who I've been given to understand (*entre nous*) is Puerto Rican.

I will be online later on tonight, around 10 PM.

Be well.

Your loving grandmother, Abigail.

Of course Sally Jessie Raphael is not Puerto Rican. She's American. She did start her radio and TV career while living there. Winnifred responded with a quick thank you note, some kisses (***). Below is a snippet of chat from a chatroom called The Authors Divan, a place where aficionados of the written word in differing stages of development gather to discuss the craft, flirt innocently, utter remarks about bodily functions, transgender issues and pop culture. Some call it, affectionately, The Authors Dive. These are not the actual names of the people. I've changed them to avoid unpleasantness. The following took place around 9:50 PM on the above date around the time that Winnifred entered this chat room.

ONLINEHOST: *** You are in "Pop Culture and Diversion - The Authors Divan". ***
SPRITZER: Picasso?
PICASSOERECTUS: Spritzer?
CRUELKAT: LOL
WHOMPAFLAMINGO: PICASSO!!!!!!!!
SHARPGRATE: http://www.images.com
PICASSOERECTUS: WHOMPA!!!!!!!
GREEKCONDUCTOR: EBJunk, I love you.
EBJUNK: Fat chance, fat broad.
CRUELKAT: LOL
WHOMPAFLAMINGO: I'm spinning.

PICASSOERECTUS: Are your panties on, Whompa?

WHOMPAFLAMINGO: I'm wearing a hoop skirt. Do you love me?

CRUELKAT: LOL

PICASSOERECTUS: I love your hoop skirt. Hahahaha.

CRUELKAT: LOL

FAROLCARSOME: I am the boss of all bosses. And I'm going to take the LSATs and go to Law School and become rich.

VONRAUGHUNCH: I've written over 800 Romance novels.

SPRITZER: VonRaghunch?

NARYMARKONME: There are questions about the athenticity of Steinbeck and his migrant research.

EBJUNK: Oh, here we go again. Authenticity, moron. First the Romance novel and now this philistine with his pseudo literary pronouncements.

CRUELKAT: LOL

WHOMPAFLAMINGO: <---- Laughing.

PICASSOERECTUS: And spinning?

CRUELKAT: LOL

LOTSOFLAUGHS: I'm almost finished with my first draft.

EBJUNK: And it's getting cold in the room.

LOTSOFLAUGHS: EBJunk, learn to punctuate.

WHOMPAFLAMINGO: Laughing, spinning and eating liverwurst.

MADHATTER: Yummy, Whompa.

LILPIPINANA: EBJunk claims that I had sex with him. I haven't even met him.

NANNYANYGOATS: Pipina, Ewwwwww!

LilPipinAna: I haven't ever written anything worth publishing.

MADHATTER: EBJunk poisons this room. Why isn't there any civility here?

EBJUNK: Hack.

SHOOSHOO: EBJunk stinks up the room. Put down the newspaper before he pees on the floor.

WHOMPAFLAMINGO: I'm laughing, spinning, eating liverwurst and singing.

CRUELKAT: LOL.

PICASSOERECTUS: You go, Whompa.

NANNYANYGOATS: He didn't write the books he claims he wrote.

EBOLAGOY: EBJunk self-publishes porno and pimps in Brooklyn and the Dominican Republic. The screen name says it all.

EBJUNK: Ebola, you're such a phony. You are such a punque.

WINNIEPOOH1: Hi, room.

PICASSOERECTUS: Hi, Winnie. How's the film?

WINNIEPOOH1: We wrapped two days ago. We're going to London soon.

PICASSOERECTUS: Good luck, Winnie. Come and see me.

WINNIEPOOH1: Hi, EB. How's the novel.

EBJUNK: Hi, Pooh. The novel is going well. The hero has managed to impregnate five women. He's in deep doodoo. It's tough not identifying with his sexual vigor.

LOXNMANGO: I note with interest that this EBJunk is now attempting to mate with the indefatigable and sexually inadequate WinnieLaPooh, Yalie and Indie film producer.

WINNIEPOOH1: LOL, Lox.

CRUELKAT: LOL

LOXNMANGO: The grossly cherubic WinnieLaPooh laughs while spreading her cetacean thighs in preparation for the herpeletic EBJunk's intromission into her mawing genitals.

PICASSOERECTUS: Hahahahaha, Lox.

SPRITZER: Picasso?

PICASSOERECTUS: Spritzer?

WHOMPAFLAMINGO: Spinning, laughing, eating liverwurst, singing and tap dancing.

CRUELKAT: LOL.

USGRANT: If EBJunk wants to write we should get him a new box of crayons.

SHOOSHOO: Get the newspaper. Shub his face in it.

WHICHEPOOH07: Good evening. Do you have your Instant Messages turned off?

WINNIEPOOH1: Hi, Which. *** Yes, let me open them up.

LOXNMANGO: EBJunk, isn't this Puritan septuagenarian WhichEPooh more your speed? I can envision the two of you giving each other toothless oral sex.

WHICHEPOOH07: That's quite enough, young lady. Have you no decency?

FAROLCARSOME: WhichEPooh, shut up!

WHICHEPOOH07: Farolcarsome <click>. You're on ignore.

CRUELKAT: LOL.

WHOMPAFLAMINGO: I've stopped spinning. I'm sitting down, doing my nails.

PICASSOERECTUS: Can I do your nails, Whompa?

WHOMPAFLAMINGO: Only if you beg.

PICASSOERECTUS: Please, can I do your nails?

WHOMPAFLAMINGO: Before or after the crucifixion?

EBJUNK: Joke. Grandson asks his grandfather if he still has sex with his grandmother. Grandpa explains that they have oral sex. "Grandpa," asks the grandson, "How? You're 93 and grandma's 91." The grandfather replies: "Well,

I get into my bed and turn off my night table lamp. She gets into her bed and turns off her light. I yell Fuck You! And she yells back Fuck You, too."

CRUELKAT: ROFLMAO

PICASSOERECTUS: Hahahaha.

WHOMPAFLAMINGO: I am spinning again.

WHICHEPOOH07: EBJunk <click>. In the box.

WINNIEPOOH1: Gotta go. Bye. IM me WhichE!

WHICHEPOOH07: I must leave as well.

EBJUNK: I'm off to continue to compose works of lasting literary signifi-cance. Have a nice evening although it is likely some of you have made other plans. Buona notte, bambini.

PICASSOERECTUS: Bye, EB.

CRUELKAT: LOL, bye, EB.

EBOLAGOY: The idiot porno king with a press in the Bronx and Puerto Rico is leaving. What a relief.

LOXNMANGO: I note with interest that this EBJunk is leaving in the company of the sexually dysfunctional Winnie and this nervous Puritan nellie WhichE. Are they headed for some sort of cross-generational *menage à trois* cyberama?

PICASSOERECTUS: Lox, Hahahahaha.

And so it went. Winnifred and her grandmother retired to the instant-message mode of AOL which provides a window for private chat. As much criticism as there is of this system, and without wishing to endorse it, AOL chatting is a very passable form of communication, and it provides an excel-lent opportunity to improve one's writing skills, a fact that many people ignore, excusing themselves by saying, "It's just chat," when in fact it offers them the chance to write well. Despite the limitations of the online life, Winnifred spent the next hour getting instruction from her grandmother on a number of issues. The most important one was how to get into someone's mind and place doubt in them about their abilities. This came in handy when Winnifred disguised herself as a Rican homegirl and from a distance of nearly a hundred feet placed in Maruquita's mind a vibrant image of Omaha going at Winnifred doggie style. Winnifred was grinning like the *perra puta* (bitch dog) she was, thought Maruquita.

Coño! What was she going to do now? Needless to say Maruquita was a bit shaken when this happened. She was now seven months into her pregnancy, wearing dresses that were like tents, feeling as if she were about to tip forward, practically needing a crane to get out of bed, and waddling everywhere she went without being able to see her feet. And now this gringa whitegirl doing her man and he enjoying himself like a pig in the mud. *Cabrón.* Sure, she thought, but she was the one with the horns in her head.

Cabrona was more like it.

MARUQUITA WADDLED HOME IN A RAGE. SHE WAS COMING OUT OF HER Aunt Ronquita's beauty parlor on Avenue B when all of a sudden she saw them together in her mind. Everything was so vivid. The gringa whitegirl was naked on all fours with her perfect tits and big butt shining like two moons in this really nice, Hollywood-looking bedroom with the lights on like it was daylight, and Omaha was there with his *bohango* all big and swollen and jumping up and down like it did. And then this gringa *pendeja* barks like a big pitbull bitch, and Omaha gets on her and sticks his *bohango* into her *papaya*, and he starts pumping her, and she's going yes, yes, yes, Omaha, and he has her by the hair and grabbing her tits, and she's having so much fun and then he comes, and he makes that real funny face that he makes, and she screams, and he falls on top of her. He's kissing her and telling her how much he loves her.

Maruquita couldn't help herself. She started crying uncontrollably. When she got back to her apartment, she fell on her bed in utter desolation, which she had learned from watching *novelas*. She couldn't believe it. She sat up on the bed and pounded her pillow. The phone next to her bed rang. She grabbed it immediately before it sounded a second time.

"Hello," she said, a bit shrilly.

"Yo, homegirl," said a girl's voice on the other end. "I got some shit to tell you."

"Who is this?" Maruquita screamed.

"You don't need to know that," the girl said, an obvious homegirl.

"Then why you calling me?"

"Cauze I got something to tell you."

"Go ahead, then. What you waiting for?"

"What you need to know is that you ain't the only one that's gonna have a Gringorican baby. And it was your man that gave it to me."

"Niggah, tell me who you be so I can fuck you up. Who you be, bitch?"

"That's for me to know and for you to find out," the girl said.

"You mothafockin bitch *maricona*. I'm gonna find you and kill you. I'ma turn you into a little chihuahua with a little pussy so a big ass pitbull can fuck you and then eat you up."

"Homegirl, you ain't shit. I axed around and as long as you pregnant, you can't do shit."

"Bitch, I'ma kill you," Maruquita responded. "So what! You having a Gringorican baby! Probably some dirty-ass squasher over there on Avenue C gave it to you, you ho. I bet it was that big redheaded dude wif da dreads that mess with the cops when they come to kick the squashers outta their house. The one they call Cheese or something. Maybe his friend Webbie. Maybe you be fuckin them and they gave you the Gringorican baby."

"No way, homegirl," said the voice. "It was our boyfriend with the big *gringo bohango*. The one that used to have green hair. He the one who gave me the Gringorican baby."

"Omagaw Boogaloo? Booshit, bitch. No way."

"Yeah, he did."

"Prove it, ho."

"I can prove it."

"Go ahead."

"His *bohango* is crooked to the left."

"I'ma kill you, bitch," Maruquita said, feeling crazy. "Stay away from my man."

"He everybody's man, *pendeja.*"

"Fuck you, *cobarde*. Why don't you tell me that shit to my face, *puta?*"

"See you, *cabrona*. *Te pegó los cuernos bien pegaos,*" she said, meaning that Omaha had placed two big horns on Maruquita's forehead, that he had been unfaithful.

"Bitch," Maruquita said, but the girl was gone.

She screamed and almost did a radical *mucura* to turn herself into a hawk and go looking for this bitch. Instead she got her keys and marched upstairs to see her mother. Before she left, the phone rang again. She picked it up and screamed into it. "What you want, bitch?" she said.

"Yo, ease up, mama," a deep voice said. "It's Rocky."

"I'm sorry, *papito,*" Maruquita said. "I didn't know it was you. Wassup?"

"Nothing, mama. Me and Chuckie found some shit out."

"About Omagaw Boogaloo?"

"Yeah, and about the blonde."

"What about her?"

"She's pregnant. We was waiting for your guy where he be staying at night. We was waiting to get paid, and the blonde was talking to some friend of hers and told her she was gonna have a baby."

"That mothafocka," Maruquita said. "That lying mothafocka. I'ma kill the niggah. First he quits working at Kinko's and he don't tell me about it. And then he tells me he got another job and then he gives me a whole lotta money and buys me nice things and he says he's making a movie. Is that shit true?"

"It's true."

"Some low *bollo* movie."

"That's right."

"With the blonde."

"Yeah, the blonde is paying for the whole thing. We found out."

"She a rich bitch?"

"Yeah."

"I can't believe this shit."

"Well, we just wanted to let you know. You want this whiteboy taken out?"

"No, I'll take care of it."

"See you around."

"Okay, thanks, Rocky. Say hello to Chuckie. Bye."

Maruquita hung up the phone and now she was even more crazed than before. She let herself out of the apartment and took the elevator up to her mother's. When she got there, she told her mother what was going on. Her mother's response was typical. She explained that she was finishing SBS's script and couldn't be bothered.

"But, Mama," Maruquita pleaded. "He's cheating on me."

"Didn't I tell you it wasn't a good idea?" Flaquita said, slamming the script on the coffee table. "I told you, didn't I? I told you to stay away from that gringo whiteboy. But no! You said, 'Mami, he's the one. I want him. Please,' you said. *¿Quién te manda?* Who told you to be a crazy? And then I agree to take you up to El Yunque and see Yukiyú and perform the *bohango*-growing ceremony and everything, and I still got a bad taste in my mouth from that."

"I'm sorry, Mami. What I'm suppose to do now?"

"Let me finish reading your brother's script. Make yourself a *ponche* with *malta.*"

"Ma! This is like the ten time you're reading that play," Maruquita complained.

"Twelfth. And it's tenth, not ten."

"Whatever. What about me? SBS's not the only kid you gots, you know."

"Don't remind me, please," Flaquita said. "Let me read. I'm analyzing the poetic symbolism of the play. And don't put too much sugar in the *ponche*. You don't wanna get your butt too fat."

To make a *ponche*, you separate the egg white, then add two or three spoonfuls of sugar to the yolk and beat it until you have a paste. You then take a cold Malta Goya or any other brand of the malt beer and mix it into the egg-and-sugar paste. This makes the mixture foam up and then you drink it. Malta has no alcoholic content, but it might as well have, because you get high from the sugar content. *Ponche* is supposed to be healthy. It's supposed to give men sexual vigor and make women's butts get bigger. I can deny the former and affirm the latter from personal observation.

Flaquita returned to reading the script. El Gato and Matalina are in bed. They are discussing Nalgas going to talk to the man with the briefcase. From there, they discuss whether the others around them are loyal. It seems that neither Ladroncito nor Manny Morongo are loyal to El Gato, but Matalina trusts them. She warns him about trusting Nalgas. In the next scene Nalgas has bad news for El Gato. It turns out that Matalina is sleeping with Ladroncito. "It's much worse," Nalgas says. "It's a *menage à trois* with Manny Morongo." El Gato tells Nalgas that he believes that Matalina is very homophobic and he should be careful. Nalgas replies that the Artists Dalliance has gone to see the local politician, Margafrida Locust.

Flaquita was puzzled. She underlined several places on the script. She meant to ask SBS what he was doing. The places in question were the following. In Scene 5 on pages 21–22 the following dialogue is held by Nalgas and El Gato, in which Nalgas reveals Matalina's disloyalty and her homophobia.

EL GATO

The plot thickens. Can I ask you something? Have you heard anything about a Puerto Rican Navy?

NALGAS

No, I haven't.

EL GATO

I heard a rumor about it. I think I could be a terrific admiral. What do you think?

NALGAS

I'm sure you could, your majesty. I've always looked at you as perfect for the Village People.

In the next scene the politician, who is also Puerto Rican, is talking about the Puerto Rican Navy. Why was she talking about the Navy? Had word gotten out and was now in the wrong hands? Margafrida Locust is totally out of her mind, thought Flaquita. This was serious. What did it mean? It was obvious that Samuel Beckett Salsipuedes was making a statement about the deceptive nature of politicians. But this was well known. What happened in Florida worried her. The Bush people had stolen the election and had paid off the Supreme Court. And these people had the guts to talk about Latin America and banana republics. Of course it had to be Florida where the Cubans run the show. The politician talks about being a submarine commander.

(*Scene Six, cont.*)

MARGAFRIDA LOCUST

Leave him to me. I have influences in high places.

BETRAYUS

We need your support.

PARCHAFLACA

We can contribute.

MARGAFRIDA LOCUST

With dollars?

PARCHAFLACA

Of course. But we need your help.

MARGAFRIDA LOCUST

It's always about money. But what can I do for you for the glory of America and all its 142 colonies in Latin America, Europe, Africa, Asia, and Israel?

BETRAYUS

Don't forget Puerto Rico.

MARGAFRIDA LOCUST

Oh, forget Puerto Rico.

(*There is an interlude here. The chorus comes out in their dollar outfits and they do a tap dance sequence to the tune of "New York, New York."*)

CHORUS

New York, New York it's a hell of a town. The Bronx is up and the Battery's down. Etc. and yadda yadda yadda. (*When they're done, the actors on stage applaud and encourage the audience to join in.*)

MARGAFRIDA LOCUST

That was excellent. One question. Have you heard something about a Puerto Rican Navy?

BETRAYUS

A Puerto Rican Navy? That is too funny.

MARGAFRIDA LOCUST

Don't laugh, you nitwit. I would make a wonderful admiral in the Puerto Rican Navy Submarine Service. I can go under. Did you see *The Hunt for Red October*? I liked the Russian uniforms better, but I'm not supposed to say that. People will think I am a Communist. I am not. I am a right wing patriot and a represser of the people.

(The stage goes dark and the music rises.)

Flaquita was left baffled by SBS's revealing the Puerto Rican Navy in his play. Was it a satirical device and part of the clown play, or was he guarding the identity of the navy? Who would believe that Puerto Ricans could put together a navy? But they could. She relaxed and once again trusted her son's genius. He was the head of the Naval Intelligence Service. What he was doing suddenly seemed brilliant, like everything else he did. Maruquita worried her, however. She tapped the script and set it down on the coffee table. She looked up. Maruquita was gone.

You couldn't blame Maruquita. She had left, insulted that her mother was so disrespectful and blamed her for what the gringo whiteboy had done. Maruquita had no choice about her next move. She simply had to take action.

Flaquita walked down the hall and knocked on Samuel Beckett Salsipuedes's door. He asked her to enter. SBS was at his computer.

"Hi, honey," Flaquita said. "How's it going?"

"Hi, Ma," SBS said, turning from the computer, removing his tinted glasses, and rubbing his eyes. "I'm having second thoughts."

"About?"

"The dialogue in the play."

"The dialogue? Why? It's wonderful."

"I don't know."

"What part?"

"The business of the Puerto Rican Navy."

"Oh, I just finished reading that part again."

"Well?" SBS said.

"It's terrific. You're a brilliant artist. You can't keep life from intruding into the artistic process. How are things going on that front?"

"The navy? That's another problem."

"The cloaking device from *Star Trek?*"

"No, that was elementary. I figured it out, and I'm having it installed on all the ships."

"How did you do it?"

"It was pretty simple, in fact. I just took the instances on *Star Trek* when the cloaking device was used and simply scanned the photos of the ships into the *Star Trek* scenes and reversed the process. You should have seen it. We were up in the Hudson River past the George Washington Bridge, and all of a sudden I asked one of our destroyers to switch the cloaking device on. One minute the destroyer was there, and *poof,* it was gone. We kept in close communication until we were down by the World Trade Center. I asked the captain of the destroyer, Fatboy Alex, Doña Marta's grandson, to turn off the cloaking device, and the destroyer showed up again down by the Statue of Liberty. That shit was def, Mami."

"I'm assuming the ships haven't been painted in our colors yet."

"No, not yet. They're still gray so they look like gringo navy ships."

"So what's the problem?"

"Grandma."

"What about her?"

"She's so controlling. She wants to name the ships all kinds of dopey things like *El Grito de Lares. Lolita Lebrón. La masacre de Ponce. Que Viva Puerto Rico Libre.* You know? All kinds of old-fashioned political rhetoric. Our strength is our popular culture."

"I understand. She's a little conservative. What do you suggest?"

"We should go with more popular names. I don't know, I was listening to this Cortijo CD, and I thought maybe one of our cruisers could be *El Chivo de la Campana.* It's an excellent example of the *plena.* I think we could play the song as we go into battle, and the crew would be really inspired. What do you think?"

"That is brilliant."

"You think so?"

"Of course. Let me talk to your grandmother. By the way, it was great including our navy in the play. I'm curious about why you did that."

"It's my own cloaking device."

"What do you mean?"

"Who's going to believe that we have a navy?"

"Great. That's what I thought. One thing about the play."

"What is that?"

"We shouldn't mount a production until we regain Vieques from the United States. After our victory, when we've taken Vieques and sunk all the American ships, we'll stage the play."

"Okay, Ma," SBS said. "I was thinking the same thing. Are you going to be on board?"

"At some point. Your grandmother thinks I should be Secretary of the Navy."

"You see? In that I agree with Grandma."

"I made *ensalada de pulpo*, honey. You should eat. The octopus is very tender."

"Maybe later, Ma," SBS said, putting on his glasses and turning back to the computer.

Flaquita shook her head and thought of how thin SBS had always been. She went out of the room and called Maruquita. The phone was busy. She tried her cell phone. A message that she was out of the area came on. She went downstairs and knocked on the door. No answer. She worried that Maruquita would do something crazy. Maruquita was heading in exactly that direction. *Calle Locura, Esquina Arrebate.* Madness Street on the Corner of Whacked-Out Avenue.

PASSING AS J-LO AND A CONFRONTATION

MARUQUITA COULDN'T BELIEVE IT. HER OWN MOTHER DIDN'T LOVE HER. Here she was, suffering because this ungrateful gringo whiteboy had cheated on her, and her mother just kept reading that stupid play that her brother had written. And then she was correcting her like she was a stupid idiot. But maybe she was stupid. And then that girl had called her and said she was pregnant with another baby from Omagaw Boogaloo. Who was the girl? Maruquita walked up Avenue B, turned at Houston, looked at Chico's mural of Selena, Princess Diana, and that poor little girl whose mother had killed her, and went into Kinko's. Maybe her mother wanted her dead, too. Maybe her mother was jealous that she could do so many things with magic and was a better *bruja*. Maybe she was jealous of her peacock. She walked up to the counter and Ludmilla, one of the Russian girls, came over.

"You want to making copies?" she said, looking industrial and Slavic.

"No, I'm looking for my boyfriend."

"Sorry, we not have KGB office in this people's collective."

"I ain't looking for no KBG shit, Frenchie. What is that, French MTV?"

"Please not comparing great effort Russian people making for protecting motherland to French postmodernist cabbage heads of capitalism."

"I ain't comparing nothing. His name is Omagaw Boogaloo."

At that point Valery Molotov came over. "Greetings, wonderful looking comrade friend with healthy revolutionary impregnation," Molotov said. "What can I be of helping?"

"Hi, I'm looking for Omagaw Boogaloo."

"Comrade Omaha not present now at this copying collective. He is producting glorious film of struggle of proletariat musician in corrupt capitalist environment."

"You talking about the movie he's making?"

"Correct. Is very much cinematographic triumph, I hearing. This information from secret sources. Not KGB."

"Shit, what's with the KGB again?"

"No, KGB never again. We are speaking in past tensing up. KGB buried in shadow of history, in fog of Stalinism, in supreme victory of *glasnost*, in triumph of *perestroika*."

"Whatever. Where is Omagaw Boogaloo?"

"Red Square. Apartment 10A. Please give him fraternal kissing from Molotov."

"Thanks," Maruquita said. "I don't know about no kissing, but I'ma kick his bony gringo whiteboy ass."

Maruquita left Kinko's and headed for Red Square. She entered the building, rushed towards the elevator, but was called back by the young Puerto Rican man at the desk. Maruquita explained that she needed to go up to 10A.

"The guy making the movie?" the young man said, his attitude severe.

"Yeah, that bozo."

"Are you his friend?"

"I ain't delivering no pizza. Yeah, I'm his friend."

"You don't gotta get nasty," said the guy at the desk, and then he stared at Maruquita. "Oh, wait," he said, his attitude totally different, smiling and pointing at her. "Wait, wait. Wow."

"What?"

"You're J-Lo."

Maruquita was suddenly aware that she could use her resemblance to the actress.

"No I'm not," she said, knowing that she wasn't going to convince this guy otherwise.

"Don't play yourself, homegirl," he said. "You're Jennifer Lopez."

"Well, I don't got no limo outside."

"I know that. You're so cool. Let me tell you something," said the young man touching his palm to his chest with great reverence. "We're proud of you, J-Lo."

"Thank you, *papito.*"

"You doing good and making big bucks, but you don't forget that you Rican."

"Never."

"Right on! Some folks be forgetting when they was Rican. You're pregnant. That's very cool. I'm not gonna ask who's the father. I don't wanna get personal."

"It's for a movie," Maruquita said, smiling and patting her belly. "It's like a thing they put on you to make you look like you pregnant. I be playing a pregnant girl. I'm trying to get used to it."

"Oh, no little J-Lo coming?"

"No, not yet. Can I go up?" Maruquita said, smiling at the young guy.

"Sure, no problem," he said. "Just sign the book." And then he pulled out a magazine with Jennifer Lopez's picture in it and had Maruquita sign the magazine.

The young man looked at the signature, looked at J-Lo's name, and nodded.

"You use one N in your name?" he said.

"Only for special people, *papito,*" she said.

"Oh, cool," the young man said, reassured.

Maruquita took the elevator, got off on the tenth floor, and looked for the apartment. When she found it, she knocked on the door. She waited and knocked again. Finally Omaha came to the door looking like he had been sleeping. Maruquita, now furious, pushed past him.

"Is she here?"

"Who?"

"Who? You saying who to me, niggah? You gonna say boo hoo if you don't tell me the truf."

"Who are you talking about?"

"Omagaw Boogaloo, don't play yourself. You know who I'm talking about. That bitch you be fucking behind my back. That's who. Don't try to mess wif my mind."

"Maruquita, what are you talking about?"

"I'm talking about the blonde," Maruquita screamed. "I'm talking about the gringa whitegirl, *perra puta sinvergüenza cabrona maricona* blondie bitch mothafocka, that's who."

"I'm all alone. She doesn't live here anymore."

"I'm gonna kill the niggah when I see her," Maruquita said, kicking a cushion on the floor. "She's dead meat, Omagaw Boogaloo. I heard you gave her a baby, and then this other girl call me up and she tole me you gave her a baby, too. Are you crazy? Don't you know what can happen to you, playing me dirty like that?"

"Maruquita, that girl is lying."

"And the blonde?"

"We're just friends. She's helping me with the film."

"You are such a liar, Omagaw Boogaloo."

"I'm not."

"I love you, you bozo," Maruquita said, starting to break up. "I love you, and you playing me like a fool," she said. "Why you cheating on me? That's wrong. Look at me, I'm carrying your baby, and you cheating on me."

"They're lying, Maruquita," Omaha lied, the activity sort of second nature to him now. "You're the only girl I love."

"Don't play me, Omagaw Boogaloo," Maruquita said, facing him down and looking into his eyes. "Don't play me."

"I'm not," Omaha said. "You look so beautiful. I'm so looking forward to the birth of our child. I'm certain that whether it's a boy or a girl, our offspring will be a remarkable specimen of hybrid vigor with genetic attributes from both of us."

"Shut up," Maruquita screamed. "Why you talking like that? I don't understand what the fuck you're talking about. You talking like that because you be hanging out with that bitch."

"Well, I have to be professional. Suppose I have to face the press? Oprah, Larry King."

"Fuck you, Omagaw Boogaloo. You gonna be in so much trouble. I don't believe nothing that come out of you lying ass. You better come home and quit messing around. And you look like shit with your blond hair. You look like Barbie's boyfriend. Like you got Christmas tree hair."

"Maruquita, I love you. I want to give you head. Come inside the bedroom."

"Booshit," Maruquita said. "I'm out."

With that she turned, went to the door, and let herself out. She went down the elevator and rushed past the desk without acknowledging the doorman's *Goodbye and good luck, J-Lo, say hello to Puffy*.

She rushed home and immediately picked up the phone and made a very important call that very likely changed the final outcome of this novel. I had an ending that would have been agreeable to most people. Not the kind of novel that Jonathan Yardley wrote about in the *Washington Post* on December 3, 2001, in which he chastises the sameness of the American novel, but something mildly provocative and agreeable to the average American. I'm not trying to hurt the United States. It's more like prodding it to see if it'll wake up. But things have a habit of changing in novels.

We'll see.

MARUQUITA WAS ANGRIER THAN SHE HAD EVER BEEN. WHAT THE HELL did he think he was doing, messing this much with her life? It was his novel, but he had no right to put her in such conditions and under so much stress. She let the phone ring a long time, and finally the author answered. He recognized her voice and asked if she was all right.

"No, I'm not all right," she said. "I'm terrible. Why are you doing this to me?"

"I'm sorry," he said. "I have to. It's the only thing I know how to do. I explained it to you. I can't pick up a gun and open fire on someone. I'm not going to plant a bomb somewhere and kill people. I'm certainly not going to strap dynamite inside my jacket and blow myself up in a pizza shop. If I don't do this, people are going to think that we're stupid and can only write dopey books, and we'll never be free. I have to do something. I've explained that to you. Look at the stuff that these people publish by us."

"I know, Vega. I wish somebody would come along and write some really worthwhile literature instead of all that ghetto bullshit. But you're really messing with me."

"You're taking it personally, baby."

"Don't do that, Vega. Don't patronize me. I'm really hurting right now."

"I'm not being patronizing. I have great affection and respect for you."

"But you got me in all this trouble. I'm pregnant, this guy doesn't love me, my mother doesn't like me. You gave me all this power, and then you took it away from me because I'm pregnant. I know it's my fault for getting pregnant, but I have needs, too. I need affection and support. I feel totally ignored."

"I'm sorry. It's part of the plot. I can't have you morphing into squirrels and monkeys and climbing trees and flying around while you're pregnant. Who's going to believe something like that? Don't you think it's a good idea to suspend your powers during your pregnancy? It makes you more vulnerable and provides more sympathy for your character. I'm sure women will identify with your situation. I think that being vulnerable is a good idea."

"Well, you have a point, but now this son of a bitch has two other women pregnant. There are three babies coming. My aunt has three kids from three different guys, but this is one guy with three women pregnant at the same time."

"Certainly not atypical, and it's five."

"Five what?"

"There are two more girls carrying his kids."

"Are you crazy? Are you telling me that besides the blonde and this lunatic chick that called me, who's probably Dominican, that he has two more girls pregnant?"

"That's right. And she's not Dominican. Your paranoia about Dominicans is unfounded."

"Fine, she's not Dominican. Who are they?"

"Well, one is his ex-girlfriend, and the other is some girl who plays in a rock band."

"Jesus Christ, what are you trying to do? Excuse me for getting academic and analytical and whatnot, but is this some sort of metaphoric affirmation of the hegemonic power of the United States juxtaposed against the destiny of this hemisphere? First NAFTA and eventually all of Latin America. You're starting to confuse me about your politics, Vega."

"I know what I'm doing, and it's nothing like that."

"What is it, then?"

"I'll let you decide that when the project is done. You can tell me what you think. Also when you see Omaha's film, you'll get a very interesting view of all this. Although I don't know, given the subject matter, if the film will be released. I hope it is. For his sake."

"What do you mean?"

"Well, he's kind of setting himself up for a fall. He's not quite his father, you know."

"What do you mean, his father? His father was killed in Vietnam."

"Never mind. You're right. He was killed in Vietnam. I'm thinking about your metaphor. He's certainly no Uncle Sam. That's obvious."

"Oh! No, he's not. I see what you mean. But I have to ask you something. The other girl."

"What other girl?"

"You said five of us are going to have babies. Who's the one who called me?"

"That's part of the plot. I can't tell you."

"Vega, don't start that again, okay?"

"What?"

"I really don't like it when you get like this."

"Sorry."

"Sorry, isn't going to do it anymore, Vega. You are so fucking deus ex machina."

"Well . . ."

"Don't do that, you bastard. Don't play like you're sorry. I know you get pleasure out of screwing around with characters' lives."

"I'm trying to work things out in my own life. There are things I don't understand."

"Like what?"

"Like why Puerto Ricans can't be free like other people."

"Maybe Ricans don't want to be free."

"That may be. Maybe Puerto Ricans like being the chatelaine of this big dick country."

"Chatelaine? Isn't a chatelaine the mistress of a château? Maybe Puerto Rico is in control of the United States instead of the other way around. Don't you mean concubine? Just a suggestion."

"Fine, concubine then."

"Don't get upset. I'm just trying to help."

"I said fine, didn't I?"

"Vega, who is she? Who's the girl who called me and told me she was pregnant? Who's the fifth one?"

"I can't tell you."

"That is so messed up. You have somebody just call me up like that and try to bug me and make me jealous, and I'm not supposed to know who it is?"

"That's right. At this point it's not good for you to know. Eventually you'll know, and it'll give you an opportunity to behave with great nobility and fulfill the heroic nature of your character."

"Get out!"

"Really."

"But you're so controlling."

"What would you like?"

"I don't know. I feel constrained by the dopey persona of this Rican home-girl. Couldn't I undergo some sort of dramatic character transformation and speak with a modicum of intelligence?"

"I don't think it'd be a good idea at this juncture, but I can compromise."

"Compromise how?"

"Let me set up the next couple of situations, and then once they're set up you can take over and do whatever you want. It doesn't seem as if I have much control over you."

"I'm willing to take direction, but you're very heavy-handed. What situations?"

"The Bush situation and the wedding preparations."

"Bush? He's involved in this?"

"Yes, sort of."

"And the wedding? Omaha's going to marry me?"

"No, not you."

"The mystery girl?"

"No, he's going to marry the blonde. You don't know her but she's very powerful."

"Powerful how? I know she's rich."

"She has witches in her family as well."

"No way. Don't tell me she's descended from those lunatic Salem women."

"Yep."

"Shit! Vega, you are so incredibly crazy. And you're planning to make even more trouble for me? I don't believe this. He's going to marry the blonde? That is so fucked up. I am so pissed off at you right now."

"Yeah, well that's the best I can do. You can decide what you want to do about it."

"I can do anything I want?"

"Anything."

"And nobody's going to get in my way and try to prevent me from carrying this out?"

"Nobody."

"Not even my mother?"

"Not even your mother."

"Well, that sounds pretty cool."

"Deal?"

"Deal."

"Let me ask you something, then."

"What?"

"Would you like to meet her? The blonde."

"I'll probably want to kill her."

"Well . . . we can wait until you have the baby. When is it due?"

"You know when it's due."

"It's important that you know, however."

"Fine, right now I'm in my third trimester. The doctor say I'm due about the third week of May. Could be the nineteenth, twentieth, twenty-first, around there. Roughly sixty days."

"I see."

"Probably the twentieth if I know you."

"Why do you say that?"

"Well, isn't your birthday May twentieth?"

"Yes, it is."

"So why wouldn't you have the baby be born on your birthday?"

"I suppose that makes sense. So do you want to meet her or not?"

"Sure, but I'll have my powers back, and if I want to morph into a seagull and drop a load on her stupid-ass Laura Ashley sundress, I can."

"Sure, it's up to you."

"And she has magical powers?"

"Moderate ones. But she's very wealthy, and that is as good as magic."

"Terrific! What kind of budget are you giving me for this?"

"Nothing, go and ask your brother. He has unlimited funds."

"Right. Is it true about the cloaking device?"

"From *Star Trek*?"

"Yeah."

"Yes, your brother is quite amazing. He figured it all out."

"That's a little like morphing and demorphing and remaining in between so you're invisible and you can sneak into places. That's good for getting into clubs. I did that a couple of times at The Limelight, even though I was underage."

"That's right. A similar concept."

"You mean they can take a boat and make it disappear and sneak up on, let's say Vieques, appear, blast a U.S. ship out of the water, and just disappear out to sea again?"

"Yes, it's quite an effective device."

"Damn. By the way, what the hell is that play about that he's writing? I read it but it's really obscure. He's crazier than you are. I've read absurdist plays and I've gone to the Ontological at St. Mark's Church and to Nada and even to see plays over at that Rican Center below Houston a lot of times."

"On Suffolk Street."

"Yeah, over there. I saw *A Walk Across Lake Constance* and a Strindberg thing and a couple of Irish plays. I think one of them was *The Magic Glasses.* I also saw an Irish company do the only play that James Joyce ever wrote over there."

"*Exiles.*"

"Yes, that's it. Really beautiful. There was an actress, a redhead, who was incredible."

"You said *actress.*"

"Yeah, I'm an actress. She's an actor or an actress. People should call themselves whatever they want. She was great. I was a little jealous."

"I know, she was luminescent, but you're truly magnificent."

"Oh, thanks . . . gee."

"Gee?"

"Well, I'm practicing saying sort of vapid things in case I get one of those Winona Ryder roles and have to play an American ingenue."

"I see."

"One thing."

"Yes?"

"My brother's play? Why the crucifixion at the end? That's truly bizarre."

"Well, you have to ask him. I don't quite understand it myself. It seems a little contrived."

"As they say: whatevah! But back to my thing. Let me understand this. You're going to set up the Bush thing and then the wedding. I'm going to have the baby, get my powers back, and then I'm going to meet this bimbo."

"Well, more like the Bush thing, you meet Winnifred, and then the wedding. Or we can insert your meeting prior to the Bush thing and the wedding. You won't have your powers when you meet her. It's up to you."

"Yeah, the sooner the better. I can handle her. I'm really pissed at the little twit."

"Okay, right away then. But you have no powers right now."

"I can handle it."

"Fine."

"So after the wedding comes the part where I have total control."

"That's correct."

"And you're going to keep your end of the bargain. Because if you don't, word's going to get around."

"You have my word. Let's get back to work."

"Wait? The wedding is after I have the baby?"

"Yes, after you have the baby. I said that. You'll have your full powers back."

"I'm just trying to get the sequence fixed in my head so I can work on my motivation and all that. One more thing, Vega."

"What is that?"

"Is it a boy or a girl?"

"I don't know. How am I supposed to know that unless it happens? You'll go to the hospital, go through the whole birthing thing, and then the doctor'll hold the baby up to you and then we'll know if it's a boy or a girl. Okay?"

"I guess so. You are incredibly weird, Vega. Aren't you supposed to know everything?"

"I can't know everything. You know that. Wouldn't that be a little arrogant?"

"Well, you act like you know everything. I have to think about all this."

"Okay, take care. *Cuídate.*"

"You too. Bye!" she said and hung up the phone.

She shook her head. There was some weird stuff going on. She couldn't believe that she'd just had that conversation. She lay down on the bed and closed her eyes. She could feel the baby kicking and felt her belly. She saw the cloth of her dress bulge. An elbow or a foot made a little lump that she touched tenderly. She smiled and imagined holding the baby and feeding it. She started thinking about breast feeding and wondered if it would ruin her breasts. Maybe not. She smiled and drifted slowly off to sleep.

On the other side of the island of Manhattan, Winnifred Buckley was on the phone with her father, asking if he could have lunch with her during the following week. She didn't know quite how she was going to tell him that she was pregnant. She also had to find out what she was going to do about the witch that had Omaha in her grasp. Omaha had called her, and he was totally freaked out because Maruquita had come to see him. He explained how this Puerto Rican hussy had threatened him and said she was going to come after her. It took all of Winnifred's patience to calm Omaha down. With what she knew she could turn this marzipan linguistic disaster into a toad. This Puerto Rican moron validated her firm conviction that eugenics might ultimately be an option in order to refine the human race.

CONFESSION AT THE HARVARD CLUB

T HE DINING ROOM AT THE HARVARD CLUB IS RATHER IMPRESSIVE. IT HAS a high ceiling, perhaps as high as one hundred feet. The lighting is so perfect that eating there one feels regal and as if God has chosen one to rule, even if it's simply a multinational corporation. The oak paneling is dark and polished, and the room has a subdued Britannic look to it. The tables are large, the linen thick and immaculate. The silver is solid and heavy, and it makes one feel as if in wielding a fork or a knife one has the power to guide the destiny of thousands or even millions of people. The china matches the substance of the silver, large, thick and porcelain white. So large are the plates that a delicately roasted quail with new potatoes and julienne string beans with a delicate hollandaise sauce appear as a light snack. As to goblets and wine, one need imagine Olympus to gain insight as to the nectar being decanted there.

When Pierce Buckley's limousine pulled up in front of the Harvard Club, Winnifred questioned why they were there. Startled, she sat somewhat appalled and asked for an explanation. Why not the Yale Club? Pierce smiled kindly and explained that whenever the Republicans gained the White House, Yale alumni ate at the Harvard Club for half price.

"And vice versa of course," he said. "Bill Clinton has not allowed us this pleasure for eight years. We can go to the Yale club if you wish. It's practically around the corner, as you know. Or we could go someplace else if you'd like."

"No, that's all right," Winnifred said. "Is this some sort of secret male arrangement?"

"Yes, a gentleman's agreement, but a very important one."

"Like the game."

"Exactly. Like the game," Pierce Buckley said. "There is nothing like a Harvard-Yale gridiron confrontation in late fall. I haven't missed one for thirty years. So?"

"Okay, then. No more Impale Yale for a while. Let's go."

Pierce laughed, waved his hand, and the driver, Lucius Washington, a serious fiftyish, African-American man with a PhD in Sino-Russian Studies, got out of the car, straightened his uniform, pushed up the knot on his tie, and tapped his cap before going around the front of the car, opening the door, and bowing ever so lightly. Dr. Washington did not look like Morgan Freeman in *Driving Miss Daisy*. He looked more like a pissed-off James Earl Jones. A question about the resonant-voiced Mr. Jones and CNN official town crier: Why is this man consistently playing high-ranking officials in military or CIA films? Are they trying to reassure everyone that Colin Powell is not going to attempt a coup and put Jesse Jackson in the White House?

Pierce emerged from the limousine first. Bending his six-foot-four angular frame, he gave his hand to Winnifred to help her alight. They were both dressed impeccably. Pierce wore a pinstriped dark blue three-piece suit. The trousers were creased sharply and the cuffs symmetrical, his shirt perfectly laundered, starched, and ironed. His shoes were expensive and fitted to his large feet by a master shoemaker in Milan at the cost of two thousand five hundred dollars per pair. His tie alone was in the two hundred dollar price range. His overcoat was English and tailored perfectly. Winnifred wore a blue silk dress with delicate gold accents by Giovannella Ramazzotti that outlined her curvaceous body. Her stockings gave her magnificent legs a sculpted sheen. Her blue high heels brought her to a statuesque six foot one. In her right hand she carried a matching rectangular purse which contained her keys, wallet with credit cards, and a small gold makeup case. She sported delicate diamond earrings, a ruby pendant, and a delicately matching ruby ring, gifts from her grandmother, Abigail, upon Winnifred's graduation from Yale. Her nails were done in a light cerise color that matched her lipstick. She wore an ankle-length mink, in the strong belief that the small animals, if permitted to live out their lives, would suffer horribly as they aged and eventually succumb to predators and the elements. Why not live a brief life in which you were fed and bred in the comfort of warm surroundings and then gloriously serve a noble purpose by enhancing the beauty of women? She was certain that the mink had been quite happy, grateful, and had faced death bravely and proudly.

Their entrance into the Harvard Club was spectacular. Heads turned and Harvard alumni, disgruntled by the debacle in Florida four months prior, whispered circumspect innuendoes about the older man and the younger woman. Movie aficionados were certain Winnifred was a screen star but couldn't recall her name. Someone mentioned Charlize Theron and cited a golfing film many had seen. Older Harvard alumni of graduating classes of the 1920s and 1930s thought that they were hallucinating and that Carole Lombard had been resurrected in their midst. Coats checked, obeisance acknowledged to the maître d' and waiters, and polite nods made by Pierce to associates and acquaintances, they were escorted into the dining room.

Winnifred was not impressed and commented that the room looked like a preparatory school library. She felt that the high ceiling was ostentatious. Once seated at one of the center tables, Pierce smiled at his youngest child. He was pleased that she had grown into such a magnificent young woman, poised, confident, and with that aquiline look in her eyes that bespoke rapine ambition. Of all his children Winnifred was the one with whom he identified completely. It was she whose instincts were unerring and resolve deadly. He was relieved that her grandmother reported that she had calmed down, had overcome her attacks, and was no longer receiving visions of warriors. She now possessed a most spectacular radiance. His mother, Abigail, had taken her under her wing, and the tutelage was obviously working.

"You look well, Winnifred," he said. "Radiant, in fact. It's as if you're entering full bloom into your womanhood. You appear a little fuller, which is not uncommon in young women."

"Thank you, Daddy," she replied. "As usual, you are the paragon of sartorial splendor. I have never seen a man so elegant."

"You're too charming for words," Pierce replied. "Thank you. How is your film project?"

"Excellent. We wrapped two weeks ago. It's being edited and the score is being synchronized. I'm very pleased with our work. We were only one week over schedule, and we came in well under budget. With good accounting we will probably end up doing the entire film for about six-point-eight million."

"That is remarkable, Winnie," Pierce said, admiringly. "I'm duly impressed. You appear to have a remarkable facility for handling this kind of enterprise. Is film production something you'd like to essay again in the future?"

"I've thought about it, Daddy. It's truly fascinating."

"I'm open to any suggestion you may have."

"Well, it's something to consider. I'll finish law school and then think about it again."

"There are a couple of studios failing badly," Pierce said. "I would be happy to purchase one and revive it. I can explore that possibility. As it stands, you still have about twelve million to draw on. I can invest further in your future if this is what you wish."

"Oh, Daddy," Winnifred said, overcome with emotion. "Thank you so very much. I always felt, being the youngest, that I would disappoint you. Muffy is so capable. She's not quite forty but already sits on the boards of six museums, four philharmonic orchestras, seventeen foundations, the DAR, and is a trustee of eight universities, including, if one can imagine, a Negro college. And the boys are nonpareil in everything: athletics, academics, and successful in every way. *Enfants d'une puissance vraiment extraordinaire,"* she added in the perfectly accented French she'd learned at a finishing school in Switzerland.

"Yes, undoubtedly young men of extraordinary power," Pierce said, translating the French and recalling his youth when he was attached to the French Sûreté. But more recent memories of French evoked images of Dakulana Imbebwabe and her glistening ebony skin, reciting Rimbaud verses to him in French as he lay in a stupor beside her after spending himself gloriously between her long and supple legs. "You are a jewel of a young woman, Winnifred. You need never feel lacking."

"Thank you, Daddy. I adore you. No girl could be as lucky to have you as a father."

They had ordered and sat drinking from their goblets French wine of a particularly fine vintage, white, chilled, and dry. Winnifred had ordered the quail, and Pierce a broiled bass fillet with a salad. They sat, father and daughter, admiring each other. Winnifred thought that no occasion could be more perfect for letting her father know that she was with child. The food came shortly thereafter and they began eating.

"Daddy, I don't want to bring up unpleasantness during our meal, but I have to tell you something."

"Nothing from you would be unpleasant."

"Daddy, I'm going to have a child."

"Well," Pierce said, lifting his napkin from his lap, coughing lightly and dabbing his lips. "This is certainly a surprise."

"I'm sorry."

"No need for apologies," Pierce said. "The filmmaker?"

"Yes, Daddy."

"Young Bigelow."

"Yes, Omaha."

"He seems a decent sort. I can't say I have any overwhelming feeling, but what now?"

"Marriage, I suppose."

"Do you love him?"

"Madly."

"And does he love you?"

"I think so. He's a bit ambivalent."

"Ambivalent?"

"Well, there's someone else."

"Is he married?"

"In a way. He's living with a Puerto Rican girl. One of those unfortunate East Village demimondaines. Merely a technicality of the bohemian life. He is a remarkable man, Daddy. I'm not flattering you when I say that each time I think of him I'm reminded of you. It is more a compliment to him, for you are extraordinary. You're an extremely successful businessman, an accomplished yachtsman, and even astride a polo pony you stand out among the others."

"Thank you, Winnifred. Can he extricate himself from the situation?" Pierce said, returning the napkin to his lap. "Of greater importance, is he worth saving?"

"Oh, most definitely, Daddy," Winnifred said. "He is a truly talented person. Gifted. There is something about him that, given the right circumstances, could make him formidable on the world stage, so to speak."

"I see," Pierce Buckley nodded. "That is indeed high praise. Is it a fulfilling relationship?"

"In every way, Daddy," Winnifred said. "And you're not upset?"

"A bit taken aback that I'm to be a grandfather yet again. I suppose we'll have to advise your mother, and she and your sister Margaret can begin the preparations, together with whomever you choose for your maid of honor and bridesmaids."

"Yes, they've been advised."

"How far along are you? And how soon do you wish to have the wedding? I can have you flown somewhere if you need to end the pregnancy."

"Oh no, I want to have the child. I'm thinking that perhaps a late June wedding would be perfect. Out at Sag Harbor. Outdoor ceremony and reception."

"You'll be quite large by then."

"I've asked Grandmother for help and she's studying the situation," Winnifred said.

"So you've discussed this with my mother?"

"Yes, she's the one who suggested I broach the subject with you."

"So you have."

"Grandma feels she can accelerate the gestation process and I can arrive at full term at the end of the next two months, since I'm already five months along."

"You don't show it at all except in your exceptional radiance," Pierce said. "That always happened with your mother. I should've remembered. And there's no danger in this? This accelerated gestation."

"No, none."

"And the young man's parents?"

"She's a gifted pianist, and his father was killed in Vietnam. A solid upbringing. He went to Yale, of course."

"Yes, I wonder under whose auspices," Pierce said.

"One question."

"Yes, dear."

"Daddy, do you want Omaha to go through the formality of asking for my hand?"

"No, that's not necessary. I'm rather busy. I'll talk to someone at the *Times* to keep things under control, and we'll have the announcement of the engagement and upcoming vows."

"Thank you, Daddy."

Their meal was completed with *crème brulée* and coffee. They talked a few minutes more, and a short time later they left the Harvard Club after Pierce Buckley signed for the meal. Pierce activated the delicate communications device in his pocket, so by the time Winnifred and her father were coming out the front door and descending the steps into the street, Dr. Washington and the limousine were pulling up. Dr. Washington slid out of the driver's seat, came around, and held the door open for Winnifred and Pierce. Once inside, Winnifred hugged herself to her father. Pierce kissed her lightly on the forehead and patted her shoulder several times.

"Where to?"

"My new home in Soho," Winnifred said. "As soon as we've set up properly, I want you to come and have dinner with us, Daddy."

Dr. Washington started the car and began making his way downtown to the address where he had picked Winnifred up earlier that afternoon.

"Well, I'd like to meet the young man at some point," Pierce said.

"Of course, Daddy. I've been meaning to do that, but our shooting schedule and postproduction has been quite rigorous. When would you like us to come to see you and Mom?"

"Well, I'm leaving for Paris on Saturday. Business."

"By the way. How is Dakulana?"

"She's well. I'll see her again in London."

"Daddy?"

"Yes, dear."

"Do you love her?"

"She's a remarkable woman, Winnifred. Perhaps the most remarkable woman I've known."

"You love her."

"I suppose it would be difficult to deny it."

"I never imagined," Winnifred said.

"Because she's an African?"

"Well, yes. It's such a radical departure from the rest of your life."

"I suppose. There are complex factors involved."

"What do you mean?"

"Global issues. Arrangements. High finance."

"Concerning Dakulana?"

"Yes, but it's all very complicated and hush-hush. We're collaborating on the West Africa project. But there are other things involved."

"And you can't talk about them."

"No, I cannot. I'm sure you understand."

"I do, sir."

Pierce laughed dryly and patted his daughter's hand.

Soon thereafter they were back in front of Winnifred's building. She kissed and hugged her father and got out of the limousine. They would have reason to meet again soon, given the complications Winnifred was about to encounter. She went through the lobby quickly, stopping to inquire momentarily of José, the Puerto Rican doorman, whether anyone had come looking for her. José said no one had. Winnifred entered the elevator, and after a twelve-floor ascent, the elevator doors opened onto the apartment foyer. She retrieved her keys from her small bag and opened the door. As soon as she was inside and had closed the door, she sensed that something was not quite right. The place was deadly still, even though she sensed a presence. She called the cook and then the maid. No answer. Winnifred reached down and removed her high heels. She placed them silently on the polished blond floor and, without removing her coat, began tip-toeing through the apartment, apprehensive but slowly in feral fashion, much as if her lair had been invaded and she meant to oust whoever had dared to intrude. Crouched in her lustrous mink, she resembled a blonde she bear, resolute and inviolable in her aim to protect her den.

I know. It sounds like some sort of Jean Auel *Clan of the Cave Bear* sentence, but it accomplishes my aim. I love anthropology and where the hell we came from, and actually enjoyed the speculative nature of Auel's books.

MARUQUITA COULDN'T HANDLE THE PRESSURE OF CONSTANTLY SEEING the images of Omaha naked, his *bohango* erect and then sliding into the blonde's pink-and-blonde *papaya*. In and out, in and out until she moaned and he exploded in her and she inflated with his seed to make another blonde person. And then they lay there on the bed, their two blond heads next to each other, and she knew that Omaha loved this blonde girl and didn't care about her because she was Puerto Rican and stupid and had dropped out of high school. Her mother was right. She was stupid. She picked up the phone and dialed Rocky's cell phone. When Rocky came on, she asked him for the blonde's address.

"You going over there?" Rocky said.

"No, I wanna mail the bitch a letter. She be messing with my man and I'ma tell her she wrong."

"I hear you," he said and gave her the address. "Be cool, okay?"

"I'm chilling. Talk to you later," Maruquita said.

She next dialed the author and waited until he answered.

"I'm going to take control of my own destiny," she said.

"You're going to what?"

"I'm going to make some changes and I'm going after this bitch."

"We made a deal."

"And?"

"Well, you should keep up your end of the bargain. Let me set up the Bush thing first, and you can meet her, and then the wedding. After the wedding is set, you're free to do whatever you want. That was our deal."

"I'm going ahead. You do whatever you have to. This bitch is really fucking with my mind. She has powers, too, right?"

"Well yes, but nothing like yours. You should relax and let me do my work."

"I can't wait, Vega. This woman is truly evil. She's everything the *morenos* say about these people. She is a white devil."

"That is a racist position and has no room in one of my books. Anyway, you're not a prejudiced person. If you're thinking of a film career, forget about it. Look at J-Lo. She has a *moreno* boyfriend."

"I don't care. I'm not a prejudiced person, but she's a devil. I'm taking her down."

"What about the baby?"

"What about it?"

"If you start changing, it's going to affect the baby."

"No, it isn't. I'm in the seventh month of pregnancy. The baby is fully formed. Anything that happens right now is about growth and gaining weight. Babies are born after seven months, and although they're small, they survive. Nothing's going to happen."

"You don't know for sure."

"Well, don't worry about it. Talk to you later, Vega. You do what you gotta do, and I'll do what I have to do. Bye."

"Good luck, but don't say I didn't warn you."

"Bye," she said and hung up.

She felt much better. Maruquita next called Winnifred's apartment and asked for Omaha. The woman said he wasn't there. She said he was at his office. Maruquita thanked the woman and dialed the apartment in Red Square. Omaha answered the phone.

"Hi, sweetie," she said.

"Hi, baby," Omaha said.

"Can I come and see you, Omagaw Boogaloo?"

"Not now, honey. I'm busy."

"I miss you, you bozo. I'm sorry I got so ballistic and whatnot."

"That's okay. I miss you, too, but I can't right now."

"When?"

"Later. Maybe tonight."

"Are you going to be there for a while?"

"Yeah. I'll be here for a while, and then I'll come to the apartment," Omaha said.

"You're not trying to fool me, right?"

"No way."

"I'll make *chuletas* and *tostones*," Maruquita said. "You like that?"

"*Con arroz y habichuelas,*" Omaha said.

"Yeah, rice and beans. I can make that."

"Okay, I'm gonna work here until about eight o'clock, and then I'll be over there."

"Okay, honey. I love you. Bye."

"Bye. I love you, too."

Two-faced bastard, Maruquita thought. She hung up the phone and opened the window to her bedroom. She thought about a monkey, felt a slight pain in her abdomen, and changed immediately. She leaped out onto the tree, morphed into a squirrel, and ran down the tree. As soon as she hit the ground she morphed back into herself and walked to Houston Street, where she got a cab, and gave the driver the address in Soho. When she got out of the cab, she walked to the building, entered, and when the concierge asked where she was going, she gave the man Winnifred Buckley's name. The man asked her name. She lied and said it was Carmen Eléctrica. The man asked her to sign a book. The man then told her to wait and he'd call upstairs to see if anyone was home. When the man turned, she morphed into a mouse and scurried away along the wall, found the right elevator, morphed back into herself, stepped into the elevator, and pushed the button for the twelfth floor. She expected the man to follow, but he must have figured that she'd left while he was looking for the right phone code.

When the elevator doors opened, she found herself in a foyer with umbrellas and a coat tree. She morphed into Rocky and rang the doorbell. A black woman answered the door.

"Hi, Rocky," the woman said.

"Is Omaha here yet?"

"No, he's not."

"He told me to wait. Is that okay?"

"Sure, you know where the TV is. You want a sandwich or something?"

"No, I'm okay. Do you know if the lady's coming back?"

"Yes, Miss Winnifred went to have lunch with her father and said she'd be back by three. Another half-hour."

"Okay, thanks."

"Make yourself comfortable."

"Anybody else here?"

"Yes, Walteria, the girl that cleans up. She's doing laundry."

"Thanks."

When the cook had gone back into the kitchen, Maruquita morphed into the monkey and scampered away through the apartment until she was in a room that had photographs and lots of books. She morphed back into herself, looked at the photographs, and focused on one of the blonde, hoping that she could be her. She tried several times but could not make herself into the young woman. She had to find a way to get the two women out of the apartment so she could be alone when the blonde arrived. She morphed into a mouse, went into the kitchen, and squeaked. The cook looked down, let out a squeal, opened a broom closet, and threatened Maruquita with a broom. At that moment the mouse morphed into a spectacular peacock that flared its tail. The cook screamed, her eyes rolled back into her head, and she fainted. The maid came running. Maruquita flared her tail feathers again, and the maid screamed and ran to the service stairs of the apartment. The cook was now coming to. She stood up and left the apartment as well. The cook took the same route, but one floor below, pulled out her cell phone and called 911 and informed the police that they should come over immediately. Fearful that on hearing her mention the peacock the police would dismiss the call as that of a lunatic, she described what happened as a possible break-in and gave the dispatcher the address. Maruquita knew that the two women would tell the doorman, and he would call the police. She morphed back into the mouse, hid under a sofa, and peeked out from under its leather skirt.

A few minutes later she heard the blonde come in, call out, and not hearing a response, tiptoe around in her stockinged feet, crouched over as she began looking through the apartment, resembling a big brown cow with her stupid fur coat. Fifteen minutes later four policemen, the cook, and the maid came into the apartment. Maruquita watched from her blind as the sergeant with a notepad and pen began asking the blonde questions about who owned the apartment and who lived there. Maruquita scurried along the floor and hid behind a grandfather clock, where she could hear the conversation.

"I own the apartment and live here with my boyfriend," Winnifred said, removing her mink coat and handing it to the maid, a smallish Central American woman.

"And your boyfriend's name?"

"Omaha Bigelow," Winnifred said, comfortable and assured in her stewardship.

Maruquita wanted to morph into Magilla Gorilla and smack Winnifred.

"Miss Buckley, can my men look around to make sure the perp isn't hiding in the apartment?" the sergeant asked. "Your employees here say there was a peacock in your kitchen. Maybe the perp, I mean the bird, left a feather that could be tested for DNA or something."

"Yes, feel free to look around," Winnifred said. "Mrs. Washington," she added, turning to the cook, "could you show the officers around?"

The cook was Amethyst Booker, married to Pierce Buckley's driver, Lucius

Washington, and herself a PhD in Russo-Japanese History. In case it hasn't occurred to you to question why these two African American characters have such great academic preparation and are working at such seemingly lowly jobs, Lucius and Amethyst were both CIA operatives working as security to protect Pierce Buckley and Winnifred. They were paid well, Pierce advised them financially, and they each had considerable financial portfolios. Remember, it's always about the money. Likely story? Not really. In spite of the precedent of James Earl Jones's fictional roles in spy films, there were other reasons. The agency had cut back considerably on its Russian section. That it should have increased its vigilance of the Arab world is now apparent. But as they say, hindsight is always twenty-twenty. Having worked for the CIA when the President's father headed the agency and later went on to be president had its advantages. Pierce had availed himself of the perks. Seriously, I don't know about other Buckleys, but these Buckleys are an extremely important family in America, and you will see how intimately involved they are in the destiny of the country. Amethyst Booker Washington accompanied the officers to the different rooms and facilitated their search. The officers spent half of their time gawking at the luxury of the apartment. This being March, no one yet knew anything about 9/11. It saddens me to tell you, but one of the officers, working so close to so-called Ground Zero, perished heroically when he went into one of the buildings and was caught in the collapse.

At this point I need to clarify something. This is fiction. Sometimes it's easier to tell the truth through fiction. Even though it might seem insensitive to use the 9/11 tragedy so soon after it happened, I have a responsibility. Don't focus on me. In spite of money collected for the families of policemen, firemen, and others who perished, people who serve the public are still not well-paid, and the families of surviving firemen, cops, and others in the public employ, have to struggle. In other words, I'm still advocating for people who do work to get paid better. Below is what happened, and even though Winnifred is a spoiled brat, she's no different from the spin doctors and the politicians. In spite of the nice words that politicians speak about sacrifice and patriotism, the truth is that they are disdainful of people who work, and they shield big money and keep the truth from the people. Examine how Winnifred Buckley treats this policeman.

"Miss Buckley," the sergeant went on. "Did anyone leave a window open?"

"I don't believe so, Sergeant," Winnifred said. She now turned to the maid. "Walteria, *ventanas altas?*"

"*No, señorita,*" Walteria said, still shaken by the sight of the huge peacock in the kitchen. "*Todas las ventanas estaban cerradas.* All close."

From her hiding place as a mouse Maruquita snickered at the phrase *ventanas altas.* It meant *high windows.* She knew what the blonde meant, but what an idiot this chick was.

"They were all closed, Sergeant," Winnifred said, confidently.

"I see, I was thinking maybe the peacock got away from the zoo and flew into one of your windows."

"That's very interesting," Winnifred said sarcastically, beginning to grow annoyed by this sudden invasion of her home. "You have quite an imagination. Why don't we go further afield and posit that by some sort of magical realism distortion one of Gabriel García Márquez's books—all of which rest comfortably in their first-edition hardbound copies on my shelves—fell accidentally to the floor and from its pages this so-called peacock appeared to frighten my household. Could that perhaps not constitute another theory?"

"Miss, a question?"

"Yes?"

"Could you please spell the name of the person you mentioned and tell me your relation to him or her."

"Her?"

"Yes, Gabriel can be a girl's name sometimes. You know? How long have you known this person? Could you also give me the phone number, in case we need to reach this individual?"

Winnifred was starting to tune out, but in the middle of the sergeant's prattling she recalled that Omaha had said that this Malsuckita could change into animals as part of her witchery. She vaguely remembered Omaha talking about a peacock. She wasn't quite sure, but suddenly she knew that the girl was in the apartment. She narrowed her eyes and went into battle-ready alert.

Coincidentally, at that very moment on the top floor of one of the buildings of the projects on Avenue D in Loisaida, the finishing touches had been applied to an extensive renovation. Eight apartments had been converted into a war room and executive offices. The high command of the Puerto Rican Navy was meeting to begin planning a preemptive strike on the U.S. Navy on the island of Vieques and the base at Roosevelt Roads near the town of Ceiba on the eastern coast of the island. Already two battle groups had been formed, with each scheduled to engage the U.S. Navy at those locations. Winnifred looked directly into the sergeant's eyes and informed him that she was expecting company and his men should leave the apartment immediately.

"You have my phone number should you need to contact me," she said. "Good day, Sergeant."

"Miss, we're not finished."

"Of course you are, Sergeant," Winnifred said, sweetly, but imperiously.

"But . . ."

"Shall I call the precinct and speak to your superiors?"

"No, that's all right, lady. I'm just trying to help here."

"I appreciate that, Sergeant, but I'm rather busy. Goodbye, and thank you very much. Mrs. Washington will see you out. Call your men, please."

"Men, let's get moving," the sergeant shouted.

Ten minutes later the policemen were gone.

"Mrs. Washington could you please explain this breach of security?"

"Winnifred, I have no idea what happened," Amethyst Booker said. "The only person who's been here this afternoon is Rocky."

"Where is he?"

"He's gone, I guess. He figured the police would come and question him."

"Do you have his cell-phone number?"

"Yes, I do."

Winnifred went to the phone and dialed as Amethyst dictated the number.

"Rocky, this is Winnifred Buckley," she said when the connection was completed. "Were you here this afternoon?"

"No, I've been at the gym all day."

"Thank you, Rocky. Goodbye."

Winnifred hung up and shook her head.

"It's not your fault, Mrs. Washington," Winnifred said. "He hasn't come here today."

"I saw him," Mrs. Washington said, looking as if she had been caught in a lie.

"We're dealing with Caribbean witchcraft, Mrs. Washington."

"Well, I have no skills or training in that direction," Amethyst Booker said. "I'm sorry."

"I know," Winnifred said. "I think the best thing would be for you and Walteria to take the rest of the afternoon and evening off. Please tell Walteria that she can go to the movies and come back tonight."

"Will you be all right, Winnifred?" Amethyst Booker said.

"I'll be fine. I just have to think certain things out."

"Very well, Winnifred. I've cooked supper. I'll see you tomorrow."

"Thank you, Mrs. Washington. Give Walteria some money and tell her to buy herself something and go to the movies. I think there is an undubbed Almódovar film at the Angelika she'll very likely enjoy. The combination popcorn and beverage is a good deal. Tell her to stay away from the nachos and cheese sauce. It's wretched."

"I will do just that, Winnifred," Amethyst Booker said and went to find the maid.

When both women were gone, Winnifred went into her bedroom, stripped naked, admired herself in the mirror, removed her jewelry, and put on a running outfit from the Team USA Olympic team, made a couple of Tae Kwan Do kicks, sat down at her vanity, and brushed her hair. She knew that if she was patient the little Puerto Rican dingbat would appear. She must remain calm.

Maruquita, having scurried along the wall until she was in the bedroom, snickered as she watched the blonde bimbo make preparations for attempting to combat her. She morphed into herself and stood facing the mirror as Winnifred brushed her hair, amusing herself with imagining Omaha entering her. She couldn't rid herself of the animation of the exploding vagina and all the rainbow colors that burst forth to simulate an orgasm. Omaha's lovemaking was simply amazing. She was a very lucky young woman, she thought. She had looks, brains, wealth, and a soulmate.

I KNOW YOU'RE PROBABLY EXPECTING A GREAT CONFRONTATIONAL SCENE between WASP and Puerto Rican witchcraft, but that's not what happened. It's silly to think that the United States could compete with Puerto Rico in this area. You simply cannot win at everything all the time, no matter how strong you think you are. Nobody can. In 1980 in Lake Placid a bunch of American college kids with typical American names like Jim Craig and Mike Eruzione beat the elite Russian national ice hockey team to win the Olympic gold medal. Well, they beat the Russians first, and then Finland, to win the gold. It was a shock to the Russians. No matter how big and strong you are, sometimes you lose. I wasn't there, but I can tell you that the crowd had to be stunned when jockey-size David, listed at 5'3" and 132 lbs, let loose with his slingshot and clocked Goliath, listed in the program at 9'11" and 577 lbs. The rock struck Goliath just under his helmet, above his left eyebrow, and slew him. A lucky shot? Maybe. Could he do it again? I don't know, but he got the motherfletcher good that one time. Seeing Philistines lose is good fun, always. But you just can't win all the time.

The U.S. could have developed supremacy in magic had it not persecuted witches into virtual extinction and driven the craft underground, where it remains, a quaint WASP aberration used mostly for baseball—to wit, Bill Buckner permitting a routine ground ball to squirt under his glove when Boston had the World Series won in 1986. I am not at liberty to disclose whose mother on the 1986 World Series champion Mets is a witch. But this is minor witchcraft. By the way, baseball is rife with this kind of magic. There is probably a strong correlation between hitting a baseball coming at you at ninety-five mph and witchy mothers. I'm not naming names. Another area in which you see a bit of witchcraft is in the stock market. Few people understand how Wall Street works, but it controls the country through witchcraft, which nobody believes because Allan Greenspan is the guru of U.S. economics. Although he looks like he could hang around the cauldron in a Shakespeare in the Parking

Lot production of *Macbeth,* in which actors enter the scene on motorcycles, Greenspan is not a real witch. Other people in D.C. are witches, but not Greenspan. I'm not making this up about SITPL. These Shakespeare productions happen during the summer between Essex and Orchard Street off Delancey Street down in the Lower East Side in the area that is a spillover from the East Village. I've seen fine interpretations of Shakespeare there, with women of the theater at my side. I will not mention their names but simply allude to them because they think I'm a cultural cretin and philistine for applauding Shakespearean language with a Brooklyn accent. Anyway, Greenspan is not a WASP, so he cannot be a witch. Yes, I know this is not a politically correct WEOP (Wiccan Equal Opportunity Position). Puleeze! As Judy Tenuta is fond of saying: *Like I have time.*

What is left today for the common people concerning witches are mostly myths, some Wiccan hobbyists, Halloween cutouts of stereotype witches on brooms, a cartoon character by the name of Broomhilda, a silly TV show, a Kim Novak film called *Bell Book and Candle* and a Frank Sinatra song entitled "It's Witchcraft." The perception that one has of functional American witchcraft is pretty much a joke. So to cast an amateur like Winnifred Buckley against a natural like Maruquita Salsipuedes is not only unfair but cruel. How can you think that this bimbo—who, granted, displayed some managerial dexterity in supervising finances for the production of Omaha's film—could go up against a talent like Maruquita? No way.

As Winnifred finished brushing her hair, she looked into the mirror and saw behind her the peacock's reflection. The bird was truly magnificent. Winnifred was amused by the ingenuity and treated it as something a very wealthy parent could have at a child's birthday party. She rose slowly, smiled with amusement, and waved her arms at the peacock. The peacock flared its tail feathers into a magnificent fan display, stared at her and squawked twice. Winnifred waved at the peacock again. In the blink of an eye the girl was there, pregnant and rotund, staring angrily at her.

"How can I help you?" Winnifred said, her arms crossed arrogantly in front of her. "I'm not impressed with your cheap Caribbean voodoo third-world tricks," she added and threw a bolt of junior lightning at Maruquita.

Maruquita deflected the lightning bolt and turned it into a canary that flew around the room and ultimately smashed itself against a window as it tried to flee.

"Third world this, you fuckin' bitch," Maruquita replied, reaching under her sizable belly and grabbing her crotch like a homeboy. "Just leave my man alone, that's what you can do. Keep messing with him and I'ma fuck you up, girl. You don't know the shit that can happen to you. One day you be looking all blondie and Bloomingale's and then you got gray and green feathers and be going coocoo. Don't fuck wif me, *cabrona*."

"Your man? How quaint!" Winnifred replied. "Check just above his pubic area sometime and see whose name is tattooed there. It says quite clearly in blue script lettering *Winnifred,* with small red roses on either side of the name."

"You're not even pregnant," Maruquita said. "Look at you. You flat."

"Five months, and I'm not even showing."

"That's cause you ain't gonna have no baby."

"It's the genes."

"You ain't even wearing no mothafockin jeans, bitch."

"You're so ignorant."

"Shut up! You have a stupid-ass name. Like a man's dick or something."

"I could have you arrested."

"I'm gonna kill you, you bitch," Maruquita said, advancing on Winnifred. "You like them evil niggahs in the *novelas* that be stealing other niggah's men. I'ma fuck you up real bad." Winnifred moved deftly to her left, so that the large bed was now behind her. She went into her crouching-tiger stance and issued several shouts of defiance. What happened next was quite sudden. Maruquita advanced quickly, bumped Winnifred with her belly and then arced a quick left hook which caught her adversary between temple and right eye, knocking her back and making her topple onto the bed. She was out cold. "Mothafocka," Maruqita added, as punctuation. "I told you not to fuck with my man." She quickly morphed into the monkey, climbed up on the bed and grabbing its tiny, pencil-thin *bohanguito* and hopping around from Winnifred's head to her feet, urinated a long time on the recumbent and unconscious figure. When Maruquita was done, she morphed back into herself, opened the window to the bedroom, morphed into a peregrine falcon, grabbed the canary in her talons for a snack, and flew back to Loisaida, where she landed on the roof of her building, ate the canary, morphed back into herself, and went down the stairs to her apartment.

That was it. Maruquita's deadly accurate punch and the outrage of waking up soaked in monkey urine made Winnifred redouble her efforts to marry Omaha. Of course Winnifred didn't know it was monkey urine and assumed that the Evil Witch of the Colony had clambered up on the bed, lowered herself over her and moving her panties aside, had fouled her with her impure Caribbean renal waste. Winnifred was determined to triumph.

On the other side of town Omaha Bigelow was totally freaked out. He got a frantic call from Winnifred that Maruquita had been at her apartment, had struck her and urinated on her. Hysterically, she told him she'd had to shampoo and shower six times in the last hour. When was he going to come over? Omaha didn't know what to do. He remembered that he had promised Maruquita that he'd come and see her, but Winnifred was now demanding that he come home to her. What should he do?

"I can't come over right away, Winnifred," he said. "These people don't play by the same rules we do."

"What do you mean?" Winnifred screamed. "What people?"

"Puerto Ricans," Omaha said. "They're going to kill me, Winnifred."

"Are you telling me that these people are beyond the law? Are you saying they've come to our country and can simply take advantage of our benevolence and remain beyond the reach of our laws? Is that what you're saying?"

"Well, maybe they don't recognize our laws as being pertinent to their condition."

"Oh, please, darling. Don't tell me that you've bought into that?"

"You don't know them, Winnifred."

"And I don't want to. Who do these people think they are? What do they have? Coconuts, merengue music, and Sammy Sosa."

"That's the Dominicans. Puerto Ricans have *guaguancó, cha cha chá, bomba, plena,* and then at Christmas they have *aguinaldos, décimas, seis . . .*"

"Omaha?"

"What?"

"Just be quiet. Whose side are you on?"

"I'm just trying to clarify a few things regarding their musical traditions."

"Whatever. They have a wretched little island that doesn't even show up on most maps, and they think they're one of the twelve tribes of Israel. And I don't know Spanish, but I'm told they speak a patois of the language. Like the Haitians and that creole bastardization of French."

"Puerto Ricans are not a bad people," Omaha said, feeling apprehensive and hoping that perhaps God would hear that he wasn't a horrible person and would save him from Maruquita's wrath. God, however, was on overload with people wanting to win a really big Lotto jackpot. "Very kind people, as a matter of fact," Omaha added.

"They're an insufferable people. The women are so tawdry. First Rita Moreno screaming on the Electric Company HEY YOU GUYS and now this J-Lo person with her enormous buttocks. Do these women think that there's a correlation between screaming or the size of their butt and intellectual capacity? I'm going to have this Malsuckita woman prosecuted to the fullest extent of the law for what she's done. Anyway, I have a very nice derrière myself."

"Yes, you do, Winnifred," Omaha said, having to admit she was pretty spectacular. In that regard she had Charlize Theron beat. "Fomidable, I would say."

"I mean, who does she think she is with all that mumbo-jumbo magic? A peacock for crying out loud? Why not a seat on the Stock Exchange? How come they live under such wretched conditions if their magic is so powerful?"

"Winnifred, I can't come over right away," Omaha said. "The best I can do is meet you at Spring Natural about eleven o'clock tonight."

"Omaha, are you crazy?"

"What?"

"I can't go out smelling like this," Winnifred said. "My God! It's like I've been sprayed by a Spanish-speaking skunk. I was out cold, and I'm sure this Malsuckita got up on the bed and urinated all over me. I was soaked, Omaha. From head to toe. My hair and everything. I may have even inhaled some of her foulness. I'm surprised she didn't open my mouth and attempt to drown me with her urine. Please come home."

"I'll be over later," Omaha said. "It's almost eight o'clock. I'll be over in a few hours."

"We have food. We'll open a bottle of wine and we can eat together . . . if you don't mind how I smell. It's really awful. Okay?"

"Okay, I'll see you later. I love you."

"I love you, too."

He hung up the phone and realized he was in a cold sweat. He put on his jacket, turned off the computer where he was working on his next film, turned off the lights in the apartment, locked the door, and took the elevator down. He walked quickly down Houston Street until he got to Avenue D and turned left into the projects. He went into Maruquita's building, greeted a couple of homeboys coming out, and went up. He let himself into the apartment and found Maruquita finishing the meal she had promised him.

"Hi, baby," Omaha said, going behind her and kissing her cheek.

"Hi, honey," Maruquita said without turning. "You hungry?"

"Yeah."

"Sit down and we'll eat."

Omaha sat down to the pork chops and plantains and rice and beans, which Maruquita had cooked rather expertly. He had been eating rice and beans as a staple in the East Village for years, the complete protein sustaining him in hard times. He still enjoyed the food but felt the sadness that his life had produced prior to this time. Things had taken such a wonderful turn. He was making money, had completed his film, and found a girl that he truly loved. Maruquita had been wonderful, but he had to admit that Winnifred was beyond any of his expectations. He had to find the courage to tell Maruquita that he could no longer be with her.

"What's the matter, honey?" Maruquita said. "You look so sad."

"I'm okay," Omaha said, scratching his head and pushing his empty plate away. "I have a lot of things on my mind. I think I have to get married."

"To the blonde?"

"Yes, to Winnifred."

"Do you love her?"

"Yes."

"What about me?"

"I love you, too."

"You bozo. You belong to me. Don't you know that? You're my pet."

"I know, but she's pregnant, and I have to marry her."

"What about me? I'm pregnant."

"That's different."

"Different. Why different?"

"It just is."

"Why?"

"You're Rican. It's not the same. Look at your aunt. She's got three kids and never got married. Getting married is going to ruin your life. You'll have no freedom."

"What about you? You'll have no freedom."

"I'll have freedom. I'll be rich. My film came out pretty good, and it'll make money."

"And you got the blonde's money."

"That too."

"Well, you can't go," Maruquita said. Standing up, she began gathering the dishes and putting them in the sink. "You belong here."

Omaha looked at his watch. It was past ten o'clock. He went over to Maruquita and told her he had to leave. Maruquita turned to him. She had a fierce look on her face. She shook her head as if she were pitying Omaha. Her look made him feel cold.

"Go ahead and go," she said. "Go to your blonde gringa whitegirl. Go and see what's gonna happen to you."

"What's gonna happen to me? You're trying to scare me."

"Just go and find out. Go!"

"I'm not scared."

"Good, go. Get outta here."

"I can take care of you and the baby," Omaha said, but knew he sounded weak. "I'll come back and see you once in a while."

"Omagaw Boogaloo, go," Maruquita said. "There's the door. Go and see what happen."

"Fine. I'm going," Omaha said, putting on his jacket. He went over to kiss Maruquita goodbye, but she held up her hands in front of her. "I'm sorry, Maruquita," he said.

"The door. Go."

Omaha left the apartment. He felt like his feet were made out of lead. Each step he took felt like he was heading closer to his doom. He went down the elevator and out into the early April night. He walked to Houston Street and continued going west, past the alphabet avenues, in utter desolation, thinking that perhaps he had made a terrible mistake. He walked all the way to Winnifred's apartment and let himself in. She was setting the table for their meal. She knew immediately that he wasn't well.

"What's the matter?" Winnifred said.

"I'm gonna die," Omaha said.

"Did she threaten you?"

"Yes, more or less."

"And you believed her?"

"She meant it."

"Well, I'm going to put an end to this once and for all. I'm going to speak to my father, and he's going to speak to certain people in the highest offices of government, and this nonsense is going to stop posthaste. Who do these people think they are, threatening the lives of people when they've come here as chattel? Omaha Bigelow, I am annoyed, and when I am annoyed I will not stand idly by. This woman and her cohorts have gone far enough. This country did not impose itself on this continent for nothing. Say what you will about stealing the land from the Indians and slashing through the wilderness with little regard for the feelings of others, but you have to admit that we've created a good thing here. I'm not going to stand by and allow evildoers to have their way with our freedom."

This is a particularly long monologue, but I'm sure that if Charlize Theron is cast in this role, she'll do fine with it. She can feel free to change it to suit her style. I hope the director allows her such latitude. I would caution that certain directors keep away from any possible script that may be written based on this novel. I will not mention any names here, but since there is magic and witchcraft involved, you can draw your own conclusions. If you're wondering where the word *evildoers* came from, you would be safe to attribute it to Winnifred Buckley and what she conveyed to her father, which was then conveyed upward toward Pennsylvania Avenue.

Meanwhile, across the ocean in Paris, Pierce Buckley and Dakulana Imbebwabe sat in a cafe in Montmartre sipping mineral water in the early April sunlight. Sipping mineral water in Paris is not the same as sipping mineral water in some pseudosophisticated Columbus Avenue yuppie bistro frequented by ABC TV anchors and producers in Manhattan. Both may be appealing to some, but they are two different experiences. Sipping mineral water in Paris is far superior. I congratulate Pierce and Dakulana for being in love in Paris in the spring. I've had no such success. Each time I go to Paris in love, I end up breaking up. For Pierce and Dakulana, it was different. They were deeply in love, the city did not affect them adversely, and they were involved in matters of great global importance.

"Did you go?" Pierce asked, sipping from his mineral water, after they sat down.

"Yes, it was harrowing," Dakulana said, reaching out to touch Pierce's hand. "One of my most difficult assignments."

"Is it serious?" Pierce said.

"It's very serious, Pierce," Dakulana replied.

"You met with him?"

"Yes, in Khartoum."

"I was never posted to the Sudan when I was in the company. But wait. Wasn't he kicked out of that country in 1996?"

"That's right, but he's respected in the Islamic world, and that's where we met."

"Interesting."

"Pierce, I don't know how to tell you this without feeling enormous embarrassment and unfathomable guilt. We've promised to be honest with each other but it pains me when I think about what I had to do."

"That was our agreement. No secrets between us."

"I had to sleep with him. It was the only way to get him to open up."

"I figured you might have to," Pierce said, steeling himself against the hurt. "I once had to bed down Princess Margaret of England when I was on assignment there."

"Oh, Pierce," Dakulana said, her eyes mirthful once again. "Poor darling. But you do forgive me, don't you?"

"You're a consummate professional. I have no choice but to forgive you and commend you on a job well done."

"Thank you, Pierce."

"But tell me about it."

"Well, the worst of it is that I ended up with a terrible inner-thigh rash from his beard," Dakulana said. "He wanted to marry me. He said I would supplant his first wife. He was quite serious, complimented me on my Arabic, but said I would have to convert to Islam."

"And he had no idea that you work for French intelligence?"

"No, of course not. He thought I was a journalist. I listened to a number of conversations between him and his lieutenants. After a few days we flew back to Kabul."

"And you were able convince him that you were doing advance work for Christiane Amanpour?"

"Yes, of course. I promised to return with Christiane Amanpour and was escorted back into Pakistan."

"So your cover remained intact."

"Yes, for that month I enjoyed being Imogene Whitleby, the product of an English father and a Jamaican mother."

"That was brilliant," Pierce said. "You did well. Was CNN in on it?"

"Yes, of course. Something was worked out with the Sûreté. There had been some silly sexual indiscretion between Ted Turner and Simone Signoret in her later years. Perhaps Simone de Beauvoir. I'm not sure which of the two."

"Perhaps both," Pierce said. "Likely la Signoret, since he has a predilection for aging actresses."

"Perhaps. It appears that French television was preparing a documentary on it. They were asked to suppress it, in return for CNN not ever mentioning Jerry Lewis in connection with French cinema. I don't know the particulars. As you know the French don't appreciate the American jokes regarding their fascination with Jerry Lewis."

"Interesting," Pierce said, amused by Dakulana's shrewdness.

"But it was awful," Dakulana went on. "The smell of his body was a combination of a halitosal camel and badly soiled underpants. You know how hygiene-conscious I am. I was ill often and faked orgasms so I could cough and release my breath. The rash persisted for a fortnight or so."

"I understand, but I was asking about his plans when I asked you to tell me all about it."

"Oh, sorry. Yes. He's quite mad and spoke to me openly about his plans. He's determined to bring down the U.S. It's a *jihad* of major proportions. It has the backing of prominent *mullahs* all over the Islamic world. The U.S. is not well liked."

"An actual physical attack like the car bomb at the World Trade Center in 1993?"

"Yes, very much so, but more impacting."

"Car bombs and such? Men with explosives strapped to their bodies at Macy's?"

"I don't think so. They're training pilots. Jet simulators and such things."

"In France, Germany? Russia? Where?"

"No, from what I understand they're training right in the United States."

"Aha. Perhaps high-altitude bombings."

"Perhaps. I'm not quite sure. But I think more macabre yet. He was quite specific about the methods."

"A possible scenario would have them gain entry into a strategic command base, getting aircraft airborne, and dropping bombs on major urban centers."

"Possibly," Dakulana said, considering the import of what Pierce was saying. "Perhaps in the future. But this was different and aimed . . ."

"Aimed at?" Pierce said.

". . . specific targets."

"Yes, did he mention specific places?"

"Yes, he did. The White House, the U.S. Congress. The Statue of Liberty and Rockefeller Center in New York City."

"Rockefeller Center? That's odd."

"It is. From what I gathered, Sue Simmons at NBC reminds him of one of his wives who is a terrible shrew. He believes that the U.S. knows how much he dislikes this one wife and is mocking him by having Simmons on the air. In my opinion, Sue Simmons is a superior anchor. Her wry humor and lack of self-importance are quite charming. She's certainly a departure from the peroxide blondes who abound in the news industry in the United States."

"We agree on that, but that's quite a story," Pierce said. "I've met Sue. Very charming and attractive woman. Have you told your superiors at the Sûreté about all this?"

"No, I have not," Dakulana said. "I'm due to be debriefed tomorrow morning. I wanted to tell you first, in case our people decide not to release the information to your government or delay doing so for political reasons. You understand how that works."

"Yes, I do. Thank you," Pierce said. "Are you hungry?"

"Not yet. You?"

"No, I'm not. We could go back to the hotel and wait until we get hungry. I've missed you."

Dakulana smiled, the black skin of her face tight against her cheekbones, the eyes dark and filled with the sensuality and beauty of Africa, of its cheetahs and impalas, of its mountains and savannas, of trumpeting elephants and roaring lions, of majestic rivers and endless deserts, just like those you see on the nature channel. Pierce dropped some francs on the table and rose, holding his hand out to Dakulana. They walked in perfect elegance from the café and headed for their hotel.

Obviously the two characters above were talking about Osama bin Laden. In true intelligence-community protocol, they did not mention the miscreant's name. It's also obvious that the airplanes that struck the World Trade Center, one heading north and the other south, apparently were ineptly diverted from their aim, as was the airplane that struck the Pentagon and the one that crashed in Pennsylvania. It is the opinion of many analysts that these people should stick to camels and light vehicles, for they obviously missed their targets. In order to be in rhythm with the collective hatred toward this madman I've decided to fight back with humor and show that the U.S. has its own terrorists. But regardless of my politics, the U.S. should not dwell on what happened and end up injuring itself. My motto is, *Never forget, but don't obsess.* I don't know the Latin for this.

Hatred is a terrible thing, and while I can understand the collective opprobrium felt toward this man, admittedly deserved, I've compiled a list of people and things that are part of Americana and reflect the country's reality. Individually, certain things in the U.S. amuse, but collectively they create a rather sickening ethos that makes the U.S. a bit funnier than it intends to be, something which I resent, being that my children and grandchildren are Americans. Me? I'm Puerto Rican. Give me a choice on whether I want to be American or not and find out how I choose. How? Let my people go. Make my day. Let me choose whether I want to be an immigrant.

Whatever the case, here is a list of other terrorists. I hasten to add that these are cultural terrorists. For example, had Dakulana become Osama's wife, she would have become Dakulana bin Laden. So here we go with other bin Ladens. I'm sure you can come up with many more if you think about it. If it ends in an a, they fit. I didn't put Alabama on the list because some of those folks down there get very upset over nothing. If you don't know some of the names, ask someone or get counseling on your Americana and related subjects. You can choose to feel insulted or examine how truly committed you are to extricating the United States from this mess. Don't blame me. I'm just the messenger. I don't even fly a kite well, and loud noises annoy me. They fucked with my psyche as well. You're not the only wounded one. Here's a short list.

COMPENDIUM OF POSSIBLE TERRORISTS

Rock and Roll Terrorist	- Madonna bin Laden
Pop Music Terrorist	- Falana bin Laden
Jazz Terrorist	- Buhena bin Laden
Bossa Nova Terrorist	- Ipaneima bin Laden
Of Color Cereal Terrorist	- Wheatena bin Laden
White Cereal Terrorist	- Farina bin Laden
Rican Cereal Terrorist	- Marota bin Laden
Health Food Cereal Terrorist	- Granola bin Laden
Latino Time Terrorist	- Mañana bin Laden
United Fruit Terrorist	- Banana bin Laden
Beach Terrorist	- Cabana bin Laden
Docking Terrorist	- Marina bin Laden
Game Show Terrorist	- Vanna bin Laden
Card Game Terrorist	- Canasta bin Laden
Air Conditioner Terrorist	- Amana bin Laden
Headgear Terrorist	- Bandana bin Laden
Carnivorous Fish Terrorist	- Piranha bin Laden
Kissing Bandit Terrorist	- Morgana bin Laden
Breath Freshener Terrorist	- Binaca bin Laden
State Terrorist	- Montana bin Laden
Municipality Terrorist	- Valdosta bin Laden
Spanish Expression Terrorist	- Caramba bin Laden
Rican Expression Terrorist	- Puñeta bin Laden
	(Equivalent of Wanker)

You're still pissed at me for being disrespectful? They're just words, babe. You know: *Sticks and stones will break my bones but words will never hurt me.* Wait. You're telling me there's a limit? No, there isn't. I don't want to get all constitutional and whatnot, but you're mistaken. Not under U.S. law. Citizens are free to express themselves orally and in writing. This right has been extended to include action as an expression of dissent. That's what the country is supposed to be about, and certain people don't want you to be truly free. People who want to control you will try and tell you there are limits because of their own fears that you're going to wake up and see what's been done to you in the interest of so-called democracy. Did you know that there are more white people living under the poverty level than all minorities combined? I'm not kidding. Look it up. You're getting a hosing and you don't even know it. Your children are being educated to be drones. They're being given an education that is irrelevant and becomes obsolete as soon as they obtain a high-school diploma, a college degree, or even a professional degree. What? You're saying that my freedom stops at your nose? Fine, don't believe me, but you don't have to get all Percale I-got-sheets-with-holes-in-them-for eyes-Casper-the-Friendly-KKK-ghost on me. I'm just tugging on your coat to point some things out to you. Lynch my ass if you want, but don't tell me that what I'm saying doesn't ring true. You are being bamboozled by scoundrels who are in the employ of fat cats. The country is great, the people are great, but you got yahoos running it and they don't give a damn about you and less about me. I'm just saying.

MACHINATIONS, AUTHORS AND
CHARACTERS, AND AN ANALYSIS OF THE PLAY

P IERCE BUCKLEY RETURNED TO THE UNITED STATES IN EARLY APRIL 2001, his considerable johnson nearly worn out. Once back home, he placed a call to his old boss at the CIA, Papa Bush, and requested a meeting. In speaking with the Bush aide, he stressed that it was of utmost importance that he speak to the ex-president. By the end of April 2001 Pierce Buckley had met with the elder Bush. It appears certain now that the CIA and the FBI had considerable information but did not want to share it. I would have to assume that the White House was fully aware of the information that had been gathered by Dakulana Imbebwabe. The old CIA head reassured Pierce that French intelligence had provided the U.S. quite a bit of information and that the information correlated to what he was saying. He added that the Mossad, Israeli intelligence, had as well.

By May 2001, however, other matters were beginning to concern the White House as things heated up on Vieques Island off the coast of Puerto Rico. Because of 9/11, some of these issues have dissipated and appear to have less importance. But on Vieques, demonstrations became more frequent, and a good deal of the populace in the small Puerto Rican archipelago, and in the United States, were now behind the immediate exit of the U.S. Navy from the island. The governor of New York, George Pataki, himself a Republican, came out against the White House position. Al Sharpton and Robert Kennedy, Jr., went to Vieques and got themselves arrested for civil disobedience. In statements to the press they denounced the U.S. government for its abuse of the Puerto Rican people. The Puerto Rican situation was gaining momentum on a global scale. During this time the Pope canonized the first Puerto Rican. I've forgotten his name. I can't keep track of saints.

Things were getting out of hand. April and May brought more resounding support from the international community. In the U.S., after the Florida election debacle of November 2000, discontent from the left made governing more difficult. A 50–50 divided U.S. Senate presented greater problems yet for the White House. Late in May, James Jeffords, a Republican Senator from Vermont, bolted the Republican Party and declared himself an Independent, in effect placing control of the Senate in the hands of the Democrats. Below is a small item to authenticate the nonfictional nature of this fact.

May 24, 2001
Web posted at: 7:44 p.m. EDT (2344 GMT) (CNN) — The Senate prepared for a change of power and President Bush faces a new political landscape after Sen. James Jeffords of Vermont left the Republican Party on Thursday, becoming an independent and throwing control of the Senate to the Democrats for the first time since 1994.

By the beginning of June 2001 the younger Bush had begun to assess his priorities and sought to defuse the Vieques situation. A man of little capacity for language, but one possessed of considerable cunning and political acumen, he was poised to pounce at history. Remember the axiom: Every great president needs a war. Two weeks later, the Chief Executive took action.

WASHINGTON, June 15, 2001
(CBS) The White House plan to end bombing practice on the island of Vieques within two years appears to have satisfied neither side of the controversy.
    Mr. Bush's decision has been criticized by Vieques protesters who say the 2003 withdrawal is not soon enough—and by some legislators who say it could cost America readiness and eventually lives.

The last sentence is particularly eerie and ironically prophetic. You know where this is heading, don't you? Just hang on to your seat, because the ride could get rough. Just the birth of Maruquita's child should prove exciting. I have no idea how the baby's going to look. No, I'm not going to punish her for going against me. I'm not a vindictive person. Fictional characters have a life of their own. I don't know of any but the most pathetic formula novelist, who writes the same book over and over again, who could force one of his or her characters to bend to their will. I doubt seriously that Fyodor Doestoevsky could have talked Raskolnikov into going for counseling or anger management in *Crime and Punishment.* I don't know that Steinbeck could've talked the Joads in *The Grapes of Wrath* into going, let's say, to New Mexico, where there were plenty of good opportunities and ultimately no smog. No, they were hell-bent on going to California, where their descendants are still called Okies. Do you really believe that Ernest Hemingway in *For Whom the Bell Tolls* could have talked Robert Jordan out of that silly scene in which he sends Maria away with "Now you go because when you go I go with you. And wherever you go I go too"? Papa could have talked Maria into shooting Jordan in the leg, and then he couldn't go and blow up the bridge and get killed. But he didn't, because Robert Jordan was a man of principle and was part of the Lincoln Brigade fighting against fascism and would have been a shell of a man had he survived. Do you think Faulkner could have rehabilitated Popeye in *Sanctuary* so he didn't have to be a victim of his impotence and use corncobs as an instrument of rape? I know they didn't have Viagra in those days, but a good roll in the hay with one of those wide-hipped, big butt, big lip African juju women from Yoknapatawpha County could have gotten Popeye's mojo working again. However, there was no way Bill Faulkner could get that yahoo turned around. Gifted as Faulkner was, his character was as stubborn as a mule and just as stupid.

There's nothing a novelist can do when a character gets it into his or her head to do whatever they want. I am nonplused at having Maruquita suddenly take over the novel. When I invited her to participate in the project, she seemed agreeable and an easily influenced young woman looking to get a credit for working in a Puerto Rican novel. I truly thought I could write her in a direction that I thought would create some pleasure for people. I had no idea that she would rebel and simply take over my novel. I wanted to poke a little fun at the Omaha Bigelow character and truly had no idea that Maruquita would become such a powerful character in spite of her considerable skill in magical realism. Sometimes people simply wake up and they see the truth of what is being done to them. In my case I don't believe that I consciously meant to embarrass Maruquita. Talking about waking people up, her sudden rearing up was quite unexpected. So there was nothing I could do about Maruquita Salsipuedes taking matters into her own hands.

Neither was there anything I could do to prevent Winnifred Buckley from going ahead with her plans to wed Omaha Bigelow and in the process get the President of the United States involved in the insanity the country is now suffering. Women have acquired certain powers, and they're not going to give it back. Anyway, this whole War on Terrorism is more like *Ghostbusters*, and although the president and the vice president resemble Bill Murray and Dan Akroyd in their comedic approach to governing, the president's wife looks nothing like Sigourney Weaver. Who is this woman? I don't want to place a greater burden on the African American community, but is it possible that Laura Bush is folks and is merely passing? Did George W. go one better on Jeb, who married a Mexican? Ever since Florida, and even during it, African Americans have been very quiet about this administration. I can't believe just having Colin Powell and Condaleeza Rice in the Bush cabinet has satisfied this beleaguered community. I wonder. But to the matter at hand. I can tell you this. Mr. Bigelow has managed, through his own volition, to place himself between a rock and a fairly hard place. Now that he's placed himself there, let's see what these two big girls are going to do with him.

The play? I saved you the trouble of having to skip ahead. It's understandable that a mother would be so taken with her son's literary output. To her great credit, my mother always thought my writing was a nice hobby. In order to prove her wrong, I've striven to make it a career. While she smiles understandingly at my meager accomplishments, she secretly wishes I had gone to law school, as I once considered. I suppose I could've, and gone on to write best-seller courtroom dramas. Sure! But Samuel Beckett Salsipuedes's play was heading nowhere fast. It isn't really worth it to subject you to any more absurdist fare. What happened is that the Artists Dalliance keeps meeting with the Man with the Briefcase and Margafrida Locust while attempting to bankrupt the castle through a rent strike. Eventually, they maneuvered El Gato and denounced him as a scoundrel. El Gato begins spreading the fact that Matalina is homophobic and hates Nalgas. Eventually Matalina, seeing her power erode, strikes back and joins forces with Ladroncito, Madreselva, and Manny Morongo and drive El Gato to capitulate. In a final scene El Gato is placed on a large cross, tied to it, and being an atheist, he is made to hear a reading of Apocalypse until he goes mad. I've read the play several times, and as much talent as Samuel Beckett Salsipuedes has in financial matters, he should stick to his day job. I'm not convinced that the plot for this so-called play isn't based on a rather puerile political occurrence that took place somewhere in the East Village in which Puerto Ricans once again shot themselves in the foot and turned over valuable real estate to gentrifiers. That, at least, appears to be the metaphor being employed in the play. But as they say in the neighborhood, *whatevah!*

A BIRTH, TWO ESCAPES, AND A TRANSFORMATION

THE STRESS OF HAVING TO DEAL WITH OMAHA'S RAMPANT UNFAITHFULNESS, her mother's apparent disregard for her well-being, and the true dislike that she had for Winnifred Buckley became too much for Maruquita. During the second week in May, about eight o'clock in the evening, she began to have contractions. As they increased in frequency, she knew the baby was coming. She called her mother, and a half hour later they were at Gouverneur Hospital in downtown Manhattan. Her water broke and minutes later she was being prepped for delivery. It was a false alarm, and for the next fourteen hours Maruquita endured the discomfort and pain of delivery. The following day, about ten in the morning, she gave birth to her baby. She expected the doctors to hold the baby up, but they snipped the umbilical cord and immediately removed the baby from the delivery room. Maruquita, exhausted by the ordeal, didn't know what to think. She wanted to see her baby and began crying. A nurse came over and tried calming her down. She was a corpulent African American woman named Veatrice Craig.

"Is my baby okay?" Maruquita asked.

"She's going to be okay," Nurse Craig said.

"Is it a boy or a girl? I think it's a girl. Rican say if the belly is pointy it's a boy, but if it's round it's a girl, so I think it's a girl."

"Yes, a girl, honey."

"Is she cute?"

"All babies are cute," said the nurse and patted Maruquita's hand.

A half hour later Maruquita had been bathed, and wearing a pink night-gown, she was back in her room. She fell asleep quickly. When she woke up, they brought her lunch. She ate, but still no baby. Her mother, her grand-mother, and her aunts showed up while she was eating. Flaquita looked worried, as did the others. Maruquita thought that perhaps something had happened to her father, but after a few minutes she knew it was the baby.

"Did the baby die, Mami?" she said.

"No, the baby didn't die."

"Something's wrong with the baby, right?"

"Yeah," Flaquita said. "Maybe she'll be all right. Did you do *mucuras* and change while you was pregnant?"

"Yeah, but I didn't think something was gonna happen. What's wrong?"

"You don't want to know."

"Please, Mami," Maruquita pleaded. "Tell me."

"The doctors told me not to discuss it with you," Flaquita said. "You weren't supposed to be changing during the pregnancy. I told you and told you. Don't be doing no *mucuras* and changing into animals. Did you listen? Of course not."

"Does the baby have two heads?"

"No, the baby doesn't have two heads," Flaquita said. "The baby is perfect."

"It didn't cry, Mami."

"Of course it didn't cry."

"It's cute," her grandmother, Bizquita said.

"Yeah." Both of her aunts nodded, but still looked worried.

Maruquita was reassured. She finished her Jell-O and for the next fifteen minutes listened to the familiar gossip that had always been a part of her life. Doña Pancha's daughter, Valerie, had gotten out of the Women's House of Detention, and she was back in the street selling her fat butt. Tita Andrade had shot her boyfriend in the leg and left him limping in East River Park, over by the tennis courts. The lowlife deserved it for stealing her Christmas savings. Rosie Lugo was pregnant and she didn't know whether the baby belonged to her *pendejo* Rican boyfriend, the Dominican that works in the bodega on Clinton Street, or the Mexican guy that works at Two Boots Pizza. Oh, and Raquel Cisneros fell in love with this Argentinean actor in a *novela*. When the actor married this rich girl in the *novela,* Raquel went up on the roof of an abandoned building on Avenue C and threw herself into the yard. She cracked her head open on a broken toilet bowl, and some pitbulls ate some of her toes and one ear, but she was going to be okay. They then began talking about their commissions in the Puerto Rican Navy but were interrupted when an Indian doctor came in and asked them to wait outside while he spoke to Maruquita. They nodded and left to wait in the maternity ward lounge.

"How are you feeling, Ms. Salsipuedes?" the doctor said. "My name is Dr. Govindah Singh. Are you comfortable?"

"I'm okay," Maruquita said, starting to weep. "I want to see my baby. Is she okay?"

"She's fine, very healthy in fact."

"Why can't I see her?"

"Well, there are complications . . ."

"What do you mean?"

"We're running some blood tests on her."

"She has bad blood?"

"No, but there appear to be some sort of cross species complications."

"What do you mean? I don't understand what you're saying."

"Let me put it this say. She's extremely hirsute. I personally have never seen such a thing, and in speaking with my colleagues, they're unaware of such an occurrence in the medical literature."

"Hirsute? That sound like she's wearing a suit made out of hair."

"More or less," the doctor said.

"Really? Can I see her?"

"I think so. But I don't want you to be alarmed.

"I won't. I just want to see my baby."

The doctor picked up the phone next to Maruquita's bed and gave an order to bring the Salsipuedes baby to him. He gave the room number, and two minutes later a nurse walked in, cradling a little bundle in her arms. Maruquita's mother, grandmother, and aunts rushed back into the room, shushing each other as they gathered around the bed. The nurse handed the bundle to Maruquita. Everyone held their breath. Maruquita pulled back the cloth and smiled contentedly.

"Oh, she's beautiful," she said and sighed. "Look at her," she added with motherly pride.

The people in the room looked at each other and shrugged their shoulders. At that moment the baby opened her eyes and yawned. Maruquita laughed happily, because staring back at her was the most beautiful little monkey she had ever seen. She leaned down and kissed the baby monkey, opened the blanket further, touched the smooth brown fur and remarked how large and green the baby's eyes were. The baby yawned again, closed her eyes and went back to sleep. Maruquita held the baby to her breast and sighed once more. The nurse reached for the baby but Maruquita shook her head.

"We must return her to the nursery for further testing," Dr. Singh said.

"No way," Maruquita said. "You're not taking my baby."

"Ms. Salsipuedes," the doctor said, "we simply want to conduct further tests. Although you've tested negative for the HIV virus, it's possible that the birth of this child involves some sort of cross-species contamination, and we want to make sure that both mother and offspring are not affected adversely."

"Mami, what did he say?"

"Honey, the doctor thinks that maybe the baby has AIDS."

"Well, not exactly," Dr. Singh said. "We just want to give her some tests."

"Dr. Singer," Maruquita said. "You're not gonna take my baby. She don't know nothing, and she can't take no tesses like she was in school. She was just born. Leave us alone."

"Ms. Salsipuedes, you're really in no position to go against the medical profession and its responsibilities to the common good."

Maruquita thought hard, handed the baby to her grandmother, and a few minutes later a huge South American condor was sitting on the metal railing at the foot of the bed. It spread its eight-foot wingspan so that the tips reached nearly across the ten foot room. Exclamations of *Coño, Mamita!* and *You go, girl,* and *Juega Maruca!* escaped the astonished relatives as the condor squawked twice and flapped its wings. From somewhere in the background Nestor Torres was counting, and his rendition of "El Condor Pasa" filled the room with the strains of his excellent flautal imrovisations. Dr. Singh knew immediately, as if he had been thrust head first into a Salman Rushdie novel, that he was in trouble. He recalled traveling in southern India and seeing vultures scavenging the cadaver of a woman. He attempted to maintain his composure and finally managed to back away.

"Pets are not allowed in the hospital," he said.

"We are prepared to obtain legal representation," Flaquita said, with profound and menacing authority as would befit a Secretary of the Puerto Rican Navy. "We will get to the bottom of how your staff botched up my daughter's delivery. A malpractice suit of multidimensional proportions is not out of the question. One hundred million dollars in compensatory damages, plus court costs and punitive damages are within the realm of possibility, Doctor Singh."

"That's right," said the chorus, as they watched Maruquita morph back into herself and cradle her baby once again.

"Very well," Dr. Singh said. "I will talk to the chief of obstetrics and provide a suitable response. In the meantime you ought to let the nurse return the baby to the nursery, where she can be cared for more adequately. Please. We will not harm the baby in any way."

Maruquita looked questioningly at her mother, who nodded her assent. The nurse came over with a clipboard, and before taking the baby, asked Maruquita what she wanted to name the baby.

"Pitirrita," Maruquita said.

"Could you spell that? Also the last name."

"I don't know how. Mami?"

Flaquita spelled the name and reiterated that indeed it had two Rs.

The nurse wrote down the full name of Pitirrita Salsipuedes and took the baby bundle from Maruquita, who immediately began crying. The doctor followed the nurse out of the room, and the women came over and surrounded Maruquita, reassuring her that the baby would be all right.

"Isn't she beautiful?" Maruquita said, between sobs.

"Very beautiful," they all agreed, although later, as they were heading home after getting dim sum in Chinatown, each one turning down the chicken feet, they admitted that it was clearly the ugliest baby they had ever seen. And all hairy and weird, Flaquita said, with full knowledge that it was a New World monkey and had to have a prehensile tail. What other grief was this daughter going to bring into her life? she thought, filled with chagrin.

Back at the hospital Maruquita fell asleep. When she woke up it was dark. A light drizzle was falling. She went to the window and looked out into the night. The rain was falling like silver strings, the skyline hazy in the distance. The twin towers stood out in the night, lighted and imposing. She would like to fly there and stand atop the antenna. She could do so as a hawk. She promised herself that she would at some point. She stood at the window a while, and then, as if something beyond her control had taken over she knew that unless she acted now, she would never see her baby again. Call it maternal instinct, but something had kicked in and Maruquita knew she had to act. She quickly morphed into the African American nurse she had seen earlier, who had to be off duty by now, and walked out of her room. She marched to the nursery, greeted the nurse in charge, and went from one cradle to the next looking at the babies. Pitirrita was nowhere to be found.

"Excuse me, Miss McIntyre," she said in her best Afrorican accent to the nurse on duty. "Can you tell me where is the Salsipuedes baby? Dr. Singh wanted me to take some measurements."

"Over there," she said, and pointed to a smaller room. "What's your name?"

"Girl, open your eyes," Maruquita said. "What's it say on my name tag? Don't it say Miss Craig? It say Miss Craig, don't it? You can read, can't you? Veatrice Craig is what it say."

"Yes, Miss Craig, thank you."

"Okay, then."

Maruquita walked into the small room and there was her daughter, sleeping soundly. Her heart caught in her throat, and she knew that she would love her baby forever. She wouldn't be like her own mother, who was so mean to her. She went to the window, opened it, returned to the cradle, picked up her daughter and carried her to the window. Once there she morphed into *falco sparverius caribaearum*, a Caribbean kestrel. She was about to hop onto the window sill when she laughed and thought to herself, *No way. Storks brought babies. It would be silly to bring her baby home as a hawk.* She quickly morphed into *plegadis falcinellus falcinellus*, a black ibis stork. Grabbing the bundle in her beak, she leaped onto the window sill, stepped out onto the ledge, and took flight into the drizzling sky. She flew north but suddenly turned and headed south, climbing higher as if she knew she might never again have a chance to stand atop the towers. She climbed higher and higher until she was at the level of the antenna, and extending her wings, stood poised upon the receiving red-and-white rod, the wind making her footing unsteady. She surveyed the night and marveled at the magnificence of the city.

A few minutes later she took flight again and headed for home, skirting the southern tip of Manhattan and flying along the river. She flew under the Brooklyn, Manhattan, and Williamsburg bridges until she was once again opposite the Wald projects. Heading inland, she landed on the roof of her building, morphed into herself, and holding the blanket with her daughter in it, made her way downstairs to her apartment. Once there she went to the nursery and placed the bundle on the changing table. She unwrapped the small blanket, and there was her little daughter, monkey-faced and furry, her tiny tail curving behind her. She was sleeping curled up like a little ball. She picked it up gently, undid the buttons on her blouse, and brought the baby close to her breast. Instinctively, the little monkey opened its small mouth and suckled at the nipple. Maruquita went to her bed and lay down, watching her daughter until they both fell asleep.

Toward morning the phone rang, but she let the machine answer it. About eight o'clock she fed the baby, changed it, and placed it in the layette. She then listened to the message. It was her mother telling her that she was missing from the hospital and had kidnapped her own baby. The police had come but she'd told them that she hadn't seen her daughter since the previous afternoon. Maruquita shook her head and knew that she had to leave and go into the Loisaida jungle. She packed clothes, her bathing suit, and enough pampers for the trek. She made ham-and-cheese sandwiches, ate one, and packed the rest along with cans of Slice and ginger ale. She took a flashlight and a portable CD player with some CDs, including La India and Charlie Palmieri.

When she had placed everything into a knapsack, she stepped out of her mountain hut and walked along a path that brought her down near Luquillo beach. The beach was deserted that early in the morning. An old woman was walking near the palm trees a distance away. The woman did not see her. Once on the beach, she removed her clothes, fed the baby, and then, with the baby clutching at her hair and holding on with all four legs, she waded into the gentle surf and submerged the baby, baptizing it in the waters of her ancestors. Even though the baby was only two days old, she delighted in her immersion and splashed around happily, swimming easily around her mother. When they were done, Maruquita dried her daughter, put a new diaper on her, put on little rubber panties, and dressed her in a little baby frock. She spread a towel on the beach, changed into fresh clothes, and lay on the towel, holding her baby to her breast.

She was asleep an hour or so before gathering her gear, placing the baby on her hip and starting her trip into the jungle. For the next two hours she climbed higher and higher until she was at the top of El Yunque, at the ceremonial plaza of her Taino ancestors. She knelt and prayed and thanked Yukiyú for giving her such a beautiful daughter. When she was finished praying, Yukiyú appeared.

"Honored One," she said, bowing respectfully. "I have come to ask you if I have committed a wrong and to ask that you bless my daughter."

"Rise, Maruquita," said Yukiyú in a deep voice. "You have done no wrong. You have been blessed with a wonder child."

"She is a monkey, Honored One."

"Yes, but she is a magical-realism monkey. Listen to her well. Feed her the fruit of knowledge and take care of her. You will be pleasantly surprised."

Before Maruquita could thank him, the Great God of the Taino Indians was gone and in its place was the Golden Mango of Wisdom, which the legends had taught and which no one really believed in these days. She approached the shining fruit slowly, stood looking at it in wonder, and then picked it up gingerly. Her daughter was awake and smiling at her. Maruquita peeled the fruit and brought it to Pitirrita's lips. The little monkey sucked at it hungrily, growing more and more amused. She then spoke, although Maruquita wasn't sure if she hadn't stepped into a dream.

"Now you," Pitirrita said.

"Me?" Maruquita asked, a little bit apprehensively. "Are you sure?"

"You, *mamita*," the little monkey said, reaching up to touch Maruquita's face.

Maruquita sucked at the mango several times, the juice dripping on her chin. She suddenly felt an enormous headache and felt herself swoon and faint in the middle of the ceremonial plaza. When she woke up, it was as if she had been reborn. Beside her was a beautiful young girl with green eyes and brownish hair. She was dressed in jeans, a polo shirt and sparkling white Nikes.

"Hi, Mommy," she said.

"Was I asleep long?"

"Not very long. Two hours. How are you feeling?"

"I'm fine. Are you Pitirrita?"

"Yes, I am and I'm ready to join you in doing battle against the evil forces."

"Did you morph?"

"Yes, I did."

"How?"

"Easy. It's genetic. Watch!"

In a quick succession she was a young peacock, an eagle, a mongoose, and then a monkey. When she was done she jumped high in the air, and she came down as the bright-eyed girl.

"See?" she said, happily as she hugged herself to Maruquita. "But there are even more amazing changes coming."

"In you?"

"More in you, but you should get back."

"Let's go."

"No, you go. I'll stay here and learn more."

"But you're just a baby."

"I know. But I can take care of myself. Go ahead. You have work to do. I want to see Daddy."

"I never want to see that bozo again, honey."

"Please, Mami. Please. We should be together as a family. Please. Bring him back."

"Okay, give Mommy a kiss."

Pitirrita went over and kissed her mother. When she was done, she morphed back into a monkey, waved, and went scampering up a tree. She was gone through the treetops as it began to drizzle. Maruquita felt a tightening in her throat, and her eyes began to tear. She rose and began walking down the mountain. When she was once again near the beach, she put on her bathing suit and waded out into the water. She dove in and swam underwater. By the time she surfaced a few minutes later, she wore a look of profound wisdom. It was as if, through the combination of eating from the Golden Mango of Wisdom and swimming in the ocean waters of Luquillo Beach, the thick veil of innocence, which had hidden knowledge from her, had been washed away. She smiled and saw the bound volumes of the Great Books in her mother's living-room bookcase, stacked neatly in her mind, and knew she could recall anything from them: Plato, Aristotle, Kant, Shakespeare, Dante, and every humanist volume and literary book ever published. She saw great big chunks of Ortega y Gasset, Thorsten Veblen, and James Joyce. More importantly, she knew that she could see the interrelation between the subjects contained therein and the theoretical and speculative inquiries they would produce in her mind. She smiled, got dressed, and walked along the beach until she was back at her apartment. The first thing she did was to cut her hair short. She then removed her hoop earrings, and for the first time in nearly two years, she got her eyeglasses from a box in the closet and put them on. She looked at herself in the mirror, and she looked like a J-Lo nerd.

She shrugged her shoulders and smiled with satisfaction.

DNA TESTING AND
POLITICAL ALTERNATIVES

THE WEEK AFTER MARUQUITA HAD HER BABY, WINNIFRED WAS FLOWN IN her father's Lear Jet to a very exclusive maternity clinic in Quebec, Canada, accompanied by her mother, her grandmother, her sister Margaret, and Omaha. Although not yet married, she wore a diamond solitaire and a wedding band. She registered at the clinic as Mrs. Winnifred Bigelow. With the assistance of her grandmother's magic, doctors were able to induce labor, and she gave birth to a baby boy on May 18, 2001. The boy was named Christopher Harrison Bigelow. He was perfect and blond and had blue eyes. Christopher's great-grandmother, Abigail Buckley, immediately got on her laptop and through a secure server authorized an endowment of five million dollars in the baby's name. By the time the boy graduated from Yale in 2023, the interest on the five million dollars would have grown into a small fortune.

The birth accomplished, Winnifred returned to the task of completing preparations for her end-of-June wedding. She asked many question and was reassured by Margaret and her mother that everything was in order. She had already been fitted for her wedding gown, had registered for three china services and three silver ones, and had invitations sent out to five hundred select friends and relatives. On Omaha's side of the family only Olivia Bigelow received an invitation. While this seemed odd to her friends and other relatives, Winnifred explained that Omaha's family observed a very archaic religious practice that forbade them from traveling more than a hundred miles from their homes. In fact, Omaha's mother had been disowned by the family when Olivia left Hope, Arkansas, to elope with Omaha's father. One of her friends mentioned that Hope was the home of the previous president. Focused now on her upcoming nuptials, this held little meaning for Winnifred. Pierce Buckley had overheard the conversation, and this small bit of information piqued his curiosity enough for him to rekindle his interest in how this somewhat common person had managed to not only interest his daughter, a gifted and beautiful young woman, but, of even greater importance, how he had managed to enter Yale. He wondered whether a few markers from his time with the company might not be called in. Someone in the Eli Network had to know. As for Winnifred's son, he was left in the care of a staff of nurses, doctors, and financial advisors at an undisclosed location somewhere in New England.

Fate is strange. If Omaha suffered from hubris regarding his *bohango,* Winnifred was no less cursed in her need to control not only her own future but that of her future mate. A number of things took place between the birth of the child and the middle of June. The wedding was scheduled for the last Saturday in June, but those thirty days brought on a postpartum depression that was particularly deep. This type of depression is called baby blues in common parlance, and it reduces most women to mush. They cry constantly and worry that the gained weight and rending of their genitals to permit the birth of the child will cause them to lose sexual allure. Little do these poor women know that a man, when young and aroused, will insert his erect penis into almost any warm and moist place, including uncooked lukewarm liver, a tepid watermelon, or room-temperature oatmeal. Nonetheless, Winnifred sank into a profound depression.

She returned to her apartment in New York and began to see visions of Maruquita's peacock staring at her. It didn't matter where she found herself: in the gym attempting to regain her body tone, in the shower, during conversation, or in elevators—there was the majestic bird with its elegant plumage. Wherever she went, the peacock followed and displayed its magnificent feathers. She tried shooing it away, but the peacock was fearless and squawked at her. Often the bird advanced and caused her to shrink back fearfully. One day her maid, Walteria, came to her and said she had found *caca de gallina,* hen excrement, around the house. Winnifred yelled at the poor woman and fell on her bed crying. So intense was her depression that she called her broker and asked her to sell all the NBC stock that she owned.

As for Omaha, he was helpless. He knew Maruquita was working her magic. Omaha was concerned about his film and the fact that distributors were not as excited as the critics. People at private screenings turned in positive evaluations, but the distributors thought the film was too raw and certainly too explicit. For the first time in her young life Winnifred sought help from a therapist. She spoke about the peacock. The therapist made a preliminary diagnosis of schizophrenia and prescribed complex drug therapy. Winnifred sank deeper into her depression and stopped taking her medicine. Amethyst

Cooper, her cook and a CIA operative, became concerned about Winnifred's condition. She spoke to Pierce Buckley and suggested that he visit his daughter's home to assess her condition himself. One afternoon in the middle of June with only two weeks left before the wedding, Pierce Buckley arrived at his daughter's apartment a little after one in the afternoon.

Amethyst Booker came into the bedroom, where Winnifred was curled up in a nearly fetal catatonic stupor and said that her father had come to see her. Winnifred brightened for a moment. She went into the bathroom, washed her face, and brushed her hair. While she was looking in the mirror the peacock appeared and squawked three times. As often happens in such conditions, it is suppressed anger that causes nonclinical depressions. The greater the oppressive social situation, the more the individual sinks into the depression. The outburst of children at such places as Columbine come from a combination of the school milieu in which the children are seen as outcasts, the parental expectations based on a Judeo-Christian morality in which the person is either good or evil, either saint or devil, and the knowledge that their education is basically useless. Things came to a head, and like Linda Blair in *The Exorcist* Winnifred's head spun around and she spit at the peacock: *Get the fuck out of my house you birdbrain cunt motherfucker! Get out! Get out!* She opened the medicine cabinet and began firing the contents at the image of the peacock. Deodorants, colognes, cans of hair conditioners began flying and going through the peacock as if it were not present.

Her father heard the outburst and ran into the room.

"Hi, Daddy," Winnifred said sheepishly.

"Whom were you addressing, Winnifred?" Pierce asked, puzzled and hurt.

"The peacock."

"Peacock?"

"Yes, it appears and attempts to vex me."

"You were quite angry."

"Yes, it made it go away."

"Is that good?"

"It's very good, but I have to tell you that this is the work of Malsuckita Whatever, the girl with whom Omaha was involved. She's a witch of major proportions. I've underestimated her, and I think we need political clout to quell her aggression."

"Well, I want to hear all about it, and if I can be of any help, I'm at your disposal."

They had walked out of Winnifred's bedroom and were now in the large living room with its white couches and rugs, sunlight illuminating the room. Amethyst Booker brought a large pitcher of cold lemonade, which she knew Pierce loved. She set the tray on the glass coffee table, poured two glasses and exited.

"Daddy, I'm so happy to see you," Winnifred said, hugging herself to Pierce before they sat down. "I feel so much better. Do you like my apartment?"

"I'm happy to see you, Pooh," Pierce said, lifting the frosted glass and taking a long sip from the lemonade. "It's a lovely pied-à-terre. I'm relieved that my presence has had a salubrious effect on you."

"Yes, very much so. Thank you."

"What does this young woman want?"

"She's upset that Omaha prefers being with me. Daddy, he's so talented. It would be a waste to have him remain with her."

"Does she want money to leave you alone? That can be arranged quite easily."

"No, I think it's about something else. Omaha thinks that they're part of a political group and they're seeking independence for their pitiful little island. I've never heard anything so pathetic."

"I'm familiar with the situation," Pierce said.

"We keep those people afloat, here as well as there."

"That's not quite accurate from a financial point of view. We actually take a lot more capital from the island than we put in. We also sell billions of dollars worth of American goods to them, so that much of the money they earn is used for purchasing these products. To be blunt, it is a very large model of the company store, in which peons work the land, get paid, and purchase goods from the master's store, an effective economic model which ultimately benefits the owner. We are the owner. They are the peons."

"Well, that's good, isn't it?"

"It's good and bad. It provides our manufacturers a steady cash flow, but it breeds a great deal of resentment, particularly in the intelligentsia, since they're aware of the deceit."

"Why don't we just rid ourselves of the problem? Give them what they want. Let them starve and become another Haiti or Cuba. They're so insufferable. And they're always having so much fun. What are they so happy about? Traipsing around in garish outfits and yelling constantly at their children in that horrid patois of Spanish. Is their diet infused with happy juice? Let them go, I say." She gave her blond hair a dismissive flip and turned her face away from the problem.

"Well, there are many geopolitical reasons why it's important to hold on to the island."

"Whatever the situation, this must cease, Daddy," Winnifred said, turning back to him. "I will not permit a little island in the middle of the sea to interfere with my happiness. I refuse to live like this and will kill myself unless something is done."

"Winnie, please don't talk that way."

"Daddy, I can't help it. I will not live under the conditions I've experienced for the past three weeks. I simply won't."

"What do you suggest?"

"What is their biggest concern?"

"The presence of the U.S. military, particularly the navy bombing range on one of their smaller islands. Some of the people want to become a permanent part of our country. There is no chance at all that they'll become a state."

"Heaven forbid!" Winnifred said, covering her face.

"Well, about half of them want that option and lobby quite actively for statehood."

"Over my dead body."

"It's simply not a realistic option. They refuse to give up their language, and they would have two senators, eight congress persons, a governor with a seat on the Governors Council, a federal budget larger than twenty-two other states, and a lobby that would seek to obtain every advantage possible. Since they're a minority, every time they gained an advantage, every minority in the U.S. would seek an equal concession. It could bankrupt us within a decade. And now this Vieques issue with our navy."

"Oh, the nonsense with this charlatan Sharpton, and the Kennedys attempting to milk the country's sentimentalism over Jack Kennedy and his equally profligate brother? I'm sorry they were assassinated, and I feel terrible about JFK, Jr., but we should get over it and move on."

"Yes, the Vieques issue. It's causing the President a bit of embarrassment. He's still feeling the repercussions of the Florida election."

"I understand that," Winnifred said. "I strongly believe that the President would be wise to just give them their island and let them starve. With American ingenuity and get up and go, we could probably construct a floating island a few miles away, a sort of parallel Puerto Rico with this Vieques albatross next to it. I once saw an episode of *Star Trek* that had parallel universes. If someone can think up such a fiction, all it would take is really good engineering and construction to replicate the place. The competition from our tourism alone would drive them to ruin. If I were advising the President, I would say, Give the evildoers what they want and let's move on."

"Well, it's certainly something to consider," Pierce said. "By the way I have extraordinary news. I was meaning to call you later in the week to see if we could have lunch again. This time at the Yale Club."

"Oh, tell me, tell me, Daddy. Not fair to tease me like this. I couldn't wait."

"It's about Omaha."

"What about him?"

"Well, for starters, we've determined that it was Bill Clinton that got Omaha into Yale. He appears to be a talented young man who simply needed a guiding hand, which he found in you. However, I was concerned how he could've managed to enter the school."

"Daddy, *the* Bill Clinton, who nearly sank the country into a morass of deceit and immorality?"

"Yes, he went to Yale Law School and obviously had considerable clout when your Omaha entered the school in 1983."

"Well, I knew that Clinton was a graduate, and it was one of the reasons I didn't want to go to Yale Law School. If they permitted him to soil the university with his presence, I knew our values were being degraded. I chose Columbia and its harmless pseudoliberal posture. But that is quite amazing, Daddy. A little tainted, but nonetheless impressive."

"Oh, there's more."

"More, Daddy?" Winnifred said, moving closer to her father and kneeling on the sofa. "About Omaha?"

"Yes, about his pedigree."

"Oh, boy. The suspense is overwhelming. Tell me. Tell me!"

Pierce Buckley went on to detail how a special unit of the intelligence community had been working independently to learn whether Gennifer Flowers was a single occurrence or whether there was a pattern to Clinton's behavior. They talked to many people in Hope, Arkansas, about the young women with whom Bill Clinton had even the most minimal contact during his high school days. Pierce explained that there was a surprisingly large number of women who claimed to have been intimate with the future president. He wanted to be a musician, and musicians have always had a special allure for young women. Pierce added that ninety percent of these women who today claimed intimacy with Clinton, did so because of his notoriety and position as president. Through further investigation a list was made of residents of Hope,

Arkansas, who had sent children to Yale. No correlation between women on the list and offspring who went to Yale. Upon further inquiry, the investigation determined that there had been a girl, Olivia McBride, who had known young Clinton and was also a musician. Some people went as far as saying the two had dated. She had left Hope under suspicious circumstances. At the time of the investigation in 1997, no one paid much attention to the name of Olivia McBride.

"When I began inquiring several weeks ago, I read the report and saw the name, Olivia. I became curious," Pierce said and went on. "I recalled that Omaha's mother's name was Olivia, and we began to follow that lead."

Winnifred listened as her father detailed that Olivia had left Hope because she was pregnant. He and his investigators needed to learn the identity of the father. Few people would talk. They still didn't know why she took the name Bigelow. There are no marriage records indicating that Olivia McBride married, either in Arkansas or in Kansas. The investigators went back to Hope and tried to locate the McBrides but they had moved many years prior. No one knew where they had gone. Eventually, two weeks earlier, they had been located in Caramba, Oklahoma, where they ran a gas station and truckstop on the edge of town. At first the McBrides did not acknowledge having a daughter. Staunch Republicans, they were told that this was a further investigation into Bill Clinton. Mrs. McBride finally broke down, began crying, and said they hadn't seen their daughter since she left Hope. Why did she leave? They didn't know. It was obvious that they were in total denial about her pregnancy.

Pierce then told Winnifred that he had a hunch that there could be a connection between Bill Clinton helping Omaha enter Yale and Olivia McBride. During the investigation there was one man who appeared to be a bit erratic and complained about Bill Clinton. Further inquiries were made, and it turned out that Willis Carruthers, a failed country-music composer of such obscure songs as "Take Everything I Got but Don't You Touch my Pickup, my Shotgun, and my Dog," had been a suitor of Olivia McBride when they were in high school. "That Billy Clinton turned her head," he said. "He just twisted her head around with all that Nigra' music. Jazz, Jazz, Jazz," he added bitterly.

Pierce's investigators were now able to zero in on a more concrete lead. They obtained the DNA results from Monica Lewinsky's dress, and samples from Olivia Bigelow's bathroom, and Amethyst Booker provided them with Omaha's hairbrush.

"Is that where it went?" Winnifred said. "He was going crazy last week looking for it. It finally turned up again. But wait! What happened? What are you saying?"

"The test came back positive," Pierce said. "Clinton's paternity is obvious."

"No way. Are you saying that my future husband and Chelsea Clinton are siblings?"

"Exactly."

"Oh, piffle," Winnifred said, suddenly crestfallen again.

"What's the matter?" Pierce said.

"Nothing," Winnifred said, ridding herself of her momentary annoyance. "This means that my husband is presidential timber."

"Possibly. Is he a registered Democrat?"

"I don't know. I can ask him."

"If he is, it would be a good idea if he switched to the Republican Party. If he's not registered, he should do so as a Republican right away."

"Of course. Wait, let me think," Winnifred said, pressing her fingers to her forehead. "This is 2001. Twenty years from now it's 2021. He would be fifty-five by then. Maybe he could make a run in 2024, after a long and respected career in motion pictures. It wouldn't be a first, would it?"

"Certainly not," Pierce said, encouraged by his daughter's political acumen and foresight. "President Reagan had just such a beginning before entering politics, didn't he?"

"I was thinking the same thing," Winnifred said. "Oh, thank you, daddy. I feel so incredibly empowered by what you've told me. What about the press?"

"I believe that we should keep everything under wraps and observe and guide your young man until we see further signs of his development in a political direction."

"I agree, Daddy," Winnifred said, hopping over on her knees and hugging herself to her father. "Can I ask you something?"

"Of course."

"Do you have access to the President?"

"If it's important enough, I can put in a call."

"Could you please tell him to rid himself of all that trouble with Vieques?"

"I'll talk to Dakulana."

"Dakulana? Why Dakulana?"

"She knows Condoleeza Rice."

"Oh, that prissy black woman with the badly tailored outfits?"

"Yes, she's the President's national security advisor. She and Dakulana know each other. I think either from England or here. I don't know which. I'll have Dakulana talk to her about the Vieques issue."

"Thank you, Daddy," Winnifred said. "I promise you that I will not spend one more day depressed. I'm going to have a wonderful wedding and a wonderful life."

"That's certainly good news, Winnie," Pierce said. "I'm grateful and relieved."

"Daddy? May I express myself fully without incurring your disappointment?"

"Of course. You never disappoint me."

"Well, I say to these people who want to demean our country with their complaints, if they can't take a fuck, joke them."

"My sentiments exactly," Pierce said, amused by his daughter's ribald humor.

"Really!"

"Well, I better get back and continue to try and make the world a better place."

"Daddy, I need to ask you something."

"Go ahead."

"Do you think I would make a good First Lady?"

"I should think so, but . . ."

"But what?"

"You should stay in law school and graduate," Pierce said. "You never know when a law degree will come in handy. Look at Hillary Clinton. She's a U.S. senator right now."

"Point well taken, Daddy," Winnifred said. "But she's another one who could use some advice on her wardrobe. These poor women!"

"Oh, one more thing, Winnifred. Do you know who Charlize Theron is?"

"She's a movie star. Why?"

"Someone who saw us at the Harvard Club called me and congratulated me for escorting this Ms. Theron around. I assumed they thought you were Ms. Theron."

"Yes, people say I look like her."

"I see. I understand that she's made a number of films. Do you recommend one?"

"Yes, you love golf, so you might want to rent *The Legend of Bagger Vance*. She's moderately good in that one. But frankly, if truth be told, objectively speaking, I'm more attractive than Charlize Theron."

"I see," Pierce said, and took one last sip from his lemonade, fearful for a moment that his daughter's arrogance signaled an upcoming fall. "I must go. I'm glad you're feeling better."

Pierce stood up and opened his arms to Winnifred, who hopped off the sofa and hugged herself to him. With her arm through his she walked him to the vestibule. When the elevator came, she reached up and kissed him. Once he was gone the peacock appeared and squawked incessantly. She stared at it, and then she was all at once amused. She laughed, and the peacock vanished. She went to her bedroom and dialed Omaha at the apartment in Red Square. When he answered the phone, she asked him if he was ready to get married. He said nothing would please him more and he couldn't wait. He noticed immediately that Winnifred's depression had broken. He longed to be with her again. They had to wait forty days, and it had been only four weeks since the birth. Maybe they could do other things. He promised to be home early. They said their *I love yous* and hung up. Things were not quite as resolved on the other side of Manhattan island, where, deep in the recesses of the Avenue D projects, preparations were being made in the War Room of the Puerto Rican Navy.

HE OPERATIONS ROOM OF THE AIRCRAFT CARRIER *DÉJALO QUE SUBA*, designated P.R. 107, anchored and cloaked on the East River not too far from the Avenue D projects, was abuzz with activity. There is no need to concern yourself with pleasure crafts, freighters, or other ships running into the cloaked carrier. Anyone who's watched the pertinent *Star Trek* episodes knows full well that there is also a force field around a cloaked vessel. Any craft that came too close to the carrier would be diverted without damage to itself or the carrier. The psychophysical aspects of such phenomena are obvious, so please don't trouble me with inane questions. I'm not in the mood for challenges to the structure or logic of this novel. This is the point in a literary novel when the strength of the character takes over and there is little the novelist can do. I've discussed this before. Once characters realize they have the power to think and act for themselves, the novelist can do little to prevent them from doing so. I'm sure Herman Melville agonized over how to tell Captain Ahab to stop obsessing about the white whale, but Ahab was driven by his own motives and had to go after the whale. I'm using a marine example so that I can prepare you for what is coming. You refuse to read nineteenth-century American literature because it's irrelevant? That's sad, because you're missing out on understanding the history of this country. I mean, it's your country. I'm just passing through. I own nothing but a computer and some old shoes. Literature is never irrelevant if read in conjunction with history. While a novel can be analyzed for its timelessness in terms of human values, it is also a chronicle of its time, bound by the strictures of the society in which the work was written. The notion of timelessness is silly, for time doesn't have past, present, or future. It just is. But I'm lecturing. The matter at hand is the war room of the aircraft carrier *Déjalo que suba*. By the way, the phrase means *Let him come on board*. This particular *plena* tells in song of an admonition to a particular black, named Bulibén, about what will happen should he dare board the singer's boat. It's not pretty, and it warns that even his relatives who have not yet been born will feel the pain of the singer's wrath. The tune is lilting and would cause even the dead to wish to dance, but the message is extremely threatening and apocalyptic.

Present in the war room and in uniform were Admirals Bizquita and Frutita and Secretary of the Navy Flaquita. The uniforms, inspired by *Star Trek* and the U.S. Navy were designed by Costurita, the famous Loisaida creator of wedding dresses and disco apparel, with a shop and showroom in the Jacob Riis projects around twelfth Street and Avenue D. Rear Admiral Samuel Beckett Salsipuedes was standing by a table on which there was a map of the southernmost Caribbean area, with the Puerto Rican archipelago at its center, indicating distances and depths. Positioned some distance away, perhaps two-hundred miles on the west side of the island of Hispaniola, were the two battle groups that would seek to wrest control of the island of Vieques from the U.S. after disabling or sinking the U.S. ships. The forward battle group was the Cortijo battle group; the rear battle group had been named the Ramito battle group. Both Cortijo and Ramito are beloved figures of the Puerto Rican musical tradition and revered by us. I commend whoever was involved in choosing the names for the battle groups.

It is of the utmost importance to understand that there is no official definition of a battle group. Generally a battle group is composed of an aircraft carrier at the center of action, with additional ships lending support. The aircraft carrier provides a movable landing strip and, because it is at sea it is not restricted by landing treaties or other such arrangements with foreign powers. The modern battle group has two guided-missile cruisers. Each of the Puerto Rican battle groups had only one cruiser. However, as in other battle groups, it had two destroyers: one with guidedmissile capabilities and the other for antisubmarine warfare. Usually a battle group has a frigate. The two Puerto Rican battle groups had no frigates. They did, however, have two submarines each. Each battle group has its own supply ships for fuel, ammunition, and food. The Puerto Rican battle groups were no different, except that they included a special pen that held fifty healthy pigs that could be slaughtered, dressed, and delivered to each of the ships' galleys. This is important, since Puerto Ricans possibly eat more pork than anyone in the world. The playwright and wry social critic, Dolores Prida, in her play *La Botánica,* has a character allude to the fact that if there were a correlation between heart disease and eating pork, the average longeveity of Puerto Ricans would be about forty-two years. In contrast, Puerto Rico has per capita the largest number of people over a hundred years of age. I'm not telling you that you should load up on the other white meat, but it's either the pork or salsa dancing that makes us one sprightly group. I don't know. Turkey contains triptophane, a well-known soporific. Maybe pork has speed and makes Ricans sound as if they talk faster and seem weird. I'm just saying. They seem pretty normal to me. Then again I'm one of them. I'm sure the Irish sound perfectly normal to each other when they speak English.

Everyone in the war room held their breath when they heard the piping that announced that the Admiral of the Fleet was coming aboard. The piping was distinctive and in clave form. Three whistles, a pause, and then two more short bursts. A few minutes later, resplendent in her whites with the five stars on her epaulets, Admiral Maruquita Salsipuedes entered the room, followed by her aide, Commander Awilda Cortez, equally starched and crisp in her uniform. Six Royal Puerto Rican Marines in their blue-and-green dress uniforms followed and stood at parade rest in threes on either side of the room. Everyone saluted. Removing her hat, Admiral Maruquita Salsipuedes bid everyone be seated. She took the seat at the head of the table and asked her brother, Rear Admiral SBS, to begin the briefing.

For the next six hours each aspect of the operation was discussed in the most minute detail. Except for a forty-five-minute *cuchifrito* break, the admiralty staff worked diligently to ensure a successful operation. *Cuchifritos* are pork innards and other confections, such as *alcapurrias, bacalaitos, piononos, rellenos de papa,* all fried in pork lard. When the Admiralty was finished with the briefing, it was agreed that in late November 2001, after the hurricane season passed, the two battle groups would leave their Loisaida base and sail out to sea, with their destination the Caribbean Sea and the Puerto Rico archipelago. Once they had sailed beyond Mona Channel, the body of water between the Dominican Republic and Mona Island off the western coast of Puerto Rico, the battle group Cortijo would then sail along the southern coast until, cloaked, it skirted the eastern side of the island and lay at anchor between Puerto Rico and Vieques. The battle group Ramito would follow and anchor across the Roosevelt Roads Naval Station on the eastern coast.

"It is imperative that from here on in," Admiral Maruquita said, speaking for the first time since the meeting began six hours before, "the utmost care be exercised by all involved to ensure the success of this mission. Our calculations indicate that it will not be a prolonged confrontation. I'm certain that we will incur casualties, but such is the nature of naval combat. We stand on the brink of an historic event, and one that will determine the fate of our people for centuries to come. At the end of this briefing you will return to your duties, but understand that we are on twenty-four-hour call and that we will have periodic shakedown cruises. Your crews should be maintained on alert, and inspections will be carried out on schedule. The Naval Academy should continue its instruction, with equal care to train our young men and women. Thank you very much, and may the grace and benevolence of Yukiyú be with you."

Those who were present couldn't help applauding the resolve of their admiral. Maruquita smiled and nodded. She turned to her aide, Commander Cortez, and asked that the captain of the submarine *El Negro Bembón* be called in. A short time later, after the Admiralty staff had departed, Lieutenant Commander Carlos "Cano" Fuentes, came in, saluted, and stood at attention until he was asked to sit down. During the next hour Maruquita outlined a particular mission in which the submarine would leave early on the morning 29 June and, cloaked, would travel up the East River into Long Island Sound, where it would submerge and run silent with a destination of Sag Harbor. Once there, it would surface and lay cloaked at anchor.

"I will be on board, together with Commander Cortez," Maruquita said. "We will lead a landing party of Royal Puerto Rican Marine Seals. I have chosen the five young men and one young woman here present as that landing party. We will use two rubber rafts, with Commander Cortez and I in charge of each of the rafts. They have been designated Attack Raft Alpha and Attack Raft Omega.

"We will disembark from the submarine *El Negro Bembón* as soon as the sun sets on the evening of 30 June. We will then enter into the area of our objective at twenty-one hundred hours and remain hidden. With great stealth we will render the guards helpless with tranquilizing injections. Attack Group Omega, led by Commander Cortez, will disable the security guards. There will be little danger, since the guards are not armed. When we receive the communication that the subject has been equally neutralized, Attack Group Alpha will spring into action and remove the subject. We will once again board our rafts and rendezvous with *El Negro Bembón* at twenty-two hundred hours and board the submarine. Once the hatch is closed, we will submerge and sail to the mouth of the East River. Once there we will surface and sail cloaked until we reach our naval base next to the Lillian Wald projects. We will then bring our prisoner to the Operations center of our navy, where he will be disposed of.

"Will he be executed?" asked Lt. Commander Fuentes.

"He will be tried and convicted of disloyalty and will be dealt with accordingly," Maruquita said. "I have recused myself from serving as judge advocate on this case. A panel of admirals will adjudicate the case. I have outlined the mission and have given it the name Operation Groomgrab. The appropriate protocols and maps have been provided to your crew. Study them well, Commander Fuentes. We will have a shakedown cruise on Saturday, June 23, to acquaint the crew with all procedures. Is that clear?"

"Aye, aye, Ma'am," said Lt. Commander Fuentes, standing and saluting.

"Dismissed, Commander," said Maruquita. "Thank you."

Maruquita nodded at Awilda Cortez. The two rose and were followed out of the room by the detail of marines.

Observing this scene and analyzing it in detail, I have to say that I am impressed by Maruquita's transformation. However, in my opinion, the change is much too abrupt and strains probability, making anyone wonder, including me, how this could have come about. I've made appropriate inquiries, and this is what apparently took place. After Maruquita came out of the jungle she got home and immediately went to sleep. She slept nearly twelve hours. When she woke up, she felt as if she were in a fog. Her head didn't hurt but it felt quite odd. She looked at herself in the mirror and couldn't recall cutting her hair or removing her earrings, but they were gone. On the night table were her glasses. She remembered retrieving them from the closet. What seemed odd became clearer when she turned on CNN and seemed interested in the news. This had never happened before. She even sat through *Money Line* with Lou Dobbs and Willow Bay, still on before moving to Los Angeles. Maruquita actually understood what the two financial analysts were talking about. After watching the news, she showered, changed, and went upstairs to her mother's. She greeted her mother warmly, inquiring about her health.

"Never mind that," Flaquita said. "Where's my granddaughter?"

"I took her to the jungle," Maruquita said.

"And you left her there?"

"Yes, I did."

"Are you crazy? I can't believe you could leave your own baby in the jungle. What kind of mother does that? Answer me! Are you crazy?"

"No, I'm quite sane," Maruquita answered.

"What did you say?" Flaquita said, coming closer and peering into her daughter's face.

"I said that I'm quite sane and in full control of my faculties," Maruquita said. "Crazy is what I was before, acting stupidly to satisfy your need to subvert my powers. I love you, but I think you ought to sit down and stop playing the hysterical Puerto Rican grandmother stereotype. You do so rather poorly and are ill-suited for it."

Flaquita was shocked. She sat down and stared dumbly at her daughter.

"Who are you?" she finally said. "Did SBS do some more *Star Trek* magic and put Mr. Spock's brain inside of you? And you cut your hair, aren't wearing makeup, and took off your earrings. Are you an extraterrestrial who has taken over my daughter's body?"

"No, nothing like that has taken place," Maruquita replied. "I've simply taken matters into my own hands. I got tired of playing the P.R. homegirl bozo, and I'm ready to assume my rightful role in the development of our people."

"But you're so different," Flaquita said, her voice at once tremulous and awed by her daughter. "You seem so bright, so articulate, so self-assured."

"I figured it out, Mom," Maruquita said.

"Figured what out?"

"It's quite simple."

"Maybe for you."

"It's like this. I can change into a monkey or a squirrel and even a peacock of imposing presence and beauty, a presence that represents power and esthetic pleasure. If I can change into such representations, I can change into anything."

"Yes, I suppose," Flaquita said, not quite grasping the implications. "And?"

"Well, I've managed to change into a graduate of the Naval Academy, Annapolis, in political science. I also have an MA in economics and a PhD in comparative literature from Harvard University."

"From Harvard, really?"

"Yes, from Harvard and I will always remember that I'm Puerto Rican," Maruquita said. "I'm ready to assume command and make sure that everything goes according to plan. I will take command of the fleet immediately."

At that point Flaquita started crying. "I'm so happy," she said. "I don't know what to say. Can I make you something to eat?"

"Of course," Maruquita said, graciously. "We have a lot to talk about."

Among the things that mother and daughter talked about was why Flaquita kept from her that Awilda Cortez was her half-sister from an affair that her father had with a nurse when he was working maintenance at Bellevue Hospital, which caused him to be sitting on the trunk twenty years later. Maruquita was overjoyed and immediately called up Awilda and asked her to come over. Fifteen minutes later a very pregnant Awilda showed up. Aware that they were sisters, they embraced and swore allegiance to each other. Awilda admitted that she was jealous and had made the call to Maruquita. They cried together, and Maruquita was there when Awilda's Gringorican twins were born. Maruquita felt no jealousy, because her monkey daughter was quite beautiful, either as a monkey girl or a regular one. Awilda's daughters and Maruquita's would grow to resemble each other.

You see? The exchange between the mother and daughter was a good scene. I can live with the transformation because it makes absolute sense within the framework of the urban-magical-realism structure. I have to admit that Maruquita strains credibility a bit with the Annapolis degree, but she's in charge. I would have preferred that her degree had been from New York University, but that's my own desire working, being that NYU is my Alma Mater. I suppose Maruquita felt the need to have the Naval Academy in her curriculum vitae in order to justify being admiral of the fleet. As I'm recording this, I have learned that the newly appointed football coach of Notre Dame University has resigned because it has been learned that he had falsified his credentials. Maruquita graduating from the U.S. Naval Academy is not the same thing. There is a great deal of difference between football and urban magical realism.

But to other matters. Pierce Buckley was overjoyed that Winnifred had recovered from her depression. As promised, he had flown to London on June 9, met with Dakulana Imbebwabe, and explained the situation. Dakulana placed a call to the President's National Security Advisor. They exchanged pleasantries, and Dakulana went immediately to the heart of the matter. She explained that it was urgent that Pierce meet with his college classmate's son immediately. A week later, under the utmost secrecy, the two men met at an undisclosed Texas location near Crawford. The President thanked Pierce for his information from French security. Pierce then outlined his daughter's predicament with the Puerto Ricans. The president said he was also having problems with the Puerto Ricans, adding that the previous administration had left him quite a mess. Pierce and the president agreed that it was time to take action.

A day later the President announced that by 2003 the Navy would be out of Puerto Rico. Was this a hasty decision which left the President vulnerable? Some people are of that opinion. Others have gone further and said that something drastic had to take place to rescue a rapidly deteriorating presidency. I am not suggesting a macabre scenario in which Puerto Rico influenced an American president's decision. That would be far-fetched. However, what

I've reported is not simply speculative and has a basis in truth. The facts of what took place remain. Pierce Buckley did meet with the president of the United States.

Omaha, although overwhelmed by doubts concerning his film and the threat that Maruquita had made, was encouraged by Winnifred's recovery. One evening, after Walteria had retired to her room at the other end of the apartment and Amethyst Booker had served their supper and had gone home, Winnifred smiled sweetly at Omaha across the candlelit table, the linen perfect, the silver heavy, the china pristine, and the food and wine delicate to the palate.

"Why didn't you tell me about your father?" she said, sweetly. "I knew there was something quite special about you. I knew it the first time I saw you in Two Boots Pizza. Do you remember?"

"I certainly do," Omaha said. "I was at my lowest point that night."

"I know, but I saw greatness in you on that occasion. Why didn't you tell me?"

"How did you find out?"

"We're Buckleys, always vigilant," Winnifred said, and explained in general terms.

"I don't know if it was modesty or the shame of knowing he had abandoned me."

"I understand, and I would have understood."

"I'm sorry. I guess I wanted to make my way in the world without the encumbrances of power and family."

"Poor thing. You were suffering from the pedestrian attitudes of the middle class. We're all products of our conditioning. Well, all of that is now immaterial and in the past. Are you a registered Democrat?"

"No, not really," Omaha said. "I've been unconcerned with politics."

"Omaha, darling?"

"Yes, Pooh?"

"Aww, you're so sweet," Winnifred said. "That's what daddy calls me. Would you consider registering as a Republican? It would mean a great deal to me."

"Sure. I don't have a problem with that."

"Oh, that's wonderful," Winnifred said reaching between the candlesticks and squeezing Omaha's hand. "That is truly a most wonderful gift two weeks before our wedding. Has your mother agreed to stay at our house in Sag Harbor?"

"Yes, I spoke to her a few nights ago. She's very excited. A bit apprehensive, but she agreed to play the wedding march. If you can get some jazz musicians, she'll play a couple of sets."

"Super, darling. That's wonderful."

They continued eating, chatting softly about things. When they were finished, Winnifred served desert and coffee. They watched *The Perfect Storm* in her private theater. Before watching the film, she put on a cute paper hat and a red-and-white transparent miniskirt uniform and went behind the counter to sell Omaha popcorn. She flirted outrageously with him, to the point that he had no choice but to lift her cute red-and-white uniform and sock it to her on a leather banquette outside the uniplex. During their lovemaking Winnifred asked him to stop.

"Omipooh, I don't want you to indulge me but do I really look like Charlize Theron?"

"You are beyond Charlize Theron. While you may share her ineffable pulchritudinous beauty, there is something beyond the commonality of the movie star in you. That persona that often dissolves into the demands of the public is absent in you. I suspect that the core of your being will always remain erect and centered within you."

These words created such a rush of emotion in Winnifred that she had a massive orgasm that caused her to emit a moan such as the Lakota Indians describe as that of a buffalo cow in heat. Shortly thereafter Omaha exploded while thinking about Maruquita's face and body. The vision sent shivers through his body but he drove the image out of his mind.

When they were done, they walked into the air-conditioned, twenty-reclining-seat theater. Winnifred pushed a button near her chair and the film began rolling. Holding hands and periodically nuzzling each other and eating popcorn, they watched the movie.

Life was certainly grand.

AT APPROXIMATELY 4 P.M. ON JUNE 30, 2001, WINNIFRED BUCKLEY ON her father's arm walked down the cerise-carpeted aisle of the north lawn of the Buckley estate in Sag Harbor. On either side of the aisle sturdy wooden chairs had been placed upon carpeted plywood to prevent their sinking into the lawn. At the end of the carpet a latticed structure had been constructed to serve as a chapel. Awaiting them was the Right Reverend William Brunswick Asherton of the Universalist Church. Facing the minister was Omaha, his best man, Valery Molotov, and his ushers, the brothers Buckley. On the other side was the maid of honor, Margaret, sister to the bride, and her three bridesmaids: Buffy Chastain, Heather Lithgow, and Clarice Worthington Antietam. The bride wore a gown of taffeta and organdy, her face veiled in tulle under a diadem of delicate miniature marguerites which shone brilliantly against the luster of her blonde hair. As she began walking, Olivia Bigelow, at the piano, played a flourish of uncanny beauty which she had extracted from a contrapuntal Bach fugue. While the last note lingered, she slid effortlessly into the wedding march. Behind Winnifred was a train some twenty feet in length, carried by one of her nieces, equally blonde and engaging. Two other nieces walking behind the train scattered petite white rose petals in the train's wake. Behind came a ten-year-old nephew in tails, carrying a small red cushion upon which there rested the two gold wedding bands, one thin and delicate and the other thick and testosteronic.

The wedding went without a hitch, and the friends and relatives were lifted into a sense of contentment as they watched the two young people exchange their vows and enter into the bond of matrimony. It was a sublime moment. The more elderly people recalled their nuptials and regretted that they would soon exit the planet and not partake of this new century, as would these young people. The younger ones wished that they too would someday be as happy as Winnifred and Omaha looked. When the wedding was over, everyone gathered on the south lawn, where an enormous tent had been erected and a buffet of mammoth proportions had been laid out. Three dozen waiters and waitresses of varied third-world descendancies had been employed to bring canapés and wines to the guests, decanting the vintages from delicate carafes into crystal goblets.

Among the waiters was Lieutenant Junior Grade Kevin Vega (no relation), an intelligence officer of the Puerto Rican Navy, who had been assigned the task of strict surveillance on the groom. Unobtrusively he was to keep an eye on his every move. Dressed in white pants and a short red jacket, he was ostensibly employed by the catering service. Lt. JG Vega was wired directly to the intelligence officer aboard the submarine *El Negro Bembón,* at this time submerged in Gardiner's Bay. The reception was a complete success. At least four new engagements would surface from the celebration. Only one unexpected pregnancy would occur, and save some minor disagreements on the merits of the Yankees versus the Mets, no unpleasantness of any sort took place. The jazz musicians, led by Olivia Bigelow, played for a while, and then a disc jockey began offering more popular tunes, and people whirled and shimmied on the dance floor that had been constructed on the lawn. Omaha and Winnifred couldn't have been happier.

Shortly after the sun went down the cake-cutting ceremony began. At that very moment the submarine *El Negro Bembón* surfaced, and the two rubber rafts were lowered into the water. Landing party Alpha, headed by Maruquita Salsipuedes, and landing party Omega, headed by Awilda Cortez, lowered themselves into the rafts. They motored inland, aided by the incoming tide, until fifteen minutes later they were in the channel near the Buckley estate. They brought the rafts closer, tied them up, and waded ashore. Having conducted a trial run, they now moved stealthily like shadows. Dressed in their camouflaged uniforms, their faces painted black and green, they approached the estate. By this time Lt. JG Vega and his team, other waiters who in reality were Ensigns Laura Tirado and Jay Delgado, and Special Ops Warrant Officer Rolando Guzmán, had swung into action by causing the bride to pass out by spiking her champagne. Additionally, they made sure that the alarm system and major telephone lines had been disabled. The first task for the landing party was to eliminate the private security detail hired to oversee the safety of the wedding guests. Led by Commander Cortez of Attack Group Omega, Marine Seals Lt. Blinky Torres, Sgt. Carmen Quiñones, and Cpl. Pito Encarnación moved quickly to immobilize the twelve security guards for the Buckley estate, rendering them somnolent with tranquilizing injections. The security guards were carefully concealed in the bushes around the property, where they would awaken three hours later, at midnight. By that time the search for Omaha would begin in earnest when Winnifred woke up from drinking too much champagne and realized her groom was missing. By then Operation Groomgrab would have been a complete success.

Omaha had been tranquilized quickly as he emerged from a first-floor bathroom near the kitchen. Lt. JG Vega, in his waiter's uniform, had bumped into him as he came out. At the same time he injected Omaha, apologized, and caught him as he began to collapse. Lt. JG Vega dragged him into the kitchen. Marine Seals Cpl. Sonny Texidor and Pfc. Bobby Rosado of Attack Group Alpha helped carry Omaha out to the back, where Maruquita was waiting with two other Seals. The rest stood guard to ensure that no one would interfere with Omaha's removal. They made their way through the estate, staying to the treeline to avoid detection because of the moonlight. They carried Omaha until they were once again near the rafts. They placed the inert Omaha in the Alpha raft, paddled out of the channel, and when both rafts were a good distance away, they started the motors and promptly at 2200 hours rendezvoused with the submarine *El Negro Bembón*. They boarded the vessel, and fifteen minutes later they were once again out on Long Island Sound at some 14 fathoms, periscope down and running silently.

At midnight when Winnifred, in a panic, declared that she couldn't find her husband, Omaha Bigelow, still in his tuxedo, appeared before a panel of judges at the operations center of the aircraft carrier *Déjalo que suba*. A bit unsteady and still feeling the effects of the drugs, he found himself before three judges. Bigelow recognized Maruquita's mother and aunt. The other judge was one of the women he had met in the Japanese restaurant months before. However, rather than three attractive Latin women dressed fashionably, they were dressed as if they were members of an army, or rather a navy, since he saw the anchors prominently displayed on the lapels of the uniforms. The trial lasted less than an hour. The evidence was presented. There was testimony from Awilda Cortez, from Rocky, from Maruquita's mother, and from numerous homegirls who attested to Bigelow's unfaithfulness. There was finally a verdict, and Bigelow was found guilty. The prosecuting attorney asked for the maximum sentence. The judges agreed. Maruquita observed the trial on closed-circuit TV from her office. She sat stoically with no expression on her face.

Subsequently an escort of marines blindfolded the prisoner and brought him up on the deck of the aircraft carrier and into a waiting helicopter. Maruquita was already seated in the back of the helicopter. They sat him next to her. Bigelow was not aware of her presence, since his eyes were blindfolded. When the helicopter lifted up off the deck, Bigelow asked for an explanation.

He did not receive a reply. The helicopter landed on the roof of Marquita's building, where Bigelow had lived for a time. The Marines removed him from the helicopter and brought him to the apartment that had been his home. They laid him on his bed and removed his blindfold. He tried to regain his balance and his senses. The first thing he noticed was that Maruquita was in camouflage fatigues, her face still painted in green and black but her eyes boring frighteningly into his.

"What's going on?" Omaha said. "Why am I here, Maruquita?"

"I don't really believe you deserve an explanation, Omaha," Maruquita said.

"I should go back to my wedding," Omaha said, sitting up and swinging his feet onto the floor.

"I don't think so."

"What did I do? I told you I would take care of you and the baby. Was it a boy or a girl?"

"A girl. You'll see her soon enough."

"Is she here?"

"No, she's not. Change your clothes, because we're leaving shortly."

"You can't do this, Maruquita," Omaha said, standing up from the bed unsteadily. "It's kidnapping. The authorities will come after you."

He started to go out of the room, but two very menacing marines blocked his way. They were armed and looked as steely-eyed as Maruquita.

"You should try to relax. It's going to be a long night."

"Please, Maruquita," he said. "I have to go back. Everyone is going to wonder what happened to me."

"Their wondering will never cease, Omaha Bigelow."

"What happened to you? You've changed."

"You noticed?"

"Yes, you're not the same."

"Yeah, I've been going through changes. You know how it is. The story of my life."

"No, you really changed. You talk so funny."

"You changed too. Get dressed. Your clothes are still here. Just get some jeans, shirt, and sneakers from the closet and get changed. We're leaving. As you can see, we mean business. Quickly."

Omaha changed, and then, with a marine escort, they stepped out of the apartment and went down the hill toward the beach. The moon was full and the sky was dotted with stars. When they reached the end of Luquillo Beach where there is a cape, they crossed the highway and began their ascent into the jungle. They traveled all night, stopping only to eat and relieve themselves. Higher and higher and deeper and deeper they went into the jungle. Omaha asked if they were going to the place where he had the ceremony of enlargement. Maruquita explained that they were going deeper into the Loisaida jungle, to places that were still unexplored in the northwest part of Puerto Rico.

Toward morning they stopped at a clearing, and Omaha surveyed the canopy of the jungle below and in the distance the sea. They traveled another half-hour and were at a ceremonial plaza similar to the one where he had undergone the *bohango* enlargement ceremony. In the blink of an eye there appeared again the elders and the God Yukiyú. Maruquita made her obeisance and asked Yukiyú for permission to change Omaha into a monkey. She explained his transgressions. Yukiyú assented and Maruquita said, *Mono viene y mono va y desde ahora mono será*, and Omaha became a monkey. The incantation loosely translated is: *Monkey comes and monkey goes and from now on monkey does.* Shortly thereafter Yukiyú disappeared, and the elders vanished back into the jungle. Omaha was dazed and looked around for Maruquita, but she was gone.

He felt disoriented and touched himself to make sure he wasn't dreaming. He was alone in the middle of the plaza with the trees of the jungle all about him. A minute later a female monkey approached with a baby monkey on her hip. They smelled each other and touched and then the baby monkey jumped on him and hugged itself to him.

"Your daughter, Pitirrita," the female monkey said.

"Hello, daddy," said the little monkey.

"Hi," Omaha said. "How come we can talk?"

"Don't ask so many questions, you bozo," the female monkey said and laughed.

"We're a family," the male monkey said sheepishly.

"That's right," said the female.

"When can I go home?"

"Never," the female monkey said. "This is now your home."

"Where am I?"

"You're in the impenetrable Loisaida jungle, you bozo. Didn't you believe me when I said you were my pet?"

"Yes, but I have to make films."

"Not anymore. You can make peepee, you can make kaka, and you can make cuchicuchi. But that's it. Look at it this way. There are many cute monkey girls, and you can have all the cuchicuchi you want. I won't mind. Once in a while I'll turn you into a man and you can provide me with cephalic pleasure."

"Mommy, what's cephalic?"

"It's Greek. Cephalic pertains to the head."

"Oh, okay," said the little monkey. "For thinking."

"Sometimes, but not always."

"Can't I go back to the East Village?"

"No, you can't," the female monkey said. "Now no more questions. I'm hungry. Let's climb the trees and get lunch."

"Let's go, daddy," the little girl monkey said.

"Very well," the male monkey replied.

With that, the monkey family took to the trees.

A massive search began the very first night of Omaha's abduction. No trace was found on the Buckley estate. Everyone was questioned, particularly the help. Nobody had seen anything untoward. Later, back in Manhattan, the police, the FBI, and the CIA infiltrated the neighborhood. They asked questions, interviewed people, interrogated others. They posted rewards. They enticed and they threatened. The ones who threatened were turned into pigeons. No one knew anything. Everyone played dumb. When they asked about Maruquita, everyone said she had disappeared and no one had seen her for a while. She was a crazy girl and had given birth to a monkey. No one in the government believed anything of what these crazy people said. Helicopters hovered above the projects, surveillance teams watched day and night. No sign of Omaha Bigelow. No sign of Maruquita Salsipuedes. They had vanished. Perhaps theirs was true love. Wealth, social position, and upcoming success had failed, and true love had triumphed.

No one believed this was possible.

ONE OF THE ELEMENTS OF THE NOVEL IS STRONG CHARACTERIZATION. While this aspect of a work is important, there are times when things can get out of hand. I believe this is what has taken place with this novel. I have to apologize for my failure to keep Maruquita Salsipuedes in check and instead permitting her to take over the narrative without my interfering with her extreme and radical behavior. As I'm a person who respects the rights of individuals, I am totally against Maruquita's actions in the kidnapping of Omaha Bigelow. I didn't think I'd ever hear from her again, since, in my opinion, she had to know I'd be upset with how she shanghaied not only Bigelow, but my work. As is often the case, I was wrong. In spite of her misplaced sense of justice, she's an honest person and a courageous young woman. You must have sensed this.

At the beginning of 2002, some six months after Bigelow's disappearance, I received a phone call from Maruquita. I was a bit taken aback by her tone, which was both apologetic and filled with an obvious need, if not to be forgiven, at least to have me hear her out. She explained that she was motivated by patriotism. Given the events of 9/11 and the shock everyone was still suffering, I didn't see the connection between Bigelow's abduction and Maruquita's patriotic fervor.

"Patriotism?" I said. "You've made a shambles out of another human being's life and now you're going to talk about patriotism?"

"I'm sorry. He deserved what he got."

"That's not the point. What is this patriotism?"

"For Puerto Rico," she said.

I explained that I shared her concerns regarding Puerto Rico, but I never intended for Omaha Bigelow to be humiliated as he had been by her. I told her that in writing this novel I had pulled no punches and had permitted my imagination to take me where it wished. Off the wall behavior by characters, discussions between author and protagonists, satire, commentary, cheap accents, and linguistic excesses. I said that I had chided the presidency, past and present. I had questioned the intelligence community and the government. I began to pull punches regarding George Walker Bush and felt cowardly. I went ahead with my first impulses.

I told her that when it came to the World Trade Center I felt some hesitation, but I didn't hold back. I explained that the novelist who is concerned with injustice must tell the truth, ugly as it may be, and must write without fear of the outcome. I told her that two people I knew were lost in the September 11th attack. One was inside the North Tower, the other on the plane that hit the South Tower. They left grieving families, as did all victims of the attack. A woman I had recently met was able to leave the tower where she worked fifteen minutes before it collapsed. She has suffered a nervous breakdown from which I doubt that she will ever recover fully. My grief is contained, the pain minimal. I can only imagine the profound sorrow that people who lost fathers, mothers, sisters, brothers, husbands, and wives must feel.

Maruquita listened patiently. I told her that death intrudes on everyone's life, but it usually happens singly. Death is a part of life, ever present if you're aware of your own mortality. What happened on 9/11 is about something else. I realize that the United States was attacked and a symbol of its might destroyed. I can understand the national chagrin and anguish over this outrage. The act was an affront to me as well.

Maruquita began to protest and intimated that even though she felt bad for the individuals involved, her concern was Puerto Rico. I told her to hear me out. I explained that the United States has to wage a war against terrorism, but it will do little against the desperation that was the impetus for the attack. It has been said that things will never be the same in the United States. This is an understatement. For me it's as if the destruction of the World Trade Center also obliterated part of my memories and magnified my regrets. And yet, although the towers are gone, erased, no longer there, the towers of my memory remain intact, undamaged, rising into the sky daringly as a testament to individuals' need to leave their footprint on history. I explained that my mind will not give in to the logic of their destruction. More troublesome yet is the dark awareness that I'm going to leave my children and grandchildren a world of monumental uncertainty, and that perhaps this was caused in part by my inaction. I feel helpless in the face of my ghost towers which refuse to recede into the chaos of destruction.

Maruquita's response was odd, and while I share some of her ideals I'm not sure I can support what she did to Omaha.

"Look, Vega," she said. "Am I outraged by what happened? Of course I am. But my outrage runs much deeper and it has to do with our colonial status."

"Maruquita, listen to me," I said. "As a writer, I can't turn away from what I see without responding. I am a Puerto Rican; not a Puerto Rican-American, because I have never been given the choice to be one. I am not saying I wouldn't choose to be an American, but we are not truly immigrants and cannot experience that process which all immigrants undergo. Many of us remain Puerto Rican as a way of maintaining our dignity. At least that is what I do. You don't have that problem. You were born here. I wasn't. I sometimes wish I had come to the United States yearning to be free, but I was already a citizen without choosing to be one, Americanhood foisted upon me by colonialism, by occupation."

"Then you agree with me that what we did was justified."

"I don't think taking the law into your own hands is ever justified."

"What if the laws are unjust?" Maruquita said. "We did what we had to do. The United States has to change. This country can't afford to treat its people with such disregard. There is so much wealth in the United States and it's in the hands of such few. Omaha Bigelow thought he could get away with making a fool out of the people."

"Well, I suppose he went a little overboard," I said.

"Overboard?"

"Well, it was your idea to provide him with that kind of freedom."

"Vega, don't talk to me about freedom. American people have no idea what freedom is. They've never lived under colonialism. To them freedom consists of being able to purchase goods and move about as they please without ever questioning why things like Enron can happen. It's a sign of how the fat cats function. The executives of Enron, a mammoth energy company, knowing the corporation was going under, sold off their stock surreptitiously while it was still valuable. At the same time, in order to give the appearance that the company was financially healthy, they prohibited their workers from selling their own stock. When the largest bankruptcy in United States history took place, the little people of Enron were screwed out of their savings. Billions of dollars that belonged to the people disappeared down the drain of corporate deceit. Once again the rich try to get away with ripping off the masses because they are more cunning and have more information. And still the people feel free because they can choose which CD to buy, which film to rent, which TV dinner to purchase, food that is worth pennies but for which they pay five dollars. And Omaha Bigelow was headed in the same direction. In a few years with that Buckley clan, he would have become just like them. We were justified in doing what we did."

"Maru, you made it personal," I said.

"More American silliness, Vega," Maruquita said. "Sometimes you worry the hell outta me. If people do things to you, it *is* personal. What Omaha Bigelow did to me *was* personal."

"Fine, but you're taking it to an extreme with this Puerto Rican thing."

"Puerto Rican thing? Is that what you call it? You're next going to tell me to look at how things are in other places and that I should be grateful that I'm living here."

"Well, to a certain extent that is true," I said.

"Fine, but you're being swayed by propaganda. Look, some people tell me that I should look at how bad things are in other places. There is no question that things are bad in other places, but that is a deceitful argument."

"Deceitful? You can't dispute that things are pretty good in the U.S. I don't like some of the things that go on, but overall most people have a pretty good standard of living."

"Look, Vega, you're pretty bright but you have to be realistic. The United States with its geography, its industrial might, and its considerable military power can't be compared to a less fortunate country in Asia, Latin America, or Africa. Why compare the U.S. to them? Why not compare the United States to what it purports to be? Why not hold it accountable? The U.S. has run roughshod over Latin America for a while, and it doesn't treat a lot of its own people all that well. And I'm not talking about non-whites only. I know you don't like the term people of color and I don't either because it's an attempt to coopt people, but it's not us only. It's whites as well, so comparing the country to other places doesn't get it. Compare the U.S. to what it says it is and stop posturing about how great the country is. If it was so great everyone would see. There would be no need to boast."

"Maruquita, maybe I'm mellowing in my old age, but you have to temper your passion."

"Vega, I knew all along you sounded like some sort of apologist for this country that has oppressed our homeland for over a hundred years."

"Oh, be real, Maruquita. I'm talking about the methods you've used. You've grown as a character and I'm in agreement with you that the country has to change."

"Sure, sure. Listen! Ask yourself these questions: Why is there such poverty and unemployment in the United States? Why are so many people on welfare? Why are there homeless? Why do children go hungry each night? Why are families so strained to survive? Are you saying that there are sufficient jobs for everyone in the United States? The unemployment rate is a reality."

"I know. You're preaching to the choir. We've just started 2002 and the

Ford Motor Company has already announced that it is closing five plants, discontinuing four automobile lines, and eliminating 30,000 jobs."

"You see?"

"Of course I see, but this doesn't justify your actions. I've written this book to relieve some of the resentment I feel but also as an offering to people who wish to address the reality of what we're currently facing in the world. We have to wake up. To that end I have a heartfelt suggestion that may boost the stock of the United States."

"Will you listen to yourself, Vega?" Maruquita said. "There you go defending the United States."

"I'm not defending anything. I am appealing to the human side of the people of the United States."

"Fine, let's hear it. I'll try to be objective."

"The government of the United States and its people should immediately enter into a process by which Puerto Rico can begin to fully take part in the community of nations."

"Vega, you're a dreamer. You're addressing this administration? What a joke! They're a bunch of fascists. Their main interest is hegemony over the entire world. You'd think they'd be satisfied with Latin America, but they want to bring the whole world under their thumb, and now you want to plead with them?"

"Well, you're right. In a way it's a meager effort—a supplication, an entreaty, a wish."

"From these heartless people?"

"Yes, but I also want to address our people."

"Our people? Puerto Ricans?"

"Yes, but also conscientious people all over the world."

"To do what?"

"Look, we've maintained our culture through music, literature, theater, art, language, and sports. I include language because we're accused of speaking an odd brand of Spanish."

"You don't need to explain that," Maruquita said. "Our way of speaking Spanish is a national treasure. It's how we identify each other and our heritage."

"I know that. That's what I'm trying to explain."

"Fine, then. Get to the point."

"Get to the point? Listen to you. At such a young age, too."

"What?"

"You're becoming one of these bottom-line American people that you love to criticize. Look, you've done enough damage. Even though you've now become a big shot Admiral of the Fleet in the Puerto Rican Navy, you think you can just push me around? Enough is enough. At least have a little intellectual respect and hear me out. I've been pretty fair and understanding with you."

"Fine, I'm sorry. You're right. I'm sorry I interrupted you. Go on."

"Thank you. Puerto Rico has never had a war against anyone. It is said that the Taino Indians, native to the Puerto Rican archipelago, when faced with the slavery imposed on them by the Spaniards, clutched their children to their breasts and jumped from high cliffs into the raging and rocky sea."

"I know, Vega. That is the mythical ethos of our nationhood. We would rather destroy ourselves than be enslaved."

"Mythical ethos or not, we have not yet destroyed ourselves and continue developing as a culture. Even though we've been a colony of the United States for more than a hundred years, we've maintained the Spanish language and our customs. We've come to the United States and struggled and fought to overcome prejudices and stereotypes. In spite of the small size of our geography we've maintained our integrity against the onslaught of a mammoth culture not always concerned with our well-being."

I could imagine Maruquita rolling her eyes, exasperated with what she saw as a rather conservative aging person. But thoughtfully, she told me to go on. And then suddenly I could see her nodding, beginning to understand what I was saying. I went on and explained that the issue of Puerto Rico, like many others, has been overshadowed by the horror of September 11th, but that she was right and the injustices against the common people remain. When I was done, she said the most remarkable thing, and I knew that here in this young woman of rather remarkable intellect was really the soul of not only Puerto Ricans, but the best of what young people all over the world are really about.

"Wait," she said. "Let me see if I'm understanding what you're saying."

"Go ahead," I said, enjoying the change in her tone.

"You're saying that the United States should exercise its true benevolence by bringing about the independence of Puerto Rico without cutting the ties that bind our two nations."

"In a way," I said, but felt as if I should expand on what I was saying. "There is no reason after all this time why Puerto Rico, as an independent nation, should not have preferred nation status from the United States and be permitted to manufacture and trade freely with other unfortunate nations and thus create a fair economy. By doing so the U.S. would gain the respect of many people in the world."

"The United States should renounce its need to bring the entire world under its economic thumb," Maruquita added, her voice now conciliatory. "The bounty of the world belongs to its people, not to a few who are more cunning, because everybody knows they don't work any harder than a farmer or a factory worker, a secretary or a nurse, a mechanic or a firefighter."

"That's exactly what I believe," I said.

"People in this country are going to think of you as disloyal."

"I don't care if people think that I am disloyal. They should stop and consider the suffering in their midst and what they're doing about it. I write to awaken. I am serious about my purpose. I cannot feel free if others are enslaved. Obviously, I can use my writing to entertain, but I also want to stimulate thought. People in the United States should begin addressing the suffering around them rather than focusing on what they see as my harmful ideas, which, after all, are only ideas. I'm just an author, a pretty insignificant one at that. If it's their opinion that I should go back to the place I came from, I can only say this: I'll get out of your country when you get out of mine."

"That's very good," Maruquita said. "I'm gonna have T-shirts printed up. I'LL GET OUT OF YOUR COUNTRY WHEN YOU GET OUTTA MINE. Buttons too."

I replied that I was saying this in jest because we should be friends.

"Friends? How can you say that after what they've done to us? Vega, you sound okay for a while and then you totally freak me out. It's like you're selling out and can't admit it. I'm sorry."

"Wait a minute," I said, growing a little annoyed with her attacks. "Are you saying all Americans are bad?"

"I didn't say that."

"Well? As I remember, you're the one who wanted to get involved with Bigelow and have a gringorican baby."

"Hormones."

"Hormones?"

"Teen hormones."

"You have to be joking!"

"Well, you're the one who wrote this thing."

"Oh, blame me. Sure. And you had nothing to do with what happened. As if you weren't given the opportunity to improvise. You're as much to blame for what happened in this novel as I am."

"Fine. But who are you trying to convince with this thing?"

"Basically our own people, but also reasonable Americans."

"I guess," she said dismissively.

"We should be friends. In fact, I'm beseeching them that we be friends."

"Whatever. We can all be friends if you want, but I'm not going to bend on certain things."

"I'm not going to bend either. I'm not going to be accommodating if anyone insists that I be docile."

"You're not? What you're saying, this so-called supplication, sounds pretty accommodating."

"No, I have never been docile and will go to my grave protesting injustice. Puerto Rico's condition as chattel of the United States is an injustice."

"So how are you going to convince Puerto Ricans to get up off their butts and begin persuading the U.S. that the island should be independent?"

"Well, that's really up to you. You're the one that's got your work cut out for you."

"By any means necessary?" she said.

"Well . . ."

She laughed and said her cellular phone was starting to fade and she needed to recharge it. She again apologized for her extreme measures and said she'd be in touch. We said goodbye and I was left with a feeling that no matter what Maruquita Salsipuedes would do the right thing.

And now for the finale, which is virtually impossible to pull off humorously after all this seriousness. But perhaps it is time for reflection and not just humor. Perhaps the masks of tragedy and comedy are one, and no matter how much fun this has been, it is time to address the novel, not solely as entertainment, as the merchants would have us believe, but as something much more intrinsic to the health of a culture, as an examination of life in all its myriad manifestations.

At the start of his journey Omaha Bigelow was a pretty mindless hedonist, wasting his life and accomplishing little with his moderate talent and fair education. What he became should help us reflect on our own lives. Is Omaha Bigelow a metaphor for the United States? People should not think of the novel that way. I suppose you could argue that Omaha is a metaphor and it is certainly something to think about. Is this too heavy? You say that there's no need to be moralistic and philosophy and ethics don't serve the novel well? Nothing could be further from the truth.

Reflect on this.

It is January 12, 2002, as I write this. Only 123 days have passed since September 11, 2001. As I come to the end of writing this novel another sad event has taken place. A fifteen-year-old boy by the name of Charles Bishop crashed a small plane into a forty-story building in Tampa, Florida. A student pilot, he had taken off, without clearance, in a single-engine plane. Once aloft, a helicopter signaled for him to land at a nearby airport. Instead, the boy crashed into a building. At first I thought that the boy had become frightened by the helicopter. (This is not wild speculation, since Air Force jets, had they perceived the danger sooner, would have shot down airliners filled with passengers before they struck the World Trade Center towers on September 11th.) I then thought that the boy had made a navigational error and had crashed into the building by accident. A few days ago I learned that Charles Bishop left a suicide note in which he supported the 9/11 horror and the actions of Osama bin Laden.

Something is definitely wrong, and it's not all outside the United States. This country has to come to an understanding of itself. The problems can no longer be explained by the actions of a few deranged people. There is sociopolitical import in these violent actions. Timothy McVeigh, the Oklahoma City bomber, John Walker, the American Taliban fighter, and Charles Bishop, a boy, the Tampa Al Qaeda supporter. These are all nice Norman Rockwell Euro-American kids. I don't want to be an alarmist, but this is just the tip of the iceberg. The U.S. should start listening to its own heartbeat. As for the Puerto Ricans, they should examine themselves and recognize that we could be free.

I'll do my best to wind this up now and I hope you will forgive my excesses and Maruquita's youthful exuberance, her political involvement, and her overactive sense of justice.

MARUQUITA SALSIPUEDES KEPT TRUE TO HER PROMISE THAT OMAHA Bigelow was her pet. Omaha, in turn, resigned himself to his existence in the jungle. Days blended into each other. They were signaled only by the rising and setting of the sun. The days were warm and the nights comfortable. Sometimes it rained torrentially, but Omaha was able to take cover under a large elephant-ear leaf. His fur protected him when there were sudden downpours. There were no weeks or months in his reckoning, but time did pass and summer gave way to fall and then to winter and subsequently to spring. Sometimes, now lost in the impenetrable Loisaida jungle that oscillated between the projects of Avenue D and the lush vegetation of the eternal but forlorn island of enchantment, he pondered how he had come to this limited existence when his future had seemed so promising. He knew that his film would never be released. He also knew that he would never see his children unless they were the monkeys that emerged from the female monkeys in the jungle.

He missed his life as a man. These days he contented himself with playing in the trees, leaping from one branch to another and chasing or being chased by other monkeys. It was all in fun, and he squawked at them with as much stridency as they complained to him. At times he stopped and chose a ripened fruit from a tree and sat on a branch eating it. Other times he was able to capture an insect and crunch it between his strong teeth. He was a blondish monkey, and quite often a brown female monkey presented herself to him, and his tiny penis became erect at the sight and smell of her delicate pink orifice. He rose then and entered the female and felt the pleasure emerge from his loins into his small brain. He wished these females had names and could talk to him, but all the female monkeys did was emit sounds, which he answered in sympathy. When they were born, he never knew if the baby monkeys were his or some other male's. In his heart he loved them all, but at times they annoyed him with their familiarity and chattering. He enjoyed entering the female monkeys. At times he had an urge to enter the weaker male monkeys, but the desire passed and he peeled a fruit until another female presented herself and he mounted her. At times he would induce the same pleasure in himself manually, absently stroking his small, thin penis as he contemplated in wonder the vastness of the jungle. He enjoyed sitting with other monkeys and being groomed and grooming them, finding small insects in their fur and eating them.

Other times the regal woman of his memory came and rescued him from his monkeyhood, permitted him to be a man again and to rest between her thighs and pleasure her briefly before he was ordered back to the jungle and his condition as a pet monkey. He never again walked in Tompkins Square Park or ate blueberry blintzes at Odessa. He never again ordered the Sushi DeLuxe at Esashi, or walked Avenue A eating a falafel on a warm summer night. An ice-cold Rolling Rock and dancing at The Bank became distant memories. He never again sat in a NYC Fringe Festival performance wondering why the people involved had the audacity to call their performance theater. Motion pictures at The Angelika became lost in a fog of remembrance. Television and films, magazines and newspapers were no longer part of his life. A few times he wondered if Charlize Theron was happy. After a while he couldn't recall whether he had loved the film star or if it had been Winnifred Buckley whom he had loved.

When Omaha Bigelow felt particularly lonely, he climbed to the top of the very highest tree in the jungle, and from there he scanned the horizon and saw the vastness of the sea, its surface shimmering blue and emerald in the brilliant sunlight. If he concentrated more diligently, he could make himself look beyond the sea, and in his memory he was back in the East Village, standing on the rooftop of a building in the projects. From that vantage point he could look southward. He didn't know why, but his heart ached when he saw the empty spaces of his mind where the towers had been. He could not explain their absence, but in his mind they were gone. He didn't know what had happened, but he knew that something had taken place that was surrounded by horror. He thought that perhaps it was his own failed life that saddened him. Tears came into his eyes, and he knew he would never be happy again. He was just a poor monkey mired in the complexity of a world that has lost its poetry. Perhaps, he thought in his muddled monkey mind, we are all poor confused monkeys and all of us are lost in a world devoid of poetry.

ACKNOWLEDGMENTS

A number of people deserve recognition for their part in bringing this novel into the light of day. My agent Thomas Colchie and his wife Elaine Jabbour Colchie deserve the most credit for their belief in the book and their persistence in seeing it published. I first showed this novel to Tom and Elaine when I finished it in January 2002. Although we never discussed it, we thought that the political and satirical nature of the book might prevent publishers from taking a chance on it, particularly in the climate created by government fears, both imagined and real.

Nevertheless, Tom sent the book out to publishers, and Peter Mayer of The Overlook Press called with a very enthusiastic response and expressed his wish to publish the novel. Robert Wyatt is the person who thought that Peter might be interested in *Omaha Bigelow*. My thanks to Bob Wyatt for suggesting that Peter look at the book.

To Peter Mayer, for his courage and good humor in publishing the novel, my eternal gratitude. My most sincere thanks as well to David Mulrooney, my editor, for his care and stewardship in producing the book, to Bernard Schleifer for his book design, and to my publicists, Sarah Rosenbloom and Corby Hawks.

Lastly, my thanks to the people, both my supporters and my detractors, in the Authors Lounge chatroom of America Online. To a certain extent, through their arguments, humor, cynicism, and personal attacks on me, they provided the inspiration for parts of the novel. Some, like Smoran26, MarkU, and Phippsh read either the entire manuscript as was the case with Smoran, or they read chapters, as did MarkU and Phippsh. My thanks also to DbasMiami, ChatDrivel, TRUBLVR, Epifanny, AztecKin, Clay, Hlowrld, JackatBrun, Pookington, OldAngler, VoxTango1, Ceadanmarta, Jthunder, HuckPortobello, and others.

A special thanks to Pablo71121, an artist of enormous generosity and skill, a comrade-in-arms and a wit of unparalleled inventiveness.

Ultimately, this book is dedicated to everyone who enjoys a good laugh.

AUTHOR'S NOTE

THIS BOOK IS FOR

Tim Vega
(1965–2002)

artist, writer, rebel, son

I wrote this novel for my son, who loved irreverence and laughter. He never read it because he died in April 2002, roughly three months after I finished the book and two weeks after I told him that my big jazz novel *Bill Bailey* was to be published in October 2003. He never knew about *Omaha Bigelow* because it was to be a surprise.

I believe my son died of heartache. Tim was to be at work at the World Trade Center at 8 A.M. on September 11th but didn't make it in that day. His grief at having lost more than 100 people whom he knew eventually cut his life short. He felt he should have been there to help.

Although he died in his sleep seven months after 9/11, I know that his heart was broken by the tragedy and his personal loss.

Goodbye Timothy, Timo, Timmy, Tim.

So long Timojin.

Adios, mijito.

Goodbye, baby boy.

I will miss you and grieve the rest of my life.

You were one hell of a dude.

You and Bird and Jean-Michel and all the young artists who have graced my life with your talent.

You did not go gentle into that dark night.

Your Dad, who always loved and admired you.